The View from Castle Rock

The View from Castle Rock

STORIES

Alice Munro

ALFRED A. KNOPF
NEW YORK
2006

THIS IS A BORZOI BOOK
PUBLISHED BY ALFRED A. KNOPF

www.aaknopf.com

Knopf, Borzoi Books, and the colophon are registered trademarks of
Random House, Inc.

Some of the stories in this collection were previously published, some
in slightly different form, in the following publications: "Fathers" in
The New Yorker; "Hired Girl" in *The New Yorker;* "Home" in *New
Canadian Short Stories* (Oberon Press, Ottawa, 1974) and in *The
Virginia Quarterly Review;* "Lying Under the Apple Tree" in *The New
Yorker;* "The View from Castle Rock" in *The New Yorker;* "What Do
You Want to Know For" in *The American Scholar;* and "Working for
a Living" in *Grand Street.*

Library of Congress Cataloging-in-Publication Data
Munro, Alice.
The view from Castle Rock : stories / by Alice Munro.—1st ed.
p. cm.
ISBN 1-4000-4282-8
I. Title.

PR9199.3.M8V54 2006
813'.54—DC22   2006045261

Manufactured in the United States of America
First Edition

Dedicated to Douglas Gibson,
who has sustained me through many travails,
and whose enthusiasm for this particular book
has even sent him prowling through the graveyard
of Ettrick Kirk, probably in the rain.

CONTENTS

FOREWORD

About ten or twelve years ago I began to take more than a random interest in the history of one side of my family, whose name was Laidlaw. There was a good deal of information lying around about them—really an unusual amount, considering that they were obscure and not prosperous, and living in the Ettrick Valley, which the Statistical Account of Scotland (1799) describes as having *no advantages.* I lived in Scotland for a few months, close to the Ettrick Valley, so I was able to find their names in the local histories in the Selkirk and Galashiels Public Libraries, and to find out what James Hogg had to say about them in *Blackwoods Magazine.* Hogg's mother was a Laidlaw, and he took Walter Scott to see her when Scott was collecting ballads for *The Minstrelsy of the Scottish Border.* (She supplied some, though she later took offense at their being printed.) And I was lucky, in that every generation of our family seemed to produce somebody who went in for writing long, outspoken, sometimes outrageous letters, and detailed recollections. Scotland was the country, remember, where John Knox had decided that every child should learn to read and write, in some sort of village school, so that everybody could read the Bible.

It didn't stop there.

I put all this material together over the years, and almost without my noticing what was happening, it began to shape itself, here and there, into something like stories. Some of the characters gave themselves to me in their own words, others rose out of their situations. Their words and my words, a curious re-creation of lives, in a given setting that was as truthful as our notion of the past can ever be.

During these years I was also writing a special set of stories. These stories were not included in the books of fiction I put together, at regular intervals. Why not? I felt they didn't belong. They were not memoirs but they were closer to my own life than the other stories I had written, even in the first person. In other first-person stories I had drawn on personal material, but then I did anything I wanted to with this material. Because the chief thing I was doing was making a story. In the stories I hadn't collected I was not doing exactly that. I was doing something closer to what a memoir does—exploring a life, my own life, but not in an austere or rigorously factual way. I put myself in the center and wrote about that self, as searchingly as I could. But the figures around this self took on their own life and color and did things they had not done in reality. They joined the Salvation Army, they revealed that they had once lived in Chicago. One of them got himself electrocuted and another fired off a gun in a barn full of horses. In fact, some of these characters have moved so far from their beginnings that I cannot remember who they were to start with.

These are *stories.*

You could say that such stories pay more attention to the truth of a life than fiction usually does. But not enough to swear on. And the part of this book that might be called family history has expanded into fiction, but always within the outline of a true narrative. With these developments the two streams came close enough together that they seemed to me meant to flow in one channel, as they do in this book.

PART ONE

No Advantages

No Advantages

This parish possesses no advantages. Upon the hills the soil is in many places mossy and fit for nothing. The air in general is moist. This is occasioned by the height of the hills which continually attract the clouds and the vapour that is continually exhaled from the mossy ground . . . The nearest market town is fifteen miles away and the roads so deep as to be almost impassable. The snow also at times is a great inconvenience, often for many months we can have no intercourse with mankind. And a great disadvantage is the want of bridges so that the traveller is obstructed when the waters are swelled . . . Barley oats and potatoes are the only crops raised. Wheat rye turnips and cabbage are never attempted . . .

There are ten proprietors of land in this parish: none of them resides in it.

Contribution by the Minister of Ettrick Parish,
in the county of Selkirk, to the Statistical Account
of Scotland, 1799

The Ettrick Valley lies about fifty miles due south of Edinburgh, and thirty or so miles north of the English border, which runs close to the wall Hadrian built to keep out the wild people from the north. During the reign of Antoninus the Romans pushed farther, and built a line of fortification between the Firth of Clyde and the Firth of Forth, but that was not so lasting. The land between the two walls has been occupied for a long time by a mix of people—Celtic people, some of whom came from Ireland and were called Scots, also Anglo-Saxons from the south, Norse from across the North Sea, and possibly some leftover Picts as well.

The high stony farm where my family lived for some time in the Ettrick Valley was called Far-Hope. The word *hope,* as used in the local geography, is an old word, a Norse word—Norse, Anglo-Saxon, and Gaelic words being all mixed up together in that part of the country, as you would expect, with some old Brythonic thrown in to indicate an early Welsh presence. *Hope* means a bay, not a bay filled with water but with land, partly enclosed by hills, which in this case are the high bare hills, the near mountains of the Southern Uplands. The Black Knowe, Bodesbeck Law, Ettrick Pen—there you have the three big hills, with the word *hill* in three languages. Some of these hills are now being reforested, with plantations of Sitka spruce, but in the seventeenth and eighteenth centuries they would have been bare, or mostly bare—the great Forest of Ettrick, the hunting grounds of the Kings of Scotland, having been cut down and turned into pasture or waste heath a century or two before.

The height of land above Far-Hope, which stands right at the end of the valley, is the spine of Scotland, marking the division of the waters that flow to the west into the Solway Firth and the Atlantic Ocean, from those that flow east into the North Sea. Within ten miles to the north is the country's most famous waterfall, the Grey Mare's Tail. Five miles from Moffat, which would be the market town to those living at the valley head, is the Devil's Beef Tub, a great cleft in the hills believed to be the hiding place for stolen cattle—English cattle, that is, taken by the reivers in the lawless sixteenth century. In the lower Ettrick Valley was Aikwood, the home of Michael Scott, the philosopher and wizard of the twelfth and thirteenth centuries, who appears in Dante's *Inferno*. And if that were not enough, William Wallace, the guerrilla hero of the Scots, is said to have hidden out here from the English, and there is a story of Merlin—*Merlin*—being hunted down and murdered, in the old forest, by Ettrick shepherds.

(As far as I know, my ancestors, generation after generation, were Ettrick shepherds. It may sound odd to have shepherds employed in a forest, but it seems that hunting forests were in many places open glades.)

Nevertheless the valley disappointed me the first time I saw it. Places are apt to do that when you've set them up in your imagination. The time of year was very early spring, and the hills were brown, or a kind of lilac brown, reminding me of the hills around Calgary. Ettrick Water was running fast and clear, but it was hardly as wide as the Maitland River, which flows past the farm where I grew up, in Ontario. The circles of stones which I had at first taken to be interesting remnants of Celtic worship were too numerous and well kept up to be anything but handy sheep pens.

I was travelling by myself, and I had come from Selkirk on the twice-a-week Shoppers' Bus, which took me no farther than Ettrick Bridge. There I wandered around, waiting for the postman. I'd been told that he would take me up the valley. The chief thing to be seen in Ettrick Bridge was a sign on a closed shop, advertising Silk Cut. I couldn't figure out what that might be. It turned out to be a well-known brand of cigarette.

After a while the postman came along and I rode with him

to Ettrick Church. By that time it had begun to rain, hard. The church was locked. It disappointed me, too. Having been built in 1824, it did not compare, in historic appearance, or grim character, to the churches I had already seen in Scotland. I felt conspicuous, out of place, and cold. I huddled by the wall till the rain let up for a bit, and then I explored the churchyard, with the long wet grass soaking my legs.

There I found, first, the gravestone of William Laidlaw, my direct ancestor, born at the end of the seventeenth century, and known as Will O'Phaup. This was a man who took on, at least locally, something of the radiance of myth, and he managed that at the very last time in history—that is, in the history of the people of the British Isles—when a man could do so. The same stone bears the names of his daughter Margaret Laidlaw Hogg, who upbraided Sir Walter Scott, and of Robert Hogg, her husband, the tenant of Ettrickhall. Then right next to it I saw the stone of the writer James Hogg, who was their son and Will O'Phaup's grandson. He was known as The Ettrick Shepherd. And not far from that was the stone of the Reverend Thomas Boston, at one time famous throughout Scotland for his books and preaching, though fame never took him to any more important ministry.

Also, among various Laidlaws, a stone bearing the name of Robert Laidlaw, who died at Hopehouse January 29th 1800 aged seventy-two years. Son of Will, brother of Margaret, uncle of James, who probably never knew that he would be remembered by his link to these others, any more than he would know the date of his own death.

My great-great-great-great-grandfather.

As I was reading these inscriptions the rain came on again, lightly, and I thought I had better start to walk back to Tushielaw, where I was to catch the school bus for my return ride to Selkirk. I couldn't loiter, because the bus might be early, and the rain might get heavier.

I was struck with a feeling familiar, I suppose, to many people whose long history goes back to a country far away from the place where they grew up. I was a naïve North American, in spite of my stored knowledge. Past and present lumped together here made a reality that was commonplace and yet disturbing beyond anything I had imagined.

MEN OF ETTRICK

Will O'Phaup

Here lyeth William Laidlaw, the far-famed Will o' Phaup, who for feats of frolic, agility and strength, had no equal in his day . . .

Epitaph composed by his grandson, James Hogg, on Will O'Phaup's tombstone in Ettrick Kirkyard.

His name was William Laidlaw, but his story-name was Will O'Phaup, Phaup being simply the local version of Far-Hope, the name of the farm he took over at the head of Ettrick Valley. It seems that Far-Hope had been abandoned for years when Will came to inhabit it. The house, that is, had been abandoned, because it was situated so high up at the end of the remote valley, and got the worst of the periodic winter storms and the renowned snowfall. The house of Potburn, the next one to it, lower down, was until recently said to be the highest inhabited house in all of Scotland. It now stands deserted, apart from the sparrows and finches busy around its outbuildings.

The land itself would not have belonged to Will, it would not even have been leased to him—he would have rented the house or got it as part of his shepherd's wages. It was never worldly prosperity that he was after.

Only Glory.

He was not native to the valley, though there were Laidlaws there, and had been since the first records were kept. The earliest man of that name I have come across is in the court records of the thirteenth century, and he was up on charges of murdering another Laidlaw. No prisons in those days. Just dungeons, mainly for the upper class, or people of some political importance who had fallen out with their rulers, and summary executions—but those happened mostly in times of large unrest, as during the border raids of the sixteenth century, when a marauder might be hanged at his own front door, or strung up in Selkirk Square, as were sixteen cattle thieves of the same name—Elliott—on a single day of punishment. My man got off with a fine.

Will was said to be "one of the old Laidlaws of Craik"— about whom I have not been able to discover anything at all, except that Craik is an almost disappeared village on a completely disappeared Roman road, in a nearby valley to the south of Ettrick. He must have walked over the hills, a lad in his teens, looking for work. He had been born in 1695, when Scotland was still a separate country, though it shared a monarch with England. He would have been twelve years old at the time of the controversial Union, a young man by the time of the bitter failed Jacobite Rebellion of 1715, a man deep into middle age by the time of Culloden. There is no telling what he thought of those events. I have a feeling that his life was lived in a world still remote and self-contained, still harboring its own mythology and local wonders. And he was one of them.

The first story told of Will is about his prowess as a runner. His earliest job in the Ettrick Valley was as shepherd to a Mr. Anderson, and this Mr. Anderson had noted how Will ran straight down on a sheep and not roundabout when he wanted to catch it. So he knew that Will was a fast runner, and when a champion English runner came into the valley Mr. Anderson wagered Will against him for a large sum of money. The English fellow scoffed, his backers scoffed, and Will won. Mr. Anderson collected a fine heap of coins and Will for his part got a gray cloth coat and a pair of hose.

Fair enough, he said, for the coat and hose meant as much to him as all that money to a man like Mr. Anderson.

Here is a classic story. I heard versions of it—with different names, different feats—when I was a child growing up in Huron County, in Ontario. A stranger arrives full of fame, bragging of his abilities, and is beaten by the local champion, a simple-hearted fellow who is not even interested in a reward.

These elements recur in another early story, in which Will goes over the hills to the town of Moffat on some errand, unaware that it is fair day, and is cajoled into taking part in a public race. He is not well dressed for the occasion and during the running his country breeches fall down. He lets them fall, kicks his way out of them, and continues running in nothing but a shirt, and he wins. There is a great fuss made of him and he gets invited to dinner in the public house with gentlemen and ladies. By this time he must have had his pants on, but he blushes anyway, and will not accept, claiming to be mortified in front of such *leddies*.

Maybe he was, but of course the leddies' appreciation of such a well-favored young athlete is the scandalous and enjoyable point of the story.

Will marries, at some point, he marries a woman named Bessie Scott, and they begin to raise their family. During this period the boy-hero turns into a mortal man, though there are still feats of strength. A certain spot in the Ettrick River becomes "Will's Leap" to commemorate a jump he made, to get help or medicine for someone who was sick. No feat, however, brought him any money, and the pressures of earning a living for his family, combined with a convivial nature, seem to have turned him into a casual bootlegger. His house is well situated to receive the liquor that is being smuggled over the hills from Moffat. Surprisingly this is not whiskey, but French brandy, no doubt entering the country illegally by way of the Solway Firth—as it will continue to do despite the efforts late in the century of Robert Burns, poet and exciseman. Phaup becomes well known for occasions of carousing or at least of high sociability. The hero's name still stands for honorable behavior, strength, and generosity, but no more for sobriety.

Bessie Scott dies fairly young, and it is probably after her death that the parties have begun. The children will have been banished, most likely, to some outbuilding or the sleeping loft of the house. There does not appear to have been any serious outlawry or loss of respectability. The French brandy may be worth noting, though, in the light of the adventures that come upon Will in his maturity.

He is out on the hills as the day turns to evening and he keeps hearing a sound like a chattering and a twittering. He knows all the sounds that birds can make and he understands that this is no bird. It seems to come out of a deep hollow nearby. So he creeps and creeps very softly to the edge of the hollow and flattens himself down, just raises up his head enough that he can look over.

And what does he see down below but a whole company of creatures all about as high as a two-year-old child, but none of them are children. They are little women, all dainty looking and dressed in green. And busy as they can be. Some baking bread in a bit of an oven and some pouring drink out of little kegs into glass pitchers and some fixing up the other one's hair and all the time humming and chittering away and never looking up, never raising one of their heads but just keeping their eyes on their business. But the more he keeps listening to them the more he thinks he hears something familiar. And it comes clearer and clearer—the little chirp-chirp song they make. Finally it comes clear as a bell.

Will O'Phaup, Will O'Phaup, Will O'Phaup.

His own name is all the word in their mouths. The song that sounded sweet enough to him when he first heard it is not that anymore, it is full of laughing but it is not decent laughing. It makes the cold sweat run down Will's back. And he remembers at the same time that this is All Hallows' Eve, the time in the year when these creatures can work their way however they please with any human being. So he jumps up and runs, he runs all the way back to his house faster than any devil could chase him.

All the way he hears the song of *Will O'Phaup, Will O'Phaup* ringing just behind his ears and never growing any less or any fainter. He reaches his house and he gets inside and bars the door and gathers all his children round him and he begins to pray as loud as ever he can and as long as he prays he cannot hear. But let him just stop to get his breath and it comes down the chimney, it comes through the cracks in the door, and it gets louder as the creatures fight against his prayer and he does not dare to rest till on the stroke of midnight he cries *Oh, Lord have mercy* and falls silent. And there is no more heard of the creatures, not a peep. It is a still night out as any night might be and the peace of Heaven over the whole valley.

Then another time, in the summer but around the darkening hour of the evening, he is making his way home from penning the sheep and he thinks that he sees some of his neighbors quite a distance away. It comes into his mind that they will be coming home from Moffat Fair, it being indeed the Moffat Fair Day. So he thinks he'll take the opportunity of going ahead and speaking to them, and find out what the news is, and how they got on.

As soon as he gets close enough to them he calls out.

But nobody takes any notice. And then again he calls out, but still not one of them turns around or looks towards him. He can see them plain from their backs, all country folks in their plaids and their bonnets, both men and women, and normal-sized, but he cannot get to look at their faces, they stay turned away from him. And they do not look to be hurrying, they are dawdling along and gossiping and chatting and he can hear the noise they make but not quite the words.

So he follows faster and faster and finally he takes to a run, to catch up to them, but no matter how fast he runs he cannot do that—though they are not hurrying at all, they are still just dawdling. And so busy he is, thinking about catching up to them, that it does not occur to him for some while that they are not going homeward at all.

They are not going down the valley but up a narrow kind of

little side valley with a trickle of a creek in it that flows down into the Ettrick. And with the light fading they seem to be getting dimmer but more numerous, a strange thing.

And down from the hills comes a cold draught of air though it is a warm summer evening.

And Will knows it then. These are no neighbor folk. And they are not leading him on to any place where he would want to go. And hard as he had run after them before, he turns now and runs the other way. This being an ordinary night and not All Hallows' Eve they have no powers to chase him. His fear is different from the fear he felt the other time, but just as cold, because of the notion he has that they are ghosts of humans bewitched into fairies.

It would be a mistake to think that everybody believed these stories. There was the brandy factor. But most people, believing or not, would hear them with more than a mild shiver. They might feel some curiosity, and some skepticism, but mostly a large portion of plain dread. Fairies and ghosts and religion were never mixed up together under some benign designation (*spiritual powers?*) as they often are today. Fairies were not blithe and captivating. They belonged to the olden times, not the old historical times of Flodden where every Selkirk man was killed except the one who brought the news, or of the lawless men raiding by night across the Debatable Lands, or of Queen Mary—or even of the times before that, of William Wallace or Archibald Bell-the-Cat or the Maid of Norway, but the truly dark times, before the Antonine Wall and before the first Christian missionaries came across the sea from Ireland. They belonged to times of bad powers and evil confusion, and their attentions were oftener than not malicious, or even deadly.

Thomas Boston

As a Testament of Esteem for the
Reverend Thomas Boston Senior
whose private character was highly respectable,
whose public labours were blessed to many and
whose writings have contributed much to promote
the advancement of vital Christianity.
This monument erected by a religious
and grateful public.

Strive to enter in at the strait gate: for many, I say unto
you, will seek to enter in, and will not be able.

Luke xi11, 24.

Will's sightings would certainly not stand well with the Kirk, and during the first part of the eighteenth century the Kirk was particularly powerful in the parish of Ettrick.

Its minister at that time was the preacher named Thomas Boston, who is remembered now—if he is remembered at all—as the author of a book called *Human Nature in its Fourfold State,* which was said to stand next to the Bible on the shelf of every pious home in Scotland. And every Presbyterian home in Scotland was meant to be a pious home. Constant investigation of private life and tortured reshapings of the faith went on to take care of that. There was no balm of ritual, no elegance of ceremony. Prayer was not only formal but personal, agonized. The readiness of the soul for eternal life was always in doubt and danger.

Thomas Boston kept this drama going without a break, for himself and for his parishioners. In his autobiography he speaks of his own recurring miseries, his dry spells, his sense of unworthiness and dullness even in the act of preaching the Gospel, or while praying in his study. He pleads for grace. He bares his breast to Heaven—at least symbolically—in his desperation. He would surely lacerate himself with thorned whips if such behavior would not be Popish, would not in fact constitute a further sin.

Sometimes God hears him, sometimes not. His craving for God can never leave him, but he can never count on its being satisfied. He can rise up filled with the Spirit and enter marathons of preaching, he presides at solemn festivals of Communion in which he knows himself to be the Vessel of God and witnesses the transformation of many souls. But he is careful not to take the credit himself. He knows that he is all too capable of the Sin of Pride, and knows too how swiftly Grace may be withdrawn from him.

He strives, he falls. Darkness again.

Meanwhile the roof of the manse is leaking, the walls are damp, the chimney smokes, his wife and his children and he himself are often sick with fevers. They have septic throats and rheumatic aches. Some of his children die. The very first baby is born with what sounds to me like spina bifida and she dies soon after birth. His wife is distraught, and though he does his best to comfort her he feels bound also to reprimand her for complaining against God's Will. He has to reproach himself later for lifting up the coffin lid to get one last glimpse of the face of his own favorite, a little boy of three. How wicked of him, how weak, to love this sinful scrap of flesh and to question in any way his Lord's wisdom in taking him. There must be further wrestlings, self-castigation, and bouts of prayer.

Wrestlings not only with his dullness of spirit but with a

majority of his fellow ministers, for he becomes deeply interested in a treatise called *The Marrow of Modern Divinity*. He is accused of being a marrow-man, in danger of going over to antinomianism. Antinomianism proceeds logically from the doctrine of predestination and asks a simple, direct question—why, if you are from the beginning one of the elect, should you not be able to get away with anything you like?

But wait. *Wait.* As to being one of the elect, who can ever be so sure?

And the problem for Boston must surely not be about getting away with anything, but about the compulsion, the honorable compulsion, to follow where certain lines of reasoning lead.

Just in time, however, he falls back from error. He retreats. He is safe.

His wife, in the midst of births and deaths and care of the remaining children and troubles with the roof and the continual cold rain, is overcome by some nervous disorder. She is unable to get out of her bed. Her faith is strong, but vitiated, as he says, on one essential point. He does not say what this point is. He prays with her. How he manages in the house we do not know. His wife, once the beautiful Catherine Brown, seems to stay in bed for years, except for the one touching respite when all the family is laid low by some passing infection. Then she rises from her bed and cares for them, tirelessly and tenderly, with the strength and optimism she showed in her youth, when Boston first fell in love with her. Everyone recovers, and when next heard from she is back in bed. She is well on in years but still alive when the minister himself is dying, and we can hope that she will get up then and go to live in a dry house with some agreeable relations in a civilized town. Keeping her faith but holding it at arm's length, perhaps, to enjoy a bit of secular happiness.

Her husband preaches from his chamber window when he is too feeble and close to death to get to the church and up into the pulpit. He exhorts bravely and fervently as ever and crowds gather to hear him, though it is raining, as usual.

The bleakest, the most desperate life, from any outside point of view. Only from the inside of the faith is it possible to get any idea of the prize as well as the struggle, the addictive pursuit of pure righteousness, the intoxication of a flash of God's favor.

So it seems strange to me that Thomas Boston should have been the minister whom Will O'Phaup listened to every Sunday during his young manhood, probably the minister who married him to Bessie Scott. My ancestor, a near pagan, a merry man, a brandy drinker, one upon whom wagers are set, a man who believes in the fairies, is bound to have listened to, and believed in, the strictures and hard hopes of this punishing Calvinist faith. And in fact when Will was pursued on All Hallows' Eve did he not call for protection on the same God whom Boston called upon when he begged to have the weight—of indifference, doubt, sorrow—lifted off his soul? The past is full of contradictions and complications, perhaps equal to those of the present, though we do not usually think so.

How could these people fail to take their religion seriously, with its threat of Hell inescapable, with Satan so cunning and relentless in his torments, and Heaven's population so sparse? And they did, they took it seriously. They were called up for their sins to sit on the cutty stool and bear their shame—usually for some sexual matter, solemnly referred to as Fornication—in front of the congregation. James Hogg was summoned there at least twice, charged with paternity by local girls. One case he admitted readily and in the other he would only say that it was possible. (Eighty miles or so to the west, in Mauchline in Ayrshire, Robert Burns, eleven years older than Hogg, suffered precisely the same public humiliation.) The Elders went from house to house to see that no cooking was in progress on a Sunday and at all times their harsh hands were employed in severely squeezing the breasts of any woman suspected of having borne an illegitimate child, so that a drop of milk might betray her. But the very fact that such vigilance was thought necessary shows how these believers were waylaid by Nature in their lives, as people always are. An Elder in Burns's church records "Only 26 Fornicators since the last sacrament," as if this figure is indeed a step in the right direction.

And they were waylaid also in the very practice of the faith, even by the industry of their own minds, by the arguments and interpretations that were bound to arise.

This might have had something to do with their being the best-educated peasantry in Europe. John Knox had wanted them educated so that they could read the Bible. And they read it, with piety but also with hunger, to discover God's order, the architecture of His mind. They found a lot to puzzle about. Other ministers of Boston's time complain of how disputatious their parishioners are, *even the women*. (Boston does not mention that, being too busy blaming himself.) They do not quietly accept the hours-long sermons but grab hold of them as intellectual fodder, judging as if they were involved in lifelong and deadly serious debates. They are forever worrying at points of doctrine and passages of scripture that they would be better off leaving alone, say their ministers. Better to rely on those trained to deal with such things. But they will not do so, and the fact is

that the trained ministers as well are sometimes driven to con-
clusions that other ministers must condemn. The result being
that the Church is riven by divisions, the men of God are frequently at one another's throats, as Boston's own troubles have
shown. And it may have been the stain of being a marrow-man,
of following his own unavoidable thought, that kept him so
long in remote Ettrick, never up to his death being "translated"
(as the word was then) to a moderately comfortable place.

James Hogg and James Laidlaw

He was always a singular and highly amusing character
who cherished every antiquated and exploded idea in science, religion, and politics . . . Nothing excited his indig-
nation more than the theory of the earth wheeling round
on its axis, and journeying around the sun . . .
. . . for a number of years bygone he talked and read
about America till he grew perfectly unhappy, and at last
when approaching his sixtieth year actually set out to seek
a temporary home and a grave in the new world.

James Hogg, writing about his cousin James Laidlaw.

Hogg poor man has spent most of his life in conning lies . . .

James Laidlaw, writing about his cousin James Hogg,
poet and novelist of early-nineteenth-century Scotland.

He was a gey [very] sensible man, for a' the nonsense he
wrat . . .

Tibbie Shiel, innkeeper, also buried in Ettrick Kirkyard,
speaking about James Hogg.

James Hogg and James Laidlaw were first cousins. Both men were born and raised in the Ettrick Valley, a place which had not much use for their sort—that is, for the sort of men who do not take easily to anonymity and quiet lives.

If such a man becomes famous, of course, it is another story. Alive he is booted out, dead he is welcomed home. After a generation or two, it is another story.

Hogg escaped, into the uneasy role of the naïve comedian, the bumpkin genius, in Edinburgh, and then he escaped, as the author of *Confessions of a Justified Sinner,* into lasting fame. Laidlaw, lacking his cousin's gifts, but not apparently his knack for self-dramatization and his need for another stage than Tibbie Shiel's tavern, made some mark by hauling up the more docile members of his family and carrying them off to America—actually to Canada—when he was old enough, as Hogg points out, to have one foot in the grave.

Self-dramatization got short shrift in our family. Though now that I come to think of it, it wasn't exactly that word they used. They spoke of *calling attention. Calling attention to yourself.* The opposite of which was not exactly modesty but a strenuous dignity and control, a sort of refusal. The refusal to feel any need to turn your life into a story, either for other people or for yourself. And when I study the people I know about in the family, it does seem that some of us have that need in large and irresistible measure—enough so as to make the others cringe with embarrassment and apprehension. That's why the judgment or warning had to be given out so frequently.

By the time his grandsons—James Hogg and James Laidlaw—were young men, the world of Will O'Phaup was almost gone.

There was a historical awareness of that recent past, even a treasuring or exploitation of it, which is only possible when people feel themselves most decidedly removed. James Hogg clearly felt that, though he was so much a man of Ettrick. It is mostly his writings I have to thank for what I know of Will O'Phaup. Hogg was both insider and outsider, industriously and—he hoped—profitably shaping and recording his people's stories. And he had a fine source in his mother—Will O'Phaup's eldest daughter, Margaret Laidlaw, who had grown up at Far-Hope. There would be some trimming and embroidering of material on Hogg's part. Some canny lying of the sort you can depend upon a writer to do.

Walter Scott was an outsider of sorts, an Edinburgh lawyer now appointed to a high post in his family's traditional territory. But he too understood, as outsiders sometimes do better, the importance of something that was vanishing. When he became the Sherriff of Selkirkshire—that is, the local judge—he began to go around the country collecting the old songs and ballads which had never been written down. He would publish them in *The Minstrelsy of the Scottish Border.* Margaret Laidlaw Hogg was famous locally for the number of verses she carried in her head. And Hogg—with his eye on posterity as well as present advantage—made sure he took Scott to see his mother.

She recited plenty of verses, including the newfound "Ballad of Johnie Armstrong," which she said she and her brother had got "from old Andrew Moore who had it from Bebe Mettlin [Maitland] who was housekeeper to the First Laird of Tushielaw."

(It happens that this same Andrew Moore had been Boston's servant and that it was he who had reported Boston as having "laid the ghost" who appears in one of Hogg's poems. A new light on the minister.)

Margaret Hogg made a great fuss when she saw the book Scott produced in 1802 with her contributions in it.

"They were made for singin and no for prentin," she is supposed to have said. "And noo they'll never be sung mair."

She complained further that they were "neither right settin down nor right spelt," though this may seem an odd judgment to be made by someone who had been presented—by herself or by Hogg—as a simple old countrywoman with only a minimum of education.

She was probably both simple and sharp. She had known what she was doing but could not help regretting what she had done.

And noo they'll never be sung mair.

She might also have enjoyed showing that it took more than a printed book, it took more than the Shirra of Selkirk, to make a favorable impression on her. Scots are like that, I think. My family was like that.

Fifty years after Will O'Phaup clasped his children and prayed for protection on All Hallows' Eve, Hogg and a few of his male cousins—he does not give their names—are to meet in that same high house at Phaup. By this time the house is used as a lodging by whatever bachelor shepherd is in charge of the high-feeding sheep, and the others are present that evening not to get drunk and tell stories but to *read essays.* These essays Hogg describes as flaming and bombastical, and from those words, and from what was said afterwards, it would seem that these young men deep in the Ettrick had heard about the Age of Reason, though they probably didn't call it that, and about the ideas of Voltaire and Locke and of David Hume, their fellow Scot and Lowlander. Hume had grown up at Ninewells near Chirnside, about fifty miles away, and it was to Ninewells that he retreated when he suffered a breakdown at the age of eighteen—perhaps overcome, temporarily, by the scope of the investigation he saw in front of him. He would still have been alive when these boys were born.

I could be guessing wrong, of course. What Hogg calls essays could have been stories. Tales of the Covenanters being hunted down at their outdoor services by red-coated dragoons, of witches, of the walking dead. These were lads who would try their hand at any composition, at prose or poetry. John Knox's schools had done their work, and a rash of literature, a fever of poetry, was breaking out in all classes. When Hogg had been at his lowest point, working as a shepherd on the lonely hills of Nithsdale, living in a rough shelter called a bothy, the Cunningham brothers—the stonemason's apprentice and poet Allan Cunningham, and his brother James—had come trudging over the countryside to meet him and tell him of their admiration. (Hogg was alarmed at first, thinking they came to charge him with some trouble about a woman.) The three of them left the dog Hector to guard the sheep and settled down to talk of poetry all day, then crawled into the bothy to drink whiskey and talk of poetry all night.

The shepherds' meeting at Phaup, which Hogg claims that he himself did not manage to attend, in spite of having such an essay in his pocket, was held in winter. The weather had been strangely warm. That night, however, a storm arose which turned out to be the worst in half a century. Sheep were frozen in their pens and men and horses were trapped and frozen on the roads, while houses were buried in snow up to their roofs. For three or four days the storm continued, roaring and devastating, and when it was over, and the young shepherds came down to the valley alive, their families were relieved but in no way pleased with them.

Hogg's mother told him plainly that it was a punishment brought on the whole countryside by the Devil's work being done in whatever reading and conversing was going on at Phaup that night. No doubt many other parents thought the same.

Some years later, Hogg wrote a fine description of this storm, and it was published in *Blackwoods Magazine*. *Blackwoods* was the favorite reading of the little Brontës, in the rectory at Haworth, and when they each chose a hero to impersonate in their games, Emily chose the Ettrick Shepherd, James Hogg. (Charlotte chose the Duke of Wellington.) *Wuthering Heights,* Emily's great novel, begins with a description of a terrible storm. I have often wondered if there is a connection.

I don't believe that James Laidlaw was one of those present at Phaup that night. His letters don't show anything like a skeptical, or theorizing, or poetical sort of mind. Of course the letters that I have read were written when he was old. People change.

Certainly he is a joker when we meet him first, by Hogg's account, in Tibbie Shiel's inn (which is still there, more than an hour's walk through the hills from Phaup, just as Phaup is still there, now a bothy shelter on the Southern Uplands Way, a walking trail). He is putting on a show that could be seen to be blasphemous. Blasphemous, risky, and funny. Down on his knees, he is offering up prayers for several of those present. He asks forgiveness, and specifies the sins that are outstanding, prefacing each one with *an if it be true—*

An if it be true that the bairn born a fortnight past to ———
———'s wife has an almighty look about it of ———, then
wilt Thou Lord show mercy on all the participants . . .

An if it be true that ——— ——— cheated ——— ———
out of twenty pieces of lamb siller [silver] at the last St. Bos-
well's sheep fair, then we pray Thee, O Lord, in spite of such
devil's doing . . .

Some of those named could not be held back, and his
friends had to drag James out before harm came to him.

By this time he was probably a widower, a fellow on the
loose, too poor for any likely woman to marry. His wife had
borne him a daughter and five sons, then died at the birth of
the last one. Mary, Robert, James, Andrew, William, Walter.

Writing to an emigration society around the time of Water-
loo, he presents himself as an excellent prospect, because of the
five strong sons who will accompany him to the New World.
Whether or not he was offered help to emigrate I do not know.
Probably not, because we next hear of him having trouble raising the fare. A depression has followed the end of the
Napoleonic Wars, and the price of sheep has fallen. And there
is no more boast of the five sons. Robert, the eldest, has taken
off for the Highlands. James—the younger James—has gone
to America, which includes Canada, all on his own, and it
seems he has not sent word to say where he is or what he is
doing. (He is in Nova Scotia, and he is teaching school in a
place called Economy, though he has no qualifications for this
except what he got in the Ettrick schoolhouse, and probably a
strong right arm.)

And as for William, the second youngest, a boy not yet out
of his teens who will be my great-great-grandfather—he is
gone as well. When we next hear of him he is settled in the
Highlands, a factor on one of the new sheep farms cleared of

the crofters. And so scornful is he of the place where he was born, as to write—in a letter to the girl he later marries—that it would be unthinkable for him to live in the Ettrick Valley ever again.

The poverty and the ignorance distress him, apparently. The poverty which seems to him willful, and the ignorance which he judges to be ignorant even of its own existence. He is a modern man.

The View from Castle Rock

The first time Andrew was ever in Edinburgh he was ten years old. With his father and some other men he climbed a slippery black street. It was raining, the city smell of smoke filled the air, and the half-doors were open, showing the firelit insides of taverns which he hoped they might enter, because he was wet through. They did not, they were bound somewhere else. Earlier on the same afternoon they had been in some such place, but it was not much more than an alcove, a hole in the wall, with planks on which bottles and glasses were set and coins laid down. He had been continually getting squeezed out of that shelter into the street and into the puddle that caught the drip from the ledge over the entryway. To keep that from happening, he had butted in low down between the cloaks and sheepskins, wedged himself amongst the drinking men and under their arms.

He was surprised at the number of people his father seemed to know in the city of Edinburgh. You would think the people in the drinking place would be strangers to him, but it was evidently not so. Amongst the arguing and excited queer-sounding voices his father's voice rose the loudest. *America*, he said, and slapped his hand on the plank for attention, the very way he would do at home. Andrew had heard that word spoken in that same tone long before he knew it was a land across the ocean. It

was spoken as a challenge and an irrefutable truth but sometimes—when his father was not there—it was spoken as a taunt
or a joke. His older brothers might ask each other, "Are ye awa
to America?" when one of them put on his plaid to go out and
do some chore such as penning the sheep. Or, "Why don't ye be
off to America?" when they had got into an argument, and one
of them wanted to make the other out to be a fool.

The cadences of his father's voice, in the talk that succeeded
that word, were so familiar, and Andrew's eyes so bleary with
the smoke, that in no time he had fallen asleep on his feet. He
wakened when several pushed together out of the place and his
father with them. Some one of them said, "Is this your lad here
or is it some tinker squeezed in to pick our pockets?" and his
father laughed and took Andrew's hand and they began their
climb. One man stumbled and another man knocked into him
and swore. A couple of women swiped their baskets at the
party with great scorn, and made some remarks in their unfamiliar speech, of which Andrew could only make out the
words "daecent bodies" and "public footpaths."

Then his father and the friends stepped aside into a much
broader street, which in fact was a courtyard, paved with large
blocks of stone. His father turned and paid attention to Andrew at this point.

"Do you know where you are, lad? You're in the castle yard,
and this is Edinburgh Castle that has stood for ten thousand
years and will stand for ten thousand more. Terrible deeds were
done here. These stones have run with blood. Do you know
that?" He raised his head so that they all listened to what he
was telling.

"It was King Jamie asked the young Douglases to have supper with him and when they were fair sitten down he says, oh,
we won't bother with their supper, take them out in the yard

and chop off their heads. And so they did. Here in the yard where we stand.

"But that King Jamie died a leper," he went on with a sigh, then a groan, making them all be still to consider this fate.

Then he shook his head.

"Ah, no, it wasn't him. It was King Robert the Bruce that died a leper. He died a king but he died a leper."

Andrew could see nothing but enormous stone walls, barred gates, a redcoat soldier marching up and down. His father did not give him much time, anyway, but shoved him ahead and through an archway, saying, "Watch your heads here, lads, they was wee little men in those days. Wee little men. So is Boney the Frenchman, there's a lot of fight in your wee little men."

They were climbing uneven stone steps, some as high as Andrew's knees—he had to crawl occasionally—inside what as far as he could make out was a roofless tower. His father called out, "Are ye all with me then, are ye all in for the climb?" and some straggling voices answered him. Andrew got the impression that there was not such a crowd following as there had been on the street.

They climbed far up in the roundabout stairway and at last came out on a bare rock, a shelf, from which the land fell steeply away. The rain had ceased for the present.

"Ah, there," said Andrew's father. "Now where's all the ones was tramping on our heels to get here?"

One of the men just reaching the top step said, "There's two-three of them took off to have a look at the Meg."

"Engines of war," said Andrew's father. "All they have eyes for is engines of war. Take care they don't go and blow themselves up."

"Haven't the heart for the stairs, more like," said another

man who was panting. And the first one said cheerfully, "Scairt to get all the way up here, scairt they're bound to fall off."

A third man—and that was the lot—came staggering across the shelf as if he had in mind to do that very thing.

"Where is it then?" he hollered. "Are we up on Arthur's seat?"

"Ye are not," said Andrew's father. "Look beyond you."

The sun was out now, shining on the stone heap of houses and streets below them, and the churches whose spires did not reach to this height, and some little trees and fields, then a wide silvery stretch of water. And beyond that a pale green and grayish-blue land, part in sunlight and part in shadow, a land as light as mist, sucked into the sky.

"So did I not tell you?" Andrew's father said. "America. It is only a little bit of it, though, only the shore. There is where every man is sitting in the midst of his own properties, and even the beggars is riding around in carriages."

"Well the sea does not look so wide as I thought," said the man who had stopped staggering. "It does not look as if it would take you weeks to cross it."

"It is the effect of the height we're on," said the man who stood beside Andrew's father. "The height we're on is making the width of it the less."

"It's a fortunate day for the view," said Andrew's father. "Many a day you could climb up here and see nothing but the fog."

He turned and addressed Andrew.

"So there you are my lad and you have looked over at America," he said. "God grant you one day you will see it closer up and for yourself."

. . .

Andrew has been to the Castle one time since, with a group of the lads from Ettrick, who all wanted to see the great cannon, Mons Meg. But nothing seemed to be in the same place then and he could not find the route they had taken to climb up to the rock. He saw a couple of places blocked off with boards that could have been it. But he did not even try to peer through them—he had no wish to tell the others what he was looking for. Even when he was ten years old he had known that the men with his father were drunk. If he did not understand that his father was drunk—due to his father's sure-footedness and sense of purpose, his commanding behavior—he did certainly understand that something was not as it should be. He knew he was not looking at America, though it was some years before he was well enough acquainted with maps to know that he had been looking at Fife.

Still, he did not know if those men met in the tavern had been mocking his father, or if it was his father playing one of his tricks on them.

Old James the father. Andrew. Walter. Their sister Mary. Andrew's wife Agnes, and Agnes and Andrew's son James, under two years old.

In the harbor of Leith, on the 4th of June, 1818, they set foot on board a ship for the first time in their lives.

Old James makes this fact known to the ship's officer who is checking off the names.

"The first time, serra, in all my long life. We are men of the Ettrick. It is a landlocked part of the world."

The officer says a word which is unintelligible to them but plain in meaning. Move along. He has run a line through their names. They move along or are pushed along, Young James riding on Mary's hip.

"What is this?" says Old James, regarding the crowd of people on deck. "Where are we to sleep? Where have all these rabble come from? Look at the faces on them, are they the blackamoors?"

"Black Highlanders, more like," says his son Walter. This is a joke, muttered so his father cannot hear—Highlanders being one of the sorts the old man despises.

"There are too many people," his father continues. "The ship will sink."

"No," says Walter, speaking up now. "Ships do not often sink because of too many people. That's what the fellow was there for, to count the people."

Barely on board the vessel and this seventeen-year-old whelp has taken on knowing airs, he has taken to contradicting his father. Fatigue, astonishment, and the weight of the great-coat he is wearing prevent Old James from cuffing him.

All the business of life aboard ship has already been explained to the family. In fact it has been explained by the old man himself. He was the one who knew all about provisions, accommodations, and the kind of people you would find on board. All Scotsmen and all decent folk. No Highlanders, no Irish.

But now he cries out that it is like the swarm of bees in the carcass of the lion.

"An evil lot, an evil lot. Oh, that ever we left our native land!"

"We have not left yet," says Andrew. "We are still looking at Leith. We would do best to go below and find ourselves a place."

More lamentation. The bunks are narrow, bare planks with horsehair pallets both hard and prickly.

"Better than nothing," says Andrew.

"Oh, that it was ever put in my head to bring us here, onto this floating sepulchre."

Will nobody shut him up? thinks Agnes. This is the way he will go on and on, like a preacher or a lunatic, when the fit takes him. She cannot abide it. She is in more agony herself than he is ever likely to know.

"Well, are we going to settle here or are we not?" she says.

Some people have hung up their plaids or shawls to make a half-private space for their families. She goes ahead and takes off her outer wrappings to do the same.

The child is turning somersaults in her belly. Her face is hot as a coal and her legs throb and the swollen flesh in between them—the lips the child must soon part to get out—is a scalding sack of pain. Her mother would have known what to do about that, she would have known which leaves to mash to make a soothing poultice.

At the thought of her mother such misery overcomes her that she wants to kick somebody.

Andrew folds up his plaid to make a comfortable seat for his father. The old man seats himself, groaning, and puts his hands up to his face, so that his speaking has a hollow sound.

"I will see no more. I will not harken to their screeching voices or their satanic tongues. I will not swallow a mouth of meat nor meal until I see the shores of America."

All the more for the rest of us, Agnes feels like saying.

Why does Andrew not speak plainly to his father, reminding him of whose idea it was, who was the one who harangued and borrowed and begged to get them just where they are now?

Andrew will not do it, Walter will only joke, and as for Mary she can hardly get her voice out of her throat in her father's presence.

Agnes comes from a large Hawick family of weavers, who work in the mills now but worked for generations at home. And working there they learned all the arts of cutting each other down to size, of squabbling and surviving in close quarters. She is still surprised by the rigid manners, the deference and silences in her husband's family. She thought from the beginning that they were a queer sort of people and she thinks so still. They are as poor as her own folk, but they have such a great notion of themselves. And what have they got to back this up? The old man has been a wonder in the tavern for years, and their cousin is a raggedy lying poet who had to flit to Nithsdale when nobody would trust him to tend sheep in Ettrick. They were all brought up by three witchey-women of aunts who were so scared of men that they would run and hide in the sheep pen if anybody but their own family was coming along the road.

As if it wasn't the men that should be running from them.

Walter has come back from carrying their heavier possessions down to a lower depth of the ship.

"You never saw such a mountain of boxes and trunks and sacks of meal and potatoes," he says excitedly. "A person has to climb over them to get to the water pipe. Nobody can help but spill their water on the way back and the sacks will be wet through and the stuff will be rotted."

"They should not have brought all that," says Andrew. "Did they not undertake to feed us when we paid our way?"

"Aye," says the old man. "But will it be fit for us to eat?"

"So a good thing I brought my cakes," says Walter, who is still in the mood to make a joke of anything. He taps his foot on the snug metal box filled with oat cakes that his aunts gave him as a particular present because he was the youngest and they still thought of him as the motherless one.

"You'll see how merry you'll be if we're starving," says Agnes. Walter is a pest to her, almost as much as the old man. She knows there is probably no chance of them starving, because Andrew is looking impatient, but not anxious. It takes a good deal, of course, to make Andrew anxious. He is apparently not anxious about her, since he thought first to make a comfortable seat for his father.

Mary has taken Young James back up to the deck. She could tell that he was alarmed down there in the half-dark. He does not have to whimper or complain—she knows his feelings by the way he digs his little knees into her.

The sails are furled tight. "Look up there, look up there," Mary says, and points to a sailor who is busy high up in the rigging. The boy on her hip makes his sound for bird. "Sailor-peep, sailor-peep," she says. She says the right word for *sailor* but his word for *bird*. She and he communicate in a half-and-half language—half her teaching and half his invention. She believes that he is one of the cleverest children ever born into the world. Being the eldest of her family, and the only girl, she has tended all of her brothers, and been proud of them all at one time, but she has never known a child like this. Nobody else has any idea of how original and independent and clever he is. Men have no interest in children so young, and Agnes his mother has no patience with him.

"Talk like folk," Agnes says to him, and if he doesn't, she may give him a clout. "What are you?" she says. "Are you a folk or an elfit?"

Mary fears Agnes's temper, but in a way she doesn't blame her. She thinks that women like Agnes—men's women, mother women—lead an appalling life. First with what the men do to them—even so good a man as Andrew—and then what the children do, coming out. She will never forget her own mother, who lay in bed out of her mind with a fever, not knowing any of them, till she died, three days after Walter was born. She had screamed at the black pot hanging over the fire, thinking it was full of devils.

Her brothers call Mary *Poor Mary,* and indeed the meagreness and timidity of many of the women in their family has caused that word to be attached to the names they were given at their christening—names that were themselves altered to something less substantial and graceful. Isabel became Poor Tibbie; Margaret, Poor Maggie; Jane, Poor Jennie. People in Ettrick said it was a fact that the looks and the height went to the men.

Mary is under five feet tall and has a little tight face with a lump of protruding chin, and a skin that is subject to fiery eruptions that take a long time to fade. When she is spoken to her mouth twitches as if the words were all mixed up with her spittle and her crooked little teeth, and the response she manages is a dribble of speech so faint and scrambled that it is hard for people not to think her dim-witted. She has great difficulty in looking anybody in the face—even the members of her own family. It is only when she gets the boy hitched on to the narrow shelf of her hip that she is capable of some coherent and decisive speech—and then it is mostly to him.

Somebody is saying something to her now. It is a person almost as small as herself—a little brown man, a sailor, with gray whiskers and not a tooth in his head. He is looking straight at her and then at Young James and back to her again—right in the middle of the pushing or loitering, bewildered or inquisitive crowd. At first she thinks it is a foreign language he is speaking, but then she makes out the word *cu*. She finds herself answering with the same word, and he laughs and waves his arms, pointing to somewhere farther back on the ship, then pointing at James and laughing again. Something she should take James to see. She has to say, "Aye. Aye," to stop him gabbling, and then to step off in that direction so that he won't be disappointed.

She wonders what part of the country or the world he could have come from, then realizes that this is the first time in her life that she has ever spoken to a stranger. And except for the difficulty of understanding what he was saying, she has managed it more easily than when having to speak to a neighbor in the Ettrick, or to her father.

She hears the bawling of the cow before she can see it. The press of people increases around her and James, forms a wall in front of her and squeezes her from behind. Then she hears the bawling in the sky and looking up sees the brown beast dangling in the air, all caged in ropes and kicking and roaring frantically. It is held by a hook on a crane, which now hauls it out of sight. People around her are hooting and clapping hands. Some child's voice cries out in the language she understands, wanting to know if the cow will be dropped into the sea. A man's voice tells him no, she will go along with them on the ship.

"Will they milk her then?"

"Aye. Keep still. They'll milk her," says the man reprovingly. And another man's voice climbs boisterously over his.

"They'll milk her till they take the hammer to her, and then ye'll have the blood pudding for yer dinner."

Now follow the hens swung through the air in crates, all squawking and fluttering in their confinement and pecking each other when they can, so that some feathers escape and float down through the air. And after them a pig trussed up like the cow, squealing with a human note in its distress and shitting wildly in midair, so that howls of both outrage and delight rise below, depending on whether they come from those who are hit or those who see others hit.

James is laughing too, he recognizes shite, and cries out his own word for it, which is *gruggin.*

Someday he may remember this. *I saw a cow and a pig fly through the air.* Then he may wonder if it was a dream. And nobody will be there—she will certainly not be there—to tell that it was not a dream, it happened on this ship. He will know that he was once on a ship because he will have been told that, but it's possible that he will never see a ship like this again in all his waking life. She has no idea where they will go when they reach the other shore, but imagines it will be some place inland, among the hills, some place like the Ettrick.

She does not think she will live long, wherever they go. She coughs in the summer as well as the winter and when she coughs her chest aches. She suffers from sties, and cramps in the stomach, and her bleeding comes rarely but may last a month when it does come. She hopes, though, that she will not die while James is still of a size to ride on her hip or still in need of her, which he will be for a while yet. She knows that the time will come when he will turn away as her brothers did, when he will become ashamed of the connection with her. That is what she tells herself will happen, but like anybody in love she cannot believe it.

On a trip to Peebles before they left home, Walter bought himself a book to write in, but for several days he has found too much to pay attention to, and too little space or quiet on the deck, even to open it. He has a vial of ink, as well, held in a leather pouch and strapped to his chest under his shirt. That was the trick used by their cousin, Jamie Hogg the poet, when he was out in the wilds of Nithsdale, watching the sheep. When a rhyme came on Jamie he would pull a wad of paper out of his breeks' pocket and uncork the ink which the heat of his heart had kept from freezing and write it all down, no matter where he was or in what weather.

Or so he said. And Walter had thought to put this method to the test. But it might have been an easier matter amongst sheep than amongst people. Also the wind can surely blow harder over the sea even than it could blow in Nithsdale. And it is essential of course for him to get out of the sight of his own family. Andrew might mock him mildly but Agnes would do it boldly, incensed as she could be by the thought of anybody doing anything she would not want to do. Mary, of course, would never say a word, but the boy on her hip that she idolized and spoiled would be all for grabbing and destroying both pen and paper. And there was no knowing what interference might come from their father.

Now after some investigating around the deck he has found a favorable spot. The cover of his book is hard, he has no need of a table. And the ink warmed on his chest flows as willingly as blood.

We came on board on the 4th day of June and lay the 5th, 6th, 7th, and 8th in the Leith roads getting the ship to our place where we could set sail which was on the 9th. We passed the corner of Fifeshire all well nothing occurring worth mentioning till this day the 13th in the morning when we were awakened by a cry, John

O'Groats house. We could see it plain and had a fine sail across the Pentland Firth having both wind and tide in our favour and it was in no way dangerous as we had heard tell. Their was a child had died, the name of Ormiston and its body was thrown overboard sewed up in a piece of canvas with a large lump of coal at its feet . . .

He pauses in his writing to think of the weighted sack falling down through the water. Darker and darker grows the water with the surface high overhead gleaming faintly like the night sky. Would the piece of coal do its job, would the sack fall straight down to the very bottom of the sea? Or would the current of the sea be strong enough to keep lifting it up and letting it fall, pushing it sideways, taking it as far as Greenland or south to the tropical waters full of rank weeds, the Sargasso Sea? Or some ferocious fish might come along and rip the sack and make a meal of the body before it had even left the upper waters and the region of light.

He has seen drawings of fish as big as horses, fish with horns as well, and scores of teeth each like a skinner's knife. Also some that are smooth and smiling, and wickedly teasing, having the breasts of women but not the other parts which the sight of the breasts conducts a man's thoughts to. All this in a book of stories and engravings that he got out of the Peebles Subscription Library.

These thoughts do not distress him. He always sets himself to think clearly and if possible to picture accurately the most disagreeable or shocking things, so as to reduce their power over him. As he pictures it now, the child is being eaten. Not swallowed whole as in the case of Jonah but chewed into bits as he himself would chew a tasty chunk from a boiled sheep. But there is the matter of a soul. The soul leaves the body at the moment of death. But from which part of the body does it leave, what has been its particular bodily location? The best guess seems to be that it emerges with the last breath, having been hidden somewhere in the chest around the place of the heart and the lungs. Though Walter has heard a joke they used to tell about an old fellow in the Ettrick, to the effect that he was so dirty that when he died his soul came out his arsehole, and was heard to do so, with a mighty explosion.

This is the sort of information that preachers might be expected to give you—not mentioning anything like an arsehole of course but explaining something of the soul's proper location and exit. But they shy away from it. Also they cannot explain—or he has never heard one explain—how the souls maintain themselves outside of bodies until the Day of Judgment and how on that day each one finds and recognizes the body that is its own and reunites with it, though it be not so much as a skeleton at that time. *Though it be dust.* There must be some who have studied enough to know how all this is accomplished. But there are also some—he has learned this recently—who have studied and read and thought till they have come to the conclusion that there are no souls at all. No one cares to speak about these people either, and indeed the thought of them is terrible. How can they live with the fear—indeed, the certainty—of Hell before them?

There was the man like that who came from by Berwick, Fat Davey he was called, because he was so fat the table had to be cut away so he could sit down to his meal. And when he died in Edinburgh, where he was some sort of scholar, the people stood in the street outside his house waiting to see if the

Devil would come to claim him. A sermon had been preached on that in Ettrick, which claimed as far as Walter could understand it that the Devil did not go in for displays of that sort and only superstitious and vulgar and Popish sort of people would expect him to, but that his embrace was nevertheless far more horrible and the torments that accompanied it more subtle than any such minds could imagine.

On the third day aboard ship Old James got up and started to walk around. Now he is walking all the time. He stops and speaks to anybody who seems ready to listen. He tells his name, and says that he comes from Ettrick, from the valley and forest of Ettrick, where the old Kings of Scotland used to hunt.

"And on the field at Flodden," he says, "after the battle of Flodden, they said you could walk up and down among the corpses and pick out the men from the Ettrick, because they were the tallest and the strongest and the finest-looking men on the ground. I have five sons and they are all good strong lads but only two of them are with me. One of my sons is in Nova Scotia, he is the one with my own name and the last I heard of him he was in a place called Economy, but we have not had any word of him since, and I do not know whether he is alive or dead. My eldest son went off to work in the Highlands, and the son that is next to the youngest took it into his head to go off there too, and I will never see either of them again. Five sons and by the mercy of God all grew to be men, but it was not the Lord's will that I should keep them with me. Their mother died after the last of them was born. She took a fever and she never got up from her bed after she bore him. A man's life is full of sorrow. I have a daughter as well, the oldest

of them all, but she is nearly a dwarf. Her mother was chased
by a ram when she was carrying her. I have three old sisters all
the same, all dwarfs."

His voice rises over all the hubbub of shipboard life and his
sons make tracks in some other direction in dread embarrassment, whenever they hear it.

On the afternoon of the 14th a wind came from the
North and the ship began to shake as if every board that
was in it would fly loose from every other. The buckets
overflowed from the people that were sick and vomiting
and there was the contents of them slipping all over the
deck. All people were ordered below but many of them
crumpled up against the rail and did not care if they
were washed over. None of our family was sick however
and now the wind has dropped and the sun has come
out and those who did not care if they died in the filth a
little while ago have got up and dragged themselves to
be washed where the sailors are splashing buckets of
water over the decks. The women are busy too washing
and rinsing and wringing out all the foul clothing. It is
the worst misery and the suddenest recovery I have seen
ever in my life . . .

A young girl ten or twelve years old stands watching Walter
write. She is wearing a fancy dress and bonnet and has light-
brown curly hair. Not so much a pretty face as a pert one.

"Are you from one of the cabins?" she says.

Walter says, "No. I am not."

"I knew you were not. There are only four of them and one
is for my father and me and one is for the captain and one is
for his mother and she never comes out and one is for the two

ladies. You are not supposed to be on this part of the deck unless you are from one of the cabins."

"Well, I did not know that," Walter says, but does not bestir himself to move away.

"I have seen you before writing in your book."

"I haven't seen you."

"No. You were writing, so you didn't notice."

"Well," says Walter. "I'm finished with it now anyway."

"I haven't told anybody about you," she says carelessly, as if that was a matter of choice, and she might well change her mind.

And on that same day but an hour or so on, there comes a great cry from the port side that there is a last sight of Scotland. Walter and Andrew go over to see that, and Mary with Young James on her hip and many others. Old James and Agnes do not go—she because she objects now to moving herself anywhere, and he on account of perversity. His sons have urged him to go but he has said, "It is nothing to me. I have seen the last of the Ettrick so I have seen the last of Scotland already."

It turns out that the cry to say farewell has been premature—a gray rim of land will remain in place for hours yet. Many will grow tired of looking at it—it is just land, like any other—but some will stay at the rail until the last rag of it fades, with the daylight.

"You should go and say farewell to your native land and the last farewell to your mother and father for you will not be seeing them again," says Old James to Agnes. "And there is worse yet you will have to endure. Aye, but there is. You have the curse of Eve." He says this with the mealy relish of a preacher and Agnes calls him an old shite-bag under her breath, but she has hardly the energy even to scowl.

Old shite-bag. You and your native land.

Walter writes at last a single sentence.

And this night in the year 1818 we lost sight of Scotland.

The words seem majestic to him. He is filled with a sense of grandeur, solemnity, and personal importance.

16th was a very windy day with the wind coming out of the S.W. the sea was running very high and the ship got her gib-boom broken on account of the violence of the wind. And this day our sister Agnes was taken into the cabin.

Sister, he has written, as if she were all the same to him as poor Mary, but that is hardly the case. Agnes is a tall well-built girl with thick dark hair and dark eyes. The flush on one of her cheeks slides into a splotch of pale brown as big as a handprint. It is a birthmark, which people say is a pity, because without it she would be handsome. Walter can hardly bear looking at it, but this is not because it is ugly. It is because he longs to touch it, to stroke it with the tips of his fingers. It looks not like ordinary skin but like the velvet on a deer. His feelings about her are so troubling that he can only speak unpleasantly to her if he speaks at all. And she pays him back with a good seasoning of contempt.

. . .

Agnes thinks that she is in the water and the waves are heaving her up and slamming her down again. Every time the waves slap her down it is worse than the time before and she sinks farther and deeper, with the moment of relief passing before she can grab it, for the wave is already gathering its power to hit her again.

Then sometimes she knows she is in a bed, a strange bed and strangely soft, but it is all the worse for that because when she sinks down there is no resistance, no hard place where the pain has to stop. And here or on the water people keep rushing back and forth in front of her. They are all seen sideways and all transparent, talking very fast so she can't make them out, and maliciously taking no heed of her. She sees Andrew in the midst of them, and two or three of his brothers. Some of the girls she knows are there too—the friends she used to lark around with in Hawick. And they do not give a glance or a poor penny for the plight she is in now.

She shouts at them to take themselves off but not one of them pays any attention and she sees more of them coming right through the wall. She never knew before that she had so many enemies. They are grinding her and pretending they don't even know it. Their movement is grinding her to death.

Her mother bends over her and says in a drawling, cold, lackadaisical voice, "You are not trying, my girl. You must try harder." Her mother is all dressed up and talking fine, like some Edinburgh lady.

Evil stuff is poured into her mouth. She tries to spit it out, knowing it is poison.

I will just get up and get out of this, she thinks. She starts trying to pull herself loose from her body, as if it were a heap of rags all on fire.

A man's voice is heard, giving some order.

"Hold her," he says and she is split and stretched wide open to the world and the fire.

"Ah—ah—ahh," the man's voice says, panting as if he has been running in a race.

Then a cow that is so heavy, bawling heavy with milk, rears up and sits down on Agnes's stomach.

"Now. Now," says the man's voice, and he groans at the end of his strength as he tries to heave it off.

The fools. The fools, ever to have let it in.

She was not better till the 18th when she was delivered of a daughter. We having a surgeon on board nothing happened. Nothing occurred till the 22nd this was the roughest day we had till then experienced. The gibboom was broken a second time. Nothing worth mentioning happened Agnes was mending in an ordinary way till the 29th we saw a great shoal of porpoises and the 30th (yesterday) was a very rough sea with the wind blowing from the west we went rather backwards than forwards . . .

"In the Ettrick there is what they call the highest house in Scotland," James says, "and the house that my grandfather lived in was a higher one than that. The name of the place is Phauhope, they call it Phaup, my grandfather was Will O'Phaup and fifty years ago you would have heard of him if you came from any place south of the Forth and north of the Debatable Lands."

Unless a person stops up his ears, what is to be done but listen? thinks Walter. There are people who curse to see the old man coming but there do seem to be others who are glad of any distraction.

He is telling about Will and his races, and the wagers on him, and other foolishness more than Walter can bear.

"And he married a woman named Bessie Scott and one of his sons was named Robert and that same Robert was my father. My father. And I am standing here in front of you."

"In but one leap Will could clear the river Ettrick, and the place is marked."

For the first two or three days Young James has refused to be unfastened from Mary's hip. He has been bold enough, but only if he can stay there. At night he has slept in her cloak, curled up beside her, and she has wakened aching along her left side because she lay stiffly all night not to disturb him. Then in the space of one morning he is down and running about and kicking at her if she tries to hoist him up.

Everything on the ship is calling out for his attention. Even at night he tries to climb over her and run away in the dark. So she gets up aching not only from her stiff position but from lack of sleep altogether. One night she drops off and the child gets loose but most fortunately stumbles against his father's body in his bid for escape. Henceforth Andrew insists that he be tied down every night. He howls of course, and Andrew shakes him and cuffs him and then he sobs himself to sleep. Mary lies by him softly explaining how this is necessary so that he should not fall off the ship into the ocean, but he regards her at these times as his enemy and if she puts a hand to stroke his face he tries to bite it with his baby teeth. Every night he goes to sleep in a rage, but in the morning when she unties him, still half-asleep and full of his infant sweetness, he clings to her drowsily and she is suffused with love.

The truth is that she loves even his howls and his rages and his kicks and his bites. She loves his dirty and his curdled smells as well as his fresh ones. As his drowsiness leaves him his clear blue eyes, looking into hers, fill with a marvellous intelligence and an imperious will, which seem to her to come straight from Heaven. (Though her religion has always taught her that self-will comes from the opposite direction.) She loved her brothers too when they were sweet and wild and had to be kept from falling into the burn, but surely not as passionately as she loves James.

Then one day he is gone. She is in the line for the wash water and she turns around and he is not beside her. She has just been speaking a few words to the woman ahead of her, answering a question about Agnes and the infant, she has just told its name—Isabel—and in that moment he has got away. When she was saying the name, Isabel, she felt a surprising longing to hold that new, exquisitely light bundle, and as she abandons her place in line and chases about for sight of James it seems to her that he must have felt her disloyalty and vanished to punish her.

Everything in an instant is overturned. The nature of the world is altered. She runs back and forth, crying out James's name. She runs up to strangers, to sailors who laugh at her as she begs them, "Have you seen a little boy, have you seen a little boy this high, he has blue eyes?"

"I seen a fifty or sixty of them like that in the last five minutes," a man says to her. A woman trying to be kind says that he will turn up, Mary should not worry herself, he will be playing with some of the other children. Some women even look about as if they would help her to search, but of course they cannot, they have their own responsibilities.

This is what Mary plainly sees, in those moments of anguish—that the world which has turned into a horror for her is still the same ordinary world for all these other people and will remain so even if James has truly vanished, even if he has crawled through the ship's railings—she has noticed, all over, the places where this could be possible—and is swallowed in the ocean.

The most brutal and unthinkable of all events, to her, could seem to most others like a sad but not extraordinary misadventure. It would not be unthinkable to them.

Or to God. For in fact when God makes some rare and remarkably beautiful human child, is He not particularly tempted to take His creature back, as if the world did not deserve it?

But she is praying to Him, all the time. At first she only called on the Lord's name. But as her search grows more specific and in some ways more bizarre—she is ducking under clotheslines that people have contrived for privacy, she thinks nothing of interrupting folk at any business, she flings up the lids of their boxes and roots in their bedclothes, not even hearing them when they curse her—her prayers also become more complicated and audacious. She seeks for something to offer, something that could be the price of James's being restored to her. But what does she have? Nothing of her own—not health or prospects or anybody's regard. There is no piece of luck or even a hope she can offer to give up. What she has is James.

And how can she offer James for James?

This is what is knocking around in her head.

But what about her love of James? Her extreme and perhaps idolatrous, perhaps wicked love of another creature. She will give up that, she will give it up gladly, if only he isn't gone, if only he can be found. If only he isn't dead.

. . .

She recalls all this, an hour or two after somebody has noticed the boy peeping out from under an empty bucket, listening to the hubbub. And she retracted her vow at once. She grabbed him in her arms and held him hard against her and took deep groaning breaths, while he struggled to get free.

Her understanding of God is shallow and unstable and the truth is that except in a time of terror such as she has just experienced, she does not really care. She has always felt that God or even the idea of Him was more distant from her than from other people. Also she does not fear His punishments after death as she should and she does not even know why. There is a stubborn indifference in her mind that nobody knows about. In fact, everybody may think that she clings secretly to religion because so little else is available to her. They are quite wrong, and now she has James back she gives no thanks but thinks what a fool she was and how she could not give up her love of him any more than stop her heart beating.

After that, Andrew insists that James be tied not only by night but to the post of the bunk or to their own clothesline on the deck, by day. Mary wishes him to be tethered to her but Andrew says a boy like that would kick her to pieces. Andrew has trounced him for the trick he played, but the look in James's eyes says that his tricks are not finished.

That climb in Edinburgh, that sighting across the water, was a thing Andrew did not even mention to his own brothers— America being already a sore enough matter. The oldest brother, Robert, went off to the Highlands as soon as he was grown, leaving home without a farewell on an evening when his father was at Tibbie Shiel's. He made it plain that he was doing this in order not to have to join any expedition that their father might have in mind. Then the brother James perversely set out for America on his own, saying that at least if he did that, he could save himself hearing any more about it. And finally Will, younger than Andrew but always the most contrary and the most bitterly set against the father, Will too had run away, to join Robert. That left only Walt, who was still childish enough to be thinking of adventures—he had grown up bragging about how he was going to fight the French, so maybe now he thought he'd fight the Indians.

And then there was Andrew himself, who ever since that day on the rock has felt about his father a deep bewildered sense of responsibility, much like sorrow.

But then, Andrew feels a responsibility for everybody in his family. For his often ill-tempered young wife, whom he has again brought into a state of peril, for the brothers far away and the brother at his side, for his pitiable sister and his heedless child. This is his burden—it never occurs to him to call it love.

Agnes keeps asking for salt, till they begin to fear that she will fuss herself into a fever. The two women looking after her are cabin passengers, Edinburgh ladies, who took on the job out of charity.

"You be still now," they tell her. "You have no idea what a fortunate lassie you are that we had Mr. Suter on board."

They tell her that the baby was turned the wrong way inside her, and they were all afraid that Mr. Suter would have to cut her, and that might be the end of her. But he had managed to get it turned so that he could wrestle it out.

"I need salt for my milk," says Agnes, who is not going to let them put her in her place with their reproaches and Edinburgh speech. They are idiots anyway. She has to tell them how you must put a little salt in the baby's first milk, just place a few grains on your finger and squeeze a drop or two of milk onto it and let the child swallow that before you put it to the breast. Without this precaution there is a good chance that it will grow up half-witted.

"Is she even a Christian?" says the one of them to the other.

"I am as much as you," Agnes says. But to her own surprise and shame she starts to weep aloud, and the baby howls along with her, out of sympathy or out of hunger. And still she refuses to feed it.

Mr. Suter comes in to see how she is. He asks what all the grief is about, and they tell him the trouble.

"A newborn baby to get salt on its stomach—where did she get the idea?"

He says, "Give her the salt." And he stays to see her squeeze the milk on her salty finger, lay the finger to the infant's lips, and follow it with her nipple.

He asks her what the reason is and she tells him.

"And does it work every time?"

She tells him—a little surprised that he is as stupid as they are, though kinder—that it works without fail.

"So where you come from they all have their wits about them? And are all the girls strong and good-looking like you?"

She says that she would not know about that.

Sometimes visiting young men, educated and from the town, used to hang around her and her friends, complimenting them and trying to work up a conversation, and she always thought any girl was a fool who allowed it, even if the man was handsome. Mr. Suter is far from handsome—he is too thin, and his face is badly pocked, so that at first she took him for an old fellow. But he has a kind voice, and if he is teasing her a little there could be no harm in it. No man would have the nature left to deal with a woman after looking at them spread wide, their raw parts open to the air.

"Are you sore?" he says, and she believes there is a shadow on his damaged cheeks, a slight blush rising. She says that she is no worse than she has to be, and he nods, picks up her wrist, and bows over it, strongly pressing her pulse.

"Lively as a racehorse," he says, with his hands still above her, as if he did not know where to drop them next. Then he decides to push back her hair and press his fingers to her temples, as well as behind her ears.

She will recall this touch, this curious, gentle, tingling pressure, with an addled mixture of scorn and longing, for many years to come.

"Good," he says. "No touch of a fever."

He watches, for a moment, the child sucking.

"All's well with you now," he says, with a sigh. "You have a fine daughter and she can say all her life that she was born at sea."

Andrew arrives later and stands at the foot of the bed. He has never looked on her in such a bed as this (a regular bed even though bolted to the wall). He is red with shame in front of the ladies, who have brought in the basin to wash her.

"That's it, is it?" he says, with a nod—not a glance—at the bundle beside her.

She laughs in a vexed way and asks, what did he think it was? That is all it takes to knock him off his unsteady perch, puncture his pretense of being at ease. Now he stiffens up, even redder, doused with fire. It isn't just what she has said, it is the whole scene, the smell of the infant and milk and blood, most of all the basin, the cloths, the women standing by, with their proper looks that can seem to a man both admonishing and full of derision.

He can't think of another word to say, so she has to tell him, with rough mercy, to get on his way, there's work to do here.

Some of the girls used to say that when you finally gave in and lay down with a man—even granting he was not the man of your first choice—it gave you a helpless but calm and even sweet feeling. Agnes does not recall that she felt that with Andrew. All she felt was that he was an honest lad and the one that she needed in her circumstances, and that it would never occur to him to run off and leave her.

Walter has continued to go to the same private place to write in his book and nobody has caught him there. Except the girl, of course. But things are even now with her. One day he arrived at the place and she was there before him, skipping with a red-tasselled rope. When she saw him she stopped, out of breath. And no sooner did she catch her breath but she began to cough, so that it was several minutes before she could speak. She sank down against the pile of canvas that concealed the spot, flushed and her eyes full of bright tears from the coughing. He simply stood and watched her, alarmed at this fit but not knowing what to do.

"Do you want me to fetch one of the ladies?"

He is on speaking terms with the Edinburgh women now, on account of Agnes. They take a kind interest in the mother and baby and Mary and Young James, and think that the old father is comical. They are also amused by Andrew and Walter, who seem to them so bashful. Walter is actually not so tongue-tied as Andrew is, but this business of humans giving birth (though he is used to it with sheep) fills him with dismay or outright disgust. Agnes has lost a great part of her sullen allure because of it. (As happened before, when she gave birth to Young James. But then, gradually, her offending powers returned. He thinks that unlikely to happen again. He has seen more of the world now, and on board this ship he has seen more of women.)

The coughing girl is shaking her curly head violently.

"I don't want them," she says, when she can gasp the words out. "I have never told anybody you come here. So you mustn't tell anybody about me."

"Well you are here by rights."

She shakes her head again and gestures for him to wait till she can speak more easily.

"I mean that you saw me skipping. My father hid my skipping rope but I found where he hid it—but he doesn't know that."

"It isn't the Sabbath," Walter says reasonably. "So what is wrong with you skipping?"

"How do I know?" she says, regaining her saucy tone. "Perhaps he thinks I am too old for it. Will you swear not to tell anyone?" She holds up her forefingers to make a cross. The gesture is innocent, he knows, but nevertheless he is shocked, knowing how some people might look at it.

But he says that he is willing to swear.

"I swear too," she says. "I won't tell anyone you come here." After saying this quite solemnly, she makes a face.

"Though I was not going to tell about you anyway."

What a queer self-important little thing she is. She speaks only of her father, so he thinks it must be she has no brothers or sisters and—like himself—no mother. That condition has probably made her both spoiled and lonely.

Following this swearing, the girl—her name is Nettie—becomes a frequent visitor when Walter intends to write in his book. She always says that she does not want to disturb him but after keeping ostentatiously quiet for about five minutes she will interrupt him with some question about his life or bit of information about hers. It is true that she is motherless and an only child and she has never even been to school. She talks most about her pets—those dead and those living at her house in Edinburgh— and a woman named Miss Anderson who used to travel with her and teach her. It seems she was glad to see the back of this woman, and surely Miss Anderson would be glad to depart, after all the tricks that were played on her—the live frog in her boot and the woolen but lifelike mouse in her bed. Also Nettie's stomping on books that were not in favor and her pretense of being struck deaf and dumb when she got sick of reciting her spelling exercises.

She has been back and forth to America three times. Her father is a wine merchant whose business takes him to Montreal.

She wants to know all about how Walter and his people live. Her questions are by country standards quite impertinent. But Walter does not really mind—in his own family he has never been in a position that allowed him to instruct or teach or tease anybody younger than himself, and in a way it gives him pleasure.

It is certainly true, though, that in his own world, nobody would ever have got away with being so pert and forward and inquisitive as this Nettie. What does Walter's family have for supper when they are at home, how do they sleep? Are there animals kept in the house? Do the sheep have names, and what are the sheepdogs' names, and can you make pets of them? Why not? What is the arrangement of the scholars in the schoolroom, what do they write on, are the teachers cruel? What do some of his words mean that she does not understand, and do all the people where he is talk like him?

"Oh, aye," says Walter. "Even His Majesty the Duke does. The Duke of Buccleugh."

She laughs and freely pounds her little fist on his shoulder.

"Now you are teasing me. I know it. I know that dukes are not called Your Majesty. They are not."

One day she arrives with paper and drawing pencils. She says she has brought them to keep her busy so she will not be a nuisance to him. She says that she will teach him to draw if he wants to learn. But his attempts make her laugh, and he deliberately does worse and worse, till she laughs so hard she has one of her coughing fits. (These don't bother him so much anymore because he has seen how she always manages to survive them.) Then she says she will do some drawings in the back of his notebook, so that he will have them to remember the voyage. She does a drawing of the sails up above and of a hen that has escaped its cage somehow and is trying to travel like a seabird over the water. She sketches from memory her dog that died. Pirate. At first she claims his name was Walter but relents and admits later that she was not telling the truth. And she makes a picture of the icebergs she has seen, higher than houses, on one of her past voyages with her father. The setting sun shone through these icebergs and made them look—she says—like castles of gold. Rose-colored and gold.

"I wish I had my paint box. Then I could show you. But I do not know where it is packed. And my painting is not very good anyway, I am better at drawing."

Everything that she has drawn, including the icebergs, has a look that is both guileless and mocking, peculiarly expressive of herself.

"The other day I was telling you about that Will O'Phaup that was my grandfather but there was more to him than I told you. I did not tell you that he was the last man in Scotland to speak to the fairies. It is certain that I have never heard of any other, in his time or later."

Walter has been trapped into hearing this story—which he has, of course, heard often before, though not by his father's telling. He is sitting around a corner where some sailors are mending the torn sails. They talk among themselves from time to time—in English, maybe, but not any English that Walt can well make out—and occasionally they seem to listen to a bit of what Old James is telling. By the sounds that are made throughout the story Walter can guess that the out-of-sight audience is made up mostly of women.

But there is one tall well-dressed man—a cabin passenger, certainly—who has paused to listen within Walter's view. There is a figure close to this man's other side, and at one moment in the tale this figure peeps around to look at Walter and he sees that it is Nettie. She seems about to laugh but she puts a finger to her lips as if warning herself—and Walter—to keep silent.

The man must of course be her father. The two of them stand there listening quietly till the tale is over.

Then the man turns and speaks directly, in a familiar yet courteous way, to Walter.

"There is no telling what happened to the fellow's sheep. I hope the fairies did not get them."

Walter is alarmed, not knowing what to say. But Nettie looks at him with calming reassurance and the slightest smile, then drops her eyes and waits beside her father as a demure little miss should.

"Are you writing down what you can make of this?" the man asks, nodding at Walter's notebook.

"I am writing a journal of the voyage," Walter says stiffly.

"Now that is interesting. That is an interesting fact because I too am keeping a journal of this voyage. I wonder if we find the same things worth writing of."

"I only write what happens," Walt says, wanting to make clear that this is a job for him and not any idle pleasure. Still he feels that some further justification is called for. "I am writing to keep track of every day so that at the end of the voyage I can send a letter home."

The man's voice is smoother and his manner gentler than any address Walter is used to. He wonders if he is being made sport of in some way. Or if Nettie's father is the sort of person who strikes up an acquaintance with you in the hope of getting hold of your money for some worthless investment.

Not that Walter's looks or dress would mark him out as any likely prospect.

"So you do not describe what you see? Only what—as you say—is *happening*?"

Walter is about to say no, and then yes. For he has just thought, if he writes that there is a rough wind, is that not describing? You do not know where you are with this kind of person.

"You are not writing about what we have just heard?"

"No."

"It might be worth it. There are people who go around now prying into every part of Scotland and writing down whatever these old country folk have to say. They think that the old songs and stories are disappearing and that they are worth recording. I don't know about that, it isn't my business. But I would not be surprised if the people who have written it all down will find that it was worth their trouble—I mean to say, there will be money in it."

Nettie speaks up unexpectedly.

"Oh, hush, Father. The old fellow is going to start again."

This is not what any daughter would say to her father in Walter's experience, but the man seems ready to laugh, looking down at her fondly.

"Just one more thing I have to ask," he says. "What do you think of this about the fairies?"

"I think it is all nonsense," says Walter.

"He *has* started again," says Nettie crossly.

And indeed, Old James's voice has been going this little while, breaking in determinedly and reproachfully on those of his audience who might have thought it was time for their own conversations.

". . . and still another time, but in the long days in the summer, out on the hills late in the day but before it was well dark . . ."

The tall man nods but looks as if he had something still to inquire of Walter. Nettie reaches up and claps her hand over his mouth.

"And I will tell you and swear my life upon it that Will could not tell a lie, him that in his young days went to church to the preacher Thomas Boston, and Thomas Boston put the fear of the Lord like a knife into every man and woman, till their dying day. No, never. He would not lie."

.　.　.

"So that was all nonsense?" says the tall man quietly, when he is sure that the story has ended. "Well I am inclined to agree. You have a modern turn of mind?"

Walter says yes, he has, and he speaks more stoutly than he did before. He has heard these stories his father is spouting, and others like them, for the whole of his life, but the odd thing is that until they came on board this ship he never heard them from his father. The father he has known up till a short while ago would, he is certain, have had no use for them.

"This is a terrible place we live in," his father used to say. "The people is all full of nonsense and bad habits and even our sheep's wool is so coarse you cannot sell it. The roads are so bad a horse cannot go more than four miles in an hour. And for ploughing here they use the spade or the old Scotch plough though there has been a better plough in other places for fifty years. Oh, aye, aye, they say when you ask them, oh aye but it's too steep hereabouts, the land is too heavy."

"To be born in the Ettrick is to be born in a backward place," he would say. "Where the people is all believing in old stories and seeing ghosts and I tell you it is a curse to be born in the Ettrick."

And very likely that would lead him on to the subject of America, where all the blessings of modern invention were put to eager use and the people could never stop improving the world around them.

But harken at him now.

"I don't believe those were fairies," Nettie says.

"So do you think they were his neighbors all the time?" says her father. "Do you think they were playing a trick on him?"

Never has Walter heard a father speak to a child so indulgently. And fond as he has grown of Nettie he cannot approve of it. It can only make her believe that there are no opinions on the face of the earth that are more worthy of being listened to than hers.

"No I do not," she says.

"What then?" says her father.

"I think they were dead people."

"What do you know about dead people?" her father asks her, finally speaking with some sternness. "Dead people won't rise up till the Day of Judgment. I don't care to hear you making light about things of that sort."

"I was not making light," says Nettie carelessly.

The sailors are scrambling loose from their sails and pointing at the sky, far to the west. They must see there something that excites them. Walter makes bold to ask, "Are they English? I cannot tell what they say."

"Some of them are English, but from parts that sound foreign to us. Some are Portuguese. I cannot make them out either but I think that they are saying they see the rotches. They all have very keen eyes."

Walter believes that he too has very keen eyes, but it takes him a moment or two before he can see these birds, the ones that must be called rotches. Flocks and flocks of seabirds flashing and rising overhead, mere bright speckles on the air.

"You must make sure to mention those in your journal," Nettie's father says. "I have seen them when I made this voyage before. They feed on fish and here is the great place for them. Soon you'll see the fishermen as well. But the rotches filling the sky are the very first sign that we must be on the Grand Banks of Newfoundland.

"You must come up and talk to us on the deck above," he says, in bidding good-bye to Walter. "I have business to think about and I am not much company for my daughter. She is forbidden to run around because she is not quite recovered from the cold she had in the winter but she is fond of sitting and talking."

"I don't believe it is the rule for me to go there," says Walter, in some confusion.

"No, no, that is no matter. My girl is lonely. She likes to read and draw but she likes company too. She could show you how to draw, if you like. That would add to your journal."

If Walter flushes it is not noticed. Nettie remains quite composed.

So they sit out in the open and draw and write. Or she reads aloud to him from her favorite book, which is *The Scottish Chiefs*. He already knows much about what happens in the story—who does not know about William Wallace?—but she reads smoothly and at just the proper speed and makes some things solemn and others terrifying and something else comical, so that he is as much in thrall to the book as she is herself. Even though, as she says, she has read it twelve times already.

He understands a little better now why she has all those questions to ask him. He and his folk remind her of some people in her book. Such people as there were out on the hills and valleys in the olden times. What would she think if she knew that the *old fellow,* the old tale-spinner spouting all over the boat and penning people up to listen as if they were the sheep and he was the sheepdog—if she knew that he was Walter's father?

She would be delighted, probably, more curious about Walter's family than ever. She would not look down on them, except in a way she could not help or know about.

We came on the fishing banks of Newfoundland on the 12th of July and on the 19th we saw land and it was a joyful sight to us. It was a part of Newfoundland. We sailed between Newfoundland and St. Paul's Island and having a fair wind both the 18th and the 19th we found ourselves in the river on the morning of the 20th and within sight of the mainland of North America. We were awakened at about 1 o'clock in the morning and I think every passenger was out of bed at 4 o'clock gazing at the land, it being wholly covered with wood and quite a new sight to us. It was a part of Nova Scotia and a beautiful hilly country. We saw several whales this day such creatures as I never saw in my life.

This is the day of wonders. The land is covered with trees like a head with hair and behind the ship the sun rises tipping the top trees with light. The sky is clear and shining as a china plate and the water just playfully ruffled with wind. Every wisp of fog has gone and the air is full of the resinous smell of the trees. Seabirds are flashing above the sails all golden like creatures of Heaven, but the sailors raise a few shots to keep them from the rigging.

Mary holds Young James up so that he may always remember this first sight of the continent that will forever be his home. She tells him the name of this land—Nova Scotia.

"It means New Scotland," she says.

Agnes hears her. "Then why doesn't it say so?"

Mary says, "It's Latin, I think."

Agnes snorts with impatience. The baby has been waked up early by all the hubbub and celebration, and now she is miserable, wanting to be on the breast all the time, wailing whenever Agnes tries to take her off. Young James, observing all this closely, makes an attempt to get on the other breast, and Agnes bats him off so hard that he staggers.

"Suckie-laddie," Agnes calls him. He yelps a bit, then crawls around behind her and pinches the baby's toes.

Another whack.

"You're a rotten egg, you are," his mother says. "Somebody's been spoiling you till you think you're the Laird's arse."

Agnes's roused voice always makes Mary feel as if she is about to catch a blow herself.

Old James is sitting with them on the deck, but pays no attention to this domestic unrest.

"Will you come and look at the country, Father?" says Mary uncertainly. "You can have a better view from the rail."

"I can see it well enough," Old James says. Nothing in his voice suggests that the revelations around them are pleasing to him.

"Ettrick was covered with trees in the old days," he says. "The monks had it first and after that it was the royal forest. It was the King's forest. Beech trees, oak trees, rowan trees."

"As many trees as this?" says Mary, made bolder than usual by the novel splendors of the day.

"Better trees. Older. It was famous all over Scotland. The Royal Forest of Ettrick."

"And Nova Scotia is where our brother James is," Mary continues.

"He may be or he may not. It would be easy to die here and nobody know you were dead. Wild animals could have eaten him."

"Come near this baby again and I'll skin you alive," says Agnes to Young James who is circling her and the baby, pretending that they hold no interest for him.

Agnes is thinking it would serve him right, the fellow who never even took his leave of her. But she has to hope he will show up sometime and see her married to his brother. So that he will wonder. Also he will understand that in the end he did not get the better of her.

Mary wonders how her father can talk in that way, about how wild animals could have eaten his own son. Is that how the sorrows of the years take hold on you, to turn your heart of flesh to a heart of stone, as it says in the old song? And if it is so, how carelessly and disdainfully might he talk about her, who never meant to him a fraction of what the boys did?

Somebody has brought a fiddle on to the deck and is tuning up to play. People who have been hanging onto the rail and pointing out to each other what any one of them could see on their own—likewise repeating the name that by now everyone knows, Nova Scotia—are distracted by these sounds and begin to call for dancing. They call out the names of the reels and dances they want the fiddler to play. Space is cleared and couples line up in some sort of order and after a lot of uneasy fiddle-scraping and impatient shouts of encouragement, the music comes through and gathers its authority and the dancing begins.

Dancing, at seven o'clock in the morning.

Andrew comes up from below, bearing their supply of water. He stands and watches for a little, then surprises Mary by asking, would she dance?

"Who will look after the boy?" says Agnes immediately. "I am not going to get up and chase him." She is fond of dancing, but is prevented now, not only by the nursing baby but by the soreness of the parts of her body that were so battered in the birth.

Mary is already refusing, saying she cannot go, but Andrew says, "We will put him on the tether."

"No, no," says Mary. "I've no need to dance." She believes that Andrew has taken pity on her, remembering how she used to be left on the sidelines in school games and at the dancing, though she can actually run and dance perfectly well. Andrew is the only one of her brothers capable of such consideration, but she would almost rather he behaved like the others, and left her ignored as she has always been. Pity does gall her.

Young James begins to complain loudly, having recognized the word *tether*.

"You be still," says his father. "Be still or I'll clout you."

Then Old James surprises them all by turning his attention to his grandson.

"You. Young lad. You sit by me."

"Oh, he will not sit," says Mary. "He will run off and then you cannot chase him, Father. I will stay."

"He will sit," says Old James.

"Well, settle it," says Agnes to Mary. "Go or stay."

Young James looks from one to the other, cautiously snuffling.

"Does he not know even the simplest word?" says his grandfather. "Sit. Lad. Here."

"He knows all kinds of words," says Mary. "He knows the name of the gib-boom."

Young James repeats, "Gib-boom."

"Hold your tongue and sit down," says Old James. Young James lowers himself, reluctantly, to the spot indicated.

"Now go," says Old James to Mary. And all in confusion, on the verge of tears, she is led away.

"What a suckie-laddie she's made of him," says Agnes, not

exactly to her father-in-law but into the air. She speaks almost indifferently, teasing the baby's cheek with her nipple.

People are dancing, not just in the figure of the reel but quite outside of it, all over the deck. They are grabbing anyone at all and twirling around. They are even grabbing some of the sailors if they can get hold of them. Men dance with women, men dance with men, women dance with women, children dance with each other or all alone and without any idea of the steps, getting in the way—but everybody is in everybody's way already and it is no matter. Some children dance in one spot, whirling around with their arms in the air till they get so dizzy they fall down. Two seconds later they are on their feet, recovered, and ready to begin the same thing all over again.

Mary has caught hands with Andrew, and is swung around by him, then passed on to others, who bend to her and fling her undersized body about. She has lost sight of Young James and cannot know if he has remained with his grandfather. She dances down at the level of the children, though she is less bold and carefree. In the thick of so many bodies she is helpless, she cannot pause—she has to stamp and wheel to the music or be knocked down.

"Now you listen and I will tell you," says Old James. "This old man, Will O'Phaup, my grandfather—he was my grandfather as I am yours—Will O'Phaup was sitting outside his house in the evening, resting himself, it was mild summer weather. All alone, he was.

"And there was three little lads hardly bigger than you are

yourself, they came around the corner of Will's house. They told him good evening. *Good evening to you, Will O'Phaup, they says.*

"*Well good evening to you, lads, what can I do for you?*

"*Can you give us a bed for the night or a place to lay down,* they says. And *Aye,* he says, *Aye, I'm thinking three bits of lads like yourselves should not be so hard to find the room for.* And he goes into the house with them following and they says, *And by the by could you give us the key, too, the big silver key that you had of us?* Well, Will looks around, and he looks for the key, till he thinks to himself, what key was that? And turns around to ask them. *What key was that?* For he knew he never had such a thing in his life. Big key or silver key, he never had it. *What key are you talking to me about?* And turns himself round and they are not there. Goes out of the house, all round the house, looks to the road. No trace of them. Looks to the hills. No trace.

"Then Will knew it. They was no lads at all. Ah, no. They was no lads at all."

Young James has not made any sound. At his back is the thick and noisy wall of dancers, to the side his mother, with the small clawing beast that bites into her body. And in front of him is the old man with his rumbling voice, insistent but remote, and his blast of bitter breath, his sense of grievance and importance absolute as the child's own. His nature hungry, crafty, and oppressive. It is Young James's first conscious encounter with someone as perfectly self-centered as himself.

He is barely able to focus his intelligence, to show himself not quite defeated.

"Key," he says. "Key?"

. . .

Agnes, watching the dancing, catches sight of Andrew, red in the face and heavy on his feet, linked arm to arm with various jovial women. They are doing the "Strip the Willow" now. There is not one girl whose looks or dancing gives Agnes any worries. Andrew never gives her any worries anyway. She sees Mary tossed around, with even a flush of color in her cheeks—though she is too shy, and too short, to look anybody in the face. She sees the nearly toothless witch of a woman who birthed a child a week after her own, dancing with her hollow-cheeked man. No sore parts for her. She must have dropped the child as slick as if it was a rat, then given it over to one or the other of her weedy-looking daughters to mind.

She sees Mr. Suter, the surgeon, out of breath, pulling away from a woman who would grab him, ducking through the dance and coming to greet her.

She wishes he would not. Now he will see who her father-in-law is, he may have to listen to the old fool's gabble. He will get a look at their drab, and now not even clean, country clothes. He will see her for what she is.

"So here you are," he says. "Here you are with your treasure."

That is not a word that Agnes has ever heard used to refer to a child. It seems as if he is talking to her in the way he might talk to a person of his own acquaintance, some sort of a lady, not as a doctor talks to a patient. Such behavior embarrasses her and she does not know how to answer.

"Your baby is well?" he says, taking a more down-to-earth tack. He is still catching his breath from the dancing, and his face, though not flushed, is covered with a fine sweat.

"Aye."

"And you yourself? You have your strength again?"

She shrugs very slightly, so as not to shake the child off the nipple.

"You have a fine color, anyway, that is a good sign."

She thinks that he sighs as he says this, and wonders if that may be because his own color, seen in the morning light, is sickly as whey.

He asks then if she will permit him to sit and talk to her for a few moments, and once more she is confused by his formality, but says he may do as he likes.

Her father-in-law gives the surgeon—and her as well—a despising glance, but Mr. Suter does not notice it, perhaps does not even understand that the old man, and the fair-haired boy who sits straight-backed and facing this old man, have anything to do with her.

"The dancing is very lively," he says. "And you are not given a chance to decide who you would dance with. You get pulled about by all and sundry." And then he asks, "What will you do in Canada West?"

It seems to her the silliest question. She shakes her head—what can she say? She will wash and sew and cook and almost certainly suckle more children. Where that will be does not much matter. It will be in a house, and not a fine one.

She knows now that this man likes her, and in what way. She remembers his fingers on her skin. What harm can happen, though, to a woman with a baby at her breast?

She feels stirred to show him a bit of friendliness.

"What will you do?" she says.

He smiles and says that he supposes he will go on doing what he has been trained to do, and that the people in America—so he has heard—are in need of doctors and surgeons just like other people in the world.

"But I do not intend to get walled up in some city. I'd like to get as far as the Mississippi River, at least. Everything beyond the Mississippi used to belong to France, you know, but now it belongs to America and it is wide open, anybody can go there, except that you may run into the Indians. I would not mind that either. Where there is fighting with the Indians, there'll be all the more need for a surgeon."

She does not know anything about this Mississippi River, but she knows that he does not look like a fighting man himself—he does not look as if he could stand up in a quarrel with the brawling lads of Hawick, let alone red Indians.

Two dancers swing so close to them as to put a wind into their faces. It is a young girl, a child really, whose skirts fly out—and who should she be dancing with but Agnes's brother-in-law, Walter. Walter makes some sort of silly bow to Agnes and the surgeon and his father, and the girl pushes him and turns him around and he laughs at her. She is all dressed up like a young lady, with bows in her hair. Her face is lit with enjoyment, her cheeks are glowing like lanterns, and she treats Walter with great familiarity, as if she had got hold of a large toy.

"That lad is your friend?" says Mr. Suter.

"No. He is my husband's brother."

The girl is laughing quite helplessly, as she and Walter—through her heedlessness—have almost knocked down another couple in the dance. She is not able to stand up for laughing, and Walter has to support her. Then it appears that she is not laughing but in a fit of coughing and every time the fit seems ready to stop she laughs and gets it started again. Walter is holding her against himself, half-carrying her to the rail.

"There is one lass that will never have a child to her breast," says Mr. Suter, his eyes flitting to the sucking child before resting again on the girl. "I doubt if she will live long enough to see much of America. Does she not have anyone to look after her? She should not have been allowed to dance."

He stands up so that he can keep the girl in view as Walter holds her by the rail.

"There, she has got stopped," he says. "No hemorrhaging. At least not this time."

Agnes does not pay attention to most people, but she can sense things about any man who is interested in her, and she can see now that he takes a satisfaction in the verdict he has passed on this young girl. And she understands that this must be because of some condition of his own—that he must be thinking that he is not so badly off, by comparison.

There is a cry at the rail, nothing to do with the girl and Walter. Another cry, and many people break off dancing, hurrying to look at the water. Mr. Suter rises and goes a few steps in that direction, following the crowd, then turns back.

"A whale," he says. "They are saying there is a whale to be seen off the side."

"You stay here," cries Agnes in an angry voice, and he turns to her in surprise. But he sees that her words are meant for Young James, who is on his feet.

"This is your lad then?" says Mr. Suter as if he has made a remarkable discovery. "May I carry him over to have a look?"

And that is how Mary—happening to raise her face in the crush of passengers—beholds Young James, much amazed, being carried across the deck in the arms of a hurrying stranger, a pale and determined though slyly courteous-looking dark-haired man who is surely a foreigner. A child-stealer, or child-murderer, heading for the rail.

She gives so wild a shriek that anybody would think she was in the Devil's clutches herself, and people make way for her as they would do for a mad dog.

"Stop thief, stop thief," she is crying. "Take the boy from him. Catch him. James. James. Jump down!"

She flings herself forward and grabs the child's ankles, yanking him so that he howls in fear and outrage. The man bearing him nearly topples over but doesn't give him up. He holds on and pushes at Mary with his foot.

"Take her arms," he shouts, to those around them. He is short of breath. "She is in a fit."

Andrew has pushed his way in, among people who are still dancing and people who have stopped to watch the drama. He manages somehow to get hold of Mary and Young James and to make clear that the one is his son and the other his sister and that it is not a question of fits. Young James throws himself from his father to Mary and then begins kicking to be let down.

All is shortly explained with courtesies and apologies from Mr. Suter—through which Young James, quite recovered to himself, cries out over and over again that he must see the whale. He insists upon this just as if he knew perfectly well what a whale was.

Andrew tells him what will happen if he does not stop his racket.

"I had just stopped for a few minutes' talk with your wife, to ask her if she was well," the surgeon says. "I did not take time to bid her good-bye, so you must do it for me."

There are whales for Young James to see all day and for everybody to see who can be bothered. People grow tired of looking at them.

"Is there anybody but a fine type of rascal would sit down to talk with a woman that had her bosoms bared," says Old James, addressing the sky.

Then he quotes from the Bible regarding whales.

"There go the ships and there is that leviathan whom thou hast made to play therein. That crooked serpent, the dragon that is in the sea."

But he will not stir himself to go and have a look.

Mary remains unconvinced by the surgeon's story. Of course he would have to say to Agnes that he was taking the child to look at the whale. But that does not make it the truth. Whenever the picture of that devilish man carrying Young James flashes through her mind, and she feels in her chest the power of her own cry, she is astonished and happy. It is still her own belief that she has saved him.

Nettie's father's name is Mr. Carbert. Sometimes he sits and listens to Nettie read or talks to Walter. The day after all the celebration and the dancing, when many people are in a bad humor from exhaustion and some from drinking whiskey, and hardly anybody looks at the shore, he seeks Walter out to talk to him.

"Nettie is so taken with you," he says, "that she has got the idea that you must come along with us to Montreal."

He gives an apologetic laugh, and Walter laughs too.

"Then she must think that Montreal is in Canada West," says Walter.

"No, no. I am not making a joke. I looked out for you to talk to you on purpose when she was not with us. You are a fine companion for her and it makes her happy to be with you. And I can see you are an intelligent lad and a prudent one and one who would do well in my business."

"I am with my father and my brother," says Walter, so startled that his voice has a youthful yelp in it. "We are going to get land."

"Well then. You are not the only son your father has. There may not be enough good land for all of you. And you may not always want to be a farmer."

Walter says to himself, that is true.

"My daughter now, how old do you think she is?"

Walter cannot think. He shakes his head.

"She is fourteen, nearly fifteen," Nettie's father says. "You would not think so, would you? But it does not matter, that is not what I am talking about. Not about you and Nettie, anything in years to come. You understand that? There is no question of years to come. But I would like for you to come with us and let her be the child that she is and make her happy now with your company. Then I would naturally want to repay you, and there would also be work for you and if all went well you could count on advancement."

Both of them at this point notice that Nettie is coming towards them. She sticks out her tongue at Walter, so quickly that her father apparently does not notice.

"No more now. Think about it and pick your time to tell me," says her father. "But sooner rather than later would be best."

We were becalmed the 21st and 22nd but we had rather more wind the 23rd but in the afternoon were all alarmed by a squall of wind accompanied by thunder and lightening which was very terrible and we had one of our mainsails that had just been mended torn to rags again with the wind. The squall lasted about 8 or 10 minutes and the 24th we had a fair wind which set us a good way up the River, where it became more strait so that we saw land on both sides of the River. But we becalmed again till the 31st when we had a breeze only two hours . . .

Walter has not taken long to make up his mind. He knows enough to thank Mr. Carbert, but says that he has not thought of working in a city, or any indoor job. He means to work with his family until they are set up with some sort of house and land to farm and then when they do not need his help so much he thinks of being a trader to the Indians, a sort of explorer. Or a miner for gold.

"As you will," says Mr. Carbert. They walk several steps together, side by side. "I must say I had thought you were rather more serious than that. Fortunately I said nothing to Nettie."

But Nettie has not been fooled as to the subject of their talks together. She pesters her father until he has to let her know how things have gone and then she seeks out Walter.

"I will not talk to you anymore from now on," she says, in a more grown-up voice than he has ever heard from her. "It is not because I am angry but just because if I go on talking to you I will have to think all the time about how soon I'll be saying good-bye to you. But if I stop now I will have already said good-bye so it will all be over sooner."

She spends the time that is left walking sedately with her father in her finest clothes.

Walter feels sorry to see her—in these lady's cloaks and bonnets she seems lost, she looks more of a child than ever, and her show of haughtiness is touching—but there is so much for him to pay attention to that he seldom thinks of her when she is out of sight.

Years will pass before she will reappear in his mind. But

when she does, he will find that she is a source of happiness, available to him till the day he dies. Sometimes he will even entertain himself with thoughts of what might have happened, had he taken up the offer. Most secretly, he will imagine a radiant recovery, Nettie's acquiring a tall and maidenly body, their life together. Such foolish thoughts as a man may have in secret.

Several boats from the land came alongside of us with fish, rum, live sheep, tobacco, etc. which they sold very high to the passengers. The 1st of August we had a slight breeze and on the morning of the 2nd we passed by the Isle of Orleans and about six in the morning we were in sight of Quebec in as good health I think as when we left Scotland. We are to sail for Montreal tomorrow in a steamboat . . .

My brother Walter in the former part of this letter has written a large journal which I intend to sum up in a small ledger. We have had a very prosperous voyage being wonderfully preserved in health. Out of three hundred passengers only 3 died, two of which being unhealthy when they left their native land and the other a child born in the ship. Our family has been as healthy on board as in their ordinary state in Scotland. We can say nothing yet about the state of the country. There is a great number of people landing here but wages is good. I can neither advise nor discourage people from coming. The land is very extensive and very thin-peopled. I think we have seen as much land as might serve all the people in Britain uncultivated and covered with wood. We will write you again as soon as settled.

When Andrew has added this paragraph, Old James is persuaded to add his signature to those of his two sons before this letter is sealed and posted to Scotland, from Quebec. He will write nothing else, saying, "What does it matter to me? It cannot be my home. It can be nothing to me but the land where I will die."

"It will be that for all of us," says Andrew. "But when the time comes we will think of it more as a home."

"Time will not be given to me to do that."

"Are you not well, Father?"

"I am well and I am not."

Young James is now paying occasional attention to the old man, sometimes stopping in front of him and looking straight into his face and saying one word to him, with a sturdy insistence, as if that could not help but lead to a conversation.

He chooses the same word every time. *Key.*

"He bothers me," Old James says. "I don't like the boldness of him. He will go on and on and not remember a thing of Scotland where he was born or the ship he travelled on, he will get to talking another language the way they do when they go to England, only it will be worse than theirs. He looks at me with the kind of a look that says he knows that me and my times is all over with."

"He will remember plenty of things," says Mary. Since the dancing on deck and the incident of Mr. Suter she has grown more forthright within the family.

"And he doesn't mean his look to be bold," she says. "It is just that he is interested in everything. He understands what you say, far more than you think. He takes everything in and he thinks about it. He may grow up to be a preacher."

Although she has such a stiff and distant regard for her religion, that is still the most distinguished thing that she can imagine a man to be.

Her eyes fill with tears of enthusiasm, but the rest of them look down at the child with sensible reservations.

Young James stands in the midst of them—bright-eyed, fair, and straight. Slightly preening, somewhat wary, unnaturally solemn, as if he has indeed felt descend on him the burden of the future.

The adults too feel the astonishment of the moment, as if they have been borne for these past six weeks not on a ship but on one great wave, which has landed them with a mighty thump among such clamor of the French tongue and cries of gulls and clanging of Papist church bells, altogether an infidel commotion.

Mary thinks that she could snatch up Young James and run away into some part of the strange city of Quebec and find work as a sewing-woman (talk on the boat has made her aware that such work is in demand) and bring him up all by herself as if she were his mother.

Andrew thinks of what it would be like to be here as a free man, without wife or father or sister or children, without a single burden on your back, what could you do then? He tells himself it is no use to think about it.

Agnes has heard women on the boat say that the officers you see in the street here are surely the best-looking men you can meet anywhere in the world, and she thinks now that this is surely true. A girl would have to watch herself with them. She has heard also that the men anyplace over here are ten or twenty times more numerous than the women. That must mean you can get what you want out of them. Marriage. Marriage to a man with enough money to let you ride in a carriage and buy paints to cover any birthmark on your face and send presents to your mother. If you were not married already and dragged down with two children.

Walter reflects that his brother is strong and Agnes is strong—she can help him on the land while Mary cares for the children. Whoever said that he should be a farmer? When they get to Montreal he will go and attach himself to the Hudson's Bay Company and they will send him to the frontier where he will find riches as well as adventure.

Old James has sensed defection, and begins to lament openly.

"How shall we sing the Lord's song in a strange land?"

But he recovered himself. Here he is, a year or so later, in the New World, in the new town of York which is just about to have its name changed to Toronto. He is writing to his eldest son Robert.

> . . . the people here speaks very good English there is many of our Scots words they cannot understand what we are saying and they live far more independent then King George . . . There is a Road goes Straight North from York for fifty miles and the farm Houses almost all Two Stories High. Some will have as good as 12 Cows and four or five horses for they pay no Taxes just a perfect trifell and ride in their Gigs or chire like Lords . . . there is no Presbetarian minister in this town as yet but there is a large English Chapel and Methodist Chapel . . . the English minister reads all that he Says unless it be for his Clark Craying always at the end of

every Period Good Lord Deliver us and the Methodist
prays as Loud as Ever He Can and the people is all doun
on there knees Craying Amen so you can Scarce Hear
what the Priest is Saying and I have Seen some of them
Jumping up as if they would have gone to Heaven Soul
and Body but there Body was a filthy Clog to them for
they always fell down again altho craying O Jesus O
Jesus as He had been there to pull them up threw the
Loft . . . Now Robert I do not advise you to Come Hear
so you may take your own will when you did not come
along with us I do not Expect Ever to See you again . . .
May the good will of Him that Dwelt in the Bush rest
up on you . . . if I had thought that you would have
deserted us I would not have comed hear it was my ame
to get you all Near me made me Come to America but
mans thoughts are Vanity for have Scattered you far
wider but I Can not help it now . . . I shall say no more
but wish that the God of Jacob be your god and may be
your gide for Ever and Ever is the sincer prayer of your
Loving Father till Death . . .

There is more—the whole letter passed on by Hogg's con-
nivance and printed in *Blackwoods Magazine,* where I can look
it up today.

And some considerable time after that, he writes another
letter, addressed to the Editor of *The Colonial Advocate,* and
published in that newspaper. By this time the family is settled
in Esquesing Township, in Canada West.

. . . The Scots Bodys that lives heare is all doing Tolera-
bly well for the things of this world but I am afraid that
few of them thinks about what will Come of thear Soul

when Death there Days doth End for they have found a thing they call Whiskey and a great mony of them dabbales and drinks at it till they make themselves worse than a ox or an ass . . . Now sir I could tell you bit of Stories but I am afraid you will put me in your Calonial Advocate I do not Like to be put in prent I once wrote a bit of a letter to my Son Robert in Scotland and my friend James Hogg the Poet put it in Blackwoods Magazine and had me all through North America before I knew my letter was gone Home . . . Hogg poor man has spent most of his life in conning Lies and if I read the Bible right I think it says that all Liares is to have there pairt in the Lake that Burns with Fire and Brimstone but I supose they find it a Loquarative trade for I belive that Hogg and Walter Scott has got more money for Lieing than old Boston and the Erskins got for all the Sermons ever they Wrote . . .

And I am surely one of the liars the old man talks about, in what I have written about the voyage. Except for Walter's journal, and the letters, the story is full of my invention.

The sighting of Fife from Castle Rock is related by Hogg, so it must be true.

Those travellers lie buried—all but one of them—in the graveyard of Boston Church, in Esquesing, in Halton County, almost within sight, and well within sound, of Highway 401 north of Milton, which at that spot may be the busiest road in Canada.

The church—built on what was once the farm of Andrew Laidlaw—is of course named for Thomas Boston. It is built of blackened limestone blocks. The front wall rises higher than the rest of the building—rather in the style of the false fronts on old-fashioned main streets—and it has an archway on top of it, rather than a tower—for the church bell.

Old James is here. In fact he is here twice, or at least his name is, along with the name of his wife, born Helen Scott, and buried in Ettrick in the year 1800. Their names appear on the same stone that bears the names of Andrew and Agnes. But surprisingly, the same names are written on another stone that looks older than others in the graveyard—a darkened, blotchy slab such as you are more apt to see in the churchyards of the British Isles. Anyone trying to figure this out might wonder if they carried it across the ocean, with the mother's name on it, waiting for the father's to be added—if it was perhaps an awkward burden, wrapped in sacking and tied with stout cord, borne by Walter down into the hold of the ship.

But why would someone have taken the trouble to have the names also added to those on the newer column above Andrew and Agnes's grave?

It looks as if the death and burial of such a father was a matter worth recording twice over.

Nearby, close to the graves of her father and her brother Andrew and her sister-in-law Agnes, is the grave of Little Mary, married after all and buried beside Robert Murray, her husband. Women were scarce and so were prized in the new country. She and Robert did not have any children together, but after Mary's early death he married another woman and by her he had four sons who lie here, dead at the ages of two, and three, and four, and thirteen. The second wife is there too. Her stone says *Mother.* Mary's says *Wife.*

And here is the brother James who was not lost to them, who made his way from Nova Scotia to join them, first in York and then in Esquesing, farming with Andrew. He brought a wife with him, or found her in the community. Perhaps she helped with Agnes's babies before she started having her own. For Agnes had a great number of pregnancies, and raised many children. In a letter written to his brothers Robert and William in Scotland, telling of the death of their father, in 1829 (a cancer, not much pain until near the end, though *it eat away a great part of his cheek and jaw*), Andrew mentions that his wife has been feeling poorly for the past three years. This may be a roundabout way of saying that during those years she bore her sixth, seventh, and eighth child. She must have recovered her health, for she lived into her eighties.

Andrew gave the land that the church is built on. Or possibly sold it. It is hard to measure devoutness against business sense. He seems to have prospered, though he spread himself less than Walter. Walter married an American girl from Montgomery County in New York State. Eighteen when she married him, thirty-three when she died after the birth of her ninth child. Walter did not marry again, but farmed successfully, educated his sons, speculated in land, and wrote letters to the government complaining about his taxes, also objecting to the township's participation in a proposed railway—the interest being squandered, he says, for the benefit of capitalists in Britain.

Nevertheless it is a fact that he and Andrew supported the British governor, Sir Francis Bond Head, who was surely representing those capitalists, against the rebellion led by their fellow Scot, William Lyon Mackenzie, in 1837. They wrote to the governor a letter of assiduous flattery, in the grand servile style of their times. Some of their descendants might wish this not to be true, but there is not much to be done about the politics of our relatives, living or dead.

And Walter was able to take a trip back to Scotland, where he had himself photographed wearing a plaid and holding on to a bouquet of thistles.

On the stone commemorating Andrew and Agnes (and Old James and Helen) there appears also the name of their daughter Isabel, who like her mother Agnes died an old woman. She has a married name, but there is no further sign of her husband.

Born at Sea.

And here also is the name of Andrew and Agnes's firstborn child, Isabel's elder brother. His dates as well.

Young James was dead within a month of the family's landing at Quebec. His name is here but surely he cannot be. They had not taken up their land when he died, they had not even seen this place. He may have been buried somewhere along the way from Montreal to York or in that hectic new town itself. Perhaps in a raw temporary burying ground now paved over, perhaps without a stone in a churchyard where other bodies would someday be laid on top of his. Dead of some mishap in the busy streets of York, or of a fever, or dysentery—of any of the ailments, the accidents, that were the common destroyers of little children in his time.

Illinois

A letter from his brothers reached William Laidlaw in the Highlands sometime early in the eighteen-thirties. They complained of not hearing from him for three years, and told him that his father was dead. It did not take him very long, once he was sure of that, to start making his plans to go to America. He asked for and was given a letter of reference from his employer, Colonel Munro (perhaps one of the many Highland landowners who had made sure of profitable sheep-rearing by hiring Borders men as their factors). He waited until Mary's fourth baby boy was born—this was my great-grandfather Thomas—and then he bundled up his family and set out. His father and his brothers had spoken of going to America, but when they said that, it was really Canada they meant. William spoke accurately. He had discarded the Ettrick Valley for the Highlands without the least regret, and now he was ready to get out from under the British flag altogether—he was bound for Illinois.

They settled in Joliet, near Chicago.

There in Joliet, on the 5th of January, in either 1839 or 1840, William died of cholera, and Mary gave birth to a girl. All on the one day.

She wrote to the brothers in Ontario—what else could she do?—and in the late spring when the roads were dry and the crops were planted Andrew arrived with a team of oxen and a cart, to carry her and her children and their goods back to Esquesing.

"Where is the tin box?" said Mary. "I saw it last thing before I went to bed. Is it in the cart already?"

Andrew said that it was not. He had just come back from loading the two rolls of bedding, wrapped up in canvas.

"Becky?" said Mary sharply. Becky Johnson was right there, rocking back and forth on a wooden stool with the baby in her arms, so surely she might have spoken if she knew the whereabouts of the box. But she was in a sulky mood, she had said barely a word that morning. And now she did nothing but shake her head slightly, as if the box and the packing and loading and the departure, which was close at hand, meant nothing to her.

"Does she understand?" said Andrew. Becky was half Indian and he had taken her for a servant, till Mary explained that she was a neighbor.

"We've got them too," he said, speaking as if Becky had no ears in her head. "But we don't have them coming in and sitting down in the house like that."

"She has been more help to me than anybody," Mary said, trying to shush him. "Her father was a white man."

"Well," said Andrew, as if to say there were two ways of looking at that.

Mary said, "I can't think how it would disappear from in front of my eyes."

She turned away from her brother-in-law to the son who was her chief comfort.

"Johnnie, did you happen to see the black tin box?"

Johnnie was sitting on the lower bunk, now bare of bedclothes, keeping a watch over his younger brothers Robbie and Tommy, as his mother had asked him to. He had invented a game of dropping a spoon between the slats onto the plank floor, and having them see who could pick it up first. Naturally Robbie always won, even though Johnnie had asked him to slow down and give his smaller brother a chance. Tommy was in such a state of excitement that he did not seem to mind. He was used to this situation anyway, as the youngest.

Johnnie shook his head, preoccupied. Mary expected no more than that. But in a moment he spoke, as if just recollecting her question.

"Jamie's setting on it. Out in the yard."

Not only sitting on it, Mary saw when she hurried out, but he had covered it with his father's coat, the coat Will had been married in. He must have got that out of the clothes trunk that was already in the cart.

"What are you doing?" cried Mary, as if she couldn't see. "You're not supposed to touch that box. What are you doing with your father's coat after I packed it up? I ought to smack you."

She was aware that Andrew was watching, and likely thinking that was a poor enough reprimand. He had asked Jamie to help him load the trunk and Jamie had done so, reluctantly, but then he had slipped away, instead of hanging around to see what more he could help with. And yesterday, when Andrew first arrived, the boy had pretended not to know who he was. "There's a man out in the road with a cart and an ox team," he had said to his mother, as if no such thing was expected and was of no concern to him.

Andrew had asked her if the lad was all right. All right in the head, was what he meant.

"His father's dying was a hard matter for him," she said.

Andrew said, "Aye," but added that there'd been time to get over it, by now.

The box was locked. Mary had the key to it around her

neck. She wondered if Jamie had meant to get into it, not knowing that. She was ready to weep.

"Put the coat back in the trunk," was all she could say.

In the box were Will's pistol and such papers as Andrew needed concerning the house and land, and the letter Colonel Munro had written before they left Scotland, and another letter, that Mary herself had sent to Will, before they were married. It was in reply to one from him—the first word she'd had since he left Ettrick, years before. He said in it that he remembered her well and had thought that by now he would have heard of her wedding. She had replied that in such case she would have sent him an invitation.

"Soon I will be like the old almanacks left on the shelf, that no person will buy," she wrote. (But to her shame, when he showed her this letter long afterwards, she saw that she had spelled "buy" *by*. Living with him, having books and journals around, had done a power of good for her spelling.)

It was true that she was in her twenty-fifth year when she wrote that, but she was still confident of her looks. No woman who thought herself lacking in that way would have dared such a comparison. And she had finished off by inviting him, as plain as any words could do it. *If you should come courting me,* she had said, *if you should come courting me some moonlight night, I think that you should be preferred before any.*

What a chance to take, she said when he showed her that. Did I have no pride?

Nor I, he said.

Before they left she took the children to Will's grave to say good-bye. Even the baby Jane, who would not remember but could be told later that she had been there.

"She don't know," said Becky, trying to hang onto the child for a few moments longer. But Mary took the baby out of her arms and Becky went away then. She went out of the house without ever saying good-bye. She had been there when the baby was born and had taken care of them both when Mary was beside herself, but now she didn't wait to say good-bye.

Mary had the children bid farewell to their father one by one. Even Tommy said it, eager to copy the others. Jamie's voice was weary and without expression, as if he had been made to recite something at school.

The baby fretted in Mary's arms, perhaps missing Becky and her smell. What with that, and the thought of Andrew waiting, in a hurry to be off, and the self-consciousness, the annoyance roused in her by Jamie's tone, Mary's own good-bye was quick and formal, there was no heart in it.

Jamie had a good idea of what his father would have thought of that. That business of trotting them all up there to say good-bye to a stone. His father did not believe in pretending one thing was another and he would have said that a stone was a stone and if there was any way of speaking to a dead person, and hearing back from them, this was not it.

His mother was a liar. Or if she didn't lie outright, she at least covered things up. She had said his uncle was coming but she had not said—he was sure she had not said—that they were going back with him. Then when the truth came out she claimed she had told him before. And most falsely, most despicably, she had claimed that such a thing was what his father would have wanted.

His uncle hated him. Naturally he did. When his mother

had said in her hopeful, foolish way, "This is my man of the house now," his uncle had said, "Oh, aye," as if to say that she was badly off, if that was all she could come up with.

In half a day they had left the prairie and its shallow, brushy hollows behind. And that was even with the oxen that walked no faster than a man. Not half as fast as Jamie, who was disappearing ahead of them and reappearing when they rounded a curve and disappearing again, and still seemed to be gaining.

"Don't they have any horses where you are?" Johnnie asked his uncle. Horses occasionally passed them, in a whirl of dust.

"These are the beasts have the strength," said his uncle after a pause. Then, "Did you never hear tell about keeping quiet until you're asked to speak?"

"It's because we have such a load of belongings, Johnnie," said his mother, in a voice that was both a warning and a plea, "and when you get tired of walking you can climb up here and they'll pull you along too."

She had already hauled Tommy up on her knee and was holding the baby on the other side. Robbie heard what she said and took it as an invitation, so Johnnie hefted him up to crawl onto the sacks at the back.

"You want up there with them?" said his uncle. "Now's the time to speak up if you do."

Johnnie shook his head, but apparently his uncle didn't see him, because the next thing he said was, "I need an answer when I speak to you."

Johnnie said, "No sir," the way they were taught in school.

"No, Uncle Andrew," said his mother, confusing things more because this uncle wasn't her uncle, surely.

Uncle Andrew made an impatient noise.

"Johnnie always tries to be a good boy," his mother said, and though that should have pleased Johnnie, it didn't.

They had entered a forest of great oak trees whose branches met over the road. In the branches you could hear and sometimes see the flight of the bright orioles, the cardinals, the red-winged blackbirds. The sumac had put its creamy cones out, coltsfoot and columbine were blooming, and the mullein was standing up straight as soldiers. Wild grapevine had wrapped some bushes so thickly that you would think they were feather beds, or old ladies.

"Did you hear any tales of wildcats?" said Mary to Andrew. "I mean, when you came along this road before?"

"If I did I didn't listen to them," said Andrew. "You're thinking of the young lad up ahead? He minds me of his father."

Mary did not answer.

Andrew said, "He won't be able to keep it up forever."

This proved to be the case. Around the next curve they did not see Jamie ahead. Mary did not mention it, lest Andrew think she was foolish. Then another view of a good stretch of level road, and he was not there. When they had gone some distance Andrew said, "Just turn your head like to look at the young ones in the back, don't be taking any heed of the road." Mary did so, and saw a figure trailing them. It was too far to make out his face, but she knew it was Jamie, scuffing along at a much reduced pace.

"Hid in the bush till we got by," said Andrew. "Are you easier now about the wildcats?"

In the evening they stopped near the Indiana border, at a crossroads inn. The woods were not cut far back, but there were a few fenced fields, and both log and wood-frame buildings, barns or houses. Jamie had walked all the way, getting closer to the wagon as the afternoon darkened. That happened quickly under the arch of the trees—when they came out into the clearing it was surprising to see how much of the daylight they still had left. The boys on the wagon had waked up—Johnnie had taken his place up there too, once the dark came on—and they were all holding quiet, taking in the new place and the people around. They had known about inns in Joliet—all told it had three—but they had never been let wander around such places.

Andrew spoke to the man who came out. He asked for a room for Mary and the baby and the two little boys, and arranged sleeping room on the porch for himself and the two older ones. Then he helped Mary down and the boys jumped off and he took the cart around to the back, where the man said it was safe to store their goods. The oxen could go in the pasture.

And there was Jamie in the midst of them. His boots were hanging round his neck.

"Jamie walked," said Robbie, solemnly.

Johnnie addressed Mary. "How far did Jamie walk?"

Mary said she had no idea. "Enough to wear himself out, anyway."

Jamie said, "No it wasn't. I'm not even tired. I could walk that far again and I wouldn't be tired."

Johnnie wanted to know if he'd seen any wildcats.

"No."

They all walked across the porch, where some men were sitting in chairs or on the railings, smoking. Mary said, "Good evening," and the men said, "Good evening," looking down.

Walking beside his mother, Jamie said, "I saw a person."

"Who was it?" said Johnnie. "Was it a bad person?"

Jamie paid him no attention. Mary said, "Don't tease him, Jamie."

Then with a sigh she said, "I guess you ring this bell," and did, and a woman came out of a back room. The woman led them upstairs and into a bedroom and said she would bring water for Mary to wash herself. Boys could wash out back, she said, at the cistern. There were towels out there, on a rack.

"Go on," said Mary to Jamie. "Take Johnnie with you. I'll keep Robbie and Tommy here."

"I saw a person you know," said Jamie.

The baby was wet through her soakers and would have to be changed on the floor, not the bed. Down on her knees, Mary said, "Who was that? Who that I know?"

"I saw Becky Johnson."

"Where?" said Mary, rocking back. "Where? *Becky Johnson?* Is she here?"

"I saw her in the bush."

"Where was she going? What did she say?"

"I wasn't near enough to talk to her. She never saw me."

"Was this back near home?" Mary said. "Think now. Back near home or nearer here?"

"Nearer here," said Jamie, considering. "Why do you say near home when you said we'd never go back there?"

Mary disregarded that. "Where was she going?"

"This way. She just went out of sight in a minute." He shook his head, like an old man. "She wasn't making any noise."

"That's the way Indians do," Mary said. "You didn't try to follow her?"

"She was just ducking along in and out the trees and then I couldn't see her anymore. Else I would have. I'd have followed her and asked her what she thought she was doing."

"Don't you ever do such a thing," Mary said. "You don't know the bush like they do, you could lose yourself like *that.*" She snapped her fingers at him, then busied herself again with the baby. "I expect she was on her own business," she said. "Indian people have their own business we don't ever know about. They're not telling us everything they're up to. Even Becky. Why should she?"

The woman of the inn entered with a big pitcher of water.

"What's the matter?" she said to Jamie. "You scared there's some strange boys out there? It's just my own boys, they're not going to hurt you."

Such a suggestion sent Jamie skittering down the stairs and Johnnie after him. Then the two little ones ran out as well.

"Tommy! Robbie!" Mary called, but the woman said, "Your husband's out back there, he'll watch out for them."

Mary did not bother saying anything. It was no strange person's business to know that she had no husband.

The baby fell asleep at the breast, and Mary laid her on the bed, with a bolster on either side in case she rolled. She went down to eat supper, with one aching arm hanging gratefully empty of its daylong load. There was pork to eat, with cabbage and boiled potatoes. The last of last year's potatoes, these were, and the meat had a good tough layer of fat. She filled up on fresh radishes and greens and new-baked bread which was tasty, and strong tea. The children ate at one table by themselves and were all so merry they didn't give her a glance, not even Tommy. She was tired enough to drop, and wondering how she would ever stay awake long enough to get them to bed.

There was only one other woman in the room besides the woman of the inn who was bringing in the food. That other woman never raised her head and gobbled her supper as if she was starved. She kept her bonnet on and looked like a foreigner. Her foreign husband spoke to her in businesslike grunts now and then. Other men kept up a steady conversation, mostly in the hard punishing American tone that Mary's own boys were beginning to imitate. These men were full of information and contradictions, and they waved their knives and forks in the air. In fact there were two or three conversations— one about the trouble in Mexico, another about where a railroad was going, which got mixed up with one about a gold strike. Some men smoked cigars at the table and if the spittoons were not handy they turned around and spat on the floor. The man sitting beside Mary tried to open a conversation more suited to a lady, asking if she had been to the tent meeting. She did not at first understand that he was speaking of a revival meeting, but when she did she said that she had no use for such things, and he begged her pardon and spoke no more.

She thought that she should not have spoken so shortly, especially as she was depending on him to pass her the bread. On the other hand, she was aware that Andrew, sitting on her other side, would not have liked her talking. Not to that man, maybe not to anybody. Andrew kept his head down and curtailed his answers. Just as he'd done when he was a lad at school. It had always been hard to tell whether he was disapproving, or just shy.

Will had been freer. Will might have wanted to hear about Mexico. So long as the men talking knew what they were talking about. Often, he thought that people didn't. When you considered that streak in him, Will had not been so unlike Andrew, not so unlike his family, as he himself thought.

One thing there was no word of here was religion—unless

you wanted to count the revival meeting, and Mary did not. No fierce arguments about doctrine. No mention either of ghosts or weird visitors, as in the old days in Ettrick. Here it was all down-to-earth, it was all about what you could find and do and understand about the real world under your feet, and she supposed that Will would have approved—that was the world he had thought he was heading for.

She squeezed out of her place, telling Andrew she was too tired to take another bite, and headed for the front hall.

At the screen door the little tag end of a breeze found its way between her sweaty dusty clothing and her skin, and she longed for the deep still night, though there was probably never such a thing in an inn. Besides the hubbub in the dining room she could hear the clatter in the kitchen and out the back door the splash of slops dumped into the pig trough, with the pigs squealing for them. And in the yard the rising voices of children, her own among them. *Ready-or-not-you're-sure-to-be-caught—*

She clapped her hands and shouted.

"Robbie and Tommy! Johnnie, bring the little lads in."

When she saw that Johnnie had heard her she didn't wait, but turned and climbed the stairs.

Johnnie, herding his brothers into the hall, looked up to see his mother at the top of the stairs, looking at him with terrible cold fright, as if she didn't know him. She took one step down and stumbled and righted herself just in time, grabbing hold of the bannister rail. She raised her head and met his eyes but could not speak. He cried out, running up the steps, and heard her say, almost without breath, "The baby—"

She meant that the baby was gone. The bolsters were not

disturbed, nor was the cloth that had been placed between them, on top of the quilt. The baby had been picked up with care and taken away.

Johnnie's cry brought a crowd, almost at once. The news travelled from one person to another. Andrew reached Mary and said to her, "Are you sure?" then made his way past her to the room. Thomas cried out in his piercing small child's voice that the doggies had eaten his baby.

"That's a lie," the woman of the inn shouted, as if tackling a grown man. "Those dogs never hurt anybody in their life. They won't even kill a groundhog."

Mary said, "No. No." Thomas ran to her and butted his head between her legs and she sank down on the steps.

She said she knew what had happened. Trying to get her breath steady then, she said that it was Becky Johnson.

Andrew had come back from looking around the bedroom and making sure it was as she said. He asked her what she meant.

Mary said that Becky Johnson had treated that baby almost as if it was her own. She wanted so much to keep that baby with her that she must have come and stolen her.

"She's a squaw," said Jamie, explaining to the people around him at the bottom of the stairs. "She was following us today. I saw her."

Several people, but most forcibly Andrew, wanted to know where he had seen her and was he sure it was her and why had he not said anything. Jamie said that he had told his mother. Then he repeated more or less what he had said to Mary.

"I didn't pay enough attention when he told me," Mary said.

A man said that squaws were well known for helping themselves to white baby girls.

"They bring them up like Indians and then they go and sell them to some chief or other for a big pile of wampum."

"It's not like she wouldn't take good care of her," said Mary, maybe not even hearing this. "Becky's a good Indian."

Andrew asked where Becky was likely to go now and Mary said, probably back home.

"I mean to Joliet," she said.

The innkeeper said that they could not follow that road at night, nobody could, except Indians. His wife agreed with him. She had brought Mary a cup of tea. Kindly now, she patted Tommy's head. Andrew said that they would start back as soon as it was light in the morning.

"I'm sorry," said Mary.

He said that it couldn't be helped. Like a good many things, was what he implied.

The man who had set up the sawmill in this community owned a cow, which he let wander round the settlement, sending his daughter Susie out in the evening to find her and milk her. Susie was almost always accompanied by her friend Meggie, the daughter of the local schoolteacher. These girls were thirteen and twelve years old and they were bound together in an intense relationship loaded with secret rituals and special jokes and fanatical loyalty. It was true that they had nobody else to be friendly with, being the only two girls of their age in the community, but that did not stop them from feeling as if they had chosen each other against the rest of the world.

One of the things they liked to do was to call people by wrong names. Sometimes this was simple substitution, as when they called somebody named George *Tom,* or somebody named Rachel *Edith.* Sometimes they celebrated a certain characteristic—as when they called the innkeeper Tooth, because of the long eyetooth that caught on his lip—or sometimes they picked on the very opposite of what the person wanted to be, as with the innkeeper's wife, who was very particular about her clean aprons. They called her Greasy-gravy.

The boy who looked after the horses was named Fergie, but they called him Birdie. This annoyed him quite satisfactorily. He was short and thickset, with black curly hair and wide-spaced innocent eyes, and had come out from Ireland just a year or so before. He would chase them when they imitated his way of talking. But the best thing they had managed was to write him a love letter and sign it Rose—the real name, as it happened, of the innkeeper's daughter—and leave it on the horse blanket he slept under in the barn. They had not realized that he didn't know how to read. He showed it to some men who came round the stable and it was a great joke and scandal. Rose was soon sent away to learn to be a milliner, though she was not actually suspected of having written the letter.

Neither were Susie and Meggie suspected.

One outcome was that the stable boy showed up at Meggie's father's door and demanded to be taught to read.

It was Susie, the eldest, who sat down on the stool they'd brought, and set to milking the cow, while Meggie wandered about picking and eating the last of the wild strawberries. The place the cow had chosen to browse in at the end of this day was close to the woods, at a little distance from the inn. Between the side door of the inn and the real woods was a stand of apple trees, and between the last of these apple trees and the trees of the woods was a small shack with a door hanging loose. It was called the smokehouse though it was not used for that purpose, or any purpose, at present.

What made Meggie investigate the shack at this time? She never knew. Perhaps it was that the door was shut, or pulled forward to be as nearly shut as it could be. It was not until she began to wrestle with the door to get it open that she heard a baby crying.

She carried it back to show Susie, and when she dipped her fingers in the fresh milk and offered one to the baby, it stopped crying and began to suck hard.

"Did somebody have it and hide it there?" she said, and Susie humiliated her—as she could occasionally do, with certain superior knowledge—by saying that it was nothing like a newborn, it was far too big. And it was dressed the way it wouldn't be if somebody was just getting rid of it.

"Well yes," said Meggie. "What are we going to do with it?"

Did she mean, what is the right thing to do with this? In which case the answer would be, to take it to one of their houses. Or take it to the inn, which was closer.

That was not quite what she meant.

No. She meant, how can we use this? How can we best make a joke, or fool somebody?

His plans had never been complete. He understood, when they left home, that his father—who was not under that stone but in the air or walking along the road invisibly and making his views known as well as if they had been talking together—*his father* was against their going. His mother ought to know that too, but she was ready to give in to that newcomer who looked and even sounded like his father but was entirely a sham. Who might indeed have been his father's brother but was just the same a sham.

Even when she started packing he had believed something would stop her—it was not till *Uncle Andrew* arrived that he saw no accident was going to prevent them and it was up to him.

Then when he got tired trying to keep so far ahead of them

and slipped off into the woods he started imagining he was an Indian, as he had often done before. It was an idea that came naturally from the paths you found, or the suggestions of paths, leading alongside the road or away from it. Trying his best to glide along without being heard or seen he imagined companion Indians and got so that he could almost see them and he thought of Becky Johnson, how she might have been following along trying for a chance to sneak away the baby whom she loved unreasonably. He had kept in the woods until the others had stopped in front of the inn and he had seen this shack, investigated it before he made his way among the apple trees. Those same apple trees sheltered him when he went out of the side door with the sleeping baby so light in his arms, so faintly breathing, hardly imaginable as a human person. Her eyes were open a crack as she slept. In the shack there were a couple of shelves that had not fallen down, and he put her on the top one, where wolves or wildcats if there were any would not get at her.

He came in late to supper but nobody thought anything of it. He was prepared to say he had been at the toilet, but he wasn't asked. Everything was sliding along so easily, as if it was still in his imagination.

After the fuss when the baby was found to be missing, he hadn't wanted to disappear too quickly, so it was almost dark when he ran along under the trees to get a look at her in the shack. He hoped she wouldn't be hungry already, but thought that if she was he could spit on his finger and let her suck it, and maybe she wouldn't know the difference between that and milk.

The plans had been made to turn back, just as he had foreseen, and what he was counting on was that once they got back, somehow his mother would understand that their attempts to leave were doomed to failure and would tell *Uncle Andrew* to get about his business.

Since he now credited his father with putting the whole plan into his head, he supposed his father must have foreseen that this was exactly what would happen.

But there was a flaw. His father had not put into his head any idea of how he was to get the baby back there, other than carrying her all the way, travelling through the woods as he had done part of the way today. And then what? When it turned out that Becky Johnson didn't have her, when it turned out in fact that Becky Johnson had never left home?

Something would come to him. It would have to. He could certainly carry the baby, now there was no choice. And keep far enough from them that they would not hear the crying. She would be hungry by then.

Could he figure out a way to steal some milk from the inn?

He could not continue with this problem because he noticed something.

The shack door was open, which he thought he had shut.

There was no crying, not a sound.

And there was no baby.

Most of the men staying at the inn had taken bedrooms, but a few, like Andrew, with his nephews James and John, were lying on mats on the wooden floor of the long porch.

Andrew was wakened sometime before midnight by the need to relieve himself. He got up and walked the length of the porch, glanced at the boys to see if they were asleep, then stepped down, and decided, for propriety's sake, to walk behind the building, down to the field where he could see by the moonlight that the horses were asleep on their feet and munching in their dreams.

James had heard his uncle's feet and closed his eyes, but he had not slept.

Either the baby had been really stolen this time, or it had been dragged off and mauled and probably half eaten by some animal. There was no reason that he himself should be involved, or in any way held to blame. Perhaps Becky Johnson might be blamed in some way, if he swore he'd seen her in the woods. She would swear she hadn't been there but he would swear she was.

Because they'd go back, surely. They'd have to bury the baby if they ever found anything left of her, or even if they didn't, they would have to have a funeral service, wouldn't they? So what he had wanted to happen would be accomplished. His mother would be in a bad way, though.

Her hair might turn white overnight.

If this was his father's present way of ordering or arranging things, it was a great deal more drastic than anything he would have thought of in the days when he was alive.

And operating in this pitiless or haphazard fashion, would his father even care that Jamie got the blame?

Also, his mother might see that he had something to do with it, something that he wasn't telling. She could do that sometimes, though she had easily swallowed the lie about Becky Johnson. If she knew, or even suspected anything like the truth, she would hate him forever.

He could pray, if a liar's prayers had any value. He could pray that the baby was taken by an Indian, though not Becky

Johnson, and that she would grow up in an Indian camp, and one day come to the door trying to sell some Indian trinkets and would be very beautiful and be recognized at once by his mother who would cry out with joy and look the way she used to look before his father died.

Stop that. How could he think of anything so stupid?

Andrew walked into the barn's shadow and stood there urinating. While he did so he heard a strange thin sound of distress. He thought it was some night animal, maybe a mouse in a trap. When he had buttoned himself up he heard it again, and now it was clear enough that he could follow it. Around the barn, across the barnyard, to an outbuilding which had a regular door, not a door for livestock. The sound was louder now and Andrew, the father of several children, recognized it for what it was.

He knocked on the door, twice, and when there was no answer he tried the latch. There was no bolt on, the door swung inwards. The moon shone in through a window and showed a baby. Sure enough, a baby. Lying there on a narrow cot made up with a rough blanket and a flat pillow that must be someone's bed. Hooks on the wall held a few articles of clothing and a lantern. This must be where the stable boy slept. But he wasn't home, he was still out—probably at the other, shabbier hotel, which sold beer and whiskey. Or mooning around with some girl.

In his place, on his bed, was this hungry baby.

Andrew picked it up, not noticing the bit of paper which fell away from its clothing. He had never paid a lot of attention to what Mary's baby looked like and he did not do so now. There was not much chance of there being two babies missing in the same night. He didn't fuss over it, but carried it confidently back to the hotel. It had stopped crying anyway, when it was picked up.

Nobody stirred on the porch when he mounted the steps, and he proceeded up the stairs to Mary's room. She opened the door before he could knock, as if she had heard the child's snuffling breathing, and he spoke at once, quietly, to stop her crying out.

"Is this the one you're missing?"

The stable boy found the paper on the floor when he got back. He could read it, too.

A PRESENT from one of your SWEETHEARTS.

But no present, not even a joke of a present, that he could see, anywhere around.

Jamie had heard his uncle come up on the porch, then enter the inn. Now he heard him come out, he heard his deliberate and threatening footsteps coming this way, instead of the other way. His heart thumped with the steps. Then he knew that his uncle was standing there looking down on him. He wagged his head about and opened his eyes reluctantly, as if waking up.

"I just took your sister upstairs to your mother," his uncle said matter-of-factly. "I thought I'd put your mind to rest." And he turned around to go to his own sleeping spot.

So there was no need to turn back, and they continued their journey on in the morning. Andrew thought it just as well not to interfere with the story of the Indian woman, and gave it as his opinion that she had got scared and left the baby in the stable boy's bed. He did not believe that the stable boy was in any way involved, and he did believe that James was, but he left the matter uninvestigated. The lad was sly and troublesome, but by the look of him in the night he might have learned a lesson.

Mary had been so glad to have the baby back that she didn't much question what had happened. Did she still blame Becky? Or did she have more of an inkling than she wanted to let on about the tendencies of her eldest son?

Oxen are long-suffering and reliable beasts and the only real problem with them is that once they get an idea of where they want to go it is very hard to make them change their minds. If they spot a pond that reminds them of how thirsty they are and how pleasant water is, you might as well let them go to it. And that is what happened around midday after they had left the inn. The pond was a large one close to the road, and the two older boys took off their clothes and climbed a tree with an overhanging branch and dropped again and again into the water. The little boys paddled at the water's edge and the baby slept in the long grass in the shade and Mary looked for strawberries.

A sharp-faced red fox watched them for a while from the edge of the woods. Andrew saw it but did not mention it, feeling that there had been enough excitement on this trip already.

He knew, better than they did, what lay ahead of them. Roads that were worse and inns rougher than anything they had seen yet, and the dust always rising, the days getting hotter. The refreshment of the first bit of rain and then the misery of it, with the mucky mess of the road and all their clothes soaked through.

He had seen enough of the Yankee people by now to know what had tempted Will to live among them. The push and noise and rawness of them, the need to get on the bandwagon. Though some were decent enough and some, and maybe some of the worst, were Scots. Will had had something in him drawing him to such a life.

It had proved a mistake.

Andrew knew, of course, that a man was as likely to die of cholera in Upper Canada as in the state of Illinois, and that it was foolish to blame Will's death on his choice of nationality. He did not do so. And yet. And yet—there was something about all this rushing away, loosing oneself entirely from family and past, there was something rash and self-trusting about it that might not help a man, that might put him more in the way of such an accident, such a fate. Poor Will.

And that became the way the surviving brothers spoke of him until the day they died, and the way their children spoke of him. Poor Will. His own sons, naturally, did not call him anything but Father, though they too, in time, may have felt a pall, of sadness and fatedness, that hung around any mention of his name. Mary almost never spoke of him, and how she felt about him became nobody's business but her own.

The Wilds of Morris Township

William's children grew up in Esquesing, among their cousins. They were treated well. But money would not stretch to sending them off to grammar school or to college, if any of them had wanted or been judged to have the ability to go there. And there was no land coming to them. So as soon as they were old enough they set off for another wilderness. One of their cousins went with them, one of Andrew's boys. He was named Big Rob because he had the same name as the third son of Will and Mary, who was now called Little Rob. Big Rob took up the family custom or duty of writing his memories down when he was an old man, so that the people left would know what things had been like.

On the third day of November, 1851, myself and my two cousins, Thomas Laidlaw now of Blyth, and his brother John, who went to B.C. several years ago, got a box of bed-clothes and a few cooking utensils into a wagon and started from the county of Halton to try our fortunes in the wilds of Morris Township.

We only got as far as Preston on the first day as the roads were very rough and bad across Nassagaweya and Puslinch. The next day we got to Shakespeare and the third afternoon arrived at Stratford. The roads were always getting worse as we went west, so we thought it best to get our bags and small things sent to Clinton by stage. But the stage had quit running, until the roads froze up, so we let the horses and the wagon turn back, as another cousin had come with us to take them back. John Laidlaw, Thomas and I, got our axes on our shoulders and walked to Morris. We got a place to board, though we had to sleep on the floor, with a quilt over us. It was a little cold as the winter was coming on, but we expected to have some hardships to endure and we made the best of them we could.

We began to underbrush a road to John's place, as it was the nearest to where we boarded and then we cut logs for a shanty and big scoops to roof it. The man we boarded with had a yoke of oxen and he let us have them to draw the logs and the scoops. Then we got a few men to help raise the shanty, but they were very few, as there were only five settlers in the township. However, we got the shanty up alright and the scoops on it. The next day we began to fill up the cracks between the logs, where they did not lie very close together, with mud, and stuff moss in the cracks between the scoops. We got the shanty made pretty comfortable and, as we were getting tired of walking through the snow every night and morning and the bed being hard and cold, we went to Goderich to try to get work for a few days and see if our boxes and cooking utensils had come.

We did not meet with anyone who wanted help, though we were three good looking fellows. We met in with one man who wanted some cordwood cut but he would not board us, so we came to the conclusion that we would go back to Morris, as there was plenty of chopping to do there. We decided to batch it some way.

We bought a barrel of fish in Goderich and got part of it on our backs. As we came along through Coulborne Township we got some flour from a man and as he was going to Goderich he said he would bring the rest of the fish and a barrel of flour for us as far as Manchester (now Auburn). We met him there and old Mr. Elkins ferried the fish and flour across the river and we had to carry them from there. I did not like carrying our provisions.

We went to our own shanty and got some hemlock branches for a bed and a big slab of elm for a door. A Frenchman from Quebec had once told John that in the lumber shanties the fire was in the middle of the shanty. So John said that he would have his fire in the middle of our shanty. We got four posts and were building the chimney on them. We built slats, house fashion, on top of the posts, intending to plaster them with mud, inside and outside. When we went to our hemlock bed, we put on a big fire and when some of us awoke through the night our lumber was all ablaze and some of the scoops were burning very briskly also. So we tore down the chimney and the scoops were not hard to put out as they were green basswood. That was the last we heard of building the fire in the middle of the house. And soon as daylight came we began to build the chimney in the end of the house, but Thomas often laughed at John and twitted him about the fire in the middle of the shanty. However we got the chimney up and it served its purpose well. We got along much better with the chopping, after the small trees and branches were cut out of the way.

Thus we plodded along for a while, Thomas doing the baking and cooking because he was the best of the three at it. We never washed any dishes and had a new plate every meal.

A man, by the name of Valentine Harrison, who was on the south end of Lot three, Concession 8, sent us a very large buffalo robe to spread over us in bed. We made a rough bedstead and got it woven together with withes instead of rope but the withes sagged down badly in the middle of the bed, and so we got two poles and put them lengthwise under the hemlock branches so that each of us had our own share of the bed, and did not roll in on the one in the middle. This made an improvement in the bachelor bed.

We plodded along in this way, until our chests and cooking utensils were brought to Clinton, and we got a man with his oxen and sleigh to bring them on from there. When we got our bedclothes we thought we were in clover, for we had slept on the hemlock branches for five or six weeks.

We cut down a large ash tree and split it into slabs and then hewed these for a floor to our shanty, and thus we were getting things into better shape.

It was about the beginning of February when my father brought John's and Thomas' mother and sister to stay with us. They had a pretty tough time coming in through Hullet, as there were no bridges over the many streams and they were not frozen over. They got to Kenneth Baines', where Blyth now is, and my father left the horses and Aunt and Cousin there and came on, to get us three to pilot them the rest of the way. We got through with only one upsetting, but the horses were very tired, for the snow was so deep that they would stop every few rods of the way. At last we got to the shanty and got the horses into shelter, and as father had brought provisions with him we were fairly comfortable.

Father wanted to take a load of fish home with him, so we went to Goderich the next day and got the fish. The following day he started for his home.

I got back to Morris, where Aunt and Cousin had things fixed up in fine style. Thomas got his discharge from baking and cooking and we all felt the change to be for the better.

We worked on, getting some of the huge trees down, but we were not much accustomed to the work and snow being very deep again, the going was very slow. About the beginning of April, 1852, there was a very hard crust on the snow, so that a person could run on it, anywhere.

As I was to take up a lot for an old neighbour, we started on April 5th, to look at some vacant lots that were for sale. We were five or six miles from our shanty, when a heavy fall of snow came on, and the east wind caused the snow to cover up the blaze marks on the trees, and we had great difficulty finding our way home. Aunt and Cousin were very pleased to see us, when we arrived, for they thought we would surely become lost.

I did nothing on my place that winter, neither did Thomas. He and John worked together for some years. I went back to Halton in the spring and came back to Morris in the fall of 1852 and got my own shanty up, and a piece chopped down that winter. My cousins and I worked together with one another, wherever our work was most needed.

They helped me to log some, in the fall of 1853, and I was not in Morris again until the spring of 1857, when I got a wife to share my hardships, joys and sorrows.

I have been here (1907) for sixty years and have had some hardships and have seen many changes both in the inhabitants and the country. For the first few months we carried our provisions seven miles—now there is a railroad less than a quarter of a mile from us.

On the 5th of November, 1852, I cut down the first tree on my lot, and if I had the trees on it now, which were on it then, I would be the richest man in Morris Township.

James Laidlaw, oldest brother of John and Thomas, moved to Morris in the fall of 1852. John took on the job of building a shanty for James Waldie, who later became his father-in-law. James and I went to help John with the building, and as we were falling a tree, one of its branches was broken in the falling, and thrown backwards, hitting James on the head and killing him instantly.

We had to carry his body a mile and a quarter to the nearest house, and I had to convey the sad news to his wife, mother, brother and sister. It was the saddest errand of my life. I had to get help to carry the body home, as there was only a footpath through the bush, and the snow was very deep and soft. This was on April 5th, 1853.

I have seen many ups and downs since I came to Morris. There are only three on this Concession, who were first settlers on the land here, and the descendants of five others, who were first settlers. In other words, there are only eight families living on the lots that their fathers took up between Walton and Blyth, a distance of 7 and a half miles.

Cousin John, one of the three who came here in 1851, departed this life on April 11th, 1907. The old Laidlaws are nearly all gone. Cousin Thomas and I are the only ones now (1907) living of those who first came in to Morris.

And the place that now knows us, will soon know us no more, for we are all old frail creatures.

James, once Jamie, Laidlaw died like his father in a place where no reliable burial records yet existed. It is believed that he was put into a corner of the land that he and his brothers and cousin had cleared, then sometime around 1900 his body was moved to the Blyth Cemetery.

Big Rob, who wrote this account of the settlement in Morris, was the father of many sons and daughters. Simon, John, Duncan, Forrest, Sandy, Susan, Maggie, Annie, Lizzie. Duncan left home early. (That name is correct, but I am not absolutely certain of all of the others.) He went to Guelph, and they seldom saw him. The others stayed at home. The house was big enough for them. At first their mother and father were with them, then for several years just their father, and finally they were on their own. People did not remember that they had ever been young.

They turned their backs on the world. The women wore their hair parted in the middle and slicked tight to their heads, though the style of the day ran to bangs and rolls. They wore dark homemade dresses with skinny skirts. And their hands were red because they scrubbed the pine floor of their kitchen with lye every day. It shone like velvet.

They were capable of going to church—which they did every Sunday—and returning home without having spoken to a soul.

Their religious observances were dutiful but not in any way emotional.

The men had to talk more than the women did, doing their business at the mill or the cheese factory. But they wasted no words or time. They were honest but firm in all their dealings. If they made money it was never with the aim of buying new machinery, of lessening their labor or adding comforts to their way of living. They were not cruel to their animals but they had no sentimental feelings for them.

The diet of the household was very plain, and water was what they drank at meals, instead of tea.

So without any pressure from the community, or their religion (the Presbyterian faith was still contentious and cranky but did not lay siege to the soul as fiercely as it had done in Boston's day), they had constructed a life for themselves that was monastic without any visitations of grace or moments of transcendence.

On a Sunday afternoon in the fall Susan looked out a window and saw Forrest walking back and forth in the big front field, where there was now only wheat stubble. He tramped hard. He stopped and judged what he was doing.

But what was that? She would not give him the satisfaction of asking.

It turned out that before the frost came he was set to dig a large hole. He worked by day and by lantern light. He went six feet down but the hole was much too large for a grave. It was in fact to be the cellar of a house. He brought the dirt up in a wheelbarrow, making use of a ramp he had built.

He hauled large stones from the stone pile into the barn, and there, after the winter closed in, he trimmed them with a stone chisel, for his cellar walls. He did not stop doing his share of the farm chores, but worked on this solitary project late into the night.

Next spring as soon as the hole was dry he mortared the stones in place to make the cellar walls. He put in the pipe for his drain and got the cistern built, then fashioned in plain view the stone foundation for his house. It could be seen that this was no two-room shanty he planned. It was a real and commodious house. It would require an entry road and a drainage ditch and would take up arable land.

His brothers spoke to him, finally. He said he would not dig the ditch till the fall when the crop was off and, as for the road, he had not thought of one and supposed he could walk over from the main house on a narrow path, not depriving them of any more grain than necessary.

They said there was still the house to be reckoned with, the land the house had taken from them, and he said yes, that was true. He would pay a reasonable sum, he said.

Where would he get it?

It could be worked out in terms of the labor he had done on the farm already, deducting living expenses. Also he was giving up his share in the inheritance and that altogether should make up for a hole in the field.

He proposed not to work on the farm anymore but to get a job at the planing mill.

They could not believe their ears, just as—until he fitted

those massive and permanent stones in—they had not been able to believe their eyes. Well then, they said. If you want to set yourself up to be a laughingstock. Well then you must do it.

He went to work at the planing mill, and in the long evenings he put up the frame of his house. It was to be two stories high, with four bedrooms and a back and front kitchen and pantry and double parlor. The walls were to be planked, with a brick veneer. He would have to buy the bricks, of course, but the planks he planned to use for the walls underneath were those stacked in the barn, left over from the old drive shed he and his brothers had pulled down when they built the new banked barn. Were such planks his to use? Strictly speaking, they were not. But no other use for them had been planned and there was some uneasiness in the family about how people would judge them if they quarrelled and quibbled about things. Already Forrest was eating his supper at a hotel in Blyth because of remarks that Sandy had made about his eating at the family table, eating what the labor of the others provided. They had let him have the land for the house when he claimed it as his due because they did not want him passing around stories of their meanness, and in the same spirit now they let him have the planks.

That fall he got the roof on though he didn't get it shingled, and he had a stove installed. He got help in both these undertakings from a man he worked with at the mill. It was the first time anyone from outside the family had done any work on the premises, except for the barn raising in their father's time. Their father had been annoyed at his daughters that day because they had set all the food out on trestle tables in the yard, then disappeared, rather than face waiting on strangers.

Time had not made them easier. While the helper was there—and he was not a real stranger, just a town man who did

not go to their church—Lizzie and Maggie would not go out
to the barn, though it was their turn to milk. Susan had to go.
She was the one who always spoke up when they had to enter a
store and buy something. And she was the boss of the brothers
when they were in the house. She was the one who had made it
a rule that nobody should question Forrest during the early
stages of his undertaking. She appeared to think he would give
it up if there was no interest or prohibition. He is only doing it
to get noticed, she said.

And certainly he was. Not so much by his brothers and sisters—who avoided looking out the windows on that side of
their house—as by the neighbors, and even by town people
who would make a special drive past, on Sundays. The fact
that he had got a job away from home, that he ate at the hotel
though he never took a drink there, that he had practically
moved out on his family, was a widespread subject of conversation. It was such a break with all that was known about the rest
of the family as to be almost a scandal. (Duncan's departure
was by now more or less forgotten.) People wondered about
what had happened, at first behind Forrest's back and eventually to his face.

Had there been a fight? No.

Ah then. Ah. Was he planning to get married?

If this was a joke, he did not take it so. He did not say yes or
no or maybe.

There was not a looking glass in the family home, except
for the little wavy one the men shaved by—the sisters could
tell each other when they looked decent. But in the hotel there
was a mammoth glass behind the counter, and Forrest could
have seen in it that he was a good-enough-looking man in his
late thirties, black-haired and broad and tall. (Actually the sisters were even better looking than the brothers but nobody

ever looked at them closely enough to figure that out. Such is the effect of style and manner.)

So why should he not think that marriage was possible, if he hadn't thought about it already?

That winter he lived with only the board walls between himself and the weather and with temporary boards shuttering the window spaces. He put up the inside partitions and built the stairs and closets and laid the final floorboards of oak and pine.

Next summer he built the brick chimney to replace the stovepipe sticking out of the roof. And he covered the whole structure with fresh red bricks, set together as well as any bricklayer might have done them. Windows were put into place, plank doors removed and ready-made doors hung, back and front. An up-to-date stove installed, with baking oven and warming oven and the reservoir for heating water. The pipes fitted into the new chimney. The big job left was the plastering of the inside walls, and he was ready for that when the weather grew chilly. A coat of rough plaster first, then the painstakingly smoothed plaster on top. He understood that wallpaper should go over that but could not think how to choose it. Meanwhile all the rooms looked wonderfully bright, with the plaster shining indoors and the snow without.

The need for furnishings took him by surprise. In the house where he had lived with his brothers and sisters, Spartan preferences ruled. No curtains, only dark-green blinds, bare floors, hard chairs, no sofas, shelves instead of cupboards. Clothing hanging from hooks on the back of doors instead of in wardrobes—more clothes than could be managed that way being seen as excessive. He did not necessarily wish to copy this style, but he had such small experience of other houses that he did not know what other way to manage. He could hardly afford—or wish—to make the place look like the hotel.

He made do, for the present, with the discards placed in the barn. A chair with two rungs missing, some rough shelving, a table that chickens had been plucked on, a cot with horse blankets laid on it for a mattress. All this was set up in the same room as the stove, the other rooms being left entirely bare.

Susan had decreed, when they all lived together, that Maggie should take care of Sandy's clothing, Lizzie of Forrest's, Annie of Simon's, she herself of John's. This meant ironing and mending and darning socks, and knitting scarves and vests and making new shirts as might be needed. Lizzie was not supposed to continue looking after Forrest—or to have anything at all to do with him—after he moved out. But a time came—five or six years after his house had been finished—when she took it upon herself to see how he was getting on. Susan was ill by this time, greatly weakened by pernicious anemia, so that her rules were not always enforced.

Forrest had quit his job at the planing mill. The reason being, so people said, that he could not bear the razzing he got all the time about marrying. Stories circulated, about his going to Toronto on the train, and sitting in Union Station all day long, looking for a woman who would fill the bill but not finding her. Also a story of his writing to an agency in the United States, then hiding in his cellar when some hefty female came knocking on his door. The younger fellows at the mill were particularly hard on him, with their preposterous advice.

He got a job as a janitor at the Presbyterian church, where he did not have to see anybody except the minister or an occasional officious Member of the Session—neither of these being the sort to make crude or personal remarks.

Lizzie crossed the field on a spring afternoon and knocked on his door. No answer. It was not locked, however, and she went in.

Forrest was not asleep. He was lying fully dressed on the cot, with his arms behind his head.

"Are you sick?" said Lizzie. None of them ever lay down in the daytime unless they were sick.

Forrest said no. He did not reproach her for coming in without being asked, but he did not welcome her either.

The place smelled bad. No wallpaper had ever been put up and there was still some whiff of raw plaster. Also the smell of horse blankets and of other clothing not washed for a long time, if ever. And of ancient grease in the frying pan and bitter tea leaves in the pot (Forrest had taken up the fancy habit of drinking tea instead of just hot water). The windows were bleary in the spring sunlight and dead flies lay on their sills.

"Did Susan send you?" Forrest said.

"No," said Lizzie. "She's not herself."

He didn't have anything to say to that. "Did Simon?"

"I came on my own." Lizzie put down the parcel she was carrying and looked about for a broom. "We are all well at the house," she said, just as if he had asked. "Except for Susan."

In the parcel was a new shirt of blue cotton, and half a loaf of bread and a fresh chunk of butter. All bread that the sisters made was excellent, and the butter tasty, being made from the milk of Jersey cows. Lizzie had taken these things without permission.

This was the beginning of a new disposition of the family. Susan did rouse herself when Lizzie got home, enough to tell her she must go or stay. Lizzie said she would go, but to Susan's surprise, and everybody's, she asked for her share of household goods. Simon separated out what she should have, with severe justice, and in that way Forrest's house was, eventually, sparsely furnished. No wallpaper was put up or curtains hung, but everything was scrubbed and gleaming. Lizzie had asked for a cow and a half dozen hens and a pig to raise, and Forrest set to work as a carpenter again, to build a barn with two stalls and a haymow. When Susan died it was discovered that she had put by a surprising nest egg, and a share of that was meted out as well. A horse was bought, and a buggy, around the first time that cars were becoming a usual thing on these roads. Forrest gave up walking to his job, and on Saturday nights he and Lizzie rode to town to shop. Lizzie reigned in her own house, like any married woman.

On one Halloween night—Halloween in those days being more of a time for serious tricks than an occasion for hand-outs—a bundle was left at Forrest and Lizzie's door. Lizzie was the first to open the door in the morning. She had forgotten about Halloween, which none of the family ever paid any attention to, and when she saw the shape of the bundle she cried out, more in amazement than vexation. In its ragged wool wrappings she saw the shape of a baby, and she would have heard somehow about babies being abandoned, left on the doorstep of people who might care for them. For one whole moment she must have thought that that had happened to her, that she had actually been singled out for such a gift and duty. Then Forrest came from the back of the house to see her stoop and pick it up, and he knew at once what it was. So did she, once she felt it. A parcel of straw in sacking, tied with cords, to resemble a baby, the face marked with crayon at the appropriate place on the sacking, to crudely show a baby's face.

Less innocent than Lizzie, Forrest caught the implication, and he grabbed the bundle from her, tore it in pieces, stuffed the pieces into the stove.

She saw that this was a thing she had better not ask about, or even mention in the future, and she never did. Neither did he mention it, and the story survived only as rumor, always to be questioned and deplored by those who passed it on.

"They were devoted to each other," said my mother, who had never actually met them, but was generally in favor of brotherly-sisterly relationships, unsullied by sex.

My father had seen them at church, when he was a child, and might have visited them a couple of times, with his mother. They were only second cousins of his father's and he did not think they had ever come to his parents' house.

He did not admire them, or blame them. He wondered at them.

"To think what their ancestors did," he said. "The nerve it took, to pick up and cross the ocean. What was it squashed their spirits? So soon."

Working for a Living

When my father was twelve years old and had gone as far as he could go at the country school, he went into town to write a set of exams. Their proper name was the Entrance Examinations, but they were known collectively as the Entrance. The Entrance meant, literally, the entrance to high school, but it also meant, in an undefined way, the entrance to the world. The world of professions such as medicine or law or engineering or teaching. Country boys did enter that world in the years before the First World War, more easily than they did a generation later. It was a time of prosperity in Huron County and expansion in the country. It was 1913 and the country was not yet fifty years old.

My father passed the Entrance with high honors and went on to the Continuation School in the town of Blyth. Continuation Schools offered four years of high school, without the final year called Upper School, or Fifth Form—you would have to go to a larger town for that. It looked as if he was on his way.

During his first week at Continuation School my father heard the teacher read a poem.

Liza Grayman Ollie Minus.
We can make Eliza blind.

Andy Parting, Lee Beehinus.
Foo Prince in the Sansa Time.

He used to recite this to us as a joke, but the fact was, he did not hear it as a joke. Around the same time, he went into the stationery store and asked for Signs Snow Paper.
Signs Snow Paper.
Science notepaper.
Soon he was surprised to see the poem written on the blackboard.

Lives of Great Men all remind us,
We can make our lives sublime.
And, departing, leave behind us
Footprints on the Sands of Time.

He had not hoped for such reasonable clarification, would not have dreamed of asking for it. He had been quite willing to give the people at the school the right to have a strange language or logic. He did not ask for them to make sense on his terms. He had a streak of pride which might look like humility, making him scared and touchy, ready to bow out. I know that very well. He made a mystery there, a hostile structure of rules and secrets, far beyond anything that really existed. He felt nearby the fierce breath of ridicule, he overestimated the competition, and the family caution, the country wisdom, came to him then: stay out of it.

In those days people in town did generally look upon the people from the country as more apt to be slow-witted, tongue-tied, uncivilized, than themselves, and somewhat more docile in spite of their strength. And farmers saw people who lived in towns as having an easy life and being unlikely to survive in situations calling for fortitude, self-reliance, hard work. They believed this in spite of the fact that the hours men worked at factory jobs or in stores were long and the wages low, in spite of the fact that many houses in town had no running water or flush toilets or electricity. But the people in town had Saturday or Wednesday afternoons and the whole of Sundays off and that was enough to make them soft. The farmers had not one holiday in their lives. Not even the Scots Presbyterians; cows don't recognize the Sabbath.

The country people when they came into town to shop or to go to church often seemed stiff and shy and the town people did not realize that this could actually be seen as a superior behavior. I'm-not-going-to-let-any-of-them-make-a-fool-out-of-me behavior. Money would not make much difference. Farmers might maintain their proud and wary reserve in the presence of citizens whom they could buy and sell.

My father would say later that he had gone to Continuation School too young to know what he was doing, and that he should have stayed there, he should have made something out of himself. But he said this almost as a matter of form, not as if he cared very much. And it wasn't as if he had run off home at the first indication that there were things he didn't understand. He was never very clear about how long he had stayed. Three years and part of the fourth? Two years and part of the third? And he didn't quit suddenly—it was not a matter of going to school one day and staying away the next and never showing up again. He just began to spend more and more time in the bush and less and less time at school, so that his parents decided there was not much point in thinking about sending him to a larger town to do his Fifth Form, not much hope of university or the professions. They could have afforded that—though not easily—but it was evidently not what he wanted.

And it could not be seen as a great disappointment. He was their only son, the only child. The farm would be his.

There was no more wild country in Huron County then than there is now. Perhaps there was less. The farms had been cleared in the period between 1830 and 1860, when the Huron Tract was being opened up, and they were cleared thoroughly. Many creeks had been dredged—the progressive thing to do was to straighten them out and make them run like tame canals between the fields. The early farmers hated the very sight of a tree and admired the look of open land. And the masculine approach to the land was managerial, dictatorial. Only women were allowed to care about landscape and not to think always of its subjugation and productivity. My grandmother, for example, was famous for having saved a line of silver maples along the lane. These trees grew beside a crop field and they were getting big and old—their roots interfered with the ploughing and they shaded too much of the crop. My grandfather and my father went out one morning and made ready to cut the first of them down. But my grandmother saw what they were doing from the kitchen window and she flew out in her apron and harangued and upbraided them so that they finally had to take up the axes and the crosscut saw and leave the scene. The trees stayed and spoiled the crop at the edge of the field until the terrible winter of 1935 finished them off.

But at the back of the farms the farmers were compelled by law to leave a woodlot. They could cut trees there both for their own use and to sell. Wood of course had been their first crop— rock elm went for ships' timbers and white pine for the ships' masts, until hardly any rock elm or white pine remained. Now there was protection decreed for the poplar and ash and maple and oak and beech, the cedar and hemlock that were left.

Through the woodlot—called the bush—at the back of my

grandfather's farm ran the Blyth Creek, dredged a long time ago when the farm was first cleared. The earth dredged out then made a high, hummocky bank on which thick clumps of cedars grew. This was where my father started trapping. He eased himself out of school and into the life of a fur-trapper. He could follow the Blyth Creek for many miles in either direction, to its rising in Grey Township or to the place where it flows into the Maitland River which flows into Lake Huron. In some places—most particularly in the village of Blyth—the creek became public for a while, but for much of its length it ran through the backs of farms, with the bush on either side, so that it was possible to follow it and be hardly aware of the farms, the cleared land, the straight-laid roads and fences—it was possible to imagine that you were out in the forest as it was a hundred years ago, and for hundreds of years before that.

My father had read a lot of books by this time, books he found at home and in the Blyth Library and in the Sunday School Library. He had read books by Fenimore Cooper and he had absorbed the myths or half-myths about wilderness that most of the country boys around him knew nothing about, since few of them were readers. Most boys whose imaginations were lit up by the same notions as his would live in cities. If they were rich enough they would travel north every summer with their families, they would go on canoe trips and later on fishing and hunting trips. If their families were truly rich they would navigate the rivers of the Far North with Indian guides. People eager for this experience of the wilderness would drive right through our part of the country without noticing there was one bit of wilderness there.

But farm boys from Huron County, knowing hardly any-thing about this big deep country of the Precambrian Shield and the wild rivers, nevertheless were drawn—some of them were, for a time—drawn to the strips of bush along the creeks, where they fished and hunted and built rafts and set traps. Even if they hadn't read a word about that sort of life they might make their forays into it. But they soon gave it up to enter upon the real, heavy work of their lives, as farmers.

And one of the differences between farmers then and now was that in those days nobody expected recreation to play any regular part in the farming life.

My father, being a farm boy with that extra, inspired or romantic perception (he would not have cared for those words), with a Fenimore Cooper–cultivated hunger, did not turn aside from these juvenile pursuits at the age of eighteen or nineteen or twenty. Instead of giving up the bush, he took to it more steadily and seriously. He began to be talked about and thought about more as a trapper than as a young farmer. And as a solitary and slightly odd young man, though not a person who was in any way feared or disliked. He was edging away from the life of a farmer, just as he had edged away earlier from the idea of getting an education and becoming a professional man. He was edging towards a life he probably could not clearly visualize, since he would know what he didn't want so much better than what he wanted.

A life in the bush, away from the towns, on the edge of the farms—how could it be managed?

Even here, where men and women mostly took whatever was cut out for them, some men had managed it. Even in this tamed country there were a few hermits, a few men who had inherited farms and didn't keep them up, or who were just squatters come from God knows where. They fished and hunted and travelled around, were gone and came back, were gone and never came back—not like the farmers who when-ever they left their own localities went in buggies or sleighs or more often now by car, bound on definite errands to certain destinations.

He was making money from his trapline. Some skins could bring him as much as a fortnight's work on a threshing gang. So at home they could not complain. He paid board, and he still helped his father when it was necessary. He and his father never talked. They could work all morning cutting wood in the bush, and never say a word, except when they had to speak about the work. His father was not interested in the bush except as a woodlot. It was to him just like a field of oats, with the difference that the crop was firewood.

His mother was more curious. She walked back to the bush on Sunday afternoons. She was a tall upright woman with a stately figure, but she still had a tomboy's stride. She would bunch up her skirts and expertly swing her legs over a fence. She was knowledgeable about wildflowers and berries and she could tell you the name of any bird from its song.

He showed her the snares where he caught fish. That made her uneasy, because the fish could be caught in the snares on a Sunday, just as on any other day. She was very strict about all Presbyterian rules and observances, and this strictness had a peculiar history. She had not been brought up as a Presbyterian at all, but had led a carefree childhood and girlhood as a member of the Anglican Church, also known as the Church of England. There were not many Anglicans in that part of the country and they were sometimes thought of as next thing to Papists—but also as next door to freethinkers. Their religion often seemed to outsiders to be all a matter of bows and responses, with short sermons, easy interpretations, worldly ministers, much pomp and frivolity. A religion to the liking of her father, who had been a convivial Irishman, a storyteller, a drinker. But when my grandmother married she had wrapped herself up in her husband's Presbyterianism, becoming fiercer than many who were brought up in it. She was a born Anglican who took on the Presbyterian righteousness-competition just as she was a born tomboy who took on the farm-housewife competition, with her whole heart. People might have wondered, did she do this for love?

My father and those who knew her well did not think so. She and my grandfather were mismatched, though they didn't fight. He thoughtful, silent; she spirited, sociable. No, not for love but for pride's sake she did what she did. Not to be outdone or criticized in any way. And not to have anybody say that she regretted a decision that she had made, or wanted anything that she couldn't have.

She stayed friends with her son in spite of the Sunday fish, which she wouldn't cook. She took an interest in the animal skins he showed her, and heard how much he got for them. She washed his smelly clothes, whose smell was as much from the fish bait he carried as from the pelts and guts. She could be exasperated but tolerant with him as if he was a much younger son. And perhaps he did seem younger to her, with his traps and treks along the creek, and his unsociability. He never went after girls, and gradually lost touch with his childhood friends who were doing so. She did not mind. His behavior might have helped her to bear a disappointment that he had not gone on in school, he was not going to become a doctor or a minister. Maybe she could pretend that he might still do that, the old plans—her plans for him—being not forgotten but just postponed. At least he was not just turning into a silent farmer, a copy of his father.

As for my grandfather, he passed no opinion, did not say whether he approved or disapproved. He maintained his air of discipline and privacy. He was a man born in Morris, settled in to be a farmer, a Grit and a Presbyterian. Born to be against the English Church and the Family Compact and Bishop Strachan and saloons; to be for universal suffrage (but not for women), free schools, responsible government, the Lord's Day Alliance. To live by hard routines, and refusals.

My grandfather diverged a little—he learned to play the fiddle, he married the tall temperamental Irish girl with eyes of two colors. That done, he withdrew, and for the rest of his life was diligent, orderly, and quiet. He too was a reader. In the winter he managed to get all his work done—and well done— and then he would read. He never talked about what he read, but the whole community knew about it. And respected him for it. That is an odd thing—there was a woman too who read, she got books from the library all the time, and nobody respected her in the least. The talk was always about how the dust grew under her beds and her husband ate a cold dinner. Perhaps it was because she read novels, stories, and the books my grandfather read were heavy. Heavy books, as everybody remembered, but their titles are not remembered. They came from the library, which at that time contained Blackstone, Macauley, Carlyle, Locke, Hume's *History of England*. What about *An Enquiry Concerning Human Understanding*? What about Voltaire? Karl Marx? It's possible.

Now—if the woman with the dustballs under the beds had read the heavy books, would she have been forgiven? I don't believe so. It was women who judged her, and women judged women more harshly than they did men. Also, it must be remembered that my grandfather got his work done first—his woodpiles were orderly and his stable shipshape. In no point of behavior did his reading affect his life.

Another thing said of my grandfather was that he prospered. But prosperity was not pursued, or understood, in those days, quite in the way it is now. I remember my grandmother saying, "When we needed something done—when your father went into Blyth to school and needed books and new clothes and so on—I would say to your grandfather, well we better raise another calf or something to get a bit extra." So it would seem that if they knew what to do to get that bit extra, they could have had it all along.

That is, in their ordinary life they were not always making as much money as they could have made. They were not stretching themselves to the limit. They did not see life in those terms. Nor did they see it in terms of saving at least a part of their energies for good times, as some of their Irish neighbors did.

How, then? I believe they saw it mostly as ritual. Seasonal and inflexible, very much like housework. To try to make more money, for an increase in status or so that life could become easier, might have seemed unbecoming.

A change in outlook from that of the man who went to Illinois. Maybe a lingering influence from that setback, on his more timid or thoughtful descendants.

This must have been the life my father saw waiting for him—a life that my grandmother, in spite of her own submission to it, was not altogether sorry to see him avoid.

There is one contradiction here. When you write about real people you are always up against contradictions. My grandfather owned the first car on the Eighth Line of Morris. It was a Gray-Dorrit. And my father in his teens had a crystal set, something that all boys wanted. Of course, he may have paid for it himself.

He may have paid for it with his trapping money.

The animals my father trapped were muskrats, mink, marten, now and then a bobcat. Otter, weasels, foxes. Muskrats he trapped in the spring because their fur stays prime until about the end of April. All the others were at their best from the end of October on into winter. The white weasel does not attain its purity until around the tenth of December. He went out on snowshoes. He built up deadfalls, with a figure 4 trigger, set so the boards and branches fell onto the muskrat or mink. He nailed weasel traps to trees. He nailed boards together to make a square box trap working on the same principle as a dead-fall—something less conspicuous to other trappers. The steel traps for muskrats were staked so the animal would drown, often at the end of a sloping cedar rail. Patience and foresight and guile were necessary. For the vegetarians he set out tasty bits of apple and parsnip; for the meat-eaters, such as mink, there was delectable fish bait mixed by himself and ripened in a jar in the ground. A similar meat mix for foxes was buried in June or July and dug up in the fall; they sought it out to roll upon, revelling in the pungency of decay.

Foxes interested him more and more. He followed them away from the creeks to the little rough sandy hills that are found sometimes between bush and pasture—they love the sandy hills at night. He learned to boil his traps in water and soft maple bark to kill the smell of metal. Such traps were set out in the open with a sifting of sand over them.

How do you kill a trapped fox? You don't want to shoot him, because of the wound left in the pelt and the blood smell spoiling the trap.

You stun him with the blow of a long, strong stick, and then put your foot on his heart.

Foxes in the wild are usually red. But occasionally a black fox will occur among them as a spontaneous mutation. He had never caught one. But he knew that some of these had been caught elsewhere and bred selectively to increase the show of white hairs along the back and tail. Then they were called silver foxes. Silver-fox farming was just beginning in Canada.

In 1925 my father bought a pair, a male silver fox and a female, and built a pen for them beside the barn. At first they must have seemed just another kind of animal being raised on the farm, something more bizarre than the chickens or the pigs or even the banty rooster, something rare and showy as peacocks, interesting for visitors. When my father bought them and built the pen for them it might even have been taken as a sign that he meant to stay, to be a slightly different farmer from most, but still a farmer.

The first litter was born, and he built more pens. He took a snapshot of his mother holding the three little pups. She looks apprehensive but sporting. Two of the pups were males and one female. He killed the males in the fall when their fur was prime and sold the pelts for an impressive price. The trapline began to seem less important than these animals raised in captivity.

A young woman came to visit. A cousin on the Irish side— a schoolteacher, lively and persistent and good-looking, a few years older than he. She was immediately interested in the foxes, and not, as his mother thought, pretending to be interested in order to entice him. (Between his mother and the visitor there was an almost instant antipathy, though they were cousins.) She came from a much poorer home, a poorer farm, than this one, and she had become a schoolteacher by her own desperate efforts. The only reason she had stopped there was that schoolteaching was the best thing for women that she had come across so far. She was a hardworking popular teacher, but some gifts that she knew she had were not being used. These gifts had something to do with taking chances, making money. They were gifts as out of place in my father's house as they had been in her own, looked at askance in both places, although they were the very gifts (less often mentioned than the hard work, the perseverance) that had built the country. She looked at the foxes and she did not see any romantic connection to the wilderness; she saw a new industry, the possibility of riches. She had a little money saved to buy a place where all this could get started in earnest. She became my mother.

When I think of my parents in the time before they became my parents, after they had made their decision but before their marriage had made it—in those days—irrevocable, they seem not only touching and helpless, marvellously deceived, but more attractive than at any later time. It is as if nothing was thwarted then and life still bloomed with possibilities, as if they enjoyed all sorts of power before they bent themselves towards each other. That can't be true, of course—they must have been anxious already—my mother must certainly have been anxious about being in her late twenties and unmarried. They must have known failure already, they may have turned to each other with reservations rather than the luxuriant optimism that I imagine. But I do imagine it, as we must all like to do, so we won't think that we were born out of affection that was always stingy, or an undertaking that was always half-hearted. I think that when they came and picked out the place where they would live for the rest of their lives, on the Maitland River just west of Wingham in Turnberry Township in the

County of Huron, they were travelling in a car that ran well on dry roads on a bright spring day, and that they themselves were kind and handsome and healthy and trusting their luck.

Not very long ago I was driving with my husband on the back roads of Grey County, which is to the north and east of Huron County. We passed a country store standing empty at a crossroads. It had old-fashioned store windows, with long narrow panes. Out in front there was a stand for gas pumps which weren't there anymore. Close beside it was a mound of sumac trees and strangling vines, into which all kinds of junk had been thrown. The sumacs jogged my memory and I looked back at the store. It seemed to me that I had been here once, and that the scene was connected with some disappointment or dismay. I knew that I had never driven this way before in my adult life and I did not think I could have come here as a child. It was too far from home. Most of our drives out of town were to my grandparents' house in Blyth—they had retired there after they sold the farm. And once a summer we drove to the lake at Goderich. But even as I was saying this to my husband I remembered the disappointment. Ice cream. Then I remembered everything—the trip my father and I had made to Muskoka in 1941, when my mother was already there, selling furs at the Pine Tree Hotel north of Gravenhurst.

My father had stopped for gas at a country store and he had bought me an ice-cream cone. It was an out-of-the-way place and the ice cream must have been sitting in its tub for a long time. It had probably been partly melted at one stage, then refrozen. It had splinters of ice in it, pure ice, and its flavor was dismally altered. Even the cone was soft and stale.

"But why would he go this way to Muskoka?" my husband

said. "Wouldn't he go along No. 9 and then go up on Highway 11?"

He was right. I wondered whether I could have been mistaken. It could have been another store at another crossroads where we bought the gas and the ice cream.

As we drove west, heading over the long hills for Bruce County and Highway 21, after sunset and before dark, I talked about what any long car trip—that is, any car trip over ten miles long—used to be like for our family, how arduous and uncertain. I described to my husband—whose family, more realistic than ours, considered themselves too poor to own a car—how the car's noises and movements, the jolting and rattling, the straining of the engine and the groan of the gears, made the crowning of hills and the covering of miles an effort that everybody in the car seemed to share. Would a tire go flat, would the radiator boil over, would there be a breakdown? The use of that word—*breakdown*—made it sound as if the car was frail and skittish, with a mysterious, almost human vulnerability.

Of course it wouldn't be like that if you had a newer car, or if you could afford to keep it in good repair, I said.

And it came to me why we would have been driving to Muskoka along back roads. I was not mistaken after all. My father must have been wary of taking the car through any sizable town or on a main highway. There were too many things wrong with it. It should not have been on the road at all. There were times when he could not afford to take it to the garage and this must have been one of them. He did what he could to fix it himself, to keep it running. Sometimes a neighbor helped him. I remember my father's saying, "The man's a mechanical genius," which makes me suspect that he was no mechanical genius himself.

Now I knew why such a feeling of risk and trepidation was mixed up with my memory of the unpaved, sometimes ungravelled roads—some were ridged in such a way that my father called them washboard roads—and the one-lane plank bridges. As things came back to me I could recall my father's telling me that he had only enough money to get to the hotel where my mother was, and that if she didn't have any money he didn't know what he was going to do. He didn't tell me this at the time, of course. He bought me the ice-cream cone, he told me to push on the dashboard when we were going up the hills, and I did so, though it was a ritual now, a joke, my faith having long ago evaporated. He seemed to be enjoying himself.

He told me about the circumstances of the trip years later, after my mother was dead, when he was remembering some times that they had gone through together.

The furs that my mother was selling to American tourists (we always spoke of American tourists, as if acknowledging that they were the only kind who could be of any use to us) were not raw furs, but tanned and dressed. Some skins were cut and sewn together in strips, to make capes; others were left whole and were made into what were called scarves. A fox scarf was one whole skin, a mink scarf was two or three skins. The head of the animal was left on and was given bright golden-brown glass eyes, also an artificial jaw. Fasteners were sewn on the paws. I believe that in the case of the mink the pelts were attached tail to mouth. The fox scarf was fastened paw to paw, and the fox cape sometimes had the fox's head sewn on out of place entirely, in the middle of the back, as a decoration.

Thirty years later these furs would have found their way into second-hand clothing stores and might be bought and worn as a joke. Of all the moldering and grotesque fashions of the past, this wearing of animal skins that were undisguised animal skins would seem the most amazing and barbaric.

My mother sold the fox scarves for twenty-five, thirty-five, forty, fifty dollars, depending on the number of white hairs, the "silver," in the pelt. Capes cost fifty, seventy-five, maybe a hundred dollars. My father had started raising mink as well as foxes during the late nineteen-thirties, but she did not have many mink scarves for sale and I do not remember what she charged for them. Perhaps we had been able to dispose of them to the furriers in Montreal without taking a loss.

The colony of fox pens took up a good deal of the territory on our farm. It stretched from behind the barn to the high bank overlooking the river flats. The first pens my father had made had roofs and walls of fine wire on a framework of cedar poles. They had earth floors. The pens built later on had raised wire floors. All the pens were set side by side on intersecting "streets" so that they made a town, and around the town was a high guard fence. Inside each pen was a kennel—a large wooden box with ventilation holes and a sloping roof or lid that could be lifted up. And there was a wooden ramp along one side of the pen, for the foxes' exercise. Because the building had been done at different times and not all planned out in the beginning, there were all the differences there are in a real town—there were wide streets and narrow streets, some spacious earth-floored old-fashioned pens and some smaller wire-floored modern pens that seemed less agreeably proportioned even if more sanitary. There were two long apartment buildings called the Sheds. The New Sheds had a covered walkway between two facing rows of pens with slanting wooden roofs and high wire floors. The Old Sheds was just a short row of attached pens rather primitively patched together. The New Sheds was a hellishly noisy place full of adolescents due to be pelted—most of them—before they were a year old. The Old Sheds was a slum and contained disappointing breeders who would not be kept another year, and the occasional cripple, and even, for a time, a red female fox who was well-disposed to humans and by way of being a pet. Either because of that, or her color, all the other foxes shunned her, and her name—for they all had names—was Old Maid. How she came to be there I don't know. A sport in a litter? A wild fox who tunnelled the wrong way under the guard fence?

When the hay was cut in our field some of it was spread on top of the pens to give the foxes shelter from the sun and keep their fur from turning brown. They looked very scruffy anyway, in the summertime—old fur falling out and new fur just coming in. By November they were resplendent, the tips of their tails snowy and their back fur deep and black, with its silver overlay. They were ready to be killed—unless they were to carry on as breeders. Their skins would be stretched, cleaned, sent off to be tanned, and then to the auctions.

Up to this time everything was in my father's control, barring some disease, or the chanciness of breeding. Everything was of his making—the pens, the kennels where the foxes could hide and have their young, the water dishes—made from tins—that tipped from the outside and were filled twice a day with fresh water, the tank that was trundled down the streets, carrying water from the pump, the feed trough in the barn where meal and water and ground horse meat were mixed, the killing box where the animal's trapped head met the blast of chloroform. Then, once the pelts were dried and cleaned and peeled off the stretch boards, nothing was within his control anymore. The pelts were laid flat in shipping boxes and sent off to Montreal and there was nothing to do but wait and see how they were graded and sold at the fur auctions. The whole year's income, the money to pay the feed bill, the money to pay the bank, the money he had to pay on the loan he had from his mother after she was widowed, had to come out of that. In some years the price of the furs was fairly good, in some years not too bad, in other years terrible. Though nobody could have seen it at the time, the truth was that he had got into the business just a little too late, and without enough capital to get going in a big way during the first years when the profits were high. Before he was fairly started the Depression arrived. The effect on his business was erratic, not steadily bad, as you might think. In some years he was slightly better off than he might have been on the farm, but there were more bad years than good. Things did not pick up much with the beginning of the war—in fact, the prices in 1940 were among the worst ever. During the Depression bad prices were not so hard to take—he could look around and see that nearly everybody was in the same boat—but now, with the war jobs opening up and the country getting prosperous again, it was very hard to have worked as he had and come up with next to nothing.

He said to my mother that he was thinking of joining the Army. He was thinking of pelting and selling all his stock, and going into the Army as a tradesman. He was not too old for that, and he had skills which would make him useful. He could be a carpenter—think of all the building he had done around his place. Or he could be a butcher—think of all the old horses he had slaughtered and cut up for the foxes.

My mother had another idea. She suggested that they keep out all the best skins, not sending them to the auctions but having them tanned and dressed—that is, made into scarves and capes, provided with eyes and claws—and then take them out and sell them. People were getting some money now. There were women around who had the money and the inclination to get dressed up. And there were tourists. We were off the beaten track for tourists, but she had heard about them, how the hotel resorts of Muskoka were full of them. They came up from Detroit and Chicago with money to spend on bone china from England, Shetland sweaters, Hudson's Bay blankets. So why not silver-fox furs?

When it comes to changes, to invasions and upheavals, there are two kinds of people. If a highway is built through their front yard, some people will be affronted, they will mourn the loss of privacy, of peony bushes and lilacs and a dimension of themselves. The other sort will see an opportunity—they will put up a hotdog stand, get a fast-food franchise, open a motel. My mother was the second sort of person. The very idea of the tourists with their American money flocking to the northern woods filled her with vitality.

In the summer, then, the summer of 1941, she went off to Muskoka with her trunkload of furs. My father's mother arrived to take over our house. She was still an upright and handsome woman and she entered my mother's domain magnificent with foreboding. She hated what my mother was doing. Peddling. She said that when she thought of American tourists all she hoped was that none of them ever came near her. For one day she and my mother were together in the house and during that time my grandmother withdrew into a harsh and unforthcoming version of herself. My mother was too steamed up to notice. But after my grandmother had been in charge on her own for a day she thawed out. She decided to forgive my father his marriage, for the time being, also his exotic enterprise and its failure, and my father decided to forgive her the humiliating fact that he owed her money. She baked bread and pies, and did well by the garden vegetables, the new-laid eggs and the rich milk and cream from the Jersey cow. (Though we had no money we were never badly fed.) She scoured the inside of the cupboards and scraped away the black on the bottom of the saucepans, which we had believed to be permanent. She ferreted out many items in need of mending. In the evenings she carried pails of water to the flower border and the tomato plants. Then my father came up from his work in the barn and the fox pens and we all sat out on yard chairs, under the heavy trees.

Our nine-acre farm—no farm at all as my grandmother saw things—had an unusual location. To the east was the town, the church towers and the tower of the Town Hall visible when the leaves were off the trees, and on the mile or so of road between us and the main street there was a gradual thickening of houses, a turning of dirt paths into sidewalks, an appearance of a lone streetlight, so that you might say we were at the town's farthest edges, though beyond its legal municipal boundaries. But to the west there was only one farmhouse to be seen, and that one far away, at the top of a hill almost at the midpoint in the western horizon. We always referred to this as Roly Grain's house, but who Roly Grain might be, or what road led to his house, I had never asked or imagined. It was all too far away, across, first, a wide field planted in corn or oats, then the woods and the river flats sloping down to the great hidden curve of the river, and the pattern of overlapping bare or wooded hills beyond. It was very seldom that you could see a stretch of country so empty, so seductive to the imagination, in our thickly populated farmland.

When we sat looking out at this view my father rolled and smoked a cigarette, and he and my grandmother talked about the old days on the farm, their old neighbors, and funny things—that is, both strange and comical things—that had happened. My mother's absence brought a sort of peace—not only between them, but for all of us. Some alert and striving note was removed. An edge of ambition, self-regard, perhaps discontent, was absent. At the time, I did not know exactly what it was that was missing. I did not know either what a deprivation, rather than a relief, it would be for me, if that was gone for good.

My younger brother and sister pestered my grandmother to let them look into her window. My grandmother's eyes were a hazel color, but in one of them she had a large spot, taking up at least a third of the iris, and the color of this spot was blue. So people said that her eyes were of two different colors, though this was not quite the truth. We called the blue spot her window. She would pretend to be cross at being asked to show it, she would duck her head and beat off whoever was trying to look in, or she would screw her eyes shut, opening the plain hazel one a crack to see if she was still being watched. She was always caught out in the end and gave in to sitting still with eyes wide open, being looked into. The blue was clear, without a speck of any other color in it, a blue made brighter by the brownish-yellow at its edges, as the summer sky is by the puffs of clouds.

It was evening by the time my father turned into the hotel driveway. We drove between the stone gateposts and there it was ahead of us—a long stone building with gables and a white veranda. Hanging pots overflowing with flowers. We missed the turn into the parking lot and followed the semicircular drive, which brought us in front of the veranda, driving past the people who sat there on swings and rockers, with nothing to do but look at us, as my father said.

Nothing to do but gawk.

We spotted the inconspicuous sign and found our way to a gravel lot next to the tennis court. We got out of the car. It was covered with dust and looked like a raffish interloper amongst the other cars there.

We had travelled the whole way with the windows down and a hot wind blowing in on us, tangling and drying my hair. My father saw that there was something wrong with me and asked me if I had a comb. I got back into the car and looked for one, finding it at last wedged down against the back of the seat. It was dirty, and some teeth were missing. I tried, and he tried, and finally he said, "Maybe if you just shoved it back behind your ears." Then he combed his own hair, frowning as he bent to look in the car mirror. We walked across the lot, with my father wondering out loud whether we should try the front or the back door. He seemed to think I might have some useful opinion about this—something he had never thought in any circumstances before. I said that we should try the front, because I wanted to get another look at the lily pond in the semicircle of lawn bounded by the drive. There was a statue of a bare-shouldered girl in a tunic draped closely against her breasts, with a jug on her shoulder—one of the most elegant things I had ever seen in my life.

"Run the gauntlet," my father said softly, and we went up the steps and crossed the veranda in front of people pretending not to look at us. We entered the lobby, where it was so dark that little lights were turned on, in frosted globes, high up on the dark shiny wood of the walls. To one side was the dining room, visible through glass doors. It was all cleaned up after supper, each table covered with a white cloth. On the other side, with the doors open, was a long rustic room with a huge stone fireplace at the end of it, and the skin of a bear stretched on the floor.

"Look at that," said my father. "She must be here somewhere."

What he had noticed in the corner of the lobby was a waist-high display case, and behind its glass was a silver-fox cape beautifully spread on what looked like a piece of white velvet. A sign set on top said, *Silver Fox, the Canadian Luxury,* in a flowing script done with white and silvery paint on a black board.

"Here somewhere," my father repeated. We peered into the room with the fireplace. A woman writing at a desk looked up and said, in an agreeable but somehow distant voice, "I think that if you ring the bell somebody will come."

It seemed strange to me to be addressed by a person you had never seen before.

We backed out and crossed to the doors of the dining room. Across the acre of white tables with their laid-out silverware and turned-down glasses and bunches of flowers and napkins peaked like wigwams, we saw two figures, ladies, seated at a table near the kitchen door, finishing a late supper or having evening tea. My father turned the doorknob and they looked up. One of them rose and came towards us, between the tables.

The moment in which I did not realize that this was my mother was not long, but there was a moment. I saw a woman in an unfamiliar dress, a cream-colored dress with a pattern of little red flowers. The skirt was pleated and swishing, the material crisp, glowing as the tablecloths did in the dark-panelled room. The woman wearing it looked brisk and elegant, her dark hair parted in the middle and pinned up in a neat coronet of braids. And even when I knew this was my mother, when she had put her arms around me and kissed me, spilling out an unaccustomed fragrance and showing none of her usual hurry and regrets, none of her usual dissatisfaction with my appearance, or my nature, I felt that she was somehow still a stranger. She had crossed effortlessly, it seemed, into the world of the hotel, where my father and I stood out like tramps or scarecrows—it was as if she had always been living there. I felt first amazed, then betrayed, then excited and hopeful, my thoughts running on to advantages to be gained for myself, in this new situation.

The woman my mother had been talking to turned out to be the dining-room hostess—a tanned, tired-looking woman with dark-red lipstick and nail polish, who was subsequently revealed to have many troubles which she had confided to my mother. She was immediately friendly. I broke into the adult conversation to tell about the ice splinters and the bad taste of the ice cream, and she went out to the kitchen and brought me a large helping of vanilla ice cream covered with chocolate sauce and bearing a cherry on top.

"Is that a sundae?" I said. It looked like the sundaes I had seen in advertisements, but since it would be the first I had ever tasted I wanted to be sure of its name.

"I believe it is," she said. "A sundae."

Nobody reproved me, in fact my parents laughed, and then the woman brought fresh tea and some sort of sandwich for my father.

"Now I'll leave you to your chat," she said, and went away and left us three alone in that hushed and splendid room. My parents talked, but I paid little attention to their conversation. I interrupted from time to time to tell my mother something about the trip or about what had been happening at home. I showed her where a bee had stung me, on my leg. Neither of them told me to be quiet—they answered me with cheerfulness and patience. My mother said that we would all sleep tonight in her cabin. She had one of the little cabins behind the hotel. She said we would eat breakfast here in the morning.

She said that when I had finished I should run out and look at the lily pond.

That must have been a happy conversation. Relieved, on my father's side—triumphant, on my mother's. She had done very well, she had sold almost everything she had brought with her, the venture was a success. Vindication for her, salvation for us all. My father must have been thinking of what had to be done first, whether to get the car fixed in a garage up here or chance it once more on the back roads and take it to the garage at home, where he knew the people. Which bills should be paid at once, and which should be paid in part. And my mother must have been looking further into the future, thinking of how she could expand, which other hotels she could try this in, how many more capes and scarves they should get made up next year, and whether this could develop into a year-round business.

She couldn't have foreseen how soon the Americans were going to get into the war, and how that was going to keep them at home, how gas rationing was going to curtail the resort business. She couldn't foresee the attack on her own body, the destruction gathering within.

She would talk for years afterwards about what she had achieved in that summer. How she had known the right way to go about it, never pushing too hard, showing the furs as if it was a great pleasure to her and not a matter of money. A sale would seem to be the last thing on her mind. It was necessary to show the people who ran the hotel that she would not cheapen the impression they wanted to make, that she was anything but a huckster. A lady, rather, whose offerings added a unique distinction. She had to become a friend of the management and the employees as well as the guests.

And that was no chore for her. She had the true instinct for mixing friendship and business considerations, the instinct that all good salespersons have. She never had to calculate her advantage and coldly act upon it. Everything she did she did naturally and felt a real warmth of heart where her interests lay. She who had always had difficulty with her mother-in-law and her husband's family, who was thought stuck-up by our neighbors, and somewhat pushy by the town women at the church, had found a world of strangers in which she was at once at home.

For all this, as I grew older, I came to feel something like revulsion. I despised the whole idea of putting yourself to use in that way, making yourself dependent on the response of others, employing flattery so adroitly and naturally that you did not even recognize it as flattery. And all for money. I thought such behavior shameful, as of course my grandmother did. I took it for granted that my father felt the same way though he did not show it. I believed—or thought I believed—in working hard and being proud, not caring about being poor and indeed having a subtle contempt for those who led easeful lives.

I did, then, regret the loss of the foxes. Not of the business, but of the animals themselves, with their beautiful tails and angry golden eyes. As I grew older, and more and more aloof from country ways, country necessities, I began for the first time to question their captivity, to feel regret for their killing, their conversion into money. (I never got so far as feeling anything like this for the mink, who seemed to me mean and rat-like, deserving of their fate.) I knew this feeling to be a luxury, and when I mentioned it to my father, in later years, I spoke of it lightly. In the same spirit he said that he believed there was some religion in India that held with all animals getting into Heaven. Think, he said, if that were true—what a pack of snarling foxes he would meet there, not to mention all the other fur-bearers he had trapped, and the mink, and a herd of thundering horses he had butchered for their meat.

Then he said, not so lightly, "You get into things, you know. You sort of don't realize what you're getting into."

It was in those later years, after my mother was dead, that he spoke of my mother's salesmanship and how she had saved the day. He spoke of how he didn't know what he was going to do, at the end of that trip, if it turned out that she hadn't made any money.

"But she had," he said. "She had it." And the tone in which he said this convinced me that he had never shared those reservations of my grandmother's and mine. Or that he'd resolutely put away such shame, if he'd ever had it.

A shame that has come full circle, finally being shameful in itself to me.

On a spring evening in 1949—the last spring, in fact the last whole season, that I was to live at home—I was riding my bicycle to the Foundry, to deliver a message to my father. I seldom rode my bicycle anymore. For a while, maybe all through the fifties, it was considered eccentric for any girl to be riding a bicycle after she was old enough, say, to wear a brassiere. But to get to the Foundry I could travel on back roads, I didn't have to go through town.

My father had started working in the Foundry in 1947. It had become apparent the year before that not just our fox farm but the whole fur-farming industry was going downhill very fast. Perhaps the mink would have tided us over if we had gone more heavily into mink, or if we had not owed so much money still, to the feed company, to my grandmother, to the bank. As it was, mink could not save us. My father had made the mistake many fox farmers made just at that time. It was believed that a new paler kind of fox, called a platinum, was going to save the day, and with borrowed money my father had bought two male breeders, one an almost snowy-white Norwegian platinum and one called a pearl platinum, a lovely bluish-gray. People were sick of silver foxes, but surely with these beauties the market would revive.

Of course there is always the chance, with a new male, of how well he will perform, and how many of the offspring will have their father's color. I think there was trouble on both fronts, though my mother would not allow questions or household talk about these matters. I think one of the males had a standoffish nature and another sired mostly dark litters. It did not matter much, because the fashion went against long-haired furs altogether.

When my father went looking for a job it was necessary to find a night job, because he had to spend all day going out of business. He had to pelt all the animals and sell the pelts for whatever he could get and he had to tear down the guard fence, the Old Sheds and the New Sheds, and all the pens. I suppose he did not have to do that immediately, but he must have wanted all traces of the enterprise destroyed.

He got a job as night watchman at the Foundry, covering the hours from five in the afternoon till ten o'clock in the evening. There was not so much money in being a night watchman, but the good fortune in it was that he was able to do another job at that time as well. This extra job was called shaking down floors. He was never finished with it when his watchman's shift was over, and sometimes he got home after midnight.

The message I was taking to my father was not an important message, but it was important in our family life. It was simply a reminder that he must not forget to call in at my grandmother's house on his way home from work, no matter how late he was. My grandmother had moved to our town, with her sister, so that she could be useful to us. She baked pies and muffins and mended our clothes and darned my father's and my brother's socks. My father was supposed to go around by her house in town after work, to pick up these things, and have a cup of tea with her, but often he forgot. She would sit up knitting, dozing under the light, listening to the radio, until the Canadian radio stations went off at midnight and she would find herself picking up distant news reports, American jazz. She would wait and wait and my father wouldn't come. This had happened last night, so tonight at suppertime she had phoned and asked with painful tact, "Was it tonight or last night your father was supposed to come?"

"I don't know," I said.

I always felt that something had not been done right, or not done at all, when I heard my grandmother's voice. I felt that our family had failed her. She was still energetic, she looked after her house and yard, she could still carry armchairs upstairs, and she had my great-aunt's company, but she needed something more—more gratitude, more compliance, than she ever got.

"Well, I sat up for him last night, but he didn't come."

"He must be coming tonight then." I did not want to spend time talking to her because I was preparing for my Grade Thirteen exams on which my whole future would depend. (Even now, on cool bright spring evenings, with the leaves just out on the trees, I can feel the stirring of expectation connected with this momentous old event, my ambition roused and quivering like a fresh blade to meet it.)

I told my mother what the call was about and she said, "Oh, you'd better ride up and remind your father, or there'll be trouble."

Whenever she had to deal with the problem of my grandmother's touchiness my mother brightened up, as if she had got back some competence or importance in our family. She had Parkinson's disease. It had been overtaking her for some time with erratic symptoms but had recently been diagnosed and pronounced incurable. Its progress took up more and more of her attention. She could no longer walk or eat or talk normally—her body was stiffening out of her control. But she had a long time yet to live.

When she said something like this about the situation with my grandmother—when she said anything that showed an awareness of other people, or even of the work around the house, I felt my heart soften towards her. But when she finished up with a reference to herself, as she did this time (*and that will upset me*), I hardened again, angry at her for her abdication, sick of her self-absorption, which seemed so flagrant, so improper in a mother.

I had never been to the Foundry in the two years my father had worked there, and I did not know where to find him. Girls of my age did not hang around men's workplaces. If they did that, if they went for long walks by themselves along the railway track or the river, or if they bicycled alone on the country roads (I did these last two things) they were sometimes said to be *asking for it.*

I did not have much interest in my father's work at the Foundry, anyway. I had never expected the fox farm to make us rich, but at least it made us unique and independent. When I thought of my father working in the Foundry I felt that he had suffered a great defeat. My mother felt the same way. Your father is too *fine* for that, she would say. But instead of agreeing with her I would argue, intimating that she did not like being an ordinary workingman's wife and that she was a snob.

The thing that most upset my mother was receiving the Foundry's Christmas basket of fruit, nuts, and candy. She could not bear to be on the receiving, not the distributing, end of that sort of thing, and the first time it happened we had to put the basket in the car and drive down the road to a family she had picked out as suitable recipients. By the next Christmas her authority had weakened and I broke into the basket, declaring that we needed treats as much as anybody. She wiped away tears at my hard tone, and I ate the chocolate, which was old and brittle and turning gray.

I could not see any light in the Foundry buildings. The windows were painted blue on the inside—perhaps a light would not get through. The office was an old brick house at the end of the long main building, and there I saw a light through the Venetian blinds, and I thought that the manager or one of the office staff must be working late. If I knocked they would tell me where my father was. But when I looked through the little window in the door I saw that it was my father in there. He was alone, and he was scrubbing the floor.

I had not known that scrubbing the office floor every night was one of the watchman's duties. (This does not mean that my father had deliberately kept quiet about it—I might not have been listening.) I was surprised, because I had never seen him doing any work of this sort before. Housework. Now that my mother was sick, such work was my responsibility. He would never have had time. Besides that, there was men's work and there was women's work. I believed this, and so did everybody else I knew.

My father's scrubbing apparatus was unlike anything anybody would have at home. He had two buckets on a stand, on rollers, with attachments on either side to hold various mops and brushes. His scrubbing was vigorous and efficient—it had no resigned and ritualistic, feminine sort of rhythm. He seemed to be in a good humor.

He had to come and unlock the door to let me in.

His face changed when he saw it was me.

"No trouble at home, is there?"

I said no, and he relaxed. "I thought you were Tom."

Tom was the factory manager. All the men called him by his first name.

"Well then. You come up to see if I'm doing this right?"

I gave him the message, and he shook his head.

"I know. I forgot."

I sat on a corner of the desk, swinging my legs up out of his way. He said he was nearly finished here, and that if I wanted to wait he would show me around the Foundry. I said I would wait.

When I say that he was in a good humor here, I don't mean that his humor around home was bad, that he was sullen and irritable there. But he showed a cheerfulness now that at home might have seemed inappropriate. It seemed, in fact, as if there was a weight off him here.

When he had finished the floor to his satisfaction he hooked the mop to the side and rolled the apparatus down a slanting passageway that connected the office with the main building. He opened a door that had a sign on it.

Caretaker.

"My domain."

He emptied the water from the buckets into an iron tub, rinsed and emptied them again, swished the tub clean. There on a shelf above the tub among the tools and rubber hose and fuses and spare windowpanes was his lunch bucket, which I packed every day when I got home from school. I filled the thermos with strong black tea and put in a bran muffin with butter and jam and a piece of pie if we had any and three thick sandwiches of fried meat and ketchup. The meat was cottage roll ends or baloney, the cheapest meat you could buy.

He led the way into the main building. The lights burning there were like streetlights—that is, they cast their light at the intersections of the passageways, but didn't light up the whole inside of the building, which was so large and high that I had the sense of being in a forest with thick dark trees, or in a town with tall, even buildings. My father switched on some more lights and things shrank a bit. You could now see the brick walls, blackened on the inside, and the windows not only painted over but covered with black wire mesh. What lined the passageways were stacks of bins, one on top of the other higher than my head, and elaborate, uniform metal trays.

We came on an open area with a great heap of metal lumps on the floor, all disfigured with what looked like warts or barnacles.

"Castings," my father said. "They haven't been cleaned yet. They put them in a contraption called a wheelabrator and it blasts shot at them, takes all the bumps off."

Then a pile of black dust, or fine black sand.

"That looks like coal dust but you know what they call it? Green sand."

"*Green* sand?"

"Use it for molding. It's sand with a bonding agent in it, like clay. Or sometimes it's linseed oil. Are you any way interested in all this?"

I said yes, partly for pride's sake. I didn't want to seem like a stupid girl. And I was interested, but not so much in the particular explanations my father began to provide me with, as in the general effects—the gloom, the fine dust in the air, the idea of there being places like this all over the country, in every town and city. Places with their windows painted over. You passed them in a car or on the train and never gave a thought to what was going on inside. Something that took up the whole of people's lives. A never-ending over-and-over attention-consuming, life-consuming process.

"Like a tomb in here," my father said, as if he had picked up some of my thoughts.

But he meant something different.

"Compared to the daytime. The racket then, you can't imagine it. They try to get them to wear earplugs, but they won't do it."

"Why not?"

"I don't know. Too independent. They won't wear the fire aprons either. See here. Here's what they call the cupola."

This was an immense black pipe which did have a cupola on top. He showed me where they made the fire, and the ladles used to carry the molten metal and pour it into the molds. He showed me chunks of metal that were like grotesque stubby limbs, and told me that those were the shapes of the hollows in the castings. The air in the hollows, that is, made solid. He told me these things with a prolonged satisfaction in his voice, as if what he revealed gave him reliable pleasure.

We turned a corner and came on two men working, stripped to their pants and undershirts.

"Now here's a couple of good hardworking fellows," my father said. "You know Ferg? You know Geordie?"

I did know them, or at least I knew who they were. Geordie Hall delivered bread, but had to work in the Foundry at night to make extra money, because he had so many children. There was a joke that his wife made him work to keep him away from her. Ferg was a younger man you saw around town. He couldn't get girls because he had a wen on his face.

"She's seeing how us working fellows live," my father said, with a note of humorous apology. Apologizing to them for me, for me to them—light apologies all round. This was his style.

Working carefully together, using long, strong hooks, the two men lifted a heavy casting out of a box of sand.

"That's plenty hot," my father said. "It was cast today. Now they have to work the sand around and get it ready for the next casting. Then do another. It's piecework, you know. Paid by the casting."

We moved away.

"Two of them been together for a while," he said. "They always work together. I do the same job by myself. Heaviest job they've got around here. It took me a while to get used to it, but it doesn't bother me now."

Much that I saw that night was soon to disappear. The cupola, the hand-lifted ladles, the killing dust. (It was truly killing—around town, on the porches of small neat houses, there were always a few yellow-faced, stoical men set out to take the air. Everybody knew and accepted that they were dying of *the foundry disease,* the dust in their lungs.) Many particular skills and dangers were going to go. Many everyday risks, along with much foolhardy pride, and random ingenuity and improvisation. The processes I saw were probably closer to those of the Middle Ages than to those of today.

And I imagine that the special character of the men who worked in the Foundry was going to change, as the processes of the work changed. They would become not so different from the men who worked in the factories, or at other jobs. Up until the time I'm talking about they had seemed stronger and rougher than those other workers; they had more pride and were perhaps more given to self-dramatization than men whose jobs were not so dirty or dangerous. They were too proud to ask for any protection from the hazards they had to undergo, and in fact, as my father had said, they disdained what protection was offered. They were said to be too proud to bother about a union.

Instead, they stole from the Foundry.

"Tell you a story about Geordie," my father said, as we walked along. He was "doing a round" now, and had to punch clocks in various parts of the building. Then he would get down to shaking out his own floors. "Geordie likes to take a bit of lumber and whatnot home with him. A few crates or whatever. Anything he thinks might come in handy to fix the house or build a back shed. So the other night he had a load of stuff, and he went out after dark and put it in the back of his car so it'd be there when he went off work. And he didn't know it, but Tom was in the office and just happened to be standing by the window and watching him. Tom hadn't brought the car, his wife had the car, she'd gone somewhere, and Tom had just walked over to do a little work or pick up something he forgot. Well, he saw what Geordie was up to and he waited around till he saw him coming off work and then he stepped out and said, Hey. He said, hey, wonder if you could give me a lift home. The wife's got the car, he said. So they got in Geordie's car with the other fellows standing around spluttering and Geordie sweating buckets, and Tom never said a word. Sat there whistling while Geordie's trying to get the key in the ignition. He let Geordie drive him home and never said a word. Never turned and looked in the back. Never intended to. Just let him sweat. And told it all over the place next day."

It would be easy to make too much of this story and to suppose that between management and workers there was an easy familiarity, tolerance, even an appreciation of each other's dilemmas. And there was some of that, but it didn't mean there wasn't also plenty of rancor and callousness and of course deceit. But jokes were important. The men who worked in the evenings would gather in my father's little room, the caretaker's room, in most weather—but outside the main door when the evenings were hot—and smoke and talk while they took their unauthorized break. They would tell about jokes that had been played recently and in years past. They talked about jokes played by and upon people now long dead. Sometimes they talked seriously as well. They argued about whether there were ghosts, and talked about who claimed to have seen one. They discussed money—who had it, who'd lost it, who'd expected it and not got it, and where people kept it. My father told me about these talks years later.

One night somebody asked, when is the best time in a man's life?

Some said, it's when you are a kid and can fool around all the time and go down to the river in the summer and play hockey on the road in the winter and that's all you think about, fooling around and having a good time.

Or when you're a young fellow going out and haven't got any responsibilities.

Or when you're first married if you're fond of your wife and a bit later, too, when the children are just little and running around and haven't shown any bad characteristics yet.

My father spoke up and said, "Now. I think maybe now."

They asked him why.

He said because you weren't old yet, with one thing or another collapsing on you, but old enough that you could see that a lot of things you might have wanted out of life you would never get. It was hard to explain how you could be happy in such a situation, but sometimes he thought you were.

When he was telling me about this he said, "I think it was the company I enjoyed. Up till then I'd been so much on my own. They weren't maybe the cream of the crop, but those were some of the best fellows I ever met."

He also told me that one night not long after he had started working at the Foundry he came off work around midnight and found that there was a great snowstorm in progress. The roads were full and the snow blowing so hard and fast that the snowplows would not get out till morning. He had to leave the car where it was—even if he got it shovelled out he couldn't tackle the roads. He started to walk home. It was a distance of about two miles. The walking was heavy, in the freshly drifted snow, and the wind was coming against him from the west. He had done several floors that night, and he was just getting used to the work. He wore a heavy overcoat, an Army greatcoat, which one of our neighbors had given him, having no use for it when he got home from the war. My father did not often wear it either. Usually he wore a windbreaker. He must have put it on that night because the temperature had dropped even below the usual winter cold, and there was no heater in the car.

He felt dragged down, pushing against the storm, and about a quarter of a mile from home he found that he wasn't moving. He was standing in the middle of a drift and he could not move his legs. He could hardly stand against the wind. He was worn out. He thought perhaps his heart was giving out. He thought of his death.

He would die leaving a sick crippled wife who could not even take care of herself, an old mother full of disappointment, a younger daughter whose health had always been delicate, an older girl who was strong and bright enough but who often seemed to be self-centered and mysteriously incompetent, a son who promised to be clever and reliable but who was still only a little boy. He would die in debt, and before he had even finished pulling down the pens. They would stand there—drooping wire on the cedar poles that he had cut in Austins swamp in the summer of 1927—to show the ruin of his enterprise.

"Was that all you thought about?" I said when he told me this.

"Wasn't that enough?" he said, and went on to tell me how he pulled one leg out of the snow, and then the other: he got out of that drift and then there were no more drifts quite so deep, and before long he was in the shelter of the windbreak of pine trees that he himself had planted the year that I was born. He got home.

But I had meant, didn't he think of himself, of the boy who had trapped along the Blyth Creek, and who went into the store and asked for Signs Snow Paper, didn't he struggle for his own self? I meant, was his life now something only other people had a use for?

My father always said he didn't really grow up till he went to work in the Foundry. He never wanted to talk about the fox farm or the fur business, until he was old and could talk easily about almost anything. But my mother, walled in by increasing paralysis, was always eager to recall the Pine Tree Hotel, the friends and the money she had made there.

And my father, as it turned out, had another occupation waiting for him. I'm not talking about his raising turkeys, which came after the work at the Foundry and lasted till he was seventy or over, and which may have done damage to his heart, since he would find himself wrestling and hauling around fifty- and sixty-pound birds. It was after giving up such work that he took up writing. He began to write reminiscences and to turn some of them into stories, which were published in an excellent though short-lived local magazine. And not long before his death he completed a novel about pioneer life, called *The Macgregors.*

He told me that writing it had surprised him. He was surprised that he could do such a thing, and surprised that doing it could make him so happy. Just as if there was a future in it for him.

Here is part of a piece called "Grandfathers," part of what my father wrote about his own grandfather Thomas Laidlaw, the same Thomas who had come to Morris at the age of seventeen and been appointed to do the cooking in the shanty.

He was a frail white-haired old man, with thin longish hair and a pale skin. Too pale, because he was anemic. He took Vita-Ore, a much-advertised patent medicine. It must have helped, because he lived into his eighties . . . When I first became aware of him he had retired to the village and leased the farm to my father. He would visit the farm, or me, as I thought, and I would visit him. We would go for walks. There was a sense of security. He talked much more easily than Dad but I don't recall that we conversed at any length. He explained things much as if he were discovering them himself at the same time. Perhaps he was in a way looking at the world from a child's viewpoint.

He never spoke harshly, he never said, "Get down off that fence," or "Mind that puddle." He preferred to let nature take its course so I could learn that way. The freedom of action inspired a certain amount of caution. There was no undue sympathy when one did get hurt.

We took slow staid walks because he couldn't go very fast. We gathered stones with fossils of weird creatures of another age, for this was gravelly country in which such stones might be found. We each had a collection. I inherited his when he died and kept both assortments for many years. They were a link with him with which I was very reluctant to part.

We walked along the nearby railway tracks to the huge embankment carrying the tracks over another railway and a big creek. There was a giant stone and cement arch over these. One could look down hundreds of feet to the railway below. I was back there lately. The embankment has shrunk strangely; the railway no longer runs along it. The C.P.R. is still down there but not nearly so far down and the creek is much smaller . . .

We went to the planing mill nearby and watched the saws whirling and whining. These were the days of all sorts of gingerbread woodwork used for ornamenting the eaves of houses, the verandahs, or any place that could be decorated. There were all sort of discarded pieces with interesting designs, which one could take home.

In the evening we went to the station, the old Grand Trunk, or the Butter and Eggs, as it was known in London. One could put an ear to the track and hear the rumble of the train, far away. Then a distant whistle, and the air became tense with anticipation. The whistles became closer and louder and finally the train burst into view. The earth shook, the heavens all but opened, and the huge monster slid screaming with tortured brakes to a stop . . .

Here we got the evening daily paper. There were two London papers, the *Free Press* and the *'Tiser* (*Advertiser*). The *'Tiser* was Grit and the *Free Press* was Tory.

There was no compromise about this. Either you were right or you were wrong. Grandfather was a good Grit of the old George Brown school and took the *'Tiser*, so I also have become a Grit and have remained one up to now . . . And so in this best of all systems were governments chosen according to the number of little Grits or little Tories who got old enough to vote . . .

The conductor grasped the handhold by the steps. He shouted, "Bort!" and waved his hand. The steam shot down in jets, the wheels clanked and groaned and moved forward, faster and faster, past the way scales, past the stockyards, over the arches, and grew smaller and smaller like a receding galaxy until the train disappeared in to the unknown world to the north . . .

Once there was a visitor, my namesake from Toronto, a cousin of Grandfather. The great man was reputed to be a millionaire, but he was disappointing, not at all impressive, only a slightly smoother and more polished version of Grandfather. The two old men sat under the maples in front of our house and talked. Probably they talked of the past as old men will. I kept discreetly in the background. Grandpa didn't say outright but delicately hinted that children were to be seen and not heard.

Sometimes they talked in the broad Scots of the district from which they came. It was not the Scots of the burring R's which we hear from the singers and comedians but was rather soft and plaintive, with a lilt like Welsh or Swedish.

That is where I feel it best to leave them—my father a little boy, not venturing too close, and the old men sitting through a summer afternoon on wooden chairs placed under one of the great benevolent elm trees that used to shelter my grandparents' farmhouse. There they spoke the dialect of their childhood—discarded as they became men—which none of their descendants could understand.

PART TWO

Home

Fathers

All over the countryside, in spring, there was a sound that was soon to disappear. Perhaps it would have disappeared already if it were not for the war. The war meant that the people who had the money to buy tractors could not find any to buy, and the few who had tractors already could not always get the fuel to run them. So the farmers were out on the land with their horses for the spring ploughing, and from time to time, near and far, you could hear them calling out their commands, in which there would be degrees of encouragement, or impatience, or warning. You couldn't hear the exact words, any more than you could make out what the seagulls on their inland flights were saying, or follow the arguments of crows. From the tone of voice, though, you could generally tell which words were swearing.

With one man it was all swearing. It didn't matter which words he was using. He could have been saying "butter and eggs" or "afternoon tea," and the spirit that spilled out would have been the same. As if he was boiling over with a scalding rage and loathing.

His name was Bunt Newcombe. He had the first farm on the county road that curved southwest from town. Bunt was probably a nickname given him at school for going around with his head lowered, ready to bump and shove anybody aside. A boyish name, a holdover, not really adequate to his behavior, or to his reputation, as a grown man.

People sometimes asked what could be the matter with him. He wasn't poor—he had two hundred acres of decent land, and a banked barn with a peaked silo, and a drive shed, and a well-built square red-brick house. (Though the house, like the man himself, had a look of bad temper. There were dark-green blinds pulled most of the way, or all the way, down on the windows, no curtains visible, and a scar along the front wall where the porch had been torn away. The front door which must at one time have opened onto that porch now opened three feet above weeds and rubble.) And he was not a drunk or a gambler, being too careful of his money for that. He was mean in both senses of the word. He mistreated his horses, and it goes without saying that he mistreated his family.

In the winter he took his milk cans to town on a sleigh pulled by a team of horses—snowplows for the county roads being in short supply then, just like tractors. This was at the time in the morning when everybody was walking to school, and he never slowed down as other farmers did to let you jump on the back of the sleigh and catch a ride. He picked up the whip instead.

Mrs. Newcombe was never with him, on the sleigh or in the car. She walked to town, wearing old-fashioned galoshes even when the weather got warm, and a long drab coat and a scarf over her hair. She mumbled hello without ever looking up, or sometimes turned her head away, not speaking at all. I think she was missing some teeth. That was more common then than it is now, and it was more common also for people to make plain a state of mind, in their speech and dress and gestures, so that everything about them said, *I know how I should look and behave and if I don't do it that's my own business,* or, *I don't care, things have gone too far with me, think what you like.*

Nowadays Mrs. Newcombe might be seen as a serious case, terminally depressed, and her husband with his brutish ways might be looked on with concern and compassion. *These people need help.* In those days they were just taken as they were and allowed to live out their lives without anyone giving a thought to intervention. They were regarded in fact as a source of interest and entertainment. It might be said—it was said—that nobody had any use for him and that you had to feel sorry for her. But there was a feeling that some people were born to make others miserable and some let themselves in for being made miserable. It was simple destiny and there was nothing to be done about it.

The Newcombes had had five daughters, then one son. The girls' names were April, Corinne, Gloria, Susannah, and Dahlia. I thought these names fanciful and lovely and I would have liked the daughters' looks to match them, as if they were the daughters of an ogre in a fairy tale.

April and Corinne were gone from home some time ago, so I had no way of knowing what they looked like. Gloria and Susannah lived in town. Gloria was married and had dropped from view as married girls did. Susannah worked in the hardware store, and she was a stout girl, with slightly crossed eyes, not at all pretty, but quite normal looking (crossed eyes being a variation of normal and not a particular misfortune at that time, not a thing to be remedied, any more than dispositions were). She did not seem in any way cowed like her mother or brutal like her father. And Dahlia was a couple of years older than I was, the first of the family to go to high school. She was no wide-eyed ripply-haired beauty of an ogre's daughter either, but she was handsome and sturdy, her hair thick and fair, her shoulders strong, her breasts firm and high. She got quite respectable marks and was good at games, particularly at basketball.

During my first few months at high school I found myself walking part of the way to school with her. She walked along the county road and over the bridge to town. I lived at the end of the half-mile road that was parallel to this road, on the river's north side. Up to now she and I had lived our lives within shouting distance of each other, you might say, but the school districts were divided in such a way that I had always gone to the town school, while the Newcombes went to a country school farther out along the county road. The first two years that Dahlia was at high school and I was still at public school we must have walked the same route, though we would not have walked together—it was not done, high school and public school students walking together. But now that we were both going to high school we would usually meet where the roads joined, and if either of us saw the other coming we would wait.

This was how it was during my first fall at high school. Walking together did not mean that we became exactly friends. It was just that it would have seemed odd to walk singly now that we were both at the high school and going the same way. I don't know what we talked about. I have an idea that there were long periods of silence, due to Dahlia's senior dignity and a matter-of-factness about her that ruled out silly conversation. But I don't recall finding these silences uncomfortable.

.   .   .

One morning she didn't appear, and I went on. In the cloakroom at school she said to me, "I won't be coming in that way anymore because I'm staying in town now, I'm staying at Gloria's."

And we hardly spoke together again until one day in early spring—that time I've been talking about, with the trees bare, but reddening, and the crows and seagulls busy and the farmers hollering to their horses. She caught up to me, as we were leaving the school. She said, "You going right home?" and I said yes, and she started to walk beside me.

I asked her if she was living at home again and she said, "Nope. Still at Gloria's."

When we had walked a bit farther she said, "I'm just going out there to have a look at what's going on."

Her way of saying this was straightforward, not confidential. But I knew that *out there* must mean out at her home, and that *what's going on,* though unspecific, meant nothing good.

During the past winter Dahlia's status in the school had risen because she was the best player on the basketball team and the team had nearly won the county championship. It gave me a feeling of distinction to be walking with her and to be receiving whatever information she felt like giving me. I can't remember for sure, but I think that she must have started high school with all the business of her family dragging behind her. It was a small enough town so that all of us started that way, with favorable factors to live up to or some shadow to live down. But now she had been allowed, to a large extent, to slip free. The independence of spirit, the faith you have to have in your body, to become an athlete, won respect and discouraged anybody who would think of snubbing her. She was well dressed, too—she had very few clothes but those she had were quite all right, not like the matronly hand-me-downs that country girls often wore, or the homemade outfits my mother had labored at for me. I remember a red V-necked sweater often worn by her, and a pleated Royal Stewart skirt. Maybe Gloria and Susannah thought of her as the representative and pride of the family, and had pooled some of their resources to dress her.

We were out of town before she spoke again.

"I got to keep track of what my old man is up to," she said. "He better not be beating up on Raymond."

Raymond. That was the brother.

"Do you think he might be?" I said. I felt as if I had to pretend to know less about her family than I—and everybody—actually did.

"Yeah," she said thoughtfully. "Yeah. He might. Raymond used to get off better than the rest of us but now he's the only one left at home I got my doubts."

"Did he beat you?"

I said this almost casually, trying to sound moderately interested, not in any way horrified.

She gave a snort. "Are you kidding? Before I got away the last time he tried to brain me with the shovel."

After we had walked a bit farther, she said, "Yeah, and I just told him to come on. Come on, let's see you kill me. Let's see you, then you'll get hung. But then I took off, because I thought yeah, sure, but then I wouldn't get the satisfaction of seeing him. Hung."

She laughed. I said encouragingly, "Do you hate him?"

"Sure I hate him," she said, with not much more expression than if she had said that she hated sausages. "If somebody told me that he was drowning in the river I would go and stand on the bank and cheer."

There was no way to comment about this. But I said, "What if he takes after you now?"

"He's not going to see me. I'm just going to spy on him."

When we came to the division of our roads she said almost cheerfully, "You want to come with me? You want to see how I do my spying?"

We walked across the bridge with our heads soberly bowed, looking through the cracks between the planks at the high-flowing river. I was full of alarm and admiration.

"I used to come out here in the winter," she said. "I used to get right up against the kitchen windows when it was dark out. Now it stays light too late. And I used to think, he'll see the boot marks in the snow and know there was somebody had been spying on him and that'll drive him crazy."

I asked whether her father had a shotgun.

"Sure," she said. "So what if he comes out and shoots me? He shoots me and he gets hung and goes to Hell. Don't worry—he's not going to see us."

Before we were in sight of the Newcombes' buildings we climbed a bank on the opposite side of the road, where there was a thick growth of sumac bordering a planted windbreak of spruce. When Dahlia began to walk in a crouch, ahead of me, I did the same. And when she stopped I stopped.

There was the barn, and the barnyard, full of cows. I realized, once we stopped making our own noise among the branches, that we had been hearing the trampling and bawling of the cows all along. Unlike most farmsteads, the Newcombes' did not have a lane. House and barn and barnyard were all right along the road.

There wasn't enough fresh grass for cows to be out to pasture yet—the low places in the pastures were still mostly underwater—but they were let out of the stable to exercise before the evening milking. From behind our screen of sumac, we could look across the road and down at them as they jostled each other and blundered around in the muck, uneasy and complaining because of their full udders. Even if we snapped a branch, or spoke in normal voices, there was too much going on over there for anybody to hear us.

Raymond, a boy about ten years old, came around the corner of the barn. He had a stick but he was just tapping the cows' rumps with it, pushing them and saying, "So-boss, so-boss," in an easygoing rhythm and urging them towards the stable door. It was the sort of mixed herd most farms had at that time. A black cow, a rusty-red cow, a pretty golden cow that must have been part Jersey, others splotched brown and white and black and white in all sorts of combinations. They still had their horns, and that gave them a look of dignity and ferocity which cows have now lost.

A man's voice, Bunt Newcombe's voice, called from the stable.

"Hurry up. What's the holdup? Do you think you've got all night?"

Raymond called back, "Okay. O-*kay.*" The tone of his voice did not indicate anything to me, except that he didn't seem scared. But Dahlia said quietly, "Yah. He's giving him lip. Good for him."

Bunt Newcombe came out of another door of the stable. He was wearing overalls and a greasy barn smock, instead of the buffalo coat I thought of as his natural costume, and he moved with an odd swing of one leg.

"Bum leg," Dahlia said, in the same quiet but intensely satisfied voice. "I heard Belle kicked him but I thought it was too good to be true. Too bad it wasn't his head."

He was carrying a pitchfork. But it seemed he meant no harm to Raymond. All he used the fork for was to pitch manure out of that doorway, while the cows were driven in at the other.

Perhaps a son was abhorred less than his daughters?

"If I had a gun I could get him now," Dahlia said. "I should do it while I'm still young enough so's I'm not the one that ends up hung."

"You'd go to jail," I said.

"So what? He runs his own jail. Maybe they'd never catch me. Maybe they'd never even know it was me."

She couldn't mean what she was saying. If she had any such intentions wouldn't it be crazy of her to tell me about them? I could betray her. I would not intend to, but somebody might get it out of me. Because of the war I often thought of what it would be like to be tortured. How much could I stand? At the dentist's, when he hit a nerve, I had thought, if a pain like that went on and on unless I betrayed where my father was hiding with the Resistance, what would I do?

When the cows were all inside and Raymond and his father had shut the stable doors we walked, still bent, back through the sumacs and once out of sight we climbed down to the road. I thought that Dahlia might say now that the shooting part was only kidding, but she didn't. I wondered why she had not said anything about her mother, about being worried for her mother as she had been for Raymond. Then I thought that she probably despised her mother, for what her mother had put up with and what she had become. You would have to show some spirit to make the grade with Dahlia. I wouldn't have wanted her to know that I was afraid of the horned cows.

We must have said good-bye when she took the route back to town, to Gloria's house, and I turned onto our dead-end road. But perhaps she just walked on and left me. I kept think-ing about whether she could really kill her father. I had a strange idea that she was too young to do that—as if killing somebody was like driving a car or voting or getting married, you had to be a certain age to manage it. I also had some idea—though I would not have known how to express it—that killing wouldn't be any relief to her, hating him having got to be such a habit. I understood that she had taken me along with her not to confide in me or because I was anything like an intimate friend—she just wanted somebody to see her hating him.

On our road there had been at one time perhaps a dozen houses. Most were small cheap rental houses—until you got to our house, which was more of an ordinary farmhouse on a small farm. Some of those houses were on the floodplain of the river, but a few years ago, during the Depression, they had all had people living in them. Then the war jobs, all sorts of jobs, had taken these families away. Some of the houses had been carted elsewhere to serve as garages or chicken sheds. A couple of those left were empty, and the rest were mostly occupied by old people—the old bachelor who walked into town every day to his blacksmith shop, the old couple who used to have a grocery store and still had an Orange Crush sign in the front window, another old couple who bootlegged and buried their money, it was said, in quart sealers in the backyard. Also the old women left on their own. Mrs. Currie. Mrs. Horne. Bessie Stewart.

Mrs. Currie raised dogs who raced about barking insanely all day in a wire pen, and at night were taken inside her house which was partly built into the bank of a hill, and must have been very dark and smelly. Mrs. Horne raised flowers, and her tiny house and yard in the summer were like an embroidery sampler—clematis vines, rose of Sharon, every sort of rose and phlox and delphinium. Bessie Stewart dressed smartly and went uptown in the afternoons to smoke cigarettes and drink coffee in the Paragon Restaurant. Though unmarried, she was said to have a Friend.

One empty house had been occupied by, and still belonged to, a Mrs. Eddy. For a short while, years ago—that is, four or five years before I ever met Dahlia, a long time in my life— some people named Wainwright had lived in that house. They were related to Mrs. Eddy and she was letting them live there, but she wasn't living with them. She had already been taken away to wherever she was taken. It was called Care.

Mr. and Mrs. Wainwright came from Chicago, where they had both worked as window dressers for a department store. The store had closed down or it had been decided that it didn't need so many windows dressed—whatever had happened, they had lost their jobs and come here to live in Mrs. Eddy's house and try to set up a wallpapering business.

They had a daughter, Frances, who was a year younger than I was. She was small and thin and she got out of breath easily, because she had asthma. On the first day of my being in Grade Five, Mrs. Wainwright came out and stopped me on the road, with Frances lagging behind her. She asked me if I would take Frances to school and show her where the Grade Four room was, and if I would be her friend, because she didn't know any-body yet or where anything was.

Mrs. Wainwright stood talking to me, right out on the road, in a silky light-blue wrapper. Frances was all dolled up in a very short checked cotton dress with a flounce around the skirt and a matching checked hair ribbon.

Soon it became understood that I would walk to school with Frances and walk home with her afterwards. We both carried our lunches to school, but I had not expressly been asked to eat lunch with her so I never did.

There was one other girl in the school who lived far enough away to have to bring her lunch. Her name was Wanda Louise Palmer, and her parents owned and lived in the dance hall to the south of town. She and I had always eaten together, but we had never thought of ourselves as friends. Now, however, a kind of friendship was formed. It was all based on avoiding Frances. Wanda and I ate in the girls' basement, behind a barricade of broken old desks that were heaped up in a corner. As soon as we were finished we sneaked out and left the school grounds to walk around the nearby streets or go downtown and look in store windows. Wanda should have been an interesting companion because of living at the dance hall, but she was so apt to lose track of what she was telling me (though not to stop talking) that she was very boring. All we really had was our bond against Frances, and our desperate held-in laughter when we peered through the desks and saw her looking for us.

After a while she didn't do that anymore, she ate her lunch upstairs in the cloakroom, alone.

I would like to think that it was Wanda who pointed Frances out, when we stood in line ready to march into the classroom, as the girl we were always trying to avoid. But I could have been the one who did that, and certainly I went along with the joke, and was glad to be on the side of those who maintained the business of raised eyebrows and bitten lips and suppressed—but not *quite* suppressed—giggles. Living out at the end of that road as I did, and being easily embarrassed, yet a show-off, as I improbably was, I could never stand up for anybody who was being humiliated. I could never rise above a feeling of relief that it was not me.

The hair ribbons became part of it. Just to go up to Frances and say, "I love your hair ribbon, where did you get it?" and have her say, in innocent bewilderment, "In Chicago," was a lasting source of pleasure. For a while, "In Chicago," or just "Chicago," became the answer to everything.

"Where did you go after school yesterday?"

"Chicago."

"Where did your sister get her permanent?"

"Oh, in Chicago."

Some girls would clamp their mouths down on the very word, and their chests would heave, or they would pretend to have hiccups till they were half sick.

I didn't avoid walking home with Frances, though I certainly let it be known that I didn't choose to do that, but did it only because her mother had asked it of me. How much of this special very feminine persecution she was aware of, I don't know. She may have thought there was some place where girls of my class always went to have lunch, and that I just went on doing that. She may never have understood what the giggling was about. She never asked about it. She tried to hold my hand, crossing the street, but I pulled away and told her not to.

She said she always used to hold Sadie's hand, when Sadie walked her to school in Chicago.

"But that was different," she said. "There aren't any street-cars here."

One day she offered me a cookie left over from her lunch. I refused, so as not to feel any inconvenient obligation.

"Go on," she said. "My mother put it in for you."

Then I understood. Her mother put in this extra cookie, this treat, for me to eat when we had our lunches together. She had never told her mother that I didn't show up at lunchtime, and that she could not find me. She must have been eating the extra cookie herself, but now the dishonesty was bothering her.

So every day from then on she offered it, almost at the last minute as if she was embarrassed, and every day I accepted.

We began to have a little conversation, starting when we were almost clear of town. We were both interested in movie stars. She had seen far more movies than I had—in Chicago you could see movies every afternoon, and Sadie used to take her. But I walked past our theatre and looked at the stills every time the picture changed, so I knew something about them. And I had one movie magazine at home, which a visiting cousin had left. It had pictures of Deanna Durbin's wedding in it, so we talked about that, and what we wanted our own weddings to be like—the bridal dresses and the bridesmaids' dresses and the flowers and the going-away outfits. The same cousin had given me a present—a Ziegfeld Girls cutout book. Frances had seen the Ziegfeld Girls movie and we talked about which Ziegfeld Girl we would like to be. She chose Judy Garland because she could sing, and I chose Hedy Lamarr because she was the most beautiful.

"My father and mother used to sing in the Light Opera Society," she said. "They sang in *The Pirates of Penzance*."

Lightopra-sussciety. Pirazapenzanze. I filed those words away but would not ask what they meant. If she had said them at school, in front of others, they would have been irresistible ammunition.

When her mother came out to greet us—kissing Frances hello as she had kissed her good-bye—she might ask if I could come in and play. I always said I had to go straight home.

Shortly before Christmas, Mrs. Wainwright asked me if I could come to have supper the next Sunday. She said it would be a little thank-you party and a farewell party, now that they were going away. I was on the point of saying that I didn't think my mother would let me, but when I heard the word *farewell* I saw the invitation in a different light. The burden of Frances would be lifted, no further obligation would be involved and no intimacy enforced. Mrs. Wainwright said that she had written a little note to my mother, since they didn't have a phone.

My mother would have liked it better if I had been asked to some town girl's house, but she said yes. She took it into account, too, that the Wainwrights were moving away.

"I don't know what they were thinking of, coming here," she said. "Anybody who can afford to wallpaper is going to do it themselves."

"Where are you going?" I asked Frances.

"Burlington."

"Where's that?"

"It's in Canada too. We're going to stay with my aunt and uncle but we'll have our own toilet upstairs and our sink and a hotplate. My dad's going to get a better job."

"What doing?"

"I don't know."

Their Christmas tree was in a corner. The front room had only one window and if they had put the tree there it would have blocked off all the light. It was not a big or well-shaped tree, but it was smothered in tinsel and gold and silver beads and beautiful intricate ornaments. In another corner of the room was a parlor stove, a woodstove, in which the fire seemed just recently to have been lighted. The air was still cold and heavy, with the forest smell of the tree.

Neither Mr. nor Mrs. Wainwright was very confident about the fire. First one and then the other kept fiddling with the damper and daringly reaching in with the poker and patting the pipe to see if it was getting hot, or by any chance too hot. The wind was fierce that day—sometimes it blew the smoke down the chimney.

That was no matter to Frances and me. On a card table set up in the middle of the room there was a Chinese checkers board ready for two people to play, and a stack of movie magazines. I fell upon them at once. I had never imagined such a feast. It made no difference that they were not new and that some had been looked through so often they were almost falling apart. Frances stood beside my chair, interfering with my pleasure a little by telling me what was just ahead and what was in another magazine I hadn't opened yet. The magazines were obviously her idea and I had to be patient with her—they were her property and if she had taken it into her head to remove them I would have been more grief-stricken even than I had been when my father drowned our kittens.

She was wearing an outfit that could have come out of one of those magazines—a child star's party dress of deep red velvet with a white lace collar and a black ribbon threaded through the lace. Her mother's dress was exactly the same, and they both had their hair done the same way—a roll in front and long in the back. Frances's hair was thin and fine and what with her excitement and her jumping around to show me things, the roll was already coming undone.

It was getting dark in the room. There were wires sticking out of the ceiling but no bulbs. Mrs. Wainwright brought in a lamp with a long cord that plugged into the wall. The bulb shone through the pale-green glass of a lady's skirt.

"That's Scarlett O'Hara," Frances said. "Daddy and I gave it to Mother for her birthday."

We never got around to the Chinese checkers and in time

the board was removed. We shifted the magazines to the floor.
A piece of lace—not a real tablecloth—was laid across the
table. Dishes followed. Evidently Frances and I were to eat in
here, by ourselves. Both parents were involved in laying the
table—Mrs. Wainwright wearing a fancy apron over her red
velvet and Mr. Wainwright in shirtsleeves and silk-backed vest.
When everything was set up we were called to the table. I
had expected Mr. Wainwright to leave the serving of the food
to his wife—in fact I had been very surprised to see him hovering with knives and forks—but now he pulled out our chairs
and announced that he was our waiter. When he was that close
I could smell him, and hear his breathing. His breathing
sounded eager, like a dog's, and his smell was of talcum and
lotion, something that reminded me of fresh diapers and suggested a repulsive intimacy.

"Now my lovely young ladies," he said. "I am going to
bring you some champagne."

He brought a pitcher of lemonade, and filled our glasses. I
was alarmed, until I tasted it—I knew that champagne was an
alcoholic drink. We never had such drinks in our house and
neither did anybody I knew. Mr. Wainwright watched me taste
it and seemed to guess my feelings.

"Is that all right? Not worried now?" he said. "All satisfac-
tory to your ladyship?"

He made a bow.

"Now," he said. "What would you care for, to eat?" He
reeled off a list of unfamiliar things—all I recognized was veni-
son, which I certainly had never tasted. The list ended up with
sweetbreads. Frances giggled and said, "We'll have sweetbreads,
please. And potatoes."

I expected the sweetbreads to be like their name—some
sort of bun with jam or brown sugar, but couldn't see why that

would come with potatoes. What arrived, however, were small pads of meat wrapped in crisp bacon, and little potatoes with their skins on, that had been rolled in hot butter and crisped in the pan. Also carrots cut in thin sticks and having a slightly candied flavor. The carrots I could have done without, but I had never tasted potatoes so delicious or meat so tender. All I wished was for Mr. Wainwright to stay in the kitchen instead of hovering around us pouring out lemonade and asking if everything was to our liking.

Dessert was another wonder—a satin vanilla pudding with a sort of lid on it of golden-brown baked sugar. Tiny cakes to go with it, iced on all sides with very dark, rich chocolate.

I sat replete, when not a lick nor a crumb was left. I looked at the fairy-tale tree with the ornaments that could have been miniature castles, or angels. Drafts came in around the window and moved the branches a little, causing the showers of tinsel to wave and the ornaments to turn slightly to show new points of light. Full of this rich and delicate food, I seemed to have entered a dream in which everything I saw was potent and benign.

One of the things I saw was the firelight, a dull rusty glow up in the pipe. I said to Frances, without alarm, "I think your pipe's on fire."

She called out in a spirit of party excitement, "Pipe's on fire," and in came Mr. Wainwright, who had finally retired to the kitchen, and Mrs. Wainwright close behind him.

Mrs. Wainwright said, "Oh God, Billy. What do we do?"

Mr. Wainwright said, "Close off the draft, I guess." His voice was squeaky and scared, unfatherly.

He did that, then yelped and shook his hand, which must have got burnt. Now they both stood and looked at the red pipe, and she said shakily, "There's something you're supposed to put on it. What is it?—*baking soda.*" She ran to the kitchen and came back with the box of baking soda, half weeping. "Right on the flames!" she cried. Mr. Wainwright was still rubbing his hand on his trousers so she wrapped her apron round her own hand and used the stove lifter and scattered the powder on the flames. There was a spitting sound as they began to die down and smoke rose into the room.

"Girls," she said. "Girls. Maybe you better run outside." She was really crying now.

I remembered something from a similar crisis at home.

"You could wrap wet towels round the pipe," I said.

"Wet towels," she said. "That sounds like a good idea. Yes."

She ran to the kitchen, where we heard her pumping water. Mr. Wainwright followed her, shaking his burned hand in front of him, and both returned with towels dripping. The towels were wrapped around the pipe, and as soon as they began to heat up and dry others were put in their place. The room began to fill up more and more with smoke. Frances started coughing.

"Get some air," said Mr. Wainwright. It took him a while, with his good hand, to wrench open the unused front door, letting fly the bits of old newspapers and rotten rags that had been stuffed around it. There was a snowdrift outside, a white wave lapping at the room.

"Throw snow on the fire," said Frances, still sounding jubilant between coughs, and she and I picked up armfuls of snow and threw them at the stove. Some hit what was left of the fire and some missed and melted and ran into the puddles that the drip from the towels had already made on the floor. I would never have been allowed to make such a mess at home.

In the midst of these puddles, the danger over and the room growing frigid, stood Mr. and Mrs. Wainwright with their arms around each other, laughing and commiserating.

"Oh your poor hand," said Mrs. Wainwright. "And I wasn't the least bit sympathetic about it. I was so afraid the house was going to burn down." She tried to kiss the hand, and he said, "Ouch, ouch." He too had tears in his eyes, from the smoke or the pain.

She patted him on the arms and shoulders and down lower, even on his buttocks, saying, "Poor poor baby," and things of that sort, while he made a pouty face and kissed her with a great smack on the mouth. Then with his good hand he squeezed her behind.

It looked as if this fondling could go on for some time.

"Shut the door, it's freezing," cried Frances, all red from coughing and happy excitement. If she meant for her parents to do this, they took no notice but went on with the appalling behavior that did not seem to embarrass her or even to be worth her notice. She and I got hold of the door and pushed it against the wind that was whipping up over the drift and blowing more snow into the house.

I did not tell about any of this at home, though the food and the ornaments and the fire were so interesting. There were the other things I could not describe and that made me feel off-balance, slightly sick, so that somehow I did not like to mention any of it. The way the two adults put themselves at the service of two children. The charade of Mr. Wainwright as the waiter, his thick soapy-white hands and pale face and wings of fine glistening light-brown hair. The insistence—the too-closeness—of his soft footsteps in fat plaid slippers. Then the laughing, so inappropriate for adults, following a near disaster. The shameless hands and the smacking kiss. There was a creepy menace about all of this, starting with the falsity of corralling me to play the role of little friend—both of them had called me that—when I was nothing of the kind. To treat me as good and guileless, when I was not that either.

What was this menace? Was it just that of love, or of lovingness? If that was what it was, then you would have to say that I had made its acquaintance too late. Such slopping-over of attention made me feel cornered and humiliated, almost as if somebody had taken a peep into my pants. Even the wonderful unfamiliar food was suspect in my memory. The movie magazines alone escaped the taint.

By the end of the Christmas holidays, the Wainwrights' house was empty. The snow was so heavy that year that the kitchen roof caved in. Even after that nobody bothered to pull the house down or to put up a NO TRESPASSING sign, and for years children—I was among them—poked around in the risky ruins just to see what they could find. Nobody seemed to worry then about injuries or liability.

No movie magazines came to light.

I did tell about Dahlia. By then I was an entirely different person, to my own way of thinking, than the girl who had been in the Wainwrights' house. In my early teens I had become the entertainer around home. I don't mean that I was always trying to make the family laugh—though I did that too—but that I relayed news and gossip. I told about things that had happened at school but also about things that had happened in town. Or I just described the looks or speech of somebody I had seen on the street. I had learned how to do this in a way that would not get me rebuked for being sarcastic or vulgar or told that I was too smart for my own good. I had mastered a deadpan, even demure style that could make people laugh even when they thought they shouldn't and that made it hard to tell whether I was innocent or malicious.

That was the way I told about Dahlia's creeping around in the sumacs spying on her father, about her hatred of him and her mention of murder. And that was the way any story about the Newcombes had to be told, not just the way it had to be told by me. Any story about them ought to confirm, to everybody's satisfaction, just how thoroughly and faithfully they played out their roles. And now Dahlia, as well, was seen to belong to this picture. The spying, the threats, the melodrama. His coming after her with the shovel. Her thoughts that if he had killed her, he would have been hanged. And that she couldn't be, if she killed him while she was still a juvenile.

My father agreed.

"Hard to get a court around here to convict her."

My mother said that it was a shame, what a man like that had made of his daughter.

It seems strange to me now that we could conduct this conversation so easily, without its seeming ever to enter our heads that my father had beaten me, at times, and that I had screamed out not that I wanted to kill him, but that I wanted to die. And that this had happened not so long ago—three or four times, I would think, in the years when I was around eleven or twelve. It happened in between my knowing Frances and my knowing Dahlia. I was being punished at those times for some falling-out with my mother, some back talk or smart talk or intransigence. She would fetch my father from his outside work to deal with me, and I would await his arrival, first in balked fury, and then in a sickening despair. I felt as if it must be my very self that they were after, and in a way I think it was. The self-important disputatious part of my self that had to be beaten out of me. When my father began to remove his belt—that was what he beat me with—I would begin to scream *No, No,* and plead my case incoherently, in a way that seemed to make him despise me. And indeed my behavior then would arouse contempt, it did not show a proud or even a self-respecting nature. I did not care. And when the belt was raised—in the second before it descended—there was a moment of terrible revelation. Injustice ruled. I could never tell my side of things, my father's detestation of me was supreme. How could I not find myself howling at such perversion in nature?

If he were alive now I am sure my father would say that I exaggerate, that the humiliation he meant to inflict was not so great, and that my offenses were perplexing and whatever other way is there to handle children? I was causing trouble for him and grief for my mother and I had to be convinced to change my ways.

And I did. I grew older. I became useful around the house. I learned not to give lip. I found ways to make myself agreeable.

And when I was with Dahlia, listening to her, when I was walking home by myself, when I was telling the story to my family, I never once thought to compare my situation with hers. Of course not. We were decent people. My mother, though sometimes grieved by the behavior of her family, did not go into town with snaggly hair, or wear floppy rubber galoshes. My father did not swear. He was a man of honor and competence and humor, and he was the parent I sorely wanted to please. I did not hate him, could not consider hating him. Instead, I saw what he hated in me. A shaky arrogance in my nature, something brazen yet cowardly, that woke in him this fury.

Shame. The shame of being beaten, and the shame of cringing from the beating. Perpetual shame. Exposure. And something connects this, as I feel it now, with the shame, the queasiness, that crept up on me when I heard the padding of

Mr. Wainwright's slippered feet, and his breathing. There were demands that seemed indecent, there were horrid invasions, both sneaky and straightforward. Some that I could tighten my skin against, others that left it raw. All in the hazards of life as a child.

And as the saying goes, about this matter of what molds or warps us, if it's not one thing it will be another. At least that was a saying of my elders in those days. Mysterious, uncomforting, unaccusing.

On Friday morning last Harvey Ryan Newcombe, a well-known farmer of Shelby Township, lost his life due to electrocution. He was the beloved husband of Dorothy (Morris) Newcombe, and he leaves to mourn his passing his daughters Mrs. Joseph (April) McConachie, of Sarnia, Mrs. Evan (Corinne) Wilson of Kaslo, British Columbia, Mrs. Hugh (Gloria) Whitehead of town, Misses Susannah and Dahlia, also of town, and one son Raymond, at home, also seven grandchildren. The funeral was held Monday afternoon from Reavie Brothers Funeral Home and interment was in Bethel Cemetery.

Come unto me, all ye that labour and are heavy laden, and I will give you rest.

Dahlia Newcombe could not possibly have had anything to do with her father's accident. It happened when he reached up to turn on a light in a hanging metal socket, while standing on a wet floor in a neighbor's stable. He had taken one of his cows there to visit the bull, and he was arguing at that moment about the fee. For some reason that nobody could understand, he was not wearing his rubber boots, which everybody said might have saved his life.

Lying Under the Apple Tree

Over on the other side of town lived a woman named Miriam McAlpin, who kept horses. These were not horses that belonged to her—she boarded them and exercised them for their owners, who were harness-racing people. She lived in a house that had been the original farmhouse, close to the horse barns, with her old parents, who seldom came outside. Beyond the house and the barns was an oval track on which Miriam or her stable boy, or sometimes the owners themselves, could be seen now and then on the low seat of a flimsy-looking sulky, flying along and beating up the dust.

In one of the pasture fields for the horses, next to the town street, there were three apple trees, the remains of an old orchard. Two of them were small and bent and one was quite large, like a nearly grown maple. They were never pruned or sprayed and the apples were scabby, not worth stealing, but most years there was an abundant flowering, apple blossoms hanging on everywhere, so that the branches looked from a little way off to be absolutely clotted with snow.

I had inherited a bicycle, or at least I had the use of one left behind by our part-time hired man when he went away to work in an aircraft factory. It was a man's bike, of course, high-seated and lightweight, of some odd-looking make long discontinued.

"You're not going to ride that to school, are you?" my sister said, when I had started practice rides up and down our lane. My sister was younger than I was, but she sometimes suffered anxiety on my behalf, understanding perhaps before I did the various ways in which I could risk making a fool of myself. She was thinking not just of the look of the bike but of the fact that I was thirteen and in my first year at high school, and that this was a watershed year as far as girls riding bikes to school was concerned. All girls who wanted to establish their femininity had to quit riding them. Girls who continued to ride either lived too far out in the country to walk—and had parents who could not afford to board them in town—or were simply eccentric and unable to take account of certain unstated but far-reaching rules. We lived just beyond the town limits, so if I showed up riding a bicycle—and particularly this bicycle—it would put me in the category of such girls. Those who wore women's oxford shoes and lisle stockings and rolled their hair.

"Not to school," I said. But I did start making use of the bike, riding it out to the country along the back roads on Sunday afternoons. There was hardly a chance then of meeting anybody I knew, and sometimes I met nobody at all.

I liked to do this because I was secretly devoted to Nature. The feeling came from books, at first. It came from the girls' stories by the writer L. M. Montgomery, who often inserted some sentences describing a snowy field in moonlight or a pine forest or a still pond mirroring the evening sky. Then it had merged with another private passion I had, which was for lines of poetry. I went rampaging through my school texts to uncover them before they could be read and despised in class.

To betray either of these addictions, at home or at school,

would have put me into a condition of permanent vulnerability. Which I felt that I was in already, to some extent. All someone had to say, in a certain voice, was *you would,* or *how like you,* and I felt the taunt, the chastening air, the lines drawn. But now that I had the bike, I could ride on Sunday afternoons into territory that seemed waiting for the kind of homage I ached to offer. Here were the sheets of water from the flooded creeks flashing over the land, and here were the banks of trillium under the red-budded trees. And the chokecherries, the pin cherries, in the fencerows, breaking into tender bits of bloom before there was a leaf on them.

The cherry blossoms got me thinking about the trees in Miriam McAlpin's field. I wanted to look at them when they flowered. And not just to look at them—as you could do from the street—but to get underneath those branches, to lie down on my back with my head against the trunk of the tree and to see how it rose, as if out of my own skull, rose up and lost itself in an upside-down sea of blossom. Also to see if there were bits of sky showing through, so that I could screw up my eyes to make them foreground not background, bright-blue fragments on that puffy white sea. There was a formality about this idea that I longed for. It was almost like kneeling down in church, which in our church we didn't do. I had done it once, when I was friends with Delia Cavanaugh and her mother took us to the Catholic church on a Saturday to arrange the flowers. I crossed myself and knelt in a pew and Delia said—not even whispering—"What are you doing that for? You're not supposed to do that. Just us."

I left the bike lying in the grass. It was evening, I had ridden through town on back streets. There was nobody in the stable yard or around the house. I got myself over the fence. I tried to go as quickly as possible, without running, over the ground where the horses had been cropping the early grass. I ducked under the branches of the big tree and went on stooping and stumbling, sometimes hit in the face by the blossoms, till I reached the trunk and could do what I'd come to do.

I lay down flat on my back. There was a root of the tree making a hard ridge under me, so I had to shift around. And there were last year's apples, dark as chunks of dried meat, that I had to get out of the way before I could settle. Even then, when I composed myself, I was aware of my body's being in an odd and unnatural situation. And when I looked up at all the dangling pearly petals with their faint rosy smear, all the pre-arranged nosegays, I was not quite swept into the state of mind, of worship, that I had been hoping for. The sky was thinly clouded, and what I could see of it reminded me of dingy bits of china.

Not that this wasn't worth doing. At least—as I began to understand as I got to my feet and scrambled out of there—it was worth having done. It was along the lines of an acknowl-edgment, rather than an experience. I hurried across the field and over the fence, retrieved my bicycle, and was in fact start-ing to ride away when I heard a loud whistle, and my name.

"Hey. You. Yeah. You."

It was Miriam McAlpin.

"You come on over here for a minute."

I wheeled around. There in the driveway between the old house and the horse barns, Miriam was talking to two men, who must have driven up in the car parked beside the road. They were wearing white shirts, suit vests, and trousers—just the same thing any man who worked at a desk or behind a counter in those days would be wearing from the time he got dressed in the morning till he got undressed to go to bed. Next to them, Miriam in her work pants and loose checked shirt looked like a cocky twelve-year-old boy, though she was a woman of between twenty-five and thirty. Either that, or she looked like a jockey. Cropped hair, hunched shoulders, raw skin. She gave me a look that was threatening and derisive.

"I saw you," she said. "Over in our field."

I said nothing. I knew what the next question would be and I was trying to think of an answer.

"So. What were you doing there?"

"Looking for something," I said.

"Looking for something. Yeah. What?"

"A bracelet."

I had never owned a bracelet in my life.

"So. Why did you think it was in there?"

"I thought I'd lost it."

"Yeah. In there. How come?"

"Because I was in there the other day looking for morels," I floundered. "I had it on then and I thought it could have slipped off."

It was true enough that people looked for morels under old apple trees in the spring. Though I don't suppose they wore bracelets while they were at it.

"Unh-hunh," said Miriam. "Did you find any? Whatchama-callums? Morels?"

I said no.

"That's good. 'Cause they would've been mine."

She looked me up and down and said what she'd been wanting to say all along. "You're starting early, aren't you?"

One of the men was looking at the ground, but I thought he was smiling. The other looked straight at me, raising his eyebrows slightly in droll reproach. Men who knew who I was, men who knew my father, would probably not have let their looks say so much.

I understood. She thought—they all thought—that I had been under the tree, yesterday evening or some other evening, with a man or a boy.

"You go on home," Miriam said. "You and your bracelets go on home and don't ever come back monkeying around on my property in the future. Go on."

Miriam McAlpin was well known for her tendency to bawl people out. I had once heard her in the grocery store, carrying on at the top of her voice about some bruised peaches. The way she was treating me was predictable, and the suspicions she had of me seemed to rouse an unambiguous feeling in her—pure disgust—which did not surprise me.

It was the men who made me sick. The looks they gave me, of proper disapproval and sneaky appraisal. The slight dull droop and thickening of their features, as the level of sludge rose in their heads.

The stable boy had come out while this was going on. He was leading a horse belonging to one or both of the men. He halted in the yard, did not come closer. He seemed not to be looking at his boss, or the horse owners, or at me, not to take any interest in the scene. He would be used to Miriam's way of telling people off.

People's thoughts about me—not just the kind of thoughts the men or Miriam might be having, each kind rather dangerous in its own way—but any thoughts at all, seemed to me a mysterious threat, a gross impertinence. I hated even to hear a person say something relatively harmless.

"I seen you walking down the street the other day. Looked like you were off in the clouds."

Judgments and speculations all like a swarm of bugs trying

to get into my mouth and eyes. I could have swatted them, I could have spat.

"Dirt," my sister whispered to me when I got home. "Dirt on the back of your blouse."

She watched me take it off in the bathroom, and scrub at it with a hard bar of soap. We didn't have running hot water except in the winter, so she offered to get me some from the kettle. She didn't ask me how the dirt had got there, she was only hoping to get rid of the evidence, keep me out of trouble.

On Saturday nights there was always a crowd on the main street. At that time there wasn't such a thing as a mall anywhere in the county, and it wasn't until several years after the war that the big shopping night would shift to Friday. The year I'm talking about is 1944, when we still had ration books and there were a lot of things you couldn't buy—like new cars and silk stockings—but the farmers came into town with some money in their pockets and the stores had brightened up after the Depression doldrums and everything stayed open till ten o'clock.

Most town people did their shopping during the week and in the daytime. Unless they worked in the stores or restaurants they stayed out of the way on Saturday evenings, playing cards with their neighbors or listening to the radio. Newly married couples, engaged couples, couples who were "going out," cuddled in the movie house or drove, if they could get the gas coupons, to one of the dance halls on the lakeshore. It was the country people who took over the street and the country men and girls on the loose who went into Neddy's Night Owl, where the platform was raised above a dirt floor and every dance cost ten cents.

I stood close to the platform with some friends of my own age. Nobody came along to pay ten cents for any of us. No wonder. We laughed loudly, we criticized the dancing, the haircuts, the clothes. We sometimes spoke of a girl as a slut, or a man as a fairy, though we did not have a precise definition of either of these words.

Neddy himself, who sold the tickets, was apt to turn to us and say, "Don't you think you girls need some fresh air?" And we would swagger off. Or else we would get bored and leave on our own initiative. We bought ice-cream cones and gave each other licks to try the different flavors, and walked along the street in a haughty style, swinging around the knots of talkers and through the swarms of children squirting water at each other from the drinking fountain. Nobody was worth our notice.

The girls who took part in this parade were not out of the top drawer—as my mother would have said, with a wistful and lightly sarcastic edge to her voice. Not one of them had a sunroom on their house or a father who wore a suit on any day but Sunday. Girls of that sort were at home now, or in each other's houses, playing Monopoly or making fudge or trying out hairstyles. My mother was sorry not to see me accepted into that crowd.

But it was all right with me. This way, I could be a ringleader and a loudmouth. If that was a disguise it was one that I managed easily. Or it might not have been a disguise, but just one of the entirely disjointed and dissimilar personalities I seemed to be made up of.

On a vacant lot at the north end of town some members of the Salvation Army had set up their post. There was a preacher and a small choir to sing the hymns and a fat boy on the drum. Also a tall boy to play the trombone, a girl playing the clarinet, some half-grown children equipped with tambourines.

Salvation Army people were even less top drawer than the girls I was with. The man who was doing the preaching was the drayman who delivered coal. No doubt he had washed himself clean, but his face still had a gray shadow. Sweat was running down it from the exertion of his preaching and it seemed as if his sweat must be gray too. Some cars would honk to drown him out as they passed. (In spite of the waste of gas, there were certain cars driven, by young men, up the street to the north end, and down the street to the south end, over and over again.) Most people walked past with uneasy but respectful faces, but some halted to watch. As we did, waiting for something to laugh at.

The instruments were raised for a hymn, and I saw that the boy who lifted the trombone was the same stable boy who had stood in the yard while Miriam McAlpin was giving me the dressing-down. He smiled at me with his eyes as he began to play, and he seemed to be smiling not to recall my humiliation but with irrepressible pleasure, as if the sight of me woke the memory of something quite different from that scene, a natural happiness.

"There is Power, Power, Power, Power, Power in the Blood," sang the choir. The tambourines were waved above the players' heads. Joy and lustiness infected the bystanders, so that most people began to sing along with a jolly irony. And we permitted ourselves to sing with the others.

Soon after that the service was at an end. The stores were closing up, and we took our separate ways home. There was a shortcut for me, a footbridge over the river. When I had nearly reached the end of it I heard heavy running, some sort of thumping, behind me. The boards shuddered under my feet. I turned sideways, backing against the railing, slightly scared but concerned not to show it. There were no lights near the foot-bridge and now it was quite dark.

When he got close I saw that it was the trombone player in his heavy dark uniform. The trombone case made the thump-ing sound, knocking against the railing.

"Okay," he said, out of breath. "It's just me. I was only try-ing to catch up with you."

"How did you know it was me?" I said.

"I could see a little. I knew you lived out this way. I could tell it was you by the way you walk."

"How?" I said. With most people, such presumption would have made me too angry to ask.

"I don't know. It's just the way you walk."

His name was Russell Craik. His family belonged to the Salva-tion Army, his father being the drayman-preacher and his mother one of the hymn-singers. Because he had worked with his father and got used to horses, he had been hired by Miriam McAlpin as soon as he left school. That was after Grade Eight. It was not at all uncommon in those years for boys to do that. Because of the war, there were lots of jobs for them to take up while they were waiting, as he was, to be old enough to go into the Army. He would be old enough in September.

If Russell Craik had wanted to take me out in the usual way, to take me to the movies or to dances, there would not have been a chance of its being allowed. My mother would have pronounced that I was too young. Probably she would have felt it was not necessary to say that he worked as a stable boy and his father delivered coal and his whole family put on

Salvation Army outfits and regularly testified on the street. Those considerations would have meant something to me too, if it had come to displaying him publicly as my boyfriend. They would have meant something at least until he got into the Army and became presentable. But as it was, I didn't have to think about any of that. Russell could not take me to the movies or to a dance hall because his religion forbade him to go there himself. The arrangement that developed between us seemed easy, almost natural, to me because it was in some ways—not all—much like the casual, hardly recognized, and temporary pairing off of boys and girls of my age, not his.

We rode bicycles, for one thing. Russell did not own a car and did not have any access to one, though he could drive—he drove the horse-barn truck. He never called for me at my house and I never suggested it. We rode out of town separately on Sunday afternoons and met always at the same place, a crossroads school two or three miles out of town. All the country schools had names by which they were known, rather than by the official numbers carved above their doors. Never S.S. No. 11, or S.S. No. 5, but Lambs' School and Brewsters' School and the Red Brick School and the Stone School. The one we chose, already familiar to me, was called the School of the Flowing Well. A thin stream of water flowed continuously out of a pipe in a corner of the school yard, to justify this name.

Around that yard, which was kept mowed even in the summer holidays, there were mature maple trees that cast nearly black pools of shade. In one corner was a stone pile with long grass growing out of it, where we concealed our bikes.

The road in front of the school yard was neat and gravelled, but the side road, climbing a hill, was not much more than a lane in a field, or a dirt track. On one side of it was pasture field dotted with hawthorns and juniper, and on the other a stand of oak and pine trees, with a hollow between it and the bank of the road. In this hollow was a dump—not the official township dump, just an informal dump that the country people had made. This interested Russell, and every time we passed it we had to lean over and peer down into the hollow, to see if there was anything new in it. There never was, the dump had probably not been used for years—but quite often he could pick out something that he had not noticed before.

"See? That's the grille of a V-8."

"See under the buggy wheel? That's an old battery radio."

I had been on this road a few times by myself and had not once seen that the dump was there, but I knew about other things. I knew that when we went over the hill the oak and pine trees would be swallowed up in spruce and tamarack and cedar, and so would the bumpy pasture, and all that we would see, for a long time, would be swamp growth on either side, with glimpses of high-bush cranberries nobody could ever get to, and some formal-looking crimson flower I was not sure of the name of—I thought it was called the Devil's paintbrush. On a branch of cedar somebody had hung the skull of a small animal, and this Russell would take note of, wondering every time if it was a ferret's or a weasel's or a mink's.

It was proof anyway, he said, that somebody had been on this road before us. Probably walking, probably not in a car— the cedars grew in too close, and the plank bridge over the creek at the lowest level of the swamp was a primitive affair, springy under our feet and without railings. Beyond that the land rose slowly, and the mucky ground was left behind and finally there were farm fields on either side, glimpsed through large beech trees. Such heavy trees and so many of them that their smooth gray light seemed actually to make a change in the air, cooling it down as if you had entered some high hall or church.

And the track would end, after the usual mile and a quarter measurement of country blocks, running into another straight gravel road. We turned and walked back the same way.

There were hardly any birds to be heard in the hot middle of the day, and none to be seen, and there were not many mosquitos because the ponds in the low ground had mostly dried up. But there were dragonflies over the creek and often clouds of very small butterflies, such a pale green that you thought maybe they were just catching a reflection of the leaves.

What there was to be heard at every stage of the walk was Russell's unhurried, pleased voice. He talked about his family—there were two older sisters who were gone from home and a younger brother and two younger sisters and they were all musical, each one playing some instrument. The younger brother's name was Jackie—he was learning the trombone, to take over from Russell. The sisters at home were Mavis and Annie and the grown-up ones were Iona and Isabel. Iona was married to a man who worked on the Hydro lines, and Isabel was a chambermaid in a large hotel. Another sister, Edna, had died of polio in an iron lung after being sick for only two days at the age of twelve. She was the only one in the family to have blond hair. The brother Jackie had nearly died also, of blood poison from stepping on a board with a rusty nail. Russell himself used to have tough feet from going barefoot in the summer. He could walk on gravel or thistles or stubble and he never got any kind of wound.

He had shot up in height in Grade Eight to be nearly as tall as he was now, and he got the part of Ali Baba in the school operetta. That was because he could sing, as well as being tall.

He had learned to drive his uncle's car when his uncle came

over from Port Huron. His uncle was in the plumbing business and he traded in his car for a new one every two years. He let Russell drive before he was old enough to get a license. But Miriam McAlpin would not let him drive her truck until he got one. He drove it now, with and without the horse trailer hitched on. To Elmira, to Hamilton, once to Peterborough. It was tricky driving because a horse trailer could roll over. She came with him sometimes, but she let him drive.

His voice changed when he talked of Miriam McAlpin. It became wary, half-contemptuous, half-amused. She was a Tartar, he said. But okay if you knew how to handle her. She liked horses better than she liked people. She would have been married by now if she could have married a horse.

I did not speak much about myself and I did not listen to him all that closely. His talk was like a curtain of easy rain between me and the trees, the light and shadows on the road, the clear-running creek, the butterflies, and all that part of myself that would have paid attention to these things if I had been alone. A lot of me was under cover, as it was with my friends on Saturday nights. But the change now was not so deliberate and voluntary. I was half-hypnotized, not just by the sound of his voice but by the bright breadth of his shoulders in a clean, short-sleeved shirt, by his tawny throat and thick arms. He had washed himself with Lifebuoy soap—I knew the smell of it as everybody did—but washing was as far as most men went in those days, they didn't bother about the sweat that would accumulate in the near future. So I could smell that too. And just faintly the smell of horses, bridles, barns, and hay.

When I wasn't with him I would try to remember—was he good-looking or was he not? His body was fairly lean but he had a slight fleshiness about the face, an authoritative pout to his lips, and his wide-open clear blue eyes showed something like an obstinate naïveté, an innocent self-regard. All that I might not have cared for much in another person.

"I grind my teeth at night," he said. "I never wake up, but it wakes Jackie up and is he ever mad. He gives me a kick and I turn over in my sleep and that fixes it. Because I only do it when I'm laying on my back."

"Would you kick me?" he said, and he reached across the foot or so of air that was between us, shot full of sunlight, and picked up my hand. He said that he got so hot in bed he kicked all the covers off, and that made Jackie mad as well.

I wanted to ask him if he wore just his pyjama tops or just the bottoms, or both, or nothing at all, but the last possibility made me feel too weak to open my mouth. Our fingers worked together, all on their own, until they got so sweaty that they gave up, and separated.

It was not until we got back to the school yard and were about to pick up our bikes and ride back to town— separately—that the reason for our walk, the only reason as far as I could understand it, received our whole attention. He would pull me into the shade and put his arms around me and begin to kiss me. Hidden from the road he would press me up against a tree trunk and we would kiss chastely at first and then more fervently, and wind ourselves together—still upright— with a shaky urgency. And after—how long?—five or ten minutes of this we would separate and pick up our bikes and say good-bye. My mouth would be rubbed sore and my cheeks and chin scraped by bristles that were not visible on his face. My back would hurt from being shoved against the tree and the front of my body would ache from the pressure of his. My stomach, though quite flat, had a little give to it, but I had noted that his had none. I thought that men must have a firmness and even a protuberance to their stomachs, that was not evident until you were held very tightly against them.

It seems so strange that knowing as much as I knew, I did not realize what this pressure was. I had a fairly accurate idea of a man's body, but somehow I had missed the information that there was this change in size and condition. I seem to have believed that a penis was at maximum size all the time, and in its classic shape, but in spite of this could be kept dangling down inside the leg of the pants, not hoisted up to put pressure against another body in this way. I had heard a lot of jokes, and I had seen animals coupling, but somehow, when education is informal, gaps can occur.

Now and then he would speak about God. His tone at such times was firm and factual, as if God were a superior officer, was occasionally gracious but often inflexible and impatient, in a manly way. When the war was over and he was out of the Army ("If I'm not killed," he said cheerfully), there would still be the commands of God and *his* Army to be reckoned with.

"I'll have to do what God wants me to."

That struck me. What terrible docility it took, to be such a believer.

Or—when you considered the war and the ordinary Army—just to be a man.

The thought of his future might have come to him because we had noticed, on the trunk of a beech tree—those trees whose gray bark is ideal for messages—a carved face and a date. The year was 1909. During the time since, the tree had been growing, its trunk had been widening, so that the outlines of the face had broadened at the sides to become blotches wider than the face itself. The rest of the date had been blotched out entirely, and the numbers of the year might soon be illegible as well.

"That was before the First World War," I said. "Whoever did it might be dead now. He might've been killed in that war.

"Or he could just be dead anyway," I added hastily.

It was on that day, I believe, that we got so hot on the way back that we took off our shoes and socks and lowered ourselves from the planks to stand in the knee-high water of the creek. We splashed our arms and faces.

"You know that time I got caught coming out from under the apple tree?" I said, to my own surprise.

"Yeah."

"I told her I was looking for a bracelet, but it wasn't true. I went in there for another reason."

"Is that right?"

By now I wished I had not started this.

"I wanted to get under the big tree when it was all in bloom and look up at it from underneath."

He laughed. "That's funny," he said. "I wanted to do that too. I never did, but I thought about it."

I was surprised, and somehow not quite pleased, to find that we had had this urge in common. But surely I would not have told him if I hadn't hoped that it was something he would understand?

"Come to our place for supper," he said.

"Don't you have to ask your mother if it's all right?"

"She don't care."

My mother would have cared, if she had known. But she didn't know, because I lied and said I was going to my friend Clara's. Now that my father had to be at the Foundry by five o'clock—even on Sundays, because he was the watchman— and my mother was so often not feeling well, our suppers had become rather haphazard. If I cooked, there were things that I liked. One was sliced bread and cheese with milk and beaten eggs poured over it, baked in the oven. Another, also oven-baked, was a loaf of tinned meat coated with brown sugar. Or heaps of slices of raw potato that had been fried to a crisp. Left to themselves, my brother and sister would make a supper of something like sardines on soda crackers or peanut butter on graham wafers. Erosion of regular customs in our house seemed to make my deception easier.

Perhaps my mother, if she had known, would have found a way to say to me that once you went into certain houses as an equal and a friend—and this was true even if they were in a way perfectly respectable houses—you showed that the value you put on yourself was not very high, and after that others would value you accordingly. I would have argued with her, of course, and the more fiercely because I would have known that what she was saying was true, as far as life in that town went. I was the one, after all, who would make any excuse now not to go with my friends past the corner where Russell and his family stationed themselves on Saturday nights.

I sometimes thought ahead hopefully to the time when Russell would have put away that slightly comic dark-blue red-piped uniform and replaced it with khaki. It seemed as if much more than the uniform might be changed, that an identity itself could be peeled away and a fresh one shine out, unassailable, once he was dressed as a fighting man.

The Craiks lived on a narrow diagonal street only a block long, not far from the horse barns. I had never had any reason to walk along this street before. The houses were close to the sidewalk and close to each other with no room for driveways or side yards in between. The people who owned cars had to park them partly on the sidewalk and partly on the strips of grass that served as front lawns. The Craiks' large wooden house was painted yellow—Russell had told me to look for the yellow house—but the paint was weathered and blistered.

Just as the brown paint was, that had once, ill-advisedly, covered the red brick of the house that I lived in. When it came to ready money our two families were not so far apart. Not far apart at all.

Two little girls were sitting on the front step, maybe stationed there in case I should have forgotten the house's description.

They jumped up, however, without a word, and ran into the house as if I'd been a wildcat after them. The screen door banged in my face and I was left staring down a long bare hallway. I could hear a subdued commotion in the back of the house, perhaps having to do with who should go to greet me. And then Russell himself came down the stairs, his hair dark from a recent wetting, and let me in.

"So you got here okay," he said. He backed off from touching me.

Mr. and Mrs. Craik did not wear their Salvation Army uniforms around home. I don't know why I had thought they would. The father, whose street preaching was always on the ferocious side, wrathful even when he held out the hope of mercy and salvation, and whose expression when he sat hunched on the coal wagon was always one of disgruntlement, came forward now as a scrubbed and tidy man with a shining bald head, and greeted me as if he was actually glad to see me in his house. The mother was tall, like Russell, large-boned and flat-fronted, with gray hair chopped off at the level of her ears. Russell had to tell her my name twice, through the racket she was making mashing the potatoes, before he could get her to turn around. She wiped her hand on her apron as if she had thought of shaking mine, but she did not do so. She said that she was pleased to meet me. Her voice when she sang the street-corner hymns was full and sweet, but when she spoke now it cracked with embarrassment like an adolescent boy's.

Russell's father was ready to step into the breach. He asked me if I had any experience of banty hens. I said no, and he said he had thought I might have, being brought up on a farm.

"The hens are my hobby," he said. "Come and have a look."

The two girls had reappeared and were hanging around in the hall doorway. They were about to follow their father and Russell and me out into the backyard, but their mother called to them.

"Annieanmavis! You stay here an put the plates on the table."

The banty rooster was named King George.

"That's a joke," Mr. Craik said. "On account of George is my name."

The hens were named after Mae West and Tugboat Annie and Daisy Mae and other personalities from the movies or comic strips or popular folklore. This surprised me because of the fact that movies were forbidden to this family and the movie theatre was singled out in the Saturday sermons as a place to be specially abhorred. I had thought the comic strips would be out of bounds as well. Perhaps it was all right to give such names to silly hens. Or perhaps the Craiks had not always belonged to the Salvation Army.

"How do you tell which is which?" I said. I didn't have my wits about me at all, or else I would have seen that each was distinctly marked, had its own pattern of red and brown and rust and gold feathers.

Russell's brother had turned up from somewhere. He snickered.

"Oh, you learn to," the father said. He began to identify each one for me, but the hens were getting flustered by all the attention and scattered around the yard so that he couldn't keep them straight. The rooster was bold and pecked at my shoe.

"Don't be alarmed," Russell's father said. "He's just showing off."

"Do they lay eggs?" was my next foolish-sounding question.

"Oh, they do, they do, but not so's it's a common occurrence. No. Not even enough for our own table. Oh no, they're an ornamental breed, that's what they are. Ornamental breed."

"You're going to get a clout," Russell said to his brother, behind my back.

At supper, the father gave Russell a nod to ask the Blessing, and Russell did so. Blessings here were leisurely and composed on the spot to suit the occasion, nothing like the Bless-this-food-to-our-use-and-us-to-thy-service that used to be mumbled at our table at home when we ate as a family. Russell spoke slowly and confidently and mentioned the name of everyone at the table—including me, asking that the Lord should make me welcome. The chill thought came to me that the war might not rescue him entirely, that when it was through with him he might revert to the other Army and put on the old uniform, that he might even have a gift and a hankering for public preaching.

There were no bread-and-butter plates. You put your slice of bread on the oilcloth or on the side of your big plate. And you wiped your plate clean with a piece of bread before the pie was set down on it.

The rooster appeared in the doorway but was ordered away

by Mr. Craik. This caused Mavis and Annie to giggle and hold their mouths.

"Choke on your food and it'll serve you right," said Russell.

Mrs. Craik avoided saying my name—she said in a harsh whisper to Russell, "Pass her the tomatoes"—but this seemed to be the result of extreme shyness, not of ill will. Mr. Craik continued to show an unperturbed sense of social occasion, asking me how my mother's health was, and what hours my father worked at the Foundry and how he liked his job there, did he find it a change from being his own boss? His way of speaking to me was more that of a teacher or a shopkeeper or even a professional man in town, than that of the man on the coal wagon. And he seemed to take it for granted that our families were on an equal footing and had a comfortable acquaintance with each other. This was close to the truth, as far as the equal footing went, and it was also true that my father had a comfortable acquaintance with almost everybody. Nevertheless it made me feel uneasy, even a little ashamed, because I was deceiving this family and my own, I was at this table under false pretenses.

But it seemed to me then that Russell and I would have been under false pretenses at any family supper table where we had to sit as if we were concerned with nothing but the food and whatever conversation was offered. While in fact we were marking time, our urgent needs were not to be met here, and our only real concern was to get at each other's skin.

It never crossed my mind that a young couple in our situation did indeed belong right here, that we were entered on the first stage of a life that would turn us, soon enough, into the Father and the Mother. Russell's parents probably knew this, and may have been privately dismayed, but decently hopeful, or resigned. Russell was already a force in the family whom they did not control. And Russell knew it, if he was capable at the moment of thinking that far ahead. He hardly looked at me, but when he did it was a steady look, laying claim, and it hit me and resonated as if I'd been a drum.

It was late in the summer now, the evenings closed in early. The light was turned on in the kitchen when we did the dishes. The dishpan was set on the table, the water had been heated on the stove, which was just the way things were managed when I washed the dishes at home. The mother washed, the sisters and I dried. Perhaps relieved that the meal was over and that I would soon be going home, Russell's mother made a few statements.

"It always takes more dishes than you'd think it would for to make a meal."

"Don't bother with them pots, I'll set them on the stove."

"That looks like it's about it now."

This last sentence sounded like a thank-you that she didn't know how to say.

So close to me and to their mother, Mavis and Annie had not dared giggle. When we got in each other's way at the draining pan they had said softly, "Parmee."

Russell came in from helping his father put the banties to roost. He said, "I guess it's time for you to be getting home," as if getting me home was just another nightly chore, instead of our anticipated first walk in the dark together. Mutely, exquisitely anticipated, on my part, the thought of it growing all through the dish-drying routine and even transforming that into a feminine ritual mysteriously linked to what was to come.

. . .

It was not so dark as I had hoped. To get me home we would have to cross the town, east to west, and almost certainly we would be noticed.

But that was not where we were going. At the end of this short street Russell put his hand on my back—a quick, functional pressure, to head me not towards home but towards Miriam McAlpin's horse barn.

I turned around to see if anybody was spying on us.

"What if your brother or sisters followed us?"

"They wouldn't," he said. "I'd kill them."

The barn was painted red, the color plain in the half-dark. The stable doors were on the lower level in the back. On the upper barn doors, which faced the street, were painted two prancing white horses. A gangway of stone and earth was built up to these doors—this was the way the loads of hay were driven in. In one of these big upper doors there was an ordinary-sized door, fitted snugly so that you would hardly notice it, holding the hoof and part of one painted horse's back legs. It was locked, but Russell had the key.

He pulled me inside after him. And once he had closed the door behind us we were in what was at first pitch-black darkness. All around us, almost choking us, the smell of that summer's new hay. Russell led me by the hand just as confidently as if he could see. His hand was hotter than mine.

After a moment I could see something myself. Bales of hay set one on top of another like giant bricks. We were in some sort of loft, overlooking the stable. Now I could get a strong smell of horses, as well as of hay, and hear continual shuffling and munching and gentle bumping around in the stalls. Most horses would be out in the pasture all night at this time of year, but these were probably too valuable to be left outside in the dark.

Russell put my hand on the rung of a ladder, by which we could climb to the top of the hay bales.

"Want me to go first or after?" he whispered.

Why whisper? Would we disturb the horses? Or does it just always seem natural to whisper in the dark? Or when you have gone weak in the legs but aching, determined, in another part of your body.

Something happened then. I thought for a moment that it was an explosion. Lightning hitting. Or even an earthquake. It seemed to me that the whole barn shook as it filled with light. Of course I had never been anywhere near an explosion or within a mile of a place where lightning struck, never felt one tremor of an earthquake. I had heard guns going off but always out of doors and at some distance. I had never heard the blast of a shotgun indoors under a high roof.

That was what I had heard now. Miriam McAlpin had shot her gun off, shot it up into the mow, then at once turned on all the barn lights. The horses had gone wild, whinnying and tossing themselves about and kicking the sides of their stalls, but you could still hear Miriam yelling.

"I know you're there. I know you're there."

"Go home," Russell was hissing into my ear. He spun me around towards the door.

"Go on home," he said angrily, or at least with an urgency like anger. As if I'd been a dog following him, or one of his little sisters, who had no right to be here.

Perhaps he said that too in a whisper, perhaps not. With the noise that the horses and Miriam made together, it wouldn't have mattered. He gave me one strong and untender push, then turned towards the stable and hollered, "Don't shoot, it's me . . . Hey Miriam. It's me."

"I know you're there—"

"It's me. It's Russ." He had run to the front of the haymow.

"Who's up there? Russ? Is that you? *Russ?*"

There must have been a ladder going down to the stable. I heard Russell's voice descending. He sounded bold but shaky, as if he was not quite sure that Miriam would not start shooting again.

"It's just me. I come in the top way."

"I heard somebody," said Miriam disbelievingly.

"I know. It was me. I just come in to see Lou. How her leg was."

"It was you?"

"Yeah. I told you."

"You were up in the mow."

"I come in by the top door."

He sounded more in control now. He was able to ask a question of his own.

"How long you been in here?"

"I just came in now. I was in the house and suddenly it hit me, there's something wrong at the barn."

"What'd you fire off the gun for? You could've killed me."

"If anybody was in here I wanted to give them a scare."

"You could've waited. You could've yelled first. You could've killed me."

"It never crossed my mind it was you."

Then Miriam McAlpin cried out again, as if she'd just spotted a new intruder.

"I could've killed you. Oh, Russ. I never thought. I could've shot you."

"Okay. Calm down," Russell said. "You could've but you didn't."

"You could be shot now and I'd be the one that did it."

"You didn't."

"What if I had, though? Jesus. Jesus. What if I had?"

She was weeping and saying something like this over and over, but in a muffled voice, as if something was stuffed into her mouth.

Or as if she was being held, pressed against something, somebody, that could comfort and quiet her.

Russell's voice, swelling with mastery, soothing.

"Okay. Yeah. So okay, honey. Okay."

That was the last thing I heard. What a strange word to speak to Miriam McAlpin. *Honey.* The word he'd used to me, during our bouts of kissing. Commonplace enough, but then it had seemed something I could suck up, a sweet mouthful like the stuff itself. Why would he say it now, when I wasn't anywhere near him? And in just the same way. Just the same.

Into the hair, against the ear, of Miriam McAlpin.

I had been standing by the door. I had been afraid that the noise of opening it might be heard below in spite of the disturbance the horses were still making. Or else I had not really understood that my presence here was unwanted, my part was over. Now I had to get out. I didn't care if they heard. But I don't suppose they did. I pulled the door shut, then ran down the gangway and along the street. I would have gone on running, but I realized that somebody might see me and wonder what was the matter. I had to be content with walking very fast. It was hard to stop for a moment, even to cross the highway that was also the main street of town.

I didn't see Russell again. He did become a soldier. He was not killed in the war, and I don't think he continued in the Salvation Army. The summer after all this had happened I saw his wife—a girl I had known by sight in high school. She had been a couple of years ahead of me, and had dropped out to work in the creamery. She was with Mrs. Craik and she was heavily pregnant. They were looking through a bargain bin outside Stedman's store, one afternoon. She looked disconsolate and plain—maybe that was the effect of her pregnancy, though I had thought her plain enough before. Or at least insignificant and shy. She still looked shy, though hardly insignificant. Her body seemed abject but amazing, grotesque. And a thrill of sexual envy, of longing, went through me, at the sight of her and the thought of how she had got that way. Such submission, such necessity.

At some time after he came home from the war Russell took up carpentry and through that work he became a contractor, building houses for the ever-growing subdivisions around Toronto. I know that much because he appeared at a high-school reunion, apparently quite prosperous, joking about how he didn't have any right to be there, since he had never even gone to high school. Report of this came to me from Clara, who had kept in touch.

Clara said that his wife was blond now, rather fat, wearing a bare-backed sundress. A bun of blond hair stuck up above the hole in the crown of her sunhat. Clara had not talked to them and so she was not actually sure whether this was the same wife or a new one.

It was probably not the same wife, though it may have been. Clara and I talked about how reunions occasionally reveal how those who seemed most secure have been somewhat diminished or battered by life, and those who were at the fringes, who seemed to droop and ask pardon, have blossomed. So that might have happened with the girl I had seen in front of Stedman's.

Miriam McAlpin stayed on at the horse barn until it burned down. I don't know the reason, it could have been the usual one—damp hay, spontaneous combustion. All of the horses were saved, but Miriam was hurt, and after that she lived on a disability pension.

Everything was normal when I got home that evening. This was the summer when my brother and sister had learned to play solitaire, and played it at every opportunity. They were sitting now at either end of the dining-room table, nine and ten years old and grave as an old couple, the cards spread out in front of them. My mother had already gone to bed. She spent many hours in bed, but she never seemed to sleep as other people did, she just dozed for short periods of the day and night, maybe got up and drank tea or sorted out a drawer. Her life had stopped being securely connected at any point with the life of the family.

She called from bed to ask if I had had a nice supper at Clara's, and what did I have for dessert?

"Cottage pudding," I said.

I thought that if I said any part of the truth, if I said "pie," I would immediately betray myself. She did not care, she only wanted a bit of conversation, but I was not able to supply it. I tucked the quilt in around her feet, as she asked me to, and went downstairs and into the living room, where I sat on the low stool in front of the bookcase and took out a book. I sat there squinting at the print in the dim light that still came in the window beside me, until I had to rise and turn on the lamp. Even then I didn't settle myself in a chair to be comfortable but continued to sit hunched on the stool, filling my mind with one sentence after another, slamming them into my head just so I would not have to think about what had happened.

I don't know which book it was that I had picked up. I had read them all before, all the novels in that bookcase. There were not many. *The Sun Is My Undoing. Gone with the Wind. The Robe. Sleep in Peace. My Son, My Son. Wuthering Heights. The Last Days of Pompeii.* The selection did not reflect any particular taste, and in fact my parents often could not say how a certain book came to be there—whether it had been bought or borrowed or whether somebody had left it behind.

It must have meant something, though, that at this turn of my life I grabbed up a book. Because it was in books that I would find, for the next few years, my lovers. They were men, not boys. They were self-possessed and sardonic, with a ferocious streak in them, reserves of gloom. Not Edgar Linton, not Ashley Wilkes. Not one of them companionable or kind.

It was not as if I had given up on passion. Passion, indeed, wholehearted, even destructive passion, was what I was after. Demand and submission. I did not exclude a certain kind of brutality. But no confusion, no double-dealing, or sleazy sort of surprise or humiliation. I could wait, and all my due would come to me, I thought, when I was full-blown.

Hired Girl

Mrs. Montjoy was showing me how to put the pots and pans away. I had put some of them in the wrong places.

Above all things, she said, she hated a higgledy-piggledy cupboard.

"You waste more time," she said. "You waste more time looking for something because it wasn't where it was last time."

"That's the way it was with our hired girls at home," I said. "The first few days they were there they were always putting things away where we couldn't find them.

"We called our maids hired girls," I added. "That was what we called them, at home."

"Did you?" she said. A moment of silence passed. "And the colander on that hook there."

Why did I have to say what I had said? Why was it necessary to mention that we had hired girls at home?

Anybody could see why. To put myself somewhere near her level. As if that was possible. As if anything I had to say about myself or the house I came from could interest or impress her.

It was true, though, about the hired girls. In my early life there was a procession of them. There was Olive, a soft drowsy girl who didn't like me because I called her Olive Oyl. Even after I was made to apologize she didn't like me. Maybe she didn't like any of us much because she was a Bible Christian, which made her mistrustful and reserved. She used to sing as she washed the dishes and I dried. *There is a Balm in Gilead* . . . If I tried to sing with her she stopped.

Then came Jeanie, whom I liked, because she was pretty and she did my hair up in pin curls at night when she did her own. She kept a list of the boys she went out with and made peculiar signs after their names: x x x o o * *. She did not last long.

Neither did Dorothy, who hung the clothes on the line in an eccentric way—pinned up by the collar, or by one sleeve or one leg—and swept the dirt into a corner and propped the broom up to hide it.

And when I was around ten years old hired girls became a thing of the past. I don't know if it was because we became poorer or because I was considered old enough to be a steady help. Both things were true.

Now I was seventeen and able to be hired out myself, though only as summer help because I had one more year to go at high school. My sister was twelve, so she could take over at home.

Mrs. Montjoy had picked me up at the railway station in Pointe au Baril, and transported me in an outboard-motor boat to the island. It was the woman in the Pointe au Baril store who had recommended me for the job. She was an old friend of my mother's—they had taught school together. Mrs. Montjoy had asked her if she knew of a country girl, used to doing housework, who would be available for the summer, and the woman had thought that it would be the very thing for me. I thought so too—I was eager to see more of the world.

Mrs. Montjoy wore khaki shorts and a tucked-in shirt. Her short, sun-bleached hair was pushed behind her ears. She leapt aboard the boat like a boy and gave a fierce tug to the motor, and we were flung out on the choppy evening waters of Georgian Bay. For thirty or forty minutes we dodged around rocky and wooded islands with their lone cottages and boats bobbing beside the docks. Pine trees jutted out at odd angles, just as they do in the paintings.

I held on to the sides of the boat and shivered in my flimsy dress.

"Feeling a tad sick?" said Mrs. Montjoy, with the briefest possible smile. It was like the signal for a smile, when the occasion did not warrant the real thing. She had large white teeth in a long tanned face, and her natural expression seemed to be one of impatience barely held in check. She probably knew that what I was feeling was fear, not sickness, and she threw out this question so that I—and she—need not be embarrassed.

Here was a difference, already, from the world I was used to. In that world, fear was commonplace, at least for females. You could be afraid of snakes, thunderstorms, deep water, heights, the dark, the bull, and the lonely road through the swamp, and nobody thought any the worse of you. In Mrs. Montjoy's world, however, fear was shameful and always something to be conquered.

The island that was our destination had a name—Nausicaa. The name was written on a board at the end of the dock. I said it aloud, trying to show that I was at ease and quietly appreciative, and Mrs. Montjoy said with slight surprise, "Oh, yes. That was the name it already had when Daddy bought it. It's for some character in Shakespeare."

I opened up my mouth to say no, no, not Shakespeare, and to tell her that Nausicaa was the girl on the beach, playing ball with her friends, surprised by Ulysses when he woke up from his nap. I had learned by this time that most of the people I lived amongst did not welcome this kind of information, and I would probably have kept quiet even if the teacher had asked us in school, but I believed that people out in the world—the real world—would be different. Just in time I recognized the briskness of Mrs. Montjoy's tone when she said "some character in Shakespeare"—the suggestion that Nausicaa, and Shakespeare, as well as any observations of mine, were things she could reasonably do without.

The dress I was wearing for my arrival was one I had made myself, out of pink and white striped cotton. The material had been cheap, the reason being that it was not really meant for a dress but for a blouse or a nightgown, and the style I had chosen—the full-skirted, tight-waisted style of those days—was a mistake. When I walked, the cloth bunched up between my legs, and I kept having to yank it loose. Today was the first day the dress had been worn, and I still thought that the trouble might be temporary—with a firm enough yank the material might be made to hang properly. But I found when I took off my belt that the day's heat and my hot ride on the train had created a worse problem. The belt was wide and elasticized, and of a burgundy color, which had run. The waistline of the dress was circled with strawberry dye.

I made this discovery when I was getting undressed in the loft of the boathouse, which I was to share with Mrs. Montjoy's ten-year-old daughter, Mary Anne.

"What happened to your dress?" Mary Anne said. "Do you sweat a lot? That's too bad."

I said that it was an old dress anyway and that I hadn't wanted to wear anything good on the train.

Mary Anne was fair-haired and freckled, with a long face like her mother's. But she didn't have her mother's look of quick judgments marshalled at the surface, ready to leap out at you. Her expression was benign and serious, and she wore heavy glasses even when sitting up in bed. She was to tell me soon that she had had an operation to get her eyes straightened, but even so her eyesight was poor.

"I've got Daddy's eyes," she said. "I'm intelligent like him too so it's too bad I'm not a boy."

Another difference. Where I came from, it was generally held to be more suspect for boys to be smart than for girls to be, though not particularly advantageous for one or the other. Girls could go on to be teachers, and that was all right—though quite often they became old maids—but for boys to continue with school usually meant they were sissies.

All night long you could hear the water slapping against the boards of the boathouse. Morning came early. I wondered whether I was far enough north of home for the sun to actually be rising sooner. I got up and looked out. Through the front window, I saw the silky water, dark underneath but flashing back from its surface the light of the sky. The rocky shores of this little cove, the moored sailboats, the open channel beyond, the mound of another island or two, shores and channels beyond that. I thought that I would never, on my own, be able to find my way back to the mainland.

I did not yet understand that maids didn't have to find their way anywhere. They stayed put, where the work was. It was the people who made the work who could come and go.

The back window looked out on a gray rock that was like a slanting wall, with shelves and crevices on it where little pine and cedar trees and blueberry bushes had got a foothold. Down at the foot of this wall was a path—which I would take later on—through the woods, to Mrs. Montjoy's house. Here everything was still damp and almost dark, though if you craned you could see bits of the sky whitening through the trees on top of the rock. Nearly all of the trees were strict-looking, fragrant evergreens, with heavy boughs that didn't allow much growth underneath—no riot of grapevine and brambles and saplings such as I was used to in the hardwood forest. I had noticed that when I looked out from the train on the day before—how what we called the bush turned into the more authentic-looking *forest,* which had eliminated all lavishness and confusion and seasonal change. It seemed to me that this real forest belonged to rich people—it was their proper though sombre playground—and to Indians, who served the rich people as guides and exotic dependents, living out of sight and out of mind, somewhere that the train didn't go.

Nevertheless, on this morning I was really looking out, eagerly, as if this was a place where I would live and everything would become familiar to me. And everything did become familiar, at least in the places where my work was and where I was supposed to go. But a barrier was up. Perhaps *barrier* is too strong a word—there was not a warning so much as something like a shimmer in the air, an indolent reminder. *Not for you.* It wasn't a thing that had to be said. Or put on a sign.

Not for you. And though I felt it, I would not quite admit to myself that such a barrier was there. I would not admit that I ever felt humbled or lonely, or that I was a real servant. But I stopped thinking about leaving the path, exploring among the trees. If anybody saw me I would have to explain what I was doing, and *they*—Mrs. Montjoy—would not like it.

And to tell the truth, this wasn't so different from the way things were at home, where taking any impractical notice of the out-of-doors, or mooning around about Nature—even using that word, *Nature*—could get you laughed at.

Mary Anne liked to talk when we were lying on our cots at night. She told me that her favorite book was *Kon-Tiki* and that she did not believe in God or Heaven.

"My sister is dead," she said. "And I don't believe she is floating around somewhere in a white nightie. She is just dead, she is just nothing.

"My sister was pretty," she said. "Compared to me she was, anyway. Mother wasn't ever pretty and Daddy is really ugly. Aunt Margaret used to be pretty but now she's fat, and Nana used to be pretty but now she's old. My friend Helen is pretty but my friend Susan isn't. You're pretty, but it doesn't count because you're the maid. Does it hurt your feelings for me to say that?"

I said no.

"I'm only the maid when I'm here."

It wasn't that I was the only servant on the island. The other servants were a married couple, Henry and Corrie. They did not feel diminished by their jobs—they were grateful for them. They had come to Canada from Holland a few years before and had been hired by Mr. and Mrs. Foley, who were Mrs. Montjoy's parents. It was Mr. and Mrs. Foley who owned the island, and lived in the large white bungalow, with its awnings and verandas, that crowned the highest point of land. Henry cut the grass and looked after the tennis court and repainted the lawn chairs and helped Mr. Foley with the boats and the clearing of paths and the repairs to the dock. Corrie did the housework and cooked the meals and looked after Mrs. Foley.

Mrs. Foley spent every sunny morning sitting outside on a deck chair, with her feet stretched out to get the sun and an awning attached to the chair protecting her head. Corrie came out and shifted her around as the sun moved, and took her to the bathroom, and brought her cups of tea and glasses of iced coffee. I was witness to this when I went up to the Foleys' house from the Montjoys' house on some errand, or to put something into or remove something from the freezer. Home freezers were still rather a novelty and a luxury at this time, and there wasn't one in the Montjoys' cottage.

"You are not going to suck the ice cubes," I heard Corrie say to Mrs. Foley. Apparently Mrs. Foley paid no attention and proceeded to suck an ice cube, and Corrie said, "Bad. No. Spit out. Spit right out in Corrie's hand. Bad. You didn't do what Corrie say."

Catching up to me on the way into the house, she said, "I tell them she could choke to death. But Mr. Foley always say, give her the ice cubes, she wants a drink like everybody else. So I tell her and tell her. Do not suck ice cubes. But she won't do what I say."

Sometimes I was sent up to help Corrie polish the furniture or buff the floors. She was very exacting. She never just wiped the kitchen counters—she scoured them. Every move she made had the energy and concentration of somebody rowing a boat against the current and every word she said was flung out as if into a high wind of opposition. When she wrung out a cleaning rag she might have been wringing the neck of a chicken. I thought it might be interesting if I could get her to talk about the war, but all she would say was that everybody was very hungry and they saved the potato skins to make soup.

"No good," she said. "No good to talk about that."

She preferred the future. She and Henry were saving their money to go into business. They meant to start up a nursing home. "Lots of people like her," said Corrie, throwing her head back as she worked to indicate Mrs. Foley out on the lawn. "Soon more and more. Because they give them the medicine, that makes them not die so soon. Who will be taking care?"

One day Mrs. Foley called out to me as I crossed the lawn.

"Now, where are you off to in such a hurry?" she said. "Come and sit down by me and have a little rest."

Her white hair was tucked up under a floppy straw hat, and when she leaned forward the sun came though the holes in the straw, sprinkling the pink and pale-brown patches of her face with pimples of light. Her eyes were a color so nearly extinct I couldn't make it out and her shape was curious—a narrow flat chest and a swollen stomach under layers of loose, pale clothing. The skin of the legs she stuck out into the sunlight was shiny and discolored and covered with faint cracks.

"Pardon my not having put my stockings on," she said. "I'm afraid I'm feeling rather lazy today. But aren't you the remarkable girl. Coming all that way by yourself. Did Henry help you carry the groceries up from the dock?"

Mrs. Montjoy waved to us. She was on her way to the tennis court, to give Mary Anne her lesson. Every morning she gave Mary Anne a lesson, and at lunch they discussed what Mary Anne had done wrong.

"There's that woman who comes to play tennis," Mrs. Foley said of her daughter. "She comes every day, so I suppose it's all right. She may as well use it if she hasn't a court of her own."

Mrs. Montjoy said to me later, "Did Mrs. Foley ask you to come over and sit on the grass?"

I said yes. "She thought I was somebody who'd brought the groceries."

"I believe there was a grocery girl who used to run a boat. There hasn't been any grocery delivery in years. Mrs. Foley does get her wires crossed now and then."

"She said you were a woman who came to play tennis."

"Did she really?" Mrs. Montjoy said.

The work that I had to do here was not hard for me. I knew how to bake, and iron, and clean an oven. Nobody tracked barnyard mud into this kitchen and there were no heavy men's work clothes to wrestle through the wringer. There was just the business of putting everything perfectly in place and doing quite a bit of polishing. Polish the rims of the burners of the stove after every use, polish the taps, polish the glass door to the deck till the glass disappears and people are in danger of smashing their faces against it.

The Montjoys' house was modern, with a flat roof and a deck extending over the water and a great many windows, which Mrs. Montjoy would have liked to see become as invisible as the glass door.

"But I have to be realistic," she said. "I know if you did that you'd hardly have time for anything else." She was not by any means a slave driver. Her tone with me was firm and slightly irritable, but that was the way it was with everybody. She was always on the lookout for inattention or incompetence, which she detested. *Sloppy* was a favorite word of condemnation. Others were *wishy-washy* and *unnecessary.* A lot of things that people did were unnecessary, and some of these were also wishy-washy. Other people might have used the words *arty* or *intellectual* or *permissive*. Mrs. Montjoy swept all those distinctions out of the way.

I ate my meals alone, between serving whoever was eating on the deck or in the dining room. I had almost made a horrible mistake about that. When Mrs. Montjoy caught me heading out to the deck with three plates—held in a show-off waitress-style—for the first lunch, she said, "Three plates there? Oh, yes, two out on the deck and yours in here. Right?"

I read as I ate. I had found a stack of old magazines—*Life* and *Look* and *Time* and *Collier's*—at the back of the broom closet. I could tell that Mrs. Montjoy did not like the idea of my sitting reading these magazines as I ate my lunch, but I did not quite know why. Was it because it was bad manners to eat as you read, or because I had not asked permission? More likely she saw my interest in things that had nothing to do with my work as a subtle kind of impudence. Unnecessary.

All she said was, "Those old magazines must be dreadfully dusty."

I said that I always wiped them off.

Sometimes there was a guest for lunch, a woman friend who had come over from one of the nearby islands. I heard Mrs. Montjoy say ". . . have to keep your girls happy or they'll be off to the hotel, off to the port. They can get jobs there so easily. It's not the way it used to be."

The other woman said, "That's so true."

"So you just make allowances," said Mrs. Montjoy. "You do the best with them you can." It took me a moment to realize who they were talking about. Me. "Girls" meant girls like me. I wondered, then, how I was being kept happy. By being taken along on the occasional alarming boat ride when Mrs. Montjoy went to get supplies? By being allowed to wear shorts and a blouse, or even a halter, instead of a uniform with a white collar and cuffs?

And what hotel was this? What port?

"What are you best at?" Mary Anne said. "What sports?"

After a moment's consideration, I said, "Volleyball." We had to play volleyball at school. I wasn't very good at it, but it was my best sport because it was the only one.

"Oh, I don't mean team sports," said Mary Anne. "I mean, what are you *best* at. Such as tennis. Or swimming or riding or what? My really best thing is riding, because that doesn't depend so much on your eyesight. Aunt Margaret's best used to be tennis and Nana's used to be tennis too, and Grandad's was always sailing, and Daddy's is swimming I guess and Uncle Stewart's is golf and sailing and Mother's is golf and swimming and sailing and tennis and everything, but maybe tennis a little bit the best of all. If my sister Jane hadn't died I don't know what hers would have been, but it might have been swimming because she could swim already and she was only three."

I had never been on a tennis court and the idea of going out in a sailboat or getting up on a horse terrified me. I could swim, but not very well. Golf to me was something that silly-looking men did in cartoons. The adults I knew never played any games that involved physical action. They sat down and rested when they were not working, which wasn't often. Though on winter evenings they might play cards. Euchre. Lost Heir. Not the kind of cards Mrs. Montjoy ever played.

"Everybody I know works too hard to do any sports," I said. "We don't even have a tennis court in our town and there isn't any golf course either." (Actually we had once had both these things, but there hadn't been the money to keep them up during the Depression and they had not been restored since.) "Nobody I know has a sailboat."

I did not mention that my town did have a hockey rink and a baseball park.

"Really?" said Mary Anne thoughtfully. "What do they do then?"

"*Work.* And they never have any money, all of their lives."

Then I told her that most people I knew had never seen a flush toilet unless it was in a public building and that sometimes old people (that is, people too old to work) had to stay in bed all winter in order to keep warm. Children walked barefoot until the frost came in order to save on shoe leather, and died of stomach aches that were really appendicitis because their parents had no money for a doctor. Sometimes people had eaten dandelion leaves, nothing else, for supper.

Not one of these statements—even the one about dandelion leaves—was completely a lie. I had heard of such things. The one about flush toilets perhaps came closest to the truth, but it applied to country people, not town people, and most of those it applied to would be of a generation before mine. But as I talked to Mary Anne all the isolated incidents and bizarre stories I had heard spread out in my mind, so that I could almost believe that I myself had walked with bare blue feet on cold mud—I who had benefited from cod liver oil and inoculations and been bundled up for school within an inch of my life, and had gone to bed hungry only because I refused to eat such things as junket or bread pudding or fried liver. And this false impression I was giving seemed justified, as if my exaggerations or near lies were substitutes for something I could not make clear.

How to make clear, for instance, the difference between the Montjoys' kitchen and our kitchen at home. You could not do that simply by mentioning the perfectly fresh and shining floor surfaces of one and the worn-out linoleum of the other, or the fact of soft water being pumped from a cistern into the sink contrasted with hot and cold water coming out of taps. You would have to say that you had in one case a kitchen that followed with absolute correctness a current notion of what a kitchen ought to be, and in the other a kitchen that changed occasionally with use and improvisation, but in many ways never changed at all, and belonged entirely to one family and to the years and decades of that family's life. And when I thought of that kitchen, with the combination wood and electric stove that I polished with waxed-paper bread wrappers, the dark old spice tins with their rusty rims kept from year to year in the cupboards, the barn clothes hanging by the door, it seemed as if I had to protect it from contempt—as if I had to protect a whole precious and intimate though hardly pleasant way of life from contempt. Contempt was what I imagined to be always waiting, swinging along on live wires, just under the skin and just behind the perceptions of people like the Montjoys.

"That isn't fair," said Mary Anne. "That's awful. I didn't know people could eat dandelion leaves." But then she brightened. "Why don't they go and catch some fish?"

"People who don't need the fish have come and caught them all already. Rich people. For fun."

Of course some of the people at home did catch fish when they had time, though others, including me, found the fish from our river too bony. But I thought that would keep Mary Anne quiet, especially since I knew that Mr. Montjoy went on fishing trips with his friends.

She could not stop mulling over the problem. "Couldn't they go to the Salvation Army?"

"They're too proud."

"Well I feel sorry for them," she said. "I feel really sorry for them, but I think that's stupid. What about the little babies and the children? They ought to think about them. Are the children too proud too?"

"Everybody's proud."

When Mr. Montjoy came to the island on weekends, there was always a great deal of noise and activity. Some of that was because there were visitors who came by boat to swim and have drinks and watch sailing races. But a lot of it was generated by Mr. Montjoy himself. He had a loud blustery voice and a thick body with a skin that would never take a tan. Every weekend he turned red from the sun, and during the week the burned skin peeled away and left him pink and muddy with freckles, ready to be burned again. When he took off his glasses you could see that one eye was quick and squinty and the other boldly blue but helpless-looking, as if caught in a trap.

His blustering was often about things that he had misplaced, or dropped, or bumped into. "Where the hell is the—?" he would say, or "You didn't happen to see the—?" So it seemed that he had also misplaced, or failed to grasp in the first place, even the name of the thing he was looking for. To console himself he might grab up a handful of peanuts or pretzels or whatever was nearby, and eat handful after handful until they were all gone. Then he would stare at the empty bowl as if that too astounded him.

One morning I heard him say, "Now where in hell is that—?" He was crashing around out on the deck.

"Your book?" said Mrs. Montjoy, in a tone of bright control. She was having her midmorning coffee.

"I thought I had it out here," he said. "I was reading it."

"The Book-of-the-Month one?" she said. "I think you left it in the living room."

She was right. I was vacuuming the living room, and a few moments before I had picked up a book pushed partway under the sofa. Its title was *Seven Gothic Tales.* The title made me want to open it, and even as I overheard the Montjoys' conversation I was reading, holding the book open in one hand and guiding the vacuum cleaner with the other. They couldn't see me from the deck.

"Nay, I speak from the heart," said Mira. "I have been trying for a long time to understand God. Now I have made friends with him. To love him truly you must love change, and you must love a joke, these being the true inclinations of his own heart."

"There it is," said Mr. Montjoy, who for a wonder had come into the room without his usual bumping and banging—or none at least that I had heard. "Good girl, you found my book. Now I remember. Last night I was reading it on the sofa."

"It was on the floor," I said. "I just picked it up."

He must have seen me reading it. He said, "It's a queer kind of book, but sometimes you want to read a book that isn't like all the others."

"I couldn't make heads or tails of it," said Mrs. Montjoy, coming in with the coffee tray. "We'll have to get out of the way here and let her get on with the vacuuming."

Mr. Montjoy went back to the mainland, and to the city, that evening. He was a bank director. That did not mean, apparently, that he worked in a bank. The day after he had gone I looked everywhere. I looked under the chairs and behind the curtains, in case he might have left that book behind. But I could not find it.

"I always thought it would be nice to live up here all the year round, the way you people do," said Mrs. Foley. She must have cast me again as the girl who brought the groceries. Some days she said, "I know who you are now. You're the new girl helping the Dutch woman in the kitchen. But I'm sorry, I just can't recall your name." And other days she let me walk by without giving any greeting or showing the least interest.

"We used to come up here in the winter," she said. "The bay would be frozen over and there would be a road across the ice. We used to go snowshoeing. Now that's something people don't do anymore. Do they? Snowshoeing?"

She didn't wait for me to answer. She leaned towards me. "Can you tell me something?" she said with embarrassment, speaking almost in a whisper. "Can you tell me where Jane is? I haven't seen her running around here for the longest time."

I said that I didn't know. She smiled as if I was teasing her, and reached out a hand to touch my face. I had been stooping down to listen to her, but now I straightened up, and her hand grazed my chest instead. It was a hot day and I was wearing my halter, so it happened that she touched my skin. Her hand was light and dry as a wood shaving, but the nail scraped me.

"I'm sure it's all right," she said.

After that I simply waved if she spoke to me and hurried on my way.

On a Saturday afternoon towards the end of August, the Montjoys gave a cocktail party. The party was given in honor of the friends they had staying with them that weekend—Mr. and Mrs. Hammond. A good many small silver forks and spoons had to be polished in preparation for this event, so Mrs. Montjoy decided that all the silver might as well be done at the same time. I did the polishing and she stood beside me, inspecting it.

On the day of the party, people arrived in motorboats and sailboats. Some of them went swimming, then sat around on the rocks in their bathing suits, or lay on the dock in the sun. Others came up to the house immediately and started drinking and talking in the living room or out on the deck. Some children had come with their parents, and older children by themselves, in their own boats. They were not children of Mary Anne's age—Mary Anne had been taken to stay with her friend Susan, on another island. There were a few very young ones, who came supplied with folding cribs and playpens, but most were around the same age as I was. Girls and boys fifteen or sixteen years old. They spent most of the afternoon in the water, shouting and diving and having races to the raft.

Mrs. Montjoy and I had been busy all morning, making all the different things to eat, which we now arranged on platters and offered to people. Making them had been fiddly and exasperating work. Stuffing various mixtures into mushroom caps and sticking one tiny slice of something on top of a tiny slice of something else on top of a precise fragment of toast or bread. All the shapes had to be perfect—perfect triangles, perfect rounds and squares, perfect diamonds.

Mrs. Hammond came into the kitchen several times and admired what we were doing.

"How marvellous everything looks," she said. "You notice I'm not offering to help. I'm a perfect mutt at this kind of thing."

I liked the way she said that. *I'm a perfect mutt.* I admired her husky voice, its weary good-humored tone, and the way she seemed to suggest that tiny geometrical bits of food were not so necessary, might even be a trifle silly. I wished I could be her, in a sleek black bathing suit with a tan like dark toast, shoulder-length smooth dark hair, orchid-colored lipstick.

Not that she looked happy. But her air of sullenness and complaint seemed glamorous to me, her hints of cloudy drama enviable. She and her husband were an altogether different type of rich people from Mr. and Mrs. Montjoy. They were more like the people I had read about in magazine stories and in books like *The Hucksters*—people who drank a lot and had love affairs and went to psychiatrists.

Her name was Carol and her husband's name was Ivan. I thought of them already by their first names—something I had never been tempted to do with the Montjoys.

Mrs. Montjoy had asked me to put on a dress, so I wore the pink and white striped cotton, with the smudged material at its waist tucked under the elasticized belt. Nearly everybody else was in shorts and bathing suits. I passed among them, offering food. I was not sure how to do this. Sometimes people were laughing or talking with such vigor that they didn't notice me, and I was afraid that their gestures would send the food bits flying. So I said, "Excuse me—would you like one of these?" in a raised voice that sounded very determined or even reproving. Then they looked at me with startled amusement, and I had the feeling that my interruption had become another joke.

"Enough passing for now," said Mrs. Montjoy. She gathered up some glasses and told me to wash them. "People never keep track of their own," she said. "It's easier just to wash them and bring in clean ones. And it's time to get the meatballs out of the fridge and heat them up. Could you do that? Watch the oven—it won't take long."

While I was busy in the kitchen I heard Mrs. Hammond calling, "Ivan! Ivan!" She was roaming through the back rooms of the house. But Mr. Hammond had come in through the kitchen door that led to the woods. He stood there and did not answer her. He came over to the counter and poured gin into his glass.

"Oh, Ivan, there you are," said Mrs. Hammond, coming in from the living room.

"Here I am," said Mr. Hammond.

"Me, too," she said. She shoved her glass along the counter.

He didn't pick it up. He pushed the gin towards her and spoke to me. "Are you having fun, Minnie?"

Mrs. Hammond gave a yelp of laughter. "Minnie? Where did you get the idea her name was Minnie?"

"Minnie," said Mr. Hammond. Ivan. He spoke in an artificial, dreamy voice. "Are you having fun, Minnie?"

"Oh yes," I said, in a voice that I meant to make as artificial as his. I was busy lifting the tiny Swedish meatballs from the oven and I wanted the Hammonds out of my way in case I dropped some. They would think that a big joke and probably report on me to Mrs. Montjoy, who would make me throw the dropped meatballs out and be annoyed at the waste. If I was alone when it happened I could just scoop them up off the floor.

Mr. Hammond said, "Good."

"I swam around the point," Mrs. Hammond said. "I'm working up to swimming around the entire island."

"Congratulations," Mr. Hammond said, in the same way that he had said "Good."

I wished that I hadn't sounded so chirpy and silly. I wished that I had matched his deeply skeptical and sophisticated tone.

"Well then," said Mrs. Hammond. Carol. "I'll leave you to it."

I had begun to spear the meatballs with toothpicks and arrange them on a platter. Ivan said, "Care for some help?" and tried to do the same, but his toothpicks missed and sent meatballs skittering onto the counter.

"Well," he said, but he seemed to lose track of his thoughts, so he turned away and took another drink. "Well, Minnie."

I knew something about him. I knew that the Hammonds were here for a special holiday because Mr. Hammond had lost his job. Mary Anne had told me this. "He's very depressed about it," she had said. "They won't be poor, though. Aunt Carol is rich."

He did not seem depressed to me. He seemed impatient—chiefly with Mrs. Hammond—but on the whole rather pleased with himself. He was tall and thin, he had dark hair combed straight back from his forehead, and his mustache was an ironic line above his upper lip. When he talked to me he leaned forward, as I had seen him doing earlier, when he talked to women in the living room. I had thought then that the word for him was *courtly*.

"Where do you go swimming, Minnie? Do you go swimming?"

"Yes," I said. "Down by the boathouse." I decided that his calling me Minnie was a special joke between us.

"Is that a good place?"

"Yes." It was, for me, because I liked being close to the dock. I had never, till this summer, swum in water that was over my head.

"Do you ever go in without your bathing suit on?"

I said, "No."

"You should try it."

Mrs. Montjoy came through the living-room doorway, asking if the meatballs were ready.

"This is certainly a hungry crowd," she said. "It's the swimming does it. How are you getting on, Ivan? Carol was just looking for you."

"She was here," said Mr. Hammond.

Mrs. Montjoy dropped parsley here and there among the meatballs. "Now," she said to me. "I think you've done about all you need to here. I think I can manage now. Why don't you just make yourself a sandwich and run along down to the boathouse?"

I said I wasn't hungry. Mr. Hammond had helped himself to more gin and ice cubes and had gone into the living room.

"Well. You'd better take something," Mrs. Montjoy said. "You'll be hungry later."

She meant that I was not to come back.

On my way to the boathouse I met a couple of the guests—girls of my own age, barefoot and in their wet bathing suits, breathlessly laughing. They had probably swum partway round the island and climbed out of the water at the boathouse. Now they were sneaking back to surprise somebody. They stepped aside politely, not to drip water on me, but did not stop laughing. Making way for my body without a glance at my face.

They were the sort of girls who would have squealed and made a fuss over me, if I had been a dog or a cat.

. . .

The noise of the party continued to rise. I lay down on my cot without taking off my dress. I had been on the go since early morning and I was tired. But I could not relax. After a while I got up and changed into my bathing suit and went down to swim. I climbed down the ladder into the water cautiously as I always did—I thought that I would go straight to the bottom and never come up if I jumped—and swam around in the shadows. The water washing my limbs made me think of what Mr. Hammond had said and I worked the straps of my bathing suit down, finally pulling out one arm after the other so that my breasts could float free. I swam that way, with the water sweetly dividing at my nipples . . .

I thought it was not impossible that Mr. Hammond might come looking for me. I thought of him touching me. (I could not figure out exactly how he would get into the water—I did not care to think of him stripping off his clothes. Perhaps he would squat down on the deck and I would swim over to him.) His fingers stroking my bare skin like ribbons of light. The thought of being touched and desired by a man that old—forty, forty-five?—was in some way repulsive, but I knew I would get pleasure from it, rather as you might get pleasure from being caressed by an amorous tame crocodile. Mr. Hammond's—Ivan's—skin might be smooth, but age and knowledge and corruptness would be on him like invisible warts and scales.

I dared to lift myself partly out of the water, holding with one hand to the dock. I bobbed up and down and rose into the air like a mermaid. Gleaming, with nobody to see.

Now I heard steps. I heard somebody coming. I sank down into the water and held still.

For a moment I believed that it was Mr. Hammond, and that I had actually entered the world of secret signals, abrupt and wordless forays of desire. I did not cover myself but shrank against the dock, in a paralyzed moment of horror and submission.

The boathouse light was switched on, and I turned around noiselessly in the water and saw that it was old Mr. Foley, still in his party outfit of white trousers and yachting cap and blazer. He had stayed for a couple of drinks and explained to everybody that Mrs. Foley was not up to the strain of seeing so many people but sent her best wishes to all.

He was moving things around on the tool shelf. Soon he either found what he wanted or put back what he had intended to put back, and he switched off the light and left. He never knew that I was there.

I pulled up my bathing suit and got out of the water and went up the stairs. My body seemed such a weight to me that I was out of breath when I got to the top.

The sound of the cocktail party went on and on. I had to do something to hold my own against it, so I started to write a letter to Dawna, who was my best friend at that time. I described the cocktail party in lurid terms—people vomited over the deck railing and a woman passed out, falling down on the sofa in such a way that part of her dress slid off and exposed a purple-nippled old breast (I called it a bezoom). I spoke of Mr. Hammond as a letch, though I added that he was very good-looking. I said that he had fondled me in the kitchen while my hands were busy with the meatballs and that later he had followed me to the boathouse and grabbed me on the stairs. But I had kicked him where he wouldn't forget and he had retreated. *Scurried away,* I said.

"So hold your breath for the next installment," I wrote. "Entitled, 'Sordid Adventures of a Kitchen Maid.' Or 'Ravaged on the Rocks of Georgian Bay.'"

When I saw that I had written "ravaged" instead of "ravished," I thought I could let it go, because Dawna would never know the difference. But I realized that the part about Mr. Hammond was overdone, even for that sort of letter, and then the whole thing filled me with shame and a sense of my own failure and loneliness. I crumpled it up. There had not been any point in writing this letter except to assure myself that I had some contact with the world and that exciting things—sexual things—happened to me. And I hadn't. They didn't.

"Mrs. Foley asked me where Jane was," I had said, when Mrs. Montjoy and I were doing the silver—or when she was keeping an eye on me doing the silver. "Was Jane one of the other girls who worked here in the summer?"

I thought for a moment that she might not answer, but she did.

"Jane was my other daughter," she said. "She was Mary Anne's sister. She died."

I said, "Oh. I didn't know." I said, "Oh. I'm sorry.

"Did she die of polio?" I said, because I did not have the sense, or you might say the decency, not to go on. And in those days children still died of polio, every summer.

"No," said Mrs. Montjoy. "She was killed when my husband moved the dresser in our bedroom. He was looking for something he thought he might have dropped behind it. He didn't realize she was in the way. One of the casters caught on the rug and the whole thing toppled over on her."

I knew every bit of this, of course. Mary Anne had already told me. She had told me even before Mrs. Foley asked me where Jane was and clawed at my breast.

"How awful," I said.

"Well. It was just one of those things."

My deception made me feel queasy. I dropped a fork on the floor.

Mrs. Montjoy picked it up.

"Remember to wash this again."

How strange that I did not question my right to pry, to barge in and bring this to the surface. Part of the reason must have been that in the society I came from, things like that were never buried for good, but ritualistically resurrected, and that such horrors were like a badge people wore—or, mostly, that women wore—throughout their lives.

Also it may have been because I would never quite give up when it came to demanding intimacy, or at least some kind of equality, even with a person I did not like.

Cruelty was a thing I could not recognize in myself. I thought I was blameless here, and in any dealings with this family. All because of being young, and poor, and knowing about Nausicaa.

I did not have the grace or fortitude to be a servant.

On my last Sunday I was alone in the boathouse, packing up my things in the suitcase I had brought—the same suitcase that had gone with my mother and father on their wedding trip and the only one we had in the house. When I pulled it out from under my cot and opened it up, it smelled of home—of the closet at the end of the upstairs hall where it usually sat, close to the mothballed winter coats and the rubber sheet once used on children's beds. But when you got it out at home it always smelled faintly of trains and coal fires and cities—of travel.

I heard steps on the path, a stumbling step into the boat-house, a rapping on the wall. It was Mr. Montjoy.

"Are you up there? Are you up there?"

His voice was boisterous, jovial, as I had heard it before when he had been drinking. As of course he had been drinking—for once again there were people visiting, celebrating the end of summer. I came to the top of the stairs. He had a hand against the wall to steady himself—a boat had gone by out in the channel and sent its waves into the boathouse.

"See here," said Mr. Montjoy, looking up at me with frowning concentration. "See here—I thought I might as well bring this down and give it to you while I thought of it.

"This book," he said.

He was holding *Seven Gothic Tales.*

"Because I saw you were looking in it that day," he said. "It seemed to me you were interested. So now I finished it and I thought I might as well pass it along to you. It occurred to me to pass it along to you. I thought, maybe you might enjoy it."

I said, "Thank you."

"I'm probably not going to read it again though I thought it was very interesting. Very unusual."

"Thank you very much."

"That's all right. I thought you might enjoy it."

"Yes," I said.

"Well then. I hope you will."

"Thank you."

"Well then," he said. "Good-bye."

I said, "Thank you. Good-bye."

Why were we saying good-bye when we were certain to see each other again before we left the island, and before I got on the train? It might have meant that this incident, of his giving me the book, was to be closed, and I was not to reveal or refer to it. Which I didn't. Or it might have been just that he was drunk and did not realize that he would see me later. Drunk or not, I see him now as pure of motive, leaning against the boathouse wall. A person who could think me worthy of this gift. Of this book.

At the moment, though, I didn't feel particularly pleased, or grateful, in spite of my repeated thank-yous. I was too startled, and in some way embarrassed. The thought of having a little corner of myself come to light, and be truly understood, stirred up alarm, just as much as being taken no notice of stirred up resentment. And Mr. Mountjoy was probably the person who interested me least, whose regard meant the least to me, of all the people I had met that summer.

He left the boathouse and I heard him stumping along the path, back to his wife and his guests. I pushed the suitcase aside and sat down on the cot. I opened the book just anywhere, as I had done the first time, and began to read.

> The walls of the room had once been painted crimson, but with time the colour had faded into a richness of hues, like a glassful of dying roses . . . Some potpourri was being burned on the tall stove, on the sides of which Neptune, with a trident, steered his team of horses through high waves . . .

I forgot Mr. Mountjoy almost immediately. In hardly any time at all I came to believe that this gift had always belonged to me.

The Ticket

Sometimes I dream about my grandmother and her sister, my Aunt Charlie—who was of course not my aunt but my great-aunt. I dream that they are still living in the house where they lived for twenty years or so, until my grandmother's death and Aunt Charlie's removal to a nursing home, which happened soon afterwards. I am shocked to find that they are alive and I am amazed, ashamed, to think that I have not visited them, have not gone near them in all this time. Forty years or more. Their house is just the same, though full of twilight, and they themselves are pretty much the same—they wear the same sort of dresses and aprons and hairstyles as they always did. Coiled and drooping hair unacquainted with the hairdresser, dresses of dark rayon or cotton printed with small flowers or geometric shapes—no pantsuits or snappy slogans or turquoise or buttercup or peony-pink materials.

But they seem to be flattened out, to move hardly at all, to use their voices with difficulty. I ask them how they manage. How do they get their groceries, for instance? Do they watch television? Do they keep up with the world? They say that they do all right. Don't worry. But every day they have been waiting, waiting to see if I would come.

God help us. Every day. And even now I'm in a hurry, I

can't stay. I tell them that I have so much to do, but I'll be back soon. They say yes, yes, that will be fine. Soon.

At Christmastime I was to be married, and after that I was going to live in Vancouver. The year was 1951. My grandmother and Aunt Charlie—one younger, one older, than I am now—were packing the trunks I would take with me. One was a sturdy old humpbacked trunk that had been in the family for a long time. I wondered out loud if it had come across the Atlantic Ocean with them.

Who knows, said my grandmother.

A hunger for history, even family history, did not rate highly with her. All that sort of thing was an indulgence, a waste of time—like reading the continued story in the daily paper. Which she did herself, but still deplored.

The other trunk was new, with metal corners, bought for the purpose. It was Aunt Charlie's gift—her income was larger than my grandmother's, though that did not mean it was very large. Just enough so that it could stretch to occasional unplanned purchases. An armchair for the living room, upholstered in salmon-colored brocade (protected, unless company was coming, by a plastic cover). A reading lamp (its shade also wrapped in plastic). My marriage trunk.

"That's her wedding present?" my husband would say, later. "A *trunk*?" Because in his family something like a trunk was what you went out and bought, when you needed it. No passing it off as a present.

The things in the humpbacked trunk were breakable, wrapped in things that were not breakable. Dishes, glasses, pitchers, vases, wrapped in newspaper and further protected by dishtowels, bath towels, crocheted doilies and afghans, embroidered table mats. The big flat truck was mostly full of bed-sheets, tablecloths (one of them, too, was crocheted), quilts, pillowcases, also some large flat breakable things like a framed picture painted by Marian, the sister of my grandmother and Aunt Charlie, who had died young. It was a picture of an eagle on a lone branch, with a blue sea and feathery trees far below. Marian at the age of fourteen had copied it from a calendar, and the next summer she had died of typhoid fever.

Some of those things were wedding presents, from members of my family, arriving early, but most were things that had been made for me to start housekeeping with. The quilts, the afghans, the crocheted articles, the pillowcases with their cheek-scratching embroidery. I had not prepared a thing, but my grandmother and Aunt Charlie had been busy, even if my prospects had seemed bleak for quite a while. And my mother had put away a few fancy water goblets, some teaspoons, a willow platter, from the brief heady period when she had dealt in antiques, before the stiffness and trembling of her limbs made any business—and driving, walking, finally even talking—too difficult.

The presents from my husband's family were packed in the shops where they were purchased, and shipped to Vancouver. Silver serving dishes, heavy table linen, half a dozen crystal wineglasses. The sort of household goods that my in-laws and their friends were used to having around them.

Nothing in my trunks, as it happened, came up to scratch. My mother's goblets were pressed glass and the willow platter was heavy kitchen china. Such things did not come into vogue until years later, and for some people, never. The six teaspoons dating from the nineteenth century were not sterling. The quilts were for an old-fashioned bed, narrower than the bed my husband had bought for us. The afghans and the doilies and the cushion covers and—needless to say—the picture copied from a calendar were next thing to a joke.

But my husband did concede that a good job had been done with the packing, not a thing was broken. He was embarrassed but attempting to be kind. Afterwards when I tried putting some of those things where they could be seen by anybody coming into our place, he had to speak plainly. And I myself saw the point.

I was nineteen years old when I became engaged, twenty on my wedding day. My husband was the first boyfriend I had ever had. The outlook had not been promising. During that same autumn, my father and my brother were repairing the cover on the well in our side yard, and my brother said, "We better do a good job here. Because if this guy falls in she'll never get another."

And that became a favorite joke in the family. Of course I laughed too. But what those around me had worried about had also been a worry of mine, at least intermittently. What was wrong with me? It wasn't a matter of looks. Something else. Something else, clear as a warning bell, scattered the possible boyfriends and potential husbands out of my path. I did have faith, though, that whatever it was would die down, once I got away from home, and from this town.

And that had happened. Suddenly, overwhelmingly. Michael had fallen in love with me and was set on marrying me. A tall, good-looking, strong, black-haired, intelligent, ambitious young man had pinned his hopes on me. He had bought me a diamond ring. He had found a job in Vancouver that was certain to lead to better things, and had bound himself to support me and our children, for the rest of his life. Nothing would make him happier.

He said so, and I believed it was true.

Most of the time I could hardly credit my luck. He wrote that he loved me, and I wrote back that I loved him. I thought about how handsome he was, and smart and trustworthy. Just before he left we had slept together—no, had sex together, on the bumpy ground under a willow tree by a river's edge—and we believed that this was as serious as a marriage ceremony, because we could not possibly, now, do the same thing with anybody else.

This was the first fall since I was five years old in which I was not spending my weekdays at school. I stayed at home and did housework. I was very much needed there. My mother was no longer able to grasp the handle of a broom or pull the covers up on a bed. There would have to be somebody found to help, after I went away, but for now I took it all on myself.

The routine enveloped me, and soon it was hard to believe that a year ago I had sat at a library table on Monday mornings, instead of getting up early to heat water on the stove to fill the washing machine and later on feeding the wet clothes through the wringer and finally hanging them on the line. Or that I had eaten my supper at drugstore counters, a sandwich prepared by somebody else.

I waxed the worn linoleum. I ironed the dishtowels and pyjamas as well as the shirts and blouses, I scoured the battered pots and pans and took steel wool to the blackened metal shelves behind the stove. These were the things that counted then, in the homes of the poor. Nobody thought of replacing what was there, just of keeping everything decent, for as long as possible, and then some. Such efforts kept a line in place, between respectable striving and raggedy defeat. And I cared the more for this the closer I came to being a deserter.

Reports of housekeeping found their way into letters to Michael and he was irritated. During the brief visit he had made to my home he had seen much that surprised him in an unpleasant way and that made him all the more resolute about rescuing me. And now because I had nothing else to write about and because I wanted to explain why my letters had to be short, he was forced to read about how I was immersing myself in daily chores in the very place, the very life, that I ought to be hastening to leave.

To his way of thinking, I ought to be longing to scrape the home-dirt off my shoes. Concentrating on the life, the home, that we would make together.

I did take a couple of hours off some afternoons, but what I did then, if I had written about it, would not have satisfied him much better. I would tuck my mother in for her second nap of the day and give the kitchen counters their final wipe and walk from our house on the far edge of town to the main street, where I did a bit of shopping and went to the library to return one book and take out another. I had not given up reading, though it seemed that the books I read now were not so harsh or demanding as the books I had been reading a year before. I read the short stories of A. E. Coppard—one of them had a title I found permanently seductive, though I can't remember anything else about it. "Dusky Ruth." And I read a short novel by John Galsworthy, which had a line on the title page that beguiled me.

The apple tree, the singing and the gold . . .

My business on the main street finished, I went to visit my

grandmother and Aunt Charlie. Sometimes—most times—I would rather have walked around alone, but I felt I could not neglect them, when they were doing so much to help me. I could not walk around here in a reverie, anyway, as I could have done in the city where I went to college. In those days nobody in town went for walks, except for some proprietary old men who strode around observing and criticizing any municipal projects. People were sure to spot you if you were noticed in a part of town where you had no particular reason to be. Then somebody would say, *we seen you the other day*— and you were supposed to explain.

And yet the town was enticing to me, it was dreamy in these autumn days. It was spellbound, with a melancholy light on the gray or yellow brick walls, and a peculiar stillness, now that the birds had flown south and the reaping machines in the country round about were silent. One day as I walked up the hill on Christena Street, towards my grandmother's house, I heard some lines in my head, the beginning of a story.

All over the town the leaves fell. Softly, silently the yellow leaves fell—it was autumn.

And I actually did write a story, then or sometime later, beginning with these sentences—I can't remember what it was about. Except that somebody pointed out that naturally it was autumn, and that it was foolish and self-consciously poetic to say so. Why else would the leaves be falling, unless the trees in the town had developed some sort of leaf plague?

My grandmother had a horse named after her, when she was young. This was meant to be an honor. The horse's name, and my grandmother's name, was Selina. The horse—a mare, naturally—was said to be *a high stepper*, which meant that she was lively, energetic, and apt to prance about in her own style. So my grandmother herself must have been a high stepper. There were a lot of dances then in which this tendency could be displayed—square dances, polkas, schottisches. And my grandmother was a noticeable young woman anyway—she was tall, busty, slim-waisted, with long strong legs and dark-red, wildly curly hair. And that audacious patch of sky blue in one of the irises of her hazel eyes.

All these things would add up, and be added to, by something in her personality, and surely that was what the man would be trying to comment on, when he paid her the compliment of giving her name to his mare.

This man was not the one who was believed to be in love with her (and whom she was believed to be in love with). Just an admiring neighbor.

The man she was in love with was not the man she married, either. He was not my grandfather. But he was someone she knew all her life, and in fact I met him once. Maybe more than once, when I was a child, but once that I can remember.

It was when I was staying with my grandmother, in her house in Downey. And it was after she became a widow but before Aunt Charlie became one too. When they had both become widows they moved together to the town outside which we lived.

Usually it was summer when I stayed in Downey, but this was on a wintry day, with a light snow falling. Early winter, because there was hardly any snow on the ground. I would have been five or six years old. My parents must have left me there for the day. Perhaps they had to go to a funeral, or take my little sister, who was frail and mildly diabetic, to see a city doctor.

In the afternoon we walked across the road, to enter the

grounds of the house where Henrietta Sharples lived. It was the largest house I had ever been in and its property ran right from one street to another. I looked forward to going there, because I was allowed to run free and look at anything I liked, and Henrietta always kept a bowl full of toffees wrapped in glistening red or green or gold or violet paper. As far as Henrietta was concerned I could have eaten all of them, but my grandmother kept an eye on me and fixed a limit.

Today we made a detour. Instead of going to Henrietta's back door we turned towards a cottage on her grounds, to the side of her house. The woman who opened the door had a puff of white hair, glowing pink skin, and a great breadth of stomach, swathed in the sort of bib apron most women wore then, indoors. I was told to call her Aunt Mabel. We sat in her kitchen, which was very hot, but we did not take off our coats because it was to be just a short call. My grandmother had brought something in a bowl under a napkin which she gave to Aunt Mabel—it might have been fresh muffins, or tea biscuits, or some warm applesauce. And the fact that we had brought it did not mean that Aunt Mabel needed any special charity. If a woman had been baking or cooking she often took an offering along when she went to her neighbor's house. Very likely Aunt Mabel protested against such generosity, as was the custom, and then, accepting, made a great fuss about how good it smelled and how good whatever it was would taste.

Then she probably got busy offering something of her own, insisting on at least making a cup of tea, and I seem to hear my grandmother saying no, no, we had just dropped in for a moment. She could have explained further that we were on our way to the Sharples house. Perhaps she wouldn't say the name, or that we were going for a proper visit. She might just say that we couldn't stop, we were going to drop in across the way. As if we were on a series of errands. She always spoke of going to visit Henrietta as going across the way, so that she would never seem to be flaunting the friendship. Never *bragging.*

There was a noise in the woodshed attached to the cottage, and then a man came in, flushed from the cold or exercise, and said hello to my grandmother and shook hands with me. I hated the way old men might greet me with a poke in the stomach or a tickle under the arms, but this handshake seemed cordial and proper.

That was all I really noticed about him, except that he was tall and not large around the stomach like Aunt Mabel, though like her he had thick white hair. His name was Uncle Leo. His hand was cold, probably from splitting wood for Henrietta's fireplaces, or putting bags around her bushes to protect them from the frost.

It was later, though, that I learned about his doing such chores for Henrietta. He did her outdoor winter work—shovelling snow and knocking down icicles and keeping up the wood supply. And trimming the hedges and cutting the grass in the summer. In return he and Aunt Mabel had the cottage rent-free, and maybe he was paid something as well. He did this for a couple of years, until he died. He died of pneumonia, or a failure of the heart, the sort of thing you expected people of his age to die of.

I was told to call him Uncle, just as I had been told to call his wife Aunt, and I didn't question this or wonder how they were related to me. It wasn't the first time I had taken on board an aunt or an uncle who was mysterious and marginal.

Uncle Leo and Aunt Mabel could not have been living there very long, with Uncle Leo employed in this way, before my grandmother and I made our call. We had never taken any notice of the cottage, or of the people living there, on previous visits to Henrietta. So it seems likely that my grandmother had suggested the arrangement to Henrietta. *Put a word in,* as people would have said. Put a word in because Uncle Leo was *on his uppers?*

I don't know. I never asked anybody. Soon the call was over, and my grandmother and I were crossing the gravelled drive and knocking on the back door and Henrietta was calling through the keyhole, "Go away, I can see you, what are you peddling today?" Then she threw open the door and squeezed me in her bony arms and exclaimed, "You little rascal—why didn't you say it was you? Who's this old gypsy woman you brought along?"

My grandmother did not approve of women smoking or of anybody drinking.

Henrietta smoked and drank.

My grandmother thought that slacks on women were abominable and sunglasses an affectation. Henrietta wore both.

My grandmother played euchre but thought it was snooty to play bridge. Henrietta played bridge.

The list could go on. Henrietta was not an unusual woman of her time but she was an unusual woman in that town.

She and my grandmother sat in front of the fire in the back living room and talked and laughed through the afternoon while I roamed about, free to examine the blue-flowered toilet in the bathroom or look through the ruby glass of the china-cabinet door. Henrietta's voice was loud and it was mostly her talk I could hear. It was punctuated by hoots of laughter—very much the kind of laughter I would recognize now as accompanying a woman's confession of gigantic folly or some tale of perfidy (male perfidy?) beyond belief.

Later on I was to hear stories about Henrietta, about the man she had jilted and the man she was in love with—a married man she continued to see all her life—and I don't doubt that she talked about that, and about other things which I don't know, and probably my grandmother talked about her own life, not so freely perhaps, or raucously, but still in the same vein, as a story that amazed her, that she could hardly believe was her own. For it seems to me that my grandmother talked in that house as she did not do—or no longer did—anywhere else. But I never got to ask Henrietta what was confided, what was said, because she died in a car accident—she was always a foolhardy driver—sometime before my grandmother died. And very likely she would not have told me anyway.

This is the story, or as much as I know of it.

My grandmother, the man she loved—Leo—and the man she married—my grandfather—all lived within a few miles of each other. She would have gone to school with Leo, who was only three or four years older than she was. But not with my grandfather, who was ten years older. The two men were cousins and bore the same surname. They did not look alike— though both were good-looking, as far as I can tell. My grandfather in his wedding picture stands erect—he is only a little taller than my grandmother, who has got her waist down to twenty-four inches for the occasion, and in her flounced white dress looks chastened and demure. He is broad-shouldered, sturdy, unsmiling, with a look of being seriously intelligent, proud, committed to whatever is required of him. And he has not changed much in the enlarged snapshot I have of him, taken when he was in his fifties or early sixties. A man who still has his strength, his competence, a necessary amount of geniality and a large reserve, a man who is respected for good reason and no more disappointed than a person can expect to be, at his age.

My memories of him come from the year he spent in bed, the year before he died, or as you might say, the year when he was dying. He was seventy-five and his heart was failing, little by little. My father, at the same age, and in the same condition, chose to have an operation, and died a few days afterwards without regaining consciousness. My grandfather had not that option.

I remember that his bed was downstairs, in the dining room, that he kept a bag of peppermints under his pillow—supposedly a secret from my grandmother—and offered them to me when she was busy elsewhere. He had a pleasant smell of shaving soap and tobacco (I was wary about the way old people smelled, and relieved when it was inoffensive), and his manner with me was kindly but not intrusive.

Then he was dead, and I went to his funeral with my mother and father. I did not want to look at him so I did not have to. My grandmother's eyes were red, with the skin wrinkled up all around them. The attention she paid to me was scanty, so I went outside and rolled down the grassy hill between the house and the sidewalk. This had been a favorite thing for me to do when I stayed there and nobody had ever objected to it. But this time my mother called me in and shook bits of grass out of my dress. She was in the state of exasperation that meant I was behaving in a way that she would get the blame for.

What did my grandfather as a young man think of the fact that my grandmother as a young girl was in love with his cousin Leo? Did he have his eye on her then? Was he hopeful, were his hopes dashed by the fiery courtship going on before his eyes? For it was fiery—a notable romance carried on with spats and reconciliations that he and practically everybody in the community was bound to be aware of. How could a romance be carried on in those days except publicly, if the girl was respectable? Walks to the woods were out of the question, as was ducking out of dances. Visits to the girl's house involved the whole family, at least until the couple became engaged. Rides in an open buggy were eyed from every kitchen window along the road, and if a ride after dark was ever contrived it was within a discouraging time limit.

Nevertheless, intimacies were managed. My grandmother's younger sisters, Charlie and Marian, were sent along as her chaperones, but were sometimes tricked and bribed.

"They were as crazy about each other as a pair can be," Aunt Charlie said, when she told me about this. "They were devils."

This conversation took place during that fall before my marriage, the time of the trunk-packing. My grandmother had been forced to take time out from the work, she was upstairs in bed, suffering from her phlebitis. For years she had worn elastic bandages to support her bulging varicose veins. So ugly in her opinion—both bandages and veins—that she hated anybody to see them. Aunt Charlie told me confidentially that the veins were wrapped around her legs like big black snakes. Every dozen years or so a vein became inflamed, and then she had to lie still, lest a blood clot should break loose and find its way to her heart.

For the three or four days that my grandmother stayed in bed, Aunt Charlie did not get on well with the packing. She was used to my grandmother's making the decisions.

"Selina's the boss," she said without resentment. "I don't know where I'm at without Selina." (And this proved to be true—after my grandmother died, Aunt Charlie's grasp on daily life immediately faltered, and she had to be taken away to the nursing home, where she died at the age of ninety-eight, after a long silence.)

Instead of tackling the job together she and I sat at the kitchen table and drank coffee and talked. Or whispered. Aunt Charlie had a way of whispering. In this case there might have been a reason—my grandmother with her unimpaired hearing was just over our heads—but often there was none. Her whispering seemed merely to exercise her charm—nearly everybody found her charming—to draw you in to a cozier, more significant sort of conversation, even if the words she was saying were only something about the weather, not—as now—about the stormy young life of my grandmother.

What happened? I was half-hoping and half-afraid to discover that my grandmother, in those days when she had never dreamt of becoming my grandmother, had found herself pregnant.

Wild as she was and cunning as love makes you, she did not.

But another girl did. Another woman, you might say, because she was eight years older than the accused father.

Leo.

The woman worked in a dry-goods store in town.

"And her reputation was not what you might call Simon-pure," Aunt Charlie said, as if this was a sad reluctant revelation.

There had often been other girls, other women. That was what the spats had been about. That was what had caused my grandmother to kick her suitor in the shins and shove him out of his own buggy and drive home by herself with his horse.

That was why she had thrown a box of chocolates in his face. And then stamped on them, so they couldn't be picked up and enjoyed, if he should be so nonchalant and greedy as to try.

But this time she was calm as an iceberg.

What she said was, "Well, you'll have to go and marry her, won't you just?"

He said he wasn't all that sure it was his.

And she said, "But you're not sure it isn't."

He said that it could all be fixed up if he agreed to pay for the support. He said he was pretty sure that was all that she was after.

"But it's not all I'm after," Selina said. Then she said that what she was after was for him to do what was right.

And she won. In a very short time he and the woman from the dry-goods store were married. And not so long after that, my grandmother—Selina—was also married, to my grandfather. She chose the same time as I had done—dead of winter—for her wedding.

Leo's baby—if it was his, and it probably was—was born in late spring and by the time it was delivered it was dead. Its mother did not last more than an hour longer.

Soon a letter came, addressed to Charlie. But it wasn't for her at all. Inside was another letter, that she was to take to Selina.

Selina read it and laughed. "Tell him I'm as big as a barn," she said. Though she was hardly showing at all, and that was the first Charlie knew that she was pregnant.

"And tell him the last thing I need is any more fool letters from anybody like him."

The baby that she was carrying then was my father, born ten months after the wedding with considerable difficulty for the mother. He was the only child that she and my grandfather would ever have. I asked Aunt Charlie why. Was there some injury to my grandmother, or some inherent problem that made childbirth too risky? Obviously it wasn't that she had difficulty conceiving, I said, since my father must have been started a month after the wedding.

A silence, and then Aunt Charlie said, "I wouldn't know about that." She did not whisper but spoke in a normally raised, and slightly distant, slightly wounded or reproachful voice.

Why this withdrawal? What had wounded her? I think it was my clinical question, my use of a word like *conceiving*. It might be 1951 and I was soon to be married, and she had just been telling me a story about passion and unlucky conception. But still it would not do, it did not do, for a young woman— for any woman—to speak so coolly, knowledgeably, shamelessly, about those things. *Conceiving*, indeed.

There might have been another reason for Aunt Charlie's response, which I did not think of at the time. Aunt Charlie and Uncle Cyril had never had children. As far as I know there was never even a pregnancy. So I could have stumbled into sensitive territory.

It looked for a moment as if Aunt Charlie was not going to go on with her story. She seemed to have decided that I was not deserving of it. But after a moment she could not help herself.

Leo took off, then, he went places. He worked with a lumbering crew in Northern Ontario. He went with a harvesters' excursion and became a hired man out west. When he came back, years later, he had a wife with him and somewhere he had learned house carpentry and roofing, so he did that. The wife was a nice person, she had been a schoolteacher. Somewhere along the line she had a baby, but it died, like the other. She and Leo lived in town, and did not go to a local church—

she belonged to some freak religion of the sort they had out west. So nobody got to know her very well. Nobody even knew that she had leukemia until shortly before she died of it. It was the first case of leukemia that people had heard of in this part of the country.

Leo stayed on, he got work. He began to visit more with his relatives. He got a car, and would drive out to see them. The word got around that he was planning to marry for a third time, and that she was a widow from somewhere down near Stratford.

But before this he showed up at my grandmother's house one weekday afternoon. It was the time of year—after frost but before heavy snow—when my grandfather and my father, who was through with school by that time, were hauling firewood from the bush. They must have seen the car but they went on with what they were doing. My grandfather didn't come up to the house to greet his cousin.

And anyway, Leo and my grandmother didn't stay in the house, which they could have had all to themselves. My grandmother saw fit to put on her coat and they went out to the car. And did not stay sitting there either, but drove down the lane and then along the road to the highway, where they turned around and drove back. They did this several times, in full view of anybody who looked out the windows of any farmhouse along the road. And by this time everybody along the road knew Leo's car.

During this drive Leo asked my grandmother to come away with him. He told her that he was still a free agent, not yet committed to the widow. And presumably he mentioned that he was still in love. With her. My grandmother. Selina.

My grandmother reminded him that she herself was not

free, whatever he might be, and so the state of her feelings did not come into it.

"And the sharper she spoke," said Aunt Charlie, with one or two choppy little nods of her head, "why, the sharper she spoke to him, the more her heart cracked open. Surely it did."

Leo drove her home. He married the widow. The one I had been told to call Aunt Mabel.

"If Selina knew I told you anything about this, my name would be mud," said Aunt Charlie.

I had three marriages to study, fairly close-up, in this early part of my life. My parents' marriage—I suppose you might say that it was the most close-up, but in a way it was the most mysterious and remote, because of my childish difficulty in thinking of my parents as having any connection but the one they had through myself. My parents, like most other parents I knew, called each other Mother and Daddy. They did this even in conversations that had nothing to do with their children. They seemed to have forgotten each other's first names. And since there was never any thought of their divorcing or separating—I did not know of any parents, or any couples, who had done that—I did not have to be gauging their feelings or anxiously paying attention to the weather between them, as children often do nowadays. As far as I was concerned they were mostly caretakers—of the house, the farm, the animals, and us children.

When my mother became sick—permanently sick, not just troubled with odd symptoms—the balance was altered. This happened when I was around twelve or thirteen years old. From then on she was weighing the family down on one side,

and we—my father and brother and sister and I—were holding it up to a kind of normality on the other. So my father
seemed to belong with us more than he did with her. She was
three years older than he was, anyway—being born in the
nineteenth century while he was born in the twentieth, and as
her long siege progressed she began to seem more like his
mother than his wife, and for us more like an elderly relative in
our charge, than a mother.

I did know that her being older was one of the things that
my grandmother had thought unsuitable about my mother
from the start. Other things emerged soon enough—the fact
that my mother learned to drive the car, that her style of dress
verged on the original, that she joined the secular Women's
Institute rather than the United Church Missionary Society,
worst of all that she began to go about the countryside selling
fur scarves and capes made from foxes my father raised, and was
branching off into the antique business when her health began
to go awry. And unfair as it might be to think so—and she herself knowing that it was unfair—my grandmother still could
not help seeing this illness that went undiagnosed for so long,
and was rare at my mother's age, as being somehow another
show of willfulness, another grab at attention.

My grandparents' marriage was not one I ever saw in
action, but I heard reports. From my mother, who did not care
for my grandmother any more than my grandmother cared for
her—and as I grew older, from other people as well, who had
no axes to grind. Neighbors who had called in on their way
home from school when they were children reported on my
grandmother's homemade marshmallows and her teasing and
laughing, but said that they had been slightly afraid of my
grandfather. Not that he was bad-tempered or mean—just
silent. People had great respect for him—he served for years on

the township council and he was known as the person to go to whenever you had to have help in filling out a document, or in writing a business letter, or needed to have some new government notion explained. He was an efficient farmer, an excellent manager, but the object of his managing was not to make more money—it was to have more leisure for his reading. His silences made people uneasy, and they thought that he was not much company for a woman like my grandmother. The two of them were said to be as unalike as if they came from the opposite sides of the moon.

My father, growing up in this house of silence, never said that he found it particularly uncomfortable. On a farm there is always so much to do. Getting through the seasonal work was what made up the content of a life—or it did then—and that was what most marriages boiled down to.

He did notice, though, how his mother became a different person, how she burst into gaiety, when company came.

There was a violin in the parlor, and he was nearly grown up before he knew why it was there—that it belonged to his father, and that his father used to play it.

My mother said that her father-in-law had been a fine old gentleman, dignified and clever, and that she didn't wonder at his silence, because my grandmother was always irritated with him because of some little thing.

If I had asked Aunt Charlie bluntly whether my grandparents had been unhappy together, she would have turned reproachful again. I did ask her what my grandfather was like, besides being silent. I said that I couldn't remember him, really.

"He was very smart. And very fair. Though you wouldn't want to cross him."

"Mother said that Grandma was always annoyed with him."

"I wouldn't know where your mother got that."

If you looked at the family photograph taken when they were young, and before her sister Marian died, you would say that my grandmother had grabbed off most of the looks in the family. Her height, her proud posture, her magnificent hair. She isn't just smiling for the photographer—she seems to be biting off a laugh. Such vitality, such confidence. And she never lost the posture, or more than a quarter of an inch of the height. But at the time I am remembering (a time, as I have said, when they were both around the age that I am now), Aunt Charlie was the one people spoke of as being such a nice-looking old lady. She had those clear blue eyes, the color of chicory flowers, and a prevailing grace in her movements, a pretty tilt of the head. *Winsome,* would be the word.

Aunt Charlie's marriage was the one that I had been best able to observe, because Uncle Cyril had not died till I was twelve.

He was a heavily built man with a large head, made massive by thick curly hair. He wore glasses, with one lens of dark amber glass, hiding the eye that had been injured when he was a child. I don't know if this eye was entirely blind. I never saw it, and it made me sick to think of it—I imagined a mound of dark quivering jelly. He was allowed to drive a car, at any rate, and he drove very badly. I remember my mother coming home and saying that she had seen him and Aunt Charlie in town, he had made a U-turn in the middle of the street and she had no idea how he was allowed to get away with it.

"Charlie takes her life in her hands every time she gets into that car."

He was allowed to get away with it, I suppose, because he was an important person locally, well-known and well-liked, sociable and confident. Like my grandfather he was a farmer, but he did not spend much time farming. He was a notary public and the clerk of the township he lived in, and he was a force in the Liberal Party. There was some money that did not come from farming. From mortgages maybe—there was talk of investments. He and Aunt Charlie kept some cows, but no other livestock. I remember seeing him in the stable, turning the cream separator, wearing a shirt and his suit-vest, with his fountain pen and Eversharp pencil clipped to the vest pocket. I don't remember his actually milking the cows. Did Aunt Charlie do it all, or did they have a hired man?

If Aunt Charlie was alarmed by his driving she never showed it. Their affection was legendary. The word *love* was not used. They were said to be *fond of each other.* My father commented to me, some time after Uncle Cyril's death, that Uncle Cyril and Aunt Charlie had been truly fond of each other. I don't know what brought this up—we were driving in the car at the time, and maybe there had been some comment—some joke—about Uncle Cyril's driving. My father emphasized *truly*, as if to acknowledge that this was how married people were supposed to feel about each other, and that they might even claim to feel so, but that in fact such a condition was rare.

For one thing, Uncle Cyril and Aunt Charlie called each other by their first names. No Mother and Dad. So their being childless set them apart and linked them together not by function, but as their constant selves. (Even my grandfather and grandmother referred to each other, at least in my hearing, as Grandma and Grandpa, moving function one degree further.) Uncle Cyril and Aunt Charlie never used endearments or pet names and I never saw them touch each other. I believe now that there was harmony, a flow of satisfaction, between them, brightening the air around so that even a self-centered child could be aware of it. But perhaps it's only what I've been told, what I think I remember. I'm certain, though, that the other feelings I remember—the sense of obligation and demand that grew monstrously around my father and my mother, and the stale air of irritability, of settled unease, that surrounded my grandparents—were absent from that one marriage, and that this was seen as something to comment on, like a perfect day in an uncertain season.

Neither my grandmother nor Aunt Charlie made much mention of her dead husband. My grandmother now called hers by his name—*Will*. She spoke without rancor or sadness, as of a school acquaintance. Aunt Charlie might occasionally speak of "your Uncle Cyril" to me alone when my grandmother was not present. What she had to say might be that he would never wear woolen socks, or that his favorite cookies were oatmeal with date filling, or that he liked a cup of tea first thing in the morning. Usually she employed her confidential whisper—there was a suggestion that this was an eminent person we had both known, and that when she said *Uncle*, she was giving me the honor of being related to him.

Michael phoned me. This was a surprise. He was being careful of his money, mindful of the responsibilities coming his way, and in those days people who were being careful of their money did not make long-distance phone calls unless there was some special, usually solemn, piece of news.

Our phone was in the kitchen. Michael's call came around noon, on a Saturday, when my family was sitting a few feet away, eating their midday meal. Of course it was only nine o'clock in the morning in Vancouver.

"I couldn't sleep all night," Michael said. "I was so worried that I hadn't heard from you. What's the matter?"

"Nothing," I said. I tried to think when I'd last written to him. Surely not more than a week ago.

"I've been busy," I said. "There's been a lot to do around here."

A few days before we had filled up the hopper with sawdust. That was what we burned in our furnace—it was the cheapest fuel you could buy. But when it was first loaded into the hopper it created clouds of very fine dust which settled everywhere, even on the bedclothes. And however you tried not to, you couldn't help tracking it into the house on your shoes. It had taken a lot of sweeping and shaking to get rid of it.

"So I gathered," he said—though I hadn't yet written him anything about the sawdust problem. "Why are you doing all the work? Why don't they get a housekeeper? Won't they have to once you're gone?"

"Fine," I said. "I hope you like my dress. I told you Aunt Charlie was making my wedding dress?"

"Can you not talk?"

"Not really."

"Well okay. Just write me."

"I will. Today."

"I'm painting the kitchen."

He had been living in an attic room with a hot plate, but had recently found a one-bedroom apartment where we could begin our life together.

"Aren't you even interested what color? I'll tell you anyway.

Yellow with white woodwork. White cupboards. To get as much light in it as I can."

"That sounds really nice," I said.

When I hung up the phone my father said, "Not a lovers' spat, I trust?" He spoke in an affected, teasing way just to break the silence in the room. Nevertheless I was embarrassed.

My brother snickered.

I knew what they thought about Michael. They thought he was too brightly smiling, too nicely shaved and shiny-shoed, too well brought up and heartily polite. Unlikely to have ever mucked out a stable or mended a fence. They had a habit of poor people—perhaps especially of poor people burdened with more intelligence than their status gets them credit for—a habit or necessity of turning their betters, or those whom they suspect of thinking themselves their betters, into such caricatures.

My mother was not like that. She approved of Michael. And he was polite to her, though uneasy around her, because of her thickened desperate speech and shaky limbs and the way her eyes might go out of control and roll upwards. He wasn't used to sick people. Or poor people. But he had done his best, during a visit that must have seemed to him appalling, a dreary captivity.

From which he longed to rescue me.

These people at the table—except my mother—thought me to some extent a traitor for not staying where I belonged, in this life. Though they really didn't want me to, either. They were relieved that someone would want me. Maybe sorry or a little ashamed that it was not one of the boys around home, yet understanding how that couldn't be and this would be better for me, all round. They wanted to tease me sharply about Michael (they would have said it was only teasing), but on the whole, they were of the opinion that I should hang on to him.

I meant to hang on to him. I wished they could understand that he did have a sense of humor, he wasn't as pompous as they thought, and that he was not afraid of work. Just as I wanted him to understand that my life here was not so sad or squalid as it seemed to him.

I meant to hang on to him and to my family as well. I thought that I would be bound up with them always, as long as I lived, and that he could not shame or argue me away from them.

And I thought I loved him. Love and marriage. That was a lighted and agreeable room you went into, where you were safe. The lovers I had imagined, the bold-plumed predators, had not appeared, perhaps did not exist, and I could hardly think myself a match for them anyway.

He deserved better than me, Michael did. He deserved a whole heart.

That afternoon, I went into town, as usual. The trunks were nearly full. My grandmother, free now of her phlebitis, was just finishing the embroidery on a pillow slip, one of a pair that she meant to add to my collection. Aunt Charlie was now devoting herself to my wedding dress. She had set up the sewing machine in the front half of the living room, which was divided by sliding oak doors from the back half where the trunks were. Dressmaking was the thing she knew about—my grandmother could never equal or interfere with her there.

I was to be married in a knee-length dress of burgundy velvet, with a gathered skirt and tight waist and what was called a sweetheart neckline, and puffed sleeves. I realize now that it looked homemade—not because of any fault in Aunt Charlie's dressmaking but just because of the pattern, which was quite flattering in its way, but had an artlessness about it, a soft droop, a lack of assertive style. I was so used to homemade clothes as to be quite unaware of this.

After I had tried on the dress and was putting on my ordinary clothes again my grandmother called to us to come into the kitchen and have coffee. If she and Aunt Charlie had been by themselves they would have been drinking tea, but for my sake they had taken to buying Nescafé. It was Aunt Charlie who had started this, when my grandmother was in bed.

Aunt Charlie told me that she would join us in a moment—she was pulling out some basting.

While I was alone with my grandmother, I asked her how she had felt before her wedding.

"This is too strong," she said, referring to the Nescafé, and she got to her feet with the dutiful slight grunt that now accompanied any sudden movement. She put on the kettle for more hot water. I thought she wasn't going to answer me, but she said, "I don't remember feeling any way at all. I remember not eating, because I had to get my waist down to fit in that dress. So I expect I was feeling hungry."

"Didn't you ever feel scared of—" I wanted to say *of living your life with that one person.* But before I could say anything more she answered briskly, "That business will sort itself out in time, never mind."

She thought I was talking about sex, the one matter on which I believed I was in no need of instruction or reassurance.

And her tone suggested to me that perhaps there was something distasteful in my having brought the subject up and that she had no intention of providing any fuller answer.

Aunt Charlie's joining us as she did at that moment would have made further comment unlikely anyway.

"I am still concerned about the sleeves," Aunt Charlie said. "I'm wondering should I shorten them a quarter of an inch?"

After she had her coffee she went back and did so, basting just one sleeve to see how it would look. She called me to come and try the dress on again and when I had done so she surprised me, looking intently into my face instead of at my arm. She had something in her fist, that she was wanting to give to me. I put out my hand and she whispered, "Here."

Four fifty-dollar bills.

"If you change your mind," she said, still in a shaky urgent whisper. "If you don't want to get married, you'll need some money to get away."

When she'd said *change your mind*, I had thought she was teasing me, but when she got to *you'll need some money*, I knew she was in earnest. I stood transfixed in my velvet dress, with an ache in my temples, as if I had got a mouthful of something far too cold or too sweet.

Aunt Charlie's eyes had gone pale with alarm at what she'd just said. And at what she still had to say, with more emphasis, though her lips were trembling.

"It might not be just the right ticket for you."

I had never heard her use the word *ticket* in that way before—it seemed as if she was trying to speak the way a younger woman would. The way she thought I would, but not to her.

We could hear my grandmother's heavy oxfords in the hall.

I shook my head and slipped the money under a piece of the wedding cloth lying on the sewing machine. It didn't even look real to me—I wasn't used to the sight of fifty-dollar bills.

I couldn't let a soul see into me, let alone a person as simple as Aunt Charlie.

The ache and the clarity in the room and within my temples receded. The moment of danger passed like an attack of hiccoughs.

"Well then," Aunt Charlie said in a cheering-up sort of voice, hastily clutching at the sleeve. "Maybe they'd look better just the way they were."

That was for my grandmother's ears. For mine, a broken whisper.

"Then you must be—you must promise—*you must be a good wife.*"

"Naturally," I said, as if there was no need to whisper. And my grandmother, coming into the room, put a hand on my arm.

"Get her out of that dress before she ruins it," she said. "She's all broke out in a sweat."

Home

I come home as I have done several times in the past year, travelling on three buses. The first bus is large, air-conditioned, fast, and comfortable. People on it pay little attention to each other. They look out at the highway traffic, which the bus negotiates with superior ease. We travel west then north from the city, and after fifty miles or so reach a large, prosperous market-and-manufacturing town. Here with those passengers who are going in my direction, I switch to a smaller bus. It is already fairly full of people whose journey home starts in this town—farmers too old to drive anymore, and farmers' wives of all ages; nursing students and agricultural college students going home for the weekend; children being transferred between parents and grandparents. This is an area with a heavy population of German and Dutch settlers, and some of the older people are speaking in one or another of those languages. On this leg of the trip you may see the bus stop to deliver a basket or a parcel to somebody waiting at a farm gate.

The thirty-mile trip to the town where the last change is made takes as long as, or longer than, the fifty-mile lap from the city. By the time we reach that town the large good-humored descendants of Germans, and the more recent Dutch, have all got off, the evening has grown darker and chillier and the farms less tended and rolling. I walk across the road with one or two survivors from the first bus, two or three from the second—here we smile at each other, acknowledging a comradeship or even a similarity that would not have been apparent to us in the places we started from. We climb onto the small bus waiting in front of a gas station. No bus depot here.

This is an old school bus, with very uncomfortable seats which cannot be adjusted in any way, and windows cut by horizontal metal frames. That makes it necessary to slump down or to sit up very straight and crane your neck, in order to get an unobstructed view. I find this irritating, because the countryside here is what I most want to see—the reddening fall woods and the dry fields of stubble and the cows crowding the barn porches. Such unremarkable scenes, in this part of the country, are what I have always thought would be the last thing I would care to see in my life.

And it does strike me that this might turn out to be true, and sooner than I had expected, as the bus is driven at what seems a reckless speed, bouncing and swerving, over the remaining twenty miles of roughly paved road.

This is great country for accidents. Boys too young to have a license will come to grief driving at ninety miles an hour over gravel roads with blind hills. Celebrating drivers will roar through villages late at night without their lights on, and most grown males seem to have survived at least one smashed telephone pole and one roll in the ditch.

My father and stepmother may tell me of these casualties when I get home. My father simply speaks of a terrible accident. My stepmother takes it further. Decapitation, a steering-wheel stove into the chest, the bottle somebody was drinking from pulping the face.

"Idiots," I say shortly. It's not just that I have no sympathy with the gravel-runners, the blind drunks. It's that I think this conversation, my stepmother's expansion and relish, may be embarrassing my father. Later I'll understand that this probably isn't so.

"That's the very word for them," says my stepmother. "Idiots. They have nobody but themself to blame."

I sit with my father and my stepmother—whose name is Irlma—at the kitchen table, drinking whiskey. Their dog Buster lies at Irlma's feet. My father pours rye into three juice glasses until they are about three-quarters full, then fills them up with water. While my mother was alive there was never a bottle of liquor in this house, or even a bottle of beer or wine. She had made my father promise, before they were married, that he would never take a drink. This was not because she had suffered from men's drinking in her own home—it was just the promise that many self-respecting women required before they would bestow themselves on a man in those days.

The wooden kitchen table that we always ate from, and the chairs we sat on, have been taken to the barn. The chairs did not match. They were very old, and a couple of them were supposed to have come from what was called the chair factory—it was probably just a workshop—at Sunshine, a village that had passed out of existence by the end of the nineteenth century. My father is ready to sell them for next to nothing, or give them away, if anybody wants them. He can never understand an admiration for what he calls old junk, and thinks that people who profess it are being pretentious. He and Irlma have bought a new table with a plastic surface that looks something like wood and will not mark, and four chairs with plastic-covered cushions that have a pattern of yellow flowers and are, to tell the truth, much more comfortable than the old wooden chairs to sit on.

Now that I am living only a hundred miles away I come home every couple of months or so. Before this, for a long time, I lived more than a thousand miles away and would go for years without seeing this house. I thought of it then as a place I might never see again and I was greatly moved by the memory of it. I would walk through its rooms in my mind. All those rooms are small, and as is usual in old farmhouses, they are not designed to take advantage of the out-of-doors but, if possible, to ignore it. People may not have wanted to spend their time of rest or shelter looking out at the fields they had to work in, or at the snowdrifts they had to shovel their way through in order to feed their stock. People who openly admired nature—or who even went so far as to use that word, *Nature*—were often taken to be slightly soft in the head.

In my mind, when I was far away, I would also see the kitchen ceiling, made of narrow, smoke-stained, tongue-in-groove boards, and the frame of the kitchen window gnawed by some dog that had been locked in before my time. The wallpaper was palely splotched by a leaking chimney, and the linoleum was repainted by my mother every spring, as long as she was able. She painted it a dark color—brown or green or navy—then, using a sponge, she made a design on it, with bright speckles of yellow or red.

That ceiling is hidden now behind squares of white tiles, and a new metal window frame has replaced the gnawed wooden one. The window glass is new as well, and doesn't contribute any odd whorls or waves to what there is to see through it. And what there is to see, anyway, is not the bush of golden glow that was seldom cut back and that covered both bottom

panes, or the orchard with the scabby apple trees and the two
pear trees that never bore much fruit, being too far north.
There is now only a long, gray, windowless turkey barn and a
turkey yard, for which my father sold off a strip of land.

The front rooms have been repapered—a white paper with
a cheerful but formal red embossed design—and wall-to-wall
moss-green carpeting has been put down. And because my
father and Irlma both grew up and lived through part of their
adult lives in houses lit by coal-oil lamps, there is light everywhere—ceiling lights and plug-in lights, long blazing tubes
and hundred-watt bulbs.

Even the outside of the house, the red brick whose crumbling mortar was particularly penetrable by an east wind, is
going to be covered up with white metal siding. My father is
thinking of putting it on himself. So it seems that this peculiar
house—the kitchen part of it built in the eighteen-sixties—can
be dissolved, in a way, and lost, inside an ordinary comfortable
house of the present time.

I do not lament this loss as I would once have done. I do
say that the red brick has a beautiful, soft color, and that I've
heard of people (*city* people) paying a big price for just such
old bricks, but I say this mostly because I think my father
expects it. I am now a city person in his eyes, and when was I
ever practical? (This is not accounted such a fault as it used to
be, because I have made my way, against expectations, among
people who are probably as impractical as myself.) And he is
pleased to explain again about the east wind and the cost of
fuel and the difficulty of repairs. I know that he speaks the
truth, and I know that the house being lost was not a fine or
handsome one in any way. A poor man's house, always, with
the stairs going up between walls, and bedrooms opening out
of one another. A house where people have lived close to the

bone for over a hundred years. So if my father and Irlma wish to be comfortable combining their old-age pensions, which make them richer than they've ever been in their lives, if they wish to be (they use this word without quotation marks, quite simply and positively) *modern,* who am I to complain about the loss of some rosy bricks, a crumbling wall?

But it's also true that in a way my father wants some objections, some foolishness from me. And I feel obliged to hide from him the fact that the house does not mean as much to me as it once did, and that it really does not matter to me now how he changes it.

"I know how you love this place," he says to me, apologetically yet with satisfaction. And I don't tell him that I am not sure now whether I love any place, and that it seems to me it was myself that I loved here—some self that I have finished with, and none too soon.

I don't go into the front room now, to rummage in the piano bench for old photographs and sheet music. I don't go looking for my old high-school texts, my Latin poetry, *Maria Chapdelaine.* Or for the best sellers of some year in the nineteen-forties when my mother belonged to the Book-of-the-Month Club— a great year for novels about the wives of Henry the Eighth, and for three-name women writers, and understanding books about the Soviet Union. I don't open the "classics" bound in limp imitation leather, bought by my mother before she was married, just to see her maiden name written in graceful, conventional schoolteacher's handwriting on the marbled endpaper, after the publisher's pledge: *Everyman, I will go with thee, and be thy guide, in thy most need to go by thy side.*

Reminders of my mother in this house are not so easy to locate, although she dominated it for so long with what seemed to us her embarrassing ambitions, and then with her

just as embarrassing though justified complaints. The disease
she had was so little known then, and so bizarre in its effects,
that it did seem to be just the sort of thing she might have contrived, out of perversity and her true need for attention, for
bigger dimensions in her life. Attention that her family came
to give her out of necessity, not quite grudgingly, but so rou-
tinely that it seemed—it sometimes was—cold, impatient,
untender. Never enough for her, never enough.

The books that used to lie under beds and on tables all over
the house have been corralled by Irlma, chased and squeezed
into this front-room bookcase, glass doors shut upon them.
My father, loyal to his wife, reports that he hardly reads at all
anymore, he has too much to do. (Though he does like to look
at the *Historical Atlas* that I sent him.) Irlma doesn't care for
the sight of people reading because it is not sociable and at the
end of it all what has been accomplished? She thinks people are
better off playing cards, or making things. Men can do wood-
working, women can quilt and hook rugs or crochet or do
embroidery. There is always plenty to do.

Contrarily, Irlma honors the writing that my father has
taken up in his old age. "His writing is very good excepting
when he gets too tired," she has said to me. "Anyway it's better
than yours."

It took me a moment to figure out that she was talking
about handwriting. That's what "writing" has always meant
around here. The other business was or is called "making
things up." For her they're joined together somehow and she
does not raise objections. Not to any of it.

"It keeps his head working," she says.

Playing cards, she believes, would do the same. But she
doesn't always have the time to sit down to that in the middle
of the day.

My father talks to me about putting siding on the house. "I need a job like that to get me back to the shape I was in a couple of years ago."

About fifteen months ago he had a serious heart attack.

Irlma sets out coffee mugs, a plate of soda crackers and graham crackers, cheese and butter, bran muffins, baking-powder biscuits, squares of spice cake with boiled icing.

"It's not a lot," she says. "I'm getting lazy in my old age."

I say that will never happen, she'll never get lazy.

"The cake's even a mix, I'm shamed to tell you. Next thing you know it'll be boughten."

"It's good," I say. "Some mixes are really good."

"That's a fact," says Irlma.

Harry Crofton—who works part-time at the turkey barn where my father used to work—drops in at dinnertime the next day and after some necessary and expected protests is persuaded to stay. Dinnertime is at noon. We are having round steak pounded and floured and cooked in the oven, mashed potatoes with gravy, boiled parsnips, cabbage salad, biscuits, raisin cookies, crab-apple preserves, pumpkin pie with marshmallow topping. Also bread and butter, various relishes, instant coffee, tea.

Harry passes on the message that Joe Thoms, who lives up the river in a trailer, with no telephone, would be obliged if my father would drop by with a sack of potatoes. He would pay for them, of course. He would come and pick them up if he could, but he can't.

"Bet he can't," says Irlma.

My father covers this taunt by saying to me, "He's next thing to blind, these days."

"Barely find his way to the liquor store," Harry says.

All laugh.

"He could find his way there by his nose," Irlma says. And repeats herself, with relish, as she often does. "Find his way there by his nose!"

Irlma is a stout and rosy woman, with tinted butterscotch curls, brown eyes in which there is still a sparkle, a look of emotional readiness, of being always on the brink of hilarity. Or on the brink of impatience flaring into outrage. She likes to make people laugh, and to laugh herself. At other times she will put her hands on her hips and thrust her head forward and make some harsh statement, as if she hoped to provoke a fight. She connects this behavior with being Irish and with being born on a train.

"I'm Irish, you know. I'm fighting Irish. And I was born on a moving train. I couldn't wait. Kicking Horse Railway, what do you think of that? Born on a kicking horse you know how to stick up for yourself, and that's a fact." Then, whether her listeners reply in kind or shrink back in disconcerted silence, she will throw out a challenging laugh.

She says to Harry, "Joe still got that Peggy-woman living with him?"

I don't know who Peggy is, so I ask.

"Don't you mind Peggy?" Harry says reproachfully. And to Irlma, "You bet he has."

Harry used to work for us when my father had the fox farm and I was a little girl. He gave me licorice whips, out of the fuzzy depths of his pockets, and tried to teach me how to drive the truck and tickled me up to the elastic of my bloomers.

"Peggy Goring?" he says. "Her and her brothers used to live up by the tracks this side of the Canada Packers? Part Indian. Hugh and Bud Goring. Hugh used to work at the creamery?"

"Bud was the caretaker at the Town Hall," my father puts in.

"You mind them now?" says Irlma with a slight sharpness. Forgetting local names and facts can be seen as deliberate, unmannerly.

I say that I do, though I don't, really.

"Hugh went off and he never come back," she says. "So Bud shut the house up. He just lives in the one back room of it. He's got the pension now but he's too cheap to heat the whole house all the same."

"Got a little queer," my father says. "Like the rest of us."

"So Peggy?" says Harry, who knows and always has known every story, rumor, disgrace, and possible paternity within many miles. "Peggy used to be going around with Joe? Years back. But then she took off and got married to somebody else and was living up north. Then after a while Joe took off up there too and he was living with her but they got into some big kind of a fight and he went away out west." He laughs as he has always done, silently, with a great private derision that seems to be held inside him, shuddering through his chest and his shoulders.

"That's the way they did," says Irlma. "That's the way they carried on."

"So then Peggy went out west chasing after him," Harry resumes, "and they ended up living together out there and it seems like he was beating up on her pretty bad so finally she got on the train and come back here. Beat her up so bad before she got on the train they thought they'd have to stop and put her in a hospital."

"I'd like to see that," Irlma says. "I'd like to see a man try that on me."

"Yeah, well," says Harry. "But she must've got some money or she made Bud pay her a share on the house because she bought herself the trailer. Maybe she thought she was going to travel. But Joe showed up again and they moved the trailer out to the river and went and got married. Her other husband must've died."

"Married according to what they say," says Irlma.

"I don't know," says Harry. "They say he still thumps her good when he takes the notion."

"Anybody tried that on me," Irlma says, "I'd let him have it. I'd let him have it in the you-know-where."

"Now now," says my father, in mock consternation.

"Her being part Indian might have something to do with it," Harry says. "They say the Indians thump their women every once in a while and it makes them love 'em better."

I feel obliged to say, "Oh, that's just the way people talk about Indians," and Irlma—immediately sniffing out some high-mindedness or superiority—says that what people say about the Indians has a lot of truth to it, never mind.

"Well, this conversation is way too stimulating for an old chap like me," says my father. "I think I'll go and lie down for a while upstairs."

"He's not himself," Irlma says, after we have listened to my father's slow steps on the stairs. "He's been feeling tough two or three days now."

"Has he?" I say, guilty that I haven't noticed. He has seemed to me the way he always seems now when a visit brings Irlma and me together—just a bit shaky and apprehensive, as if he had to be on guard, as if it took some energy explaining and defending us, one to the other.

"He don't feel right," Irlma says. "I can tell."

She turns to Harry, who has put on his outdoor jacket.

"Just tell me something before you go out that door," she says, getting between him and the door to block his way. "Tell me—how much string does it take to tie up a woman?"

Harry pretends to consider. "Big woman or little woman, would that be?"

"Any size woman at all."

"Oh, I couldn't tell you. Couldn't say."

"Two balls and six inches," cries Irlma, and some far gurgles reach us, from Harry's subterranean enjoyment.

"Irlma, you're a Tartar."

"I am so. I'm an old Tartar. I am so."

I go along in the car with my father, to take the potatoes to Joe Thoms.

"You aren't feeling well?"

"Not the very best."

"*How* aren't you feeling well?"

"I don't know. Can't sleep. I wouldn't be surprised if I've got the flu."

"Are you going to call the doctor?"

"If I don't get better I'll call him. Call him now I'd just be wasting his time."

Joe Thoms, a man about ten years older than I am, is alarmingly frail and shaky, with long stringy arms, an unshaven, ruined, handsome face, grayed-over eyes. I can't see how he could manage to thump anybody. He gropes to meet us and take the sack of potatoes, urges us inside the smoky trailer.

"I mean to pay you for these here," he says. "Just tell me what they're worth?"

My father says, "Now now."

An enormous woman stands at the stove, stirring something in a pot.

My father says, "Peggy, this is my daughter. Smells good, whatever you got there."

She doesn't respond, and Joe Thoms says, "It's just a rabbit we got give for a present. No use to talk to her, she's got her deaf ear to you. She's deaf and I'm blind. Isn't that the devil? It's just a rabbit but we don't mind rabbit. Rabbit's a clean feeder."

I see now that the woman is not so enormous all over. The upper part of the arm next to us is out of proportion to the rest of her body, swollen like a puffball. The sleeve has been ripped out of her dress, leaving the armhole frayed, threads dangling, and the great swelling of flesh exposed and gleaming in the smoke and shadow of the trailer.

My father says, "It can be pretty good all right, rabbit."

"Sorry not to offer you a shot," Joe says. "But we don't have it in the house. We don't drink no more."

"I'm not feeling up to it either, to tell you the truth."

"Nothing in the house since we joined the Tabernacle. Peggy and me both. You hear we joined up?"

"No, Joe. I didn't hear about that."

"We did. And it's a comfort to us."

"Well."

"I realize now I spent a lot of my life in the wrong way. Peggy, she realizes it too."

My father says, "H'm-h'm."

"I say to myself it's no wonder the Lord struck me blind. He struck me blind but I see his purpose in it. I see the Lord's purpose. We have not had a drop of liquor in the place since the first of July weekend. That was the last time. First of July."

He sticks his face close to my father's.

"You see the Lord's purpose?"

"Oh Joe," says my father with a sigh. "Joe, I think all that's a lot of hogwash."

I am surprised at this, because my father is usually a man of great diplomacy, of kind evasions. He has always spoken to me, almost warningly, about the need to *fit in,* not to rile people.

Joe Thoms is even more surprised than I am.

"You don't mean to say that. You don't mean it. You don't know what you're saying."

"Yes I do."

"Well you should read your Bible. You should see what all it says in the Bible."

My father slaps his hands nervously or impatiently on his knees.

"A person can agree or disagree with the Bible, Joe. The Bible is just a book like any other book."

"It's a sin to say that. The Lord wrote the Bible and He planned and created the world and every one of us here."

More hand slapping. "I don't know about that, Joe. I don't know. Come to planning the world, who says it has to've been planned at all?"

"Well then, who created it?"

"I don't know the answer to that. And I don't care."

I see that my father's face is not as usual, that it is not agreeable (that has been its most constant expression) and not ill-humored either. It is stubborn but not challenging, simply locked into itself in an unyielding weariness. Something has shut down in him, ground to a halt.

. . .

He drives himself to the hospital. I sit beside him with a washed-out can on my knees, ready to hold it for him if he should have to pull off the road and be sick again. He has been up all night, vomiting often. In between times he sat at the kitchen table looking at the *Historical Atlas.* He who has rarely been out of the province of Ontario knows about rivers in Asia and ancient boundaries in the Middle East. He knows where the deepest trench is in the ocean floor. He knows Alexander's route, and Napoleon's, and that the Khazars had their capital city where the Volga flows into the Caspian Sea.

He said he had a pain across his shoulders, across his back. And what he called his old enemy, his gut pain.

About eight o'clock he went upstairs to try to sleep, and Irlma and I spent the morning talking and smoking in the kitchen, hoping that he was doing that.

Irlma recalled the effect she used to have on men. It started early. A man tried to lure her off when she was watching a parade, only nine years old. And during the early years of her first marriage she found herself walking down a street in Toronto, looking for a place she'd heard about, that sold vacuum-cleaner parts. And a man, a perfect stranger, said to her, "Let me give you a piece of advice, young lady. Don't walk around in the city with a smile like that on your face. People could take that up the wrong way."

"I didn't know how I was smiling. I wasn't meaning any harm. I'd always've rather smiled than frowned. I was never so flabbergasted in my life. *Don't walk around in the city with a smile like that on your face.*" She leans back in her chair, opens her arms helplessly, laughs.

"Hot stuff," she says. "And didn't even know it."

She tells me what my father has said to her. He has said

that he wished that she'd always been his wife, and not my mother.

"That's what he said. He said I was the one what would have suited him. Should've got me the first time."

And that's the truth, she says.

When my father came downstairs he said he felt better, he had slept a little and the pain was gone, or at least he thought it was going. He could try to eat something. Irlma offered a sandwich, scrambled eggs, applesauce, a cup of tea. My father tried the cup of tea, and then he vomited and kept vomiting bile.

But before he would leave for the hospital he had to take me out to the barn and show me where the hay was, how to put it down for the sheep. He and Irlma keep two dozen or so sheep. I don't know why they do this. I don't think they make enough money on the sheep for the work that is created to be worthwhile. Perhaps it is just reassuring to have some animals around. They have Buster of course, but he is not exactly a farm animal. The sheep provide chores, farm work still to be done, the kind of work they have known all their lives.

The sheep are still out to pasture, but the grass they get has lost some of its nourishment—there have been a couple of frosts—so they must have the hay as well.

In the car I sit beside him holding the can and we follow slowly that old, usual route—Spencer Street, Church Street, Wexford Street, Ladysmith Street—to the hospital. The town, unlike the house, stays very much the same—nobody is renovating or changing it. Nevertheless it has changed for me. I have written about it and used it up. Here are more or less the same banks and hardware and grocery stores and the barbershop and the Town Hall tower, but all their secret, plentiful messages for me have drained away.

Not for my father. He has lived here and nowhere else. He has not escaped things by such use.

Two slightly strange things happen when I take my father into the hospital. They ask me how old he is, and I say immediately, "Fifty-two," which is the age of a man I am in love with. Then I laugh and apologize and run to the bed in the Emergency Ward where he is lying, and ask him if he is seventy-two or seventy-three. He looks at me as if the question bewilders him too. He says, "Beg your pardon?" in a formal way, to gain time, then is able to tell me, seventy-two. He is trembling slightly all over, but his chin is trembling conspicuously, just the way my mother's did. In the short time since he has entered the hospital some abdication has taken place. He knew it would, of course—that is why he held off coming. The nurse comes to take his blood pressure and he tries to roll up his shirtsleeve but is not able—she has to do it for him.

"You can go and sit in the room outside," the nurse says to me. "It's more comfortable there."

The second strange thing: It happens that Dr. Parakulam, my father's own doctor—known locally as the Hin-doo doctor—is the doctor on call in the Emergency Ward. He arrives after a while and I hear my father making an effort to greet him in an affable way. I hear the curtains being pulled shut around the bed. After the examination Dr. Parakulam comes out and speaks to the nurse, who is now busy at the desk in the room where I am waiting.

"All right. Admit him. Upstairs."

He sits down opposite me while the nurse gets on the phone.

"No?" she says on the phone. "Well he wants him up there. No. Okay, I'll tell him."

"They say he'll have to go in Three-C. No beds."

"I don't want him in Chronic," the doctor says—perhaps he speaks to her in a more authoritarian way, or in a more aggrieved tone, than a doctor who had been brought up in this country would use. "I want him in Intensive. I want him upstairs."

"Well maybe you should talk to them then," she says. "Do you want to talk to them?"

She is a tall lean nurse, with some air of a middle-aged tomboy, cheerful and slangy. Her tone with him is less discreet, less correct and deferential, than the tone I would expect a nurse to take with a doctor. Maybe he is not a doctor who wins respect. Or maybe it is just that country and small-town women, who are generally so conservative in opinion, can often be bossy and unintimidated in manner.

Dr. Parakulam picks up the phone.

"I do not want him in Chronic. I want him upstairs. Well can't you— Yes I know. But can't you?— This is a case— I know. But I am saying— Yes. Yes all right. All right. I see."

He puts down the phone and says to the nurse, "Get him down to Three." She takes the phone to arrange it.

"But you want him in Intensive Care," I say, thinking that there must be some way in which my father's needs can prevail.

"Yes. I want him there but there is not anything I can do about it." For the first time the doctor looks directly at me and now it is I who am perhaps his enemy, and not the person on the phone. A short, brown, elegant man he is, with large glossy eyes.

"I did my best," he says. "What more do you think I can do? What is a doctor? A doctor is not anything anymore."

I do not know who he thinks is to blame—the nurses, the hospital, the government—but I am not used to seeing doctors flare up like this and the last thing I want from him is a confession of helplessness. It seems a bad omen for my father.

"I am not blaming you—," I say.

"Well then. Do not blame me."

The nurse has finished talking on the phone. She tells me I will have to go to Admitting and fill out some forms. "You've got his card?" she says. And to the doctor, "They're bringing in somebody that banged up on the Lucknow highway. Far as I can make out it's not too bad."

"All right. All right."

"Just your lucky day."

My father has been put in a four-bed ward. One bed is empty. In the bed beside him, next to the window, there is an old man who has to lie flat on his back and receive oxygen but is able to make conversation. During the past two years, he says, he has had nine operations. He spent most of the past year in the Veterans Hospital in the city.

"They took out everything they could take out and then they pumped me full of pills and sent me home to die." He says this as if it is a witticism he has delivered successfully many times.

He has a radio, which he has tuned to a rock station. Perhaps it is all he can get. Perhaps he likes it.

Across from my father is the bed of another old man, who has been removed from it and placed in a wheelchair. He has cropped white hair, still thick, and the big head and frail body of a sickly child. He wears a short hospital gown and sits in the wheelchair with his legs apart, revealing a nest of dry brown nuts. There is a tray across the front of his chair, like the tray on a child's high chair. He has been given a washcloth to play with. He rolls up the washcloth and pounds it three times with his fist. Then he unrolls it and rolls it up again, carefully, and pounds it again. He always pounds it three times, once at each end and once in the middle. The procedure continues and the timing does not vary.

"Dave Ellers," my father says in a low voice.

"You know him?"

"Oh sure. Old railroad man."

The old railroad man gives us a quick look, without breaking his routine. "Ha," he says, warningly.

My father says, apparently without irony, "He's gone away downhill."

"Well you are the best-looking man in the room," I say. "Also the best dressed."

He does smile then, weakly and dutifully. They have let him wear the maroon and gray striped pyjamas that Irlma took out of their package for him. A Christmas present.

"Does it feel to you like I've got a bit of a fever?"

I touch his forehead, which is burning.

"Maybe a bit. They'll give you something." I lean close to whisper. "I think you've got a head start in the intellectual stakes, too."

"What?" he says. "Oh." He looks around. "I may not keep it." Even as he says this he gives me the wild helpless look I have learned today to interpret and I snatch the basin from the bedside stand and hold it for him.

As my father retches, the man who has had nine operations turns up the volume on his radio.

Sitting on the ceiling
Looking upside down
Watching all the people
Goin' roun' and roun'

I go home and eat supper with Irlma. I will go back to the hospital after supper. Irlma will go tomorrow. My father has said it would be better if she didn't come tonight.

"Wait till they get me under control," he said. "I don't want her upset."

"Buster's out somewhere," Irlma says. "I can't call him back. And if he won't come to me he won't come to nobody."

Buster is really Irlma's dog. He is the dog she brought with her when she married my father. Part German shepherd, part collie, he is very old, smelly, and generally dispirited. Irlma is right—he doesn't trust anybody but her. At intervals during our meal she gets up and calls from the kitchen door.

"Here Buster. Buster, Buster. Come on home."

"Do you want me to go out and call him?"

"Wouldn't work. He'd just not pay no attention."

It seems to me her voice is weaker and more discouraged when she calls Buster than she allows it to be when she speaks to anybody else. She whistles for him, as strongly as she can, but her whistle, too, lacks vigor.

"I bet you I know where he's gone," she says. "Down to the river."

I am thinking that, whatever she says, I will have to put on my father's rubber boots and go looking for him. Then, at no noise that I can hear, she lifts her head and hurries to the door and calls, "Here Buster old boy. There he is. There he is. Come on in now. Come on Buster. There's the old boy.

"Where you been?" she says, bending and hugging him. "Where you been, you old bugger? I know. I know. You gone and wet yourself in the river."

Buster smells of rot and river weeds. He stretches himself out on the mat between the couch and the television set.

"He's got his bowel trouble again, that's it. That's why he went in the water. It burns him and burns so he goes in the water to relieve it. But he won't get no real relief till he passes it. No he won't," she says, cuddling him in the towel she uses to wipe him. "Poor old fellow."

She explains to me as she has done before that Buster's bowel trouble comes from going poking around the turkey barn and eating whatever he finds there.

"Old dead turkey stuff. With quills in it. He gets them into his system and he can't pass them through the way a younger dog would. He can't manage them. They get all bunched up in his bowels and they block all up in there and he can't pass it out and he's in agony. Just listen to him."

Sure enough Buster is grunting, groaning. He pushes himself to his feet. *Hunh. Hunh.*

"He'll be all night like that, maybe. I don't know. Maybe never get it out at all. That's what I can't help but be scared of. Take him to the vet's I know they won't help him. They'll just tell me he's too old, and they'll want to put him down."

Hunh. Hunh.

. . .

"Nobody even goen to come to put me to bed," says Mr. Ellers the railroad man. He is in bed, propped up. His voice is harsh and strong but he does not wake my father. My father's eyelids tremble. His false teeth have been taken out so that his mouth sinks down at the corners, his lips have nearly disappeared. On his sleeping face there is a look of the most unalterable disappointment.

"Shut up that racket out there," says Mr. Ellers to the silent hall. "Shut up or I'll fine you a hunderd and eighty dollars."

"Shut up yourself, you old looney," says the man with the radio, and turns it on.

"A hunderd and eighty dollars."

My father opens his eyes, tries to sit up, sinks back, and says to me in a tone of some urgency, "How can we tell that the end product is man?"

Get yo' hans outa my pocket—

"Evolution," my father says. "We might've got the wrong end of the stick about that. Something going on we don't know the first thing about."

I touch his head. Hot as ever.

"What do you think about it?"

"I don't know, Dad."

Because I don't think—I don't think about things like that. I did at one time, but not anymore. Now I think about my work, and about men.

His conversational energy is already running out.

"May be coming—new Dark Ages."

"Do you think so?"

"Irlma's got the jump on you and me."

His voice sounds fond to me, yet rueful. Then he faintly smiles. The word I think he says is . . . *wonder.*

. . .

"Buster come through," Irlma greets me when I get home. A glow of relief and triumph has spread over her face.

"Oh. That's good."

"Just after you went to the hospital he got down to business. I'll have you a cup of coffee in a minute." She plugs in the kettle. On the table she has set out ham sandwiches, mustard pickles, cheese, biscuits, dark and light honey. It is just a couple of hours since we finished supper.

"He started grunting and pacing and worrying at the mat. He was just crazy with the misery and wasn't nothing I could do. Then about quarter past seven I heard the change. I can tell by the sound he makes when he's got it worked down into a better position where he can make the effort. There's some pie left, we never finished it, would you rather have the pie?"

"No thanks. This is fine."

I pick up a ham sandwich.

"So I open the door and try to persuade him to get outside where he can pass it."

The kettle is whistling. She pours water on my instant coffee.

"Wait a minute, I'll get you some real cream—but too late. Right on the mat there he passed it. A hunk like that." She shows me her fists bunched together. "And *hard.* Oh boy. You should of seen it. Like rock.

"And I was right," she says. "It was chock-full of turkey quills."

I stir the muddy coffee.

"And after that *whoosh,* out with the soft stuff. Bust the dam, you did." She says this to Buster, who has raised his head. "You went and stunk the place up something fierce, you did. But the most of it went on the mat so I took it outside and put the hose on it," she said, turning back to me. "Then I took the soap and the scrub-brush and then I renched it with the hose all over again. Then scrubbed up the floor too and sprayed with Lysol and left the door open. You can't smell it in here now, can you?"

"No."

"I was sure good and happy to see him get relief. Poor old fellow. He'd be the age of ninety-four if he was human."

During the first visit I made to my father and Irlma after I left my marriage and came east, I went to sleep in the room that used to be my parents' bedroom. (My father and Irlma now sleep in the bedroom that used to be mine.) I dreamed that I had just entered this room where I was really sleeping, and I found my mother on her knees. She was painting the baseboard yellow. Don't you know, I said, that Irlma is going to paint this room blue and white? Yes I do know, my mother said, but I thought if I hurried up and got it all done she would leave it alone, she wouldn't go to the trouble of covering up fresh paint. But you will have to help me, she said. You will have to help me get it done because I have to do it while she's asleep.

And that was exactly like her, in the old days—she would start something in a big burst of energy, then marshall everybody to help her, because of a sudden onslaught of fatigue and helplessness.

"I'm dead you know," she said in explanation. "So I have to do this while she's asleep."

. . .

Irlma's got the jump on you and me.

What did my father mean by that?

That she knows only the things which are useful to her, but she knows those things very well? That she could be depended upon to take what she needs, under almost any circumstances? Being a person who doesn't question her wants, doesn't question that she is right in whatever she feels or says or does.

In describing her to a friend I have said, she's a person who would take the boots off a dead body on the street. And then of course I said, what's wrong with that?

. . . wonder.

She's a wonder.

Something happened that I am ashamed of. When Irlma said what she did about my father having wished he'd been with her all the time, about his having preferred her to my mother, I said to her in a cool judicious tone—that educated tone which in itself has power to hurt—that I didn't doubt that he had said that. (Nor do I. My father and I share a habit—not too praiseworthy—of often saying to people more or less what we think they'd like to hear.) I said that I didn't doubt that he had said it but I did not think it had been tactful of her to tell me. *Tactful,* yes. That was the word I used.

She was amazed that anybody could try to singe her so, when she was happy with herself, flowering. She said that if there was one thing she could not stand it was people who took her up wrong, people who were so touchy. And her eyes filled up with tears. But then my father came downstairs and she forgot her own grievance—at least temporarily, she forgot it—in her anxiety to care for him, to provide him with something he could eat.

In her anxiety? I could say, in her love. Her face utterly soft-ened, pink, tender, suffused with love.

I talk to Dr. Parakulam on the phone.

"Why do you think he is running this temperature?"

"He has an infection somewhere." *Obviously,* is what he does not say.

"Is he on—well, I suppose he's on antibiotics for that?"

"He is on everything."

A silence.

"Where do you think the infection—"

"I'm having tests done on him today. Blood tests. Another electrocardiogram."

"Do you think it's his heart?"

"Yes. I think basically it is. That is the main trouble. His heart."

On Monday afternoon, Irlma has gone to the hospital. I was going to take her—she does not drive—but Harry Crofton has shown up in his truck and she has decided to go with him, so that I can stay at home. Both she and my father are nervous about there being *nobody on the place.*

I go out to the barn. I put down a bale of hay and cut the twine around it and separate the hay and spread it.

When I come here I usually stay from Friday night until Sunday night, no longer, and now that I have stayed on into the next week something about my life seems to have slipped out of control. I don't feel so sure that it is just a visit. The buses that run from place to place no longer seem so surely to connect with me.

I am wearing open sandals, cheap water-buffalo sandals. This type of footwear is worn by a lot of women I know and it is seen to indicate a preference for country life, a belief in what is simple and natural. It is not practical when you are doing the sort of job I am doing now. Bits of hay and sheep pellets, which are like big black raisins, get squashed between my toes.

The sheep come crowding at me. Since they were sheared in the summer, their wool has grown back, but it is not yet very long. Right after the shearing they look from a distance surprisingly like goats, and they are not soft and heavy even yet. The big hip bones stand out, the bunting foreheads. I talk to them rather self-consciously, spreading the hay. I give them oats in the long trough.

People I know say that work like this is restorative and has a peculiar dignity, but I was born to it and feel it differently. Time and place can close in on me, it can so easily seem as if I have never got away, that I have stayed here my whole life. As if my life as an adult was some kind of dream that never took hold of me. I see myself not like Harry and Irlma, who have to some extent flourished in this life, or like my father, who has trimmed himself to it, but more like one of those misfits, captives—nearly useless, celibate, rusting—who should have left but didn't, couldn't, and are now unfit for any place. I think of a man who let his cows starve to death one winter after his mother died, not because he was frozen in grief but because he couldn't be bothered going out to the barn to feed them, and there was nobody to tell him he had to. I can believe that, I can imagine it. I can see myself as a middle-aged daughter who did her duty, stayed at home, thinking that someday her chance would come, until she woke up and knew it wouldn't. Now she reads all night and doesn't answer her door, and comes out in a surly trance to spread hay for the sheep.

. . .

What happens as I'm finishing with the sheep is that Irlma's niece Connie drives into the barnyard. She has picked up her younger son from the high school and come to see how we are getting on.

Connie is a widow with two sons and a marginal farm a few miles away. She works as a nurse's aide at the hospital. As well as being Irlma's niece she is a second cousin of mine—it was through her, I think, that my father got better acquainted with Irlma. Her eyes are brown and sparkling, like Irlma's, but they are more thoughtful, less demanding. Her body is capable, her skin dried, her arms hard muscled, her dark hair cropped and graying. There is a fitful charm in her voice and her expression and she still moves like a good dancer. She fixes her lipstick and makes up her eyes before she goes to work and again when work is over, she surfaces full of what you might describe inadequately as high spirits or good humor or human kindness, from a life whose choices have not been plentiful, whose luck has not been in good supply.

She sends her son to shut the gate for me—I should have done that—to keep the sheep from straying into the lower field.

She says that she has been in to see my father at the hospital and that he seems a good deal better today, his fever is down and he ate up his dinner.

"You must be wanting to get back to your own life," she says, as if that was the most natural thing in the world and exactly what she would be wanting herself in my place. She can't know anything about my life of sitting in a room writing and going out sometimes to meet a friend or a lover, but if she did know, she would probably say that I have a right to it.

"The boys and I can run up and do what we have to for Aunt Irlma. One of them can stay with her if she doesn't like to be alone. We can manage for now, anyway. You can phone and see how things develop. You could come up again on the week-end. How about that?"

"Are you sure that would be all right?"

"I don't think this is so dire," she says. "The way it usually is, you have to go through quite a few scares before—you know, before it's curtains. Usually, anyway."

I think that I can get here in a hurry if I have to, I can always rent a car.

"I can get in to see him every day," she says. "Him and I are friends, he'll talk to me. I'll be sure and let you know anything. Any change or anything."

And that seems to be the way we're going to leave it.

I remember something my father once said to me. *She restored my faith in women.*

Faith in women's instinct, their natural instinct, something warm and active and straightforward. Something not mine, I had thought, bridling. But now talking to Connie I could see more of what was meant. Though it wasn't Connie he'd been talking about. It was Irlma.

When I think about all this later, I will recognize that the very corner of the stable where I was standing, to spread the hay, and where the beginning of panic came on me, is the scene of the first clear memory of my life. There is in that corner a flight of steep wooden steps going up to the hayloft, and in the scene I remember I am sitting on the first or second step watching my father milk the black-and-white cow. I know what year it was—the black-and-white cow died of pneumonia in the worst winter of my childhood, which was 1935. Such an expensive loss is not hard to remember.

And since the cow is still alive and I am wearing warm clothes, a woolen coat and leggings, and at milking-time it is already dark—there is a lantern hanging on a nail beside the stall—it is probably the late fall or early winter. Maybe it was still 1934. Just before the brunt of the season hit us.

The lantern hangs on the nail. The black-and-white cow seems remarkably large and definitely marked, at least in comparison with the red cow, or muddy-reddish cow, her survivor, in the next stall. My father sits on the three-legged milking stool, in the cow's shadow. I can recall the rhythm of the two streams of milk going into the pail, but not quite the sound. Something hard and light, like tiny hailstones? Outside the small area of the stable lit by the lantern are the mangers filled with shaggy hay, the water tank where a kitten of mine will drown some years into the future; the cobwebbed windows, the large brutal tools—scythes and axes and rakes—hanging out of my reach. Outside of that, the dark of the country nights when few cars came down our road and there were no outdoor lights.

And the cold which even then must have been gathering, building into the cold of that extraordinary winter which killed all the chestnut trees, and many orchards.

What Do You Want to Know For?

I saw the crypt before my husband did. It was on the left-hand side, his side of the car, but he was busy driving. We were on a narrow, bumpy road.

"What was that?" I said. "Something strange."

A large, unnatural mound blanketed with grass.

We turned around as soon as we could find a place, though we hadn't much time. We were on our way to have lunch with friends who live on Georgian Bay. But we are possessive about this country, and try not to let anything get by us.

There it was, set in the middle of a little country cemetery. Like a big woolly animal—like some giant wombat, lolling around in a prehistoric landscape.

We climbed a bank and unhooked a gate and went to look at the front end of this thing. A stone wall there, between an upper and a lower arch, and a brick wall within the lower arch. No names or dates, nothing but a skinny cross carved roughly into the keystone of the upper arch, as with a stick or a finger. At the other, lower end of the mound, nothing but earth and grass and some big protruding stones, probably set there to hold the earth in place. No markings on them, either—no clues as to who or what might be hidden inside.

We returned to the car.

. . .

About a year after this, I had a phone call from the nurse in my doctor's office. The doctor wanted to see me, an appointment had been made. I knew without asking what this would be about. Three weeks or so before, I had gone to a city clinic for a mammogram. There was no special reason for me to do this, no problem. It is just that I have reached the age when a yearly mammogram is recommended. I had missed last year's, however, because of too many other things to do.

The results of the mammogram had now been sent to my doctor.

There was a lump deep in my left breast, which neither my doctor nor I had been able to feel. We still could not feel it. My doctor said that it was shown on the mammogram to be about the size of a pea. He had made an appointment for me to see a city doctor who would do a biopsy. As I was leaving he laid his hand on my shoulder. A gesture of concern or reassurance. He is a friend, and I knew that his first wife's death had begun in just this way.

There were ten days to be put in before I could see the city doctor. I filled the time by answering letters and cleaning up my house and going through my files and having people to dinner. It was a surprise to me that I was busying myself in this way instead of thinking about what you might call deeper matters. I didn't do any serious reading or listening to music and I didn't go into a muddled trance as I so often do, looking out the big window in the early morning as the sunlight creeps into the cedars. I didn't even want to go for walks by myself, though my husband and I went for our usual walks together, or for drives.

I got it into my head that I would like to see the crypt again, and find out something about it. So we set out, sure—or reasonably sure—that we remembered which road it was on. But we did not find it. We took the next road over, and did not find it on that one either. Surely it was in Bruce County, we said, and it was on the north side of an east–west unpaved road, and there were a lot of evergreen trees close by. We spent three or four afternoons looking for it, and were puzzled and disconcerted. But it was a pleasure, as always, to be together in this part of the world looking at the countryside that we think we know so well and that is always springing some sort of surprise on us.

The landscape here is a record of ancient events. It was formed by the advancing, stationary, and retreating ice. The ice has staged its conquests and retreats here several times, withdrawing for the last time about fifteen thousand years ago.

Quite recently, you might say. Quite recently now that I have got used to a certain way of reckoning history.

A glacial landscape such as this is vulnerable. Many of its various contours are made up of gravel, and gravel is easy to get at, easy to scoop out, and always in demand. That's the material that makes these back roads passable—gravel from the chewed-up hills, the plundered terraces, that have been turned into holes in the land. And it's a way for farmers to get hold of some cash. One of my earliest memories is of the summer my father sold off the gravel on our river flats, and we had the excitement of the trucks going past all day, as well as the importance of the sign at our gate. *Children Playing*. That was *us.* Then when the trucks were gone, the gravel removed, there was the novelty of pits and hollows that held, almost into the summer, the remains of the spring floods. Such hollows will eventually grow clumps of tough flowering weeds, then grass and bushes.

In the big gravel pits you see hills turned into hollows, as if a part of the landscape had managed, in a haphazard way, to turn itself inside out. And little lakes ripple where before there were only terraces or river flats. The steep sides of the hollows grow lush, in time, bumpy with greenery. But the tracks of the glacier are gone for good.

So you have to keep checking, taking in the changes, seeing things while they last.

We have special maps that we travel with. They are maps sold to accompany a book called *The Physiography of Southern Ontario,* by Lyman Chapman and Donald Putnam—whom we refer to, familiarly but somewhat reverentially, as Put and Chap. These maps show the usual roads and towns and rivers, but they show other things as well—things that were a complete surprise to me when I first saw them.

Look at just one map—a section of southern Ontario south of Georgian Bay. Roads. Towns and rivers appear, as well as township boundaries. But look what else—patches of bright yellow, fresh green, battleship gray, and a darker mud gray, and a very pale gray, and splotches or stretches or fat or skinny tails of blue and tan and orange and rosy pink and purple and burgundy brown. Clusters of freckles. Ribbons of green like grass snakes. Narrow fluttery strokes from a red pen.

What is all this?

The yellow color shows sand, not along the lakeshore but collected inland, often bordering a swamp or a long-gone lake. The freckles are not round but lozenge-shaped, and they appear in the landscape like partly buried eggs, with the blunt end against the flow of the ice. These are drumlins—thickly packed in some places, sparse in others. Some qualifying as big smooth hills, some barely breaking through the ground. They give their name to the soil in which they appear (drumlinized till—tan) and to the somewhat rougher soil which has none of them in it (undrumlinized till—battleship gray). The glacier in fact did lay them down like eggs, neatly and economically getting rid of material that it had picked up in its bulldozing advance. And where it didn't manage this, the ground is naturally rougher.

The purple tails are end moraines, they show where the ice halted on its long retreat, putting down a ridge of rubble at its edge. The vivid green strokes are eskers, and they are the easiest of all features to recognize, when you're looking through the car window. Miniature mountain ranges, dragons' backs— they show the route of the rivers that tunnelled under the ice, at right angles to its front. Torrents loaded with gravel, which they discharged as they went. Usually there will be a little mild-mannered creek, running along beside an esker—a direct descendant of that ancient battering river.

The orange color is for spillways, the huge channels that carried off the meltwater. And the dark gray shows the swamps that have developed in the spillways and are still there. Blue shows the clay soil, where the ice water was trapped in lakes. These places are flat but not smooth and there is something sour and lumpy about clay fields. Heavy soil, coarse grass, poor drainage.

Meadow green is for the bevelled till, the wonderfully smooth surface that the old Lake Warren planed in the deposits along the shore of today's Lake Huron.

Red strokes and red interrupted lines that appear on the

bevelled till, or on the sand nearby, are remnants of bluffs and the abandoned beaches of those ancestors of the Great Lakes, whose outlines are discernible now only by a gentle lift of the land. Such prosaic, modern, authoritative-sounding names they have been given—Lake Warren, Lake Whittlesey.

Up on the Bruce peninsula there is limestone under a thin soil (pale gray), and around Owen Sound and on Cape Rich there is shale, at the bottom of the Niagara Escarpment, exposed where the limestone is worn off. Crumbly rock that can be made into brick of the same color it shows on the map—rosy pink.

My favorite of all the kinds of country is the one I've left till last. This is kame, or kame moraine, which is a chocolate burgundy color on the map and is generally in blobs, not ribbons. A big blob here, a little one there. Kame moraines show where a heap of dead ice sat, cut off from the rest of the moving glacier, earth-stuff pouring through all its holes and crevices. Or sometimes it shows where two lobes of ice pulled apart, and the crevice filled in. End moraines are hilly in what seems a reasonable way, not as smooth as drumlins, but still harmonious, rhythmical, while kame moraines are all wild and bumpy, unpredictable, with a look of chance and secrets.

I didn't learn any of this at school. I think there was some nervousness then, about being at loggerheads with the Bible in the matter of the creation of the Earth. I learned it when I came to live here with my second husband, a geographer. When I came back to where I never expected to be, in the countryside where I had grown up. So my knowledge is untainted, fresh. I get a naïve and particular pleasure from matching what I see on the map with what I can see through the car window. Also from trying to figure out what bit of landscape we're in, before I look at the map, and being right a good deal of the time. It is exciting to me to spot the boundaries, when it's a question of the different till plains, or where the kame moraine takes over from the end moraine.

But there is always more than just the keen pleasure of identification. There's the fact of these separate domains, each with its own history and reason, its favorite crops and trees and weeds—oaks and pines, for instance, growing on sand, and cedars and strayed lilacs on limestone—each with its special expression, its pull on the imagination. The fact of these little countries lying snug and unsuspected, like and unlike as siblings can be, in a landscape that's usually disregarded, or dismissed as drab agricultural counterpane. It's the fact you cherish.

I thought that the appointment I had was for a biopsy, but it turned out not to be. It was an appointment to let the city doctor decide whether he would do a biopsy, and after examining my breast and the results of the mammogram, he decided that he would. He had seen only the results of my most recent mammogram—those from 1990 and 1991 had not arrived yet from the country hospital where they had been done. The biopsy was set for a date two weeks ahead and I was given a sheet with instructions about how to prepare for it.

I said that two weeks seemed like quite a while to wait.

At this stage of the game, the doctor said, two weeks was immaterial.

That was not what I had been led to believe. But I did not complain—not after a look at some of the people in the waiting room. I am over sixty. My death would not be a disaster.

Not in comparison with the death of a young mother, a family wage-earner, a child. It would not be *apparent* as a disaster.

It bothered us that we could not find the crypt. We extended our search. Perhaps it was not in Bruce County but in next-door Grey County? Sometimes we were sure that we were on the right road, but always we were disappointed. I went to the town library to look at the nineteenth-century county atlases, to see if perhaps the country cemeteries were marked on the township maps. They appeared to be marked on the maps of Huron County, but not in Bruce or Grey. (This wasn't true, I found out later—they were marked, or some of them were, but I managed to miss the small faint C's.)

In the library I met a friend who had dropped in to see us last summer shortly after our discovery. We had told him about the crypt and given him some rough directions as to how to find it, because he is interested in old cemeteries. He said now that he had written down the directions as soon as he got home. I had forgotten ever giving them. He went straight home and found the piece of paper—found it miraculously, he said, in a welter of other papers. He came back to the library where I was still looking through the atlases.

Peabody, Scone, McCullough Lake. That was what he had written down.

Farther north than we had thought—just beyond the boundary of the territory we had been doggedly covering.

So we found the right cemetery, and the grass-grown crypt looked just as surprising, as primitive, as we remembered. Now we had enough time to look around. We saw that most of the old slabs had been collected together and placed in the form of a cross. Nearly all of these were the tombstones of children. In any of these old cemeteries the earliest dates were apt to be those of children, or young mothers lost in childbirth, or young men who had died accidentally—drowned, or hit by a falling tree, killed by a wild horse, or involved in an accident during the raising of a barn. There were hardly any old people around to die, in those days.

The names were nearly all German, and many of the inscriptions were entirely in German. *Hier ruhet in Gott.* And *Geboren,* followed by the name of some German town or province, then *Gestorben,* with a date in the sixties or seventies of the nineteenth century.

Gestorben, here in Sullivan Township in Grey County in a colony of England, in the middle of the bush.

> *Das arme Herz hienieden*
> *Von manches Sturm bewegt*
> *Erlangt den renen Frieden*
> *Nur wenn es nicht mehr schlagt.*

I always have the notion that I can read German, even though I can't. I thought that this said something about the heart, the soul, the person buried here being out of harm's way now, and altogether better off. *Herz* and *Sturm* and *nicht mehr* could hardly be mistaken. But when I got home and checked the words in a German-English dictionary—finding all of them except *renen,* which could easily be a misspelling of *reinen*—I found that the verse was not so comforting. It seemed to say something about the poor heart buried here getting no peace until it stopped beating.

Better off dead.

Maybe that came out of a book of tombstone verses, and there wasn't much choice.

Not a word on the crypt, though we searched far more thoroughly than we had done before. Nothing but that single, amateurishly drawn cross. But we did find a surprise in the northeastern corner of the cemetery. A second crypt was there, much smaller than the first one, with a smooth concrete top. No earth or grass, but a good-sized cedar tree growing out of a crack in the concrete, its roots nourished by whatever was inside.

It's something like mound burial, we said. Something that had survived in Central Europe from pre-Christian times?

In the same city where I was to have my biopsy, and where I had the mammogram, there is a college where my husband and I were once students. I am not allowed to take out books, because I did not graduate, but I can use my husband's card, and I can poke around in the stacks and the reference rooms to my heart's content. During our next visit there I went into the Regional Reference Room to read some books about Grey County and find out whatever I could about Sullivan Township.

I read of a plague of passenger pigeons that destroyed every bit of the crops, one year in the late nineteenth century. And of a terrible winter in the eighteen-forties, which lasted so long and with such annihilating cold that those first settlers were living on cow cabbages dug out of the ground. (I did not know what cow cabbages were—were they ordinary cabbages kept to be fed to animals or something wild and coarser, like skunk cabbage? And how could they be dug up in such weather, with the ground like rock? There are always puzzles.)

A man named Barnes had starved himself to death, letting his family have his share, that they might survive.

A few years after that a young woman was writing to her

friend in Toronto that there was a marvellous crop of berries, more than anybody could pick to eat or dry, and that when she was out picking them she had seen a bear, so close that she could make out the drops of berry juice sparkling on its whiskers. She was not afraid, she said—she would walk through the bush to post this letter, bears or no bears.

I asked for church histories, thinking there might be something about Lutheran or German Catholic churches that would help me. It is difficult to make such requests in reference libraries because you will often be asked what it is, exactly, that you want to know, and what do you want to know it for? Sometimes it is even necessary to write your reason down. If you are doing a paper, a study, you will of course have a good reason, but what if you are *just interested*? The best thing, probably, is to say you are doing a family history. Librarians are used to people doing that—particularly people who have gray hair—and it is generally thought to be a reasonable way of spending one's time. *Just interested* sounds apologetic, if not shifty, and makes you run the risk of being seen as an idler lounging around in the library, a person at loose ends, with no proper direction in life, *nothing better to do.* I thought of writing on my form: *research for paper concerning survival of mound burial in pioneer Ontario.* But I didn't have the nerve. I thought they might ask me to prove it.

I did locate a church that I thought might be connected with our cemetery, being a couple of country blocks west and a block north. St. Peter's Evangelical Lutheran, it was called, if it was still there.

In Sullivan Township you are reminded of what the crop fields everywhere used to look like before the advent of the big farm machinery. These fields have kept the size that can be served by the horse-drawn plough, the binder, the mower. Rail fences are still in place—here and there is a rough stone wall—and along these boundaries grow hawthorn trees, chokecherries, golden-rod, old-man's beard.

Such fields are unchanged because there is no profit to be gained in opening them up. The crops that can be grown on them are not worth the trouble. Two big rough moraines curve across the southern part of the township—the purple ribbons turning here into snakes swollen as if each of them had swallowed a frog—and there is a swampy spillway in between them. To the north, the land is clay. Crops raised here were probably never up to much, though people used to be more resigned to working unprofitable land, more grateful for whatever they could get, than is the case today. Where such land is put to any use at all now, it's pasture. The wooded areas—the bush—are making a strong comeback. In country like this the trend is no longer towards a taming of the landscape and a thickening of population, but rather the opposite. The bush will never again take over completely, but it is making a good grab. The deer, the wolves, which had at one time almost completely disappeared, have reclaimed some of their territory. Perhaps there will be bears soon, feasting again on the blackberries and thimbleberries, and in the wild orchards. Perhaps they are here already.

As the notion of farming fades, unexpected enterprises spring up to replace it. It's hard to think that they will last. SPORTS CARDS GALORE, says a sign that is already weathering. TWO-DOOR DOGHOUSES FOR SALE. A place where chairs can be re-caned. TIRE SUPERYARD. Antiques and beauty treatments are offered. Brown eggs, maple syrup, bagpipe lessons, unisex haircuts.

We arrive at St. Peter's Lutheran Church on a Sunday morning just as the bell is ringing for services and the hands on the church tower point to eleven o'clock. (We learn later that those hands do not tell the time, they always point to eleven o'clock. Church time.)

St. Peter's is large and handsome, built of limestone blocks. A high steeple on the tower and a modern glass porch to block the wind and snow. Also a long drive shed built of stone and wood—a reminder of the days when people drove to church in buggies and cutters. A pretty stone house, the rectory, surrounded by summer flowers.

We drive on to Williamsford on Highway 6, to have lunch, and to give the minister a decent interval to recover from the morning service before we knock at the rectory door to seek out information. A mile or so down the road we make a discouraging discovery. Another cemetery—St. Peter's own cemetery, with its own early dates and German names—making our cemetery, so close by, seem even more of a puzzle, an orphan.

We come back anyway, at around two o'clock. We knock on the front door of the rectory, and after a while a little girl appears and tries to unbolt the door. She can't manage it, and makes signs for us to go around to the back. She comes running out to meet us on our way.

The minister isn't home, she says. She has gone to take afternoon services in Williamsford. Just our informant and her sister are here, looking after the minister's dog and cats. But if we want to know anything about churches or cemeteries or history we should go and ask her mother, who lives up the hill in the big new log house.

She tells us her name. Rachel.

. . .

Rachel's mother does not seem at all surprised by our curiosity or put out by our visit. She invites us into her house, where there is a noisy interested dog and a self-possessed husband just finishing a late lunch. The main floor of the house is all one big room with a wide view of fields and trees.

She brings out a book that I did not see in the Regional Reference Room. An old soft-covered history of the township. She thinks it has a chapter about cemeteries.

And in fact it does. In a short time she and I are reading together a section on the Mannerow Cemetery, "famous for its two vaults." There is a grainy photograph of the larger crypt. It is said to have been built in 1895 to receive the body of a three-year-old boy, a son of the Mannerow family. Other members of the family were placed there in the years that followed. One Mannerow husband and wife were put into the smaller crypt in the corner of the cemetery. What was originally a family graveyard later became public and the name of it was changed, from Mannerow to Cedardale.

The vaults were roofed with concrete on the inside.

Rachel's mother says that there was only one descendant of the family living in the township today. He lives in Scone.

"Next door to the house my brother's in," she says. "You know how there's just the three houses in Scone? That's all there is. There's the yellow brick house and that's my brother's, then the one in the middle, that's Mannerows'. So maybe they might tell you something more, if you went there and asked them."

While I was talking to Rachel's mother and looking at the history book, my husband sat at the table and talked to her husband. That is the proper way for conversations to go in our part of the country. The husband asked where we came from, and on hearing that we came from Huron County, he said that he knew it very well. He went there straight off the boat, he said, when he came out from Holland not long after the war. In 1948, yes. (He is a man considerably older than his wife.) He lived for a while near Blyth and he worked on a turkey farm.

I overhear him saying this and when my own conversation has drawn to a close I ask him if it was the Wallace Turkey Farm that he worked on.

Yes, he says, that was the one. And his sister married Alvin Wallace.

"Corrie Wallace," I say.

"That's right. That's her."

I ask him if he knew any Laidlaws from around that area, and he says no.

I say that if he worked at Wallaces' (another rule in our part of the country is that you never say *the* so-and-so's, just the name), then he must have known Bob Laidlaw.

"He raised turkeys too," I tell him. "And he knew Wallaces from when they'd gone to school together. Sometimes he worked with them."

"Bob Laidlaw?" he says, on a rising note. "Oh, sure, I knew him. But I thought you meant around Blyth. He had a place up by Wingham. West of Wingham. Bob Laidlaw."

I say that Bob Laidlaw grew up near Blyth, on the Eighth Line of Morris Township, and that was how he knew the Wallace brothers, Alvin's father and uncle. They had all gone to school at S.S. No. 1, Morris, right beside the Wallace farm.

He takes a closer look at me, and laughs.

"You're not telling me he was your dad, are you? You're not Sheila?"

"Sheila's my sister. I'm the older one."

"I didn't know there was an older one," he says. "I didn't know that. But Bill and Sheila. I knew them. They used to be down working at the turkeys with us, before Christmas. You never were there?"

"I was away from home by then."

"Bob Laidlaw. Bob Laidlaw was your dad. Well. I should have thought of that right away. But when you said from around Blyth I didn't catch on. I was thinking, Bob Laidlaw was from up at Wingham. I never knew he was from Blyth in the first place."

He laughs and reaches across the table to shake my hand.

"Well now. I can see it in you. Bob Laidlaw's girl. 'Round the eyes. That's a long time ago. A long time ago."

I am not sure whether he means it's a long time ago that my father and the Wallace boys went to school in Morris Township, or a long time since he himself was a young man fresh from Holland, and worked with my father and my brother and sister preparing the Christmas turkeys. But I agree with him, and then we both say that it is a small world. We say this, as people usually do, with a sense of wonder and refreshment. (People who are not going to be comforted by this discovery usually avoid making it.) We explore the connection as far as it will go, and soon find that there is not much more to be got out of it. But we are both happy. He is happy to be reminded of himself as a young man, fresh in the country and able to turn himself to any work that was offered, with confidence in what lay ahead of him. And by the looks of this well-built house with its wide view, and his lively wife, his pretty Rachel, his own still alert and useful body, it does look as if things have turned out pretty well for him.

And I am happy to find somebody who can see me still as part of my family, who can remember my father and the place where my parents worked and lived for all of their married lives, first in hope and then in honorable persistence. A place that I seldom drive past and can hardly relate to the life I live now, though it is not much more than twenty miles away.

It has changed, of course, it has changed utterly, becoming a car-wrecking operation. The front yard and the side yard and the vegetable garden and the flower borders, the hayfield, the mock-orange bush, the lilac trees, the chestnut stump, the pasture and the ground once covered by the fox pens, are all swept under a tide of car parts, gutted car bodies, smashed headlights, grilles, and fenders, overturned car seats with rotten bloated stuffing—heaps of painted, rusted, blackened, glittering, whole or twisted, defiant and surviving metal.

But that is not the only thing that deprives it of meaning for me. No. It is the fact that it *is* only twenty miles away, that I could see it every day if I wanted to. The past needs to be approached from a distance.

Rachel's mother asks us if we would like to look at the inside of the church, before we head off to Scone, and we say that we would. We walk down the hill and she takes us hospitably into the red-carpeted interior. It smells a little damp or musty as stone buildings often do, even when they are kept quite clean.

She talks to us about how things have been going with this building and its congregation.

The whole church was raised up some years ago, to add on the Sunday School and the kitchen underneath.

The bell still rings out to announce the death of every church member. One ring for every year of life. Everybody within hearing distance can listen and count the times it rings

and try to figure out who it must be for. Sometimes it's easy—
a person who was expected to die. Sometimes it's a surprise.

She mentions that the front porch of the church is modern,
as we must have noticed. There was a big argument when it was
put on, between those who thought it was necessary and even
liked it, and those who disagreed. Finally there was a split. The
ones who didn't like it went off to Williamsford and formed
their own church there, though with the same minister.

The minister is a woman. The last time a minister had to be
hired, five out of the seven candidates were women. This one is
married to a veterinarian, and used to be a veterinarian herself.
Everybody likes her fine. Though there was a man from Faith
Lutheran in Desboro who got up and walked out of a funeral
when he found she was preaching at it. He could not stand the
idea of a woman preaching.

Faith Lutheran is part of the Missouri Synod, and that is
the way they are.

There was a great fire in the church some time ago. It gutted much of the inside but left the shell intact. When the surviving inside walls were scrubbed down afterwards, layers of
paint came off with the smoke and there was a surprise underneath. A faint text in German, in the Gothic German lettering,
which did not entirely wash off. It had been hidden under the
paint.

And there it is. They touched up the paint, and there it is.

*Ich hebe meine Augen auf zu den Bergen, von welchen mir
Hilfe Kommt.* That is on one side wall. And on the opposite
wall: *Dein Wort ist meines Fusses Leuchte und ein Licht auf
meinem Wege.*

*I will lift up my eyes unto the hills, from whence cometh my
help.*

Thy word is a lamp unto my feet and a light unto my path.

Nobody had known, nobody had remembered that the German words were there, until the fire and the cleaning revealed them. They must have been painted over at some time, and afterwards nobody spoke of them, and so the memory that they were there had entirely died out.

At what time? Very likely it happened at the beginning of the First World War, the 1914–18 war. Not a time to show German lettering, even spelling out holy texts. And not a thing to be mentioned for many years afterwards.

Being in the church with this woman as guide gives me a slightly lost feeling, or a feeling of bewilderment, of having got things the wrong way round. The words on the wall strike me to the heart, but I am not a believer and they do not make me a believer. She seems to think of her church, including those words, as if she were its vigilant housekeeper. In fact she mentions critically that a bit of the paint—in the ornate "L" of Licht—has faded or flaked off, and should be replaced. But she is the believer. It seems as if you must always take care of what's on the surface, and what is behind, so immense and disturbing, will take care of itself.

In separate panes of the stained-glass windows are displayed these symbols:

The Dove (over the altar).

The letters Alpha and Omega (in the rear wall).

The Holy Grail.

The Sheaf of Wheat.

The Cross in the Crown.

The Ship at Anchor.

The Lamb of God bearing the Cross.

The Mythical Pelican, with golden feathers, believed to feed its young on the blood of its own torn breast, as Christ the

Church. (The Mythical Pelican as represented here resembles the real pelican only by way of being a bird.)

Just a few days before I am to have my biopsy I get a call from the city hospital to say that the operation has been cancelled.

I am to keep the appointment anyway, to have a talk with the radiologist, but I do not need to fast in preparation for surgery.

Cancelled.

Why? Information on the other two mammograms?

I once knew a man who went into the hospital to have a little lump cut out of his neck. He put my hand on it, on that silly little lump, and we laughed about how we could exaggerate its seriousness and get him a couple of weeks off work, to go on a holiday together. The lump was examined, but further surgery was cancelled because there were so many, many other lumps that were discovered. The verdict was that any operation would be useless. All of a sudden, he was a marked man. No more laughing. When I went to see him he stared at me in nearly witless anger, he could not hide it. It was *all through him*, they said.

I used to hear that same thing said when I was a child, always said in a hushed voice that seemed to throw the door open, half-willingly, to calamity. Half-willingly, even with an obscene hint of invitation.

We do stop at the middle house in Scone, not after visiting the church but on the day after the hospital phoned. We are looking for some diversion. Already something has changed—we notice how familiar the landscape of Sullivan Township and the church and the cemeteries and the villages of Desboro and Scone and the town of Chesley are beginning to seem to us, how the distances between places have shortened. Perhaps we had found out all we are going to find out. There might be a bit more explanation—the idea of the vault might have come from somebody's reluctance to put a three-year-old child under the ground—but what has been so compelling is drawn now into a pattern of things we know about.

Nobody answers the outside door. The house and yard are tidily kept. I look around at the bright beds of annuals and a rose of Sharon bush and a little black boy sitting on a stump with a Canadian flag in his hand. There are not so many little black boys in people's yards as there used to be. Grown children, city dwellers, may have cautioned against them—though I don't believe that a racial insult was ever a conscious intention. It was more as if people felt that a little black boy added a touch of sportiness, and charm.

The outside door opens into a narrow porch. I step inside and sound the house doorbell. There is just room to move past an armchair with an afghan on it and a couple of wicker tables with potted plants.

Still nobody comes. But I can hear loud religious singing inside the house. A choir, singing "Onward, Christian Soldiers." Through the window in the door I see the singers on television in an inner room. Blue robes, many bobbing faces against a sunset sky. The Mormon Tabernacle Choir?

I listen to the words, all of which I used to know. As far as I can tell these singers are about at the end of the first verse.

I let the bell alone till they finish.

I try again, and Mrs. Mannerow comes. A short, competent-looking woman with tight grayish-brown curls, wearing a flowered blue top to match her blue slacks.

She says that her husband is very hard of hearing, so it wouldn't do much good to talk to him. And he has just come home from the hospital a few days ago, so he isn't really feeling like talking. She doesn't have much time to talk herself, because she is getting ready to go out. Her daughter is coming from Chesley to pick her up. They are going to a family picnic to celebrate her daughter's husband's parents' fiftieth wedding anniversary.

But she wouldn't mind telling me as much as she knows.

Though being only married into the family she never knew too much.

And even they didn't know too much.

I notice something new in the readiness of both this older woman and the energetic younger woman in the log house. They do not seem to find it strange that anybody should wish to know about things that are of no particular benefit or practical importance. They do not suggest that they have better things to think about. Real things, that is. Real work. When I was growing up an appetite for impractical knowledge of any kind did not get encouragement. It was all right to know which field would suit certain crops, but not all right to know anything about the glacial geography that I have mentioned. It was necessary to learn to read but not in the least desirable to end up with your nose in a book. If you had to learn history and foreign languages to pass out of school it was only natural to forget that sort of thing as quickly as you could. Otherwise you would *stand out*. And that was not a good idea. And wondering about *olden days*—what used to be here, what happened there, why, why?—was as sure a way to make yourself stand out as any.

Of course some of this kind of thing would be expected in outsiders, city people, who have time on their hands. Maybe this woman thinks that's what I am. But the younger woman found out differently, and still seemed to think my curiosity understandable.

Mrs. Mannerow says that she did use to wonder. When she was first married she used to wonder. Why did they put their people in there like that, where did they get the idea? Her husband didn't know why. The Mannerows all took it for granted. They didn't know why. They took it for granted because that was the way they had always done it. That was their way and they never thought to ask why or where their family got the idea.

Did I know the vault was all concrete on the inside?

The smaller one on the outside too. Yes. She hadn't been in the cemetery for a while and she had forgotten about that one.

She did remember the last funeral they had when they put the last person in the big vault. The last time they had opened it up. It was for Mrs. Lempke, who had been born a Mannerow. There was just room for one more and she was the one. Then there was no room for anybody else.

They dug down at the end and opened up the bricks and then you could see some of the inside, before they got her coffin in. You could see there were coffins in there before her, along either side. Put in nobody knows how long a time ago.

"It gave me a strange feeling," she says. "It did so. Because you get used to seeing the coffins when they're new, but not so much when they're old."

And the one little table sitting straight ahead of the entranceway, a little table at the far end. A table with a Bible opened up on it.

And beside the Bible, a lamp.

It was just an ordinary old-fashioned lamp, the kind they used to burn coal oil in.

Sitting there the same today, all sealed up and nobody going to see it ever again.

"Nobody knows why they did it. They just did."

She smiles at me with a sociable sort of perplexity, her almost colorless eyes enlarged, made owlish, by her glasses. She gives a couple of tremulous nods. As if to say, it's beyond us, isn't it? A multitude of things, beyond us. Yes.

The radiologist says that when she looked at the mammograms that had come in from the country hospital, she could see that the lump had been there in 1990 and in 1991. It had not changed. Still in the same place, still the same size. She says that you can never be absolutely one hundred percent certain that such a lump is safe, unless you do a biopsy. But you can be sure enough. A biopsy in itself is an intrusive procedure and if she were in my place she would not have it. She would have a mammogram in another six months, instead. If it were her breast she would keep an eye on it, but for the time being she would let it alone.

I ask why nobody had told me about the lump when it first appeared.

Oh, she says, they must not have seen it.

So this is the first time.

Such frights will come and go.

Then there'll be one that won't. One that won't go.

But for now, the corn in tassel, the height of summer passing, time opening out with room again for tiffs and trivialities. No more hard edges on the days, no sense of fate buzzing around in your veins like a swarm of tiny and relentless insects.

Back to where no great change seems to be promised beyond the change of seasons. Some raggedness, carelessness, even a casual possibility of boredom again in the reaches of earth and sky.

On our way home from the city hospital I say to my husband, "Do you think they put any oil in that lamp?"

He knows at once what I am talking about. He says that he has wondered the same thing.

Epilogue

Messenger

My father wrote that the countryside created by the efforts of the pioneers had changed very little in his time. The farms were still the size that had been manageable in that time and the woodlots were in the same places and the fences, though repaired many times, were still where they used to be. So were the great bank barns—not the first barns but buildings created around the end of the nineteenth century, chiefly for the storage of hay and the shelter of livestock through the winters. And many of the houses—brick houses succeeding the first log structures—had been there since sometime in the eighteen-seventies or -eighties. Cousins of ours had in fact retained the log house built by the first Laidlaw boys in Morris Township, simply building additions to it at different times. The inside of this house was baffling and delightful, with so many turns and odd little sets of steps.

Now that house is gone, the barns have been pulled down (also the original cow byre built of logs). The same thing has happened to the house my father was born in, and to the house my grandmother lived in as a child, to all the barns and sheds. The land the buildings stood on can be identified perhaps by a slight rise in the ground, or by a clump of lilacs—otherwise it has become just a patch of field.

In the early days in Huron County there was a great trade

in apples—hundreds of thousands of bushels shipped out, so
I've been told, or sold to the evaporator in Clinton. That trade
died off many years ago when the orchards in British Columbia went into operation, with their advantage of a longer growing season. Now there might be one or two trees left, with their
scabby little apples. And those everlasting lilac bushes. These
the only survivors of the lost farmstead; not another sign that
people have ever lived here. Fences have been pulled down
wherever there are crops instead of livestock. And of course
just in the recent decade the low barns as long as city blocks, as
forbidding and secretive as penitentiaries have appeared, with
the livestock housed inside of them, never to be seen—chickens
and turkeys and hogs raised in the efficient and profitable
modern way.

The removal of so many of the fences, and of orchards and
houses and barns, seems to me to have had the effect of making the countryside look smaller, instead of larger—the way
the space once occupied by a house looks astonishingly small,
once you see only the foundation. All those posts and wires
and hedges and windbreaks, those rows of shade trees, those
varied uses of plots of land, those particular colonies of occupied houses and barns and useful outbuildings every quarter of
a mile or so—all that arrangement and shelter for lives that
were known and secret. It made every fence corner or twist of a
creek seem remarkable.

As if you could see more then, though now you can see
farther.

In the summer of 2004 I visited Joliet, looking for some trace
of the life of William Laidlaw, my great-great-grandfather, who
died there. We drove from Ontario through Michigan along

what was once the Chicago Turnpike and before that the route of La Salle and many generations of First Nations travellers, and is now Highway 12, passing through the old towns of Coldwater and Sturgis and White Pigeon. The oak trees were magnificent. White oak, red oak, burr oak, their limbs arching over the town streets and stretches of the country roads. Also great walnut trees, maples, of course, all the luxuriance of the Carolinian zone which is just slightly unfamiliar to me, being south of the region that I know. Poison ivy here grows three feet high instead of being a carpet on the forest floor, and vines seem to envelop every tree trunk, so that you can't look into the roadside woods—everywhere are wreaths and curtains of green.

We listened to music on National Public Radio, and then when that signal faded we listened to a preacher answering questions about demons. Demons can possess animals and houses and features of the landscape as well as people. Sometimes whole congregations and denominations. The world is aswarm with them and the prophecies are proving true that they will proliferate during the Last Days. Which are come upon us now.

Flags everywhere. Signs. God Bless America.

Then the freeways south of Chicago, road repairs, unexpected tolls, the restaurant that was built on an overpass and that is now empty and dark, a wonder of former times. And Joliet rimmed with new suburban houses, as every city is these days, acres of houses, miles of houses, joined or separate, all alike. And even these are preferable, I think, to the grander sort of new houses which are here too—set apart, not quite the same but all related, with vast shelter for cars and windows high enough for a cathedral.

·   ·   ·

No deaths recorded in Joliet until 1843. No Laidlaw listed in the earliest list of the settlers or those buried in the first cemeteries. What singular folly of mine, to come to a place like this—that is, to any place that has prospered, or even grown, during the last century—hoping to find some notion of what things were like more than a hundred and fifty years ago. Looking for a grave, a memory. There is only one listing that gets my attention.

Unknown Cemetery.

In a certain corner of Homer Township, a burial ground in which only two stones have been found, but in which as many as twenty were said to have existed at one time. The two stones remaining, according to the lists, bear the names of people who died in the year 1837. There is speculation that some of the others might have been those of soldiers who died in the Black Hawk war.

This means that there was a graveyard in existence before Will died.

We go there, we drive to the corner of 143rd and Parker. On the northwest corner is a golf course, on the northeast and southeast corners are recently built houses with landscaped lots. On the southwest corner there are houses, also fairly new, but with the difference that their lots on the corner do not reach the street, being separated from it by a high fence. Between this fence and the street is a patch of land gone completely wild.

I clamber into it, brushing aside the vigorous poison ivy. In among the half-grown trees and almost impenetrable undergrowth, hidden from the street, I peer all around—I cannot straighten up, because of the tree branches. I do not see any leaning or fallen or broken gravestones, or any plants growing—

rosebushes, for instance—that might be a sign that graves had once been here. It is useless. I become apprehensive about the poison ivy. I grope my way out.

But why has the wild land remained there? Human burial is one of the very few reasons that any land is undisturbed, nowadays, when all the land around it is put to use.

I could pursue this. It's what people do. Once they get started they'll follow any lead. People who have done little reading in their whole lives will immerse themselves in documents, and some who would have trouble telling you the years in which the First World War was begun and ended will toss about dates from past centuries. We are beguiled. It happens mostly in our old age, when our personal futures close down and we cannot imagine—sometimes cannot believe in—the future of our children's children. We can't resist this rifling around in the past, sifting the untrustworthy evidence, linking stray names and questionable dates and anecdotes together, hanging on to threads, insisting on being joined to dead people and therefore to life.

Another cemetery, in Blyth. Where the body of James was moved for burial, decades after he had been killed by the falling tree. And here is where Mary Scott is buried. Mary who wrote the letter from Ettrick to lure the man she wanted to come and marry her. On her stone is the name of that man, *William Laidlaw.*

Died in Illinois. And buried God knows where.

Beside her is the body and stone of her daughter Jane, the girl born on the day of her father's death, who was carried as a baby from Illinois. She died when she was twenty-six years old, giving birth to her first child. Mary did not die until two years later. So she had that loss, as well, to absorb before she was finished.

Jane's husband lies nearby. His name was Neil Armour and he too died young. He was a brother of Margaret Armour who was Thomas Laidlaw's wife. They were the children of John Armour, the first teacher at S.S. No.1 Morris Township, where many of the Laidlaws went to school. The baby that cost Jane her life was named James Armour.

And here a live memory comes twitching through my mind. Jimmy Armour. *Jimmy Armour.* I don't know what happened to him but I know his name. And not only that—I think I saw him once or more than once, an old man come on a visit from wherever he lived then to the place where he had been born, an old man among other old people—my grandfather and grandmother, my grandfather's sisters. And now it occurs to me that he must have been brought up with those people—my grandfather and my great-aunts, the children of Thomas Laidlaw and Margaret Armour. They were his first cousins, after all, his double first cousins. My Aunt Annie, Aunt Jenny, Aunt Mary, my grandfather William Laidlaw, the "Dad" of my father's memoir.

Now all these names I have been recording are joined to the living people in my mind, and to the lost kitchens, the polished nickel trim on the commodious presiding black stoves, the sour wooden drainboards that never quite dried, the yellow light of the coal-oil lamps. The cream cans on the porch, the apples in the cellar, the stovepipes going up through the holes in the ceiling, the stable warmed in winter by the bodies and breath of the cows—those cows whom we still spoke to in words common in the days of Troy. *So bos. So bos.* The cold waxed parlor where the coffin was put when people died.

And in one of these houses—I can't remember whose—a magic doorstop, a big mother-of-pearl seashell that I recognized as a messenger from near and far, because I could hold it to my ear—when nobody was there to stop me—and discover the tremendous pounding of my own blood, and of the sea.

Alice Munro grew up in Wingham, Ontario, and attended the University of Western Ontario. She has published ten previous collections of stories—*Dance of the Happy Shades; Something I've Been Meaning to Tell You; The Beggar Maid; The Moons of Jupiter; The Progress of Love; Friend of My Youth; Open Secrets; The Love of a Good Woman; Hateship, Friendship, Courtship, Loveship, Marriage;* and *Runaway*—as well as a novel, *Lives of Girls and Women,* and a *Selected Stories.*

During her distinguished career she has been the recipient of many awards and prizes, including three of Canada's Governor General's Literary Awards; two of its Giller Prizes; the Rea Award for the Short Story; the Lannan Literary Award; the W. H. Smith Award, given to *Open Secrets* as the best book published in the United Kingdom in 1995; the United States' National Book Critics Circle Award; and the Edward MacDowell Medal in Literature. Her stories have appeared in *The New Yorker, The Atlantic Monthly, The Paris Review,* and other publications, and her collections have been translated into thirteen languages.

Alice Munro and her husband divide their time between Clinton, Ontario, near Lake Huron, and Comox, British Columbia.

A NOTE ABOUT THE TYPE

This book was set in Adobe Garamond. Designed for the Adobe Corporation by Robert Slimbach, the fonts are based on types first cut by Claude Garamond (c. 1480–1561). Garamond was a pupil of Geoffroy Tory and is believed to have followed the Venetian models, although he introduced a number of important differences, and it is to him that we owe the letter we now know as "old style." He gave to his letters a certain elegance and feeling of movement that won their creator an immediate reputation and the patronage of Francis I of France.

Composed by Stratford Publishing Services,
Brattleboro, Vermont
Printed and bound by R. R. Donnelley & Sons,
Harrisonburg, Virginia
Designed by Virginia Tan